# NECROTIC CITY

Leland Lydecker

Lyken Publishing
PO Box 72024
Fairbanks, Alaska 99707
www.LykenPublishing.com

Necrotic City/ Leland Lydecker -- 1st Edition October 2017

ISBN: 978-1-947948-03-7

For everyone who lent their advice and support– thank you.

# Contents

# CHAPTER ONE

The lights in the small living space brightened, signaling the end of his scheduled sleep cycle and causing Adrian to reluctantly open his eyes. An image of colorful rock walls and sparkling green water lingered in his mind, glittering under bright sunlight, before being replaced by the stylized infinity symbol that indicated his neural interface was waking up.

Adrian blinked, relegating the loading symbol to the edge of his vision. Bright sunshine? Green water? Those things existed nowhere in the world he knew.

He rolled off the narrow cot, faced the blank white wall across from his bed, and stretched. A field of text scrolled across his vision as the tiny sensors implanted in his eyes, ears, and other organs ran through their startup sequences. The extensive network of nano-prosthetic implants fed into the processor core of his neural interface, providing him with senses heightened far beyond those of the average citizen.

At the dawn of the computing age, an entire skyscraper full of super-computers would have been required to replicate the processing power and storage capacity that resided on a few atom-thick nanochips within his skull. During that same era, it would have taken a dozen separate devices to serve the same function as his neural interface's communication module. Adrian smiled. He did not consider himself a technophile, but the sophistication of the Company technology he carried never failed to fill him with a sense of pride.

An average Hero returned his gaze when he stepped in front of the mirror; he was square-jawed and solidly built, and years of service had molded his features into a perpetually kind expression. Like all Heroes, his eyes were a pale morning blue, his hair was light brown, and he tanned easily. At five-foot-eleven he was a little shorter than many of his counterparts, yet still taller than most of the city's population.

A short, pale scar crossed his left eyebrow, souvenir of an attack by an illegally augmented citizen. His right cheek bore a tattoo of a shield, with a bar code and his ten digit identification number in the center. Around the upper border, tiny letters proclaimed the motto of the Company's Safety Division: "For Life, Liberty, and Happiness."

The shield served as both his badge and a visible reminder that he was genetically engineered Company property. Adrian barely glanced at it as he removed the night's growth of stubble. It had been there his entire life.

He checked the time on his visual display as he pulled on his uniform. In an hour and twenty minutes, his shift would begin.

The exterior of the heavy gray jacket and matching pants consisted of a tear-resistant, waterproof outer shell, while the lining enclosed a state of the art thermal management system. Sandwiched between the two, heat-resistant, non-conductive aramid fabric infused with shear-thickening fluid provided a flexible layer of nearly impenetrable armor.

The jacket zipped up the front, and a collar could be raised to protect the wearer's throat. A bright blue band circled both sleeves just below the shoulder, denoting that the wearer belonged to the Company's Safety Division.

Adrian pulled on the sturdy dark gray boots that went with the uniform and stepped out into the communal living area. A handful of rooms like his own opened into the same space, the quarters of the Heroes of his home group. Instead of windows, the walls held screens displaying motivational posters and soothing generic landscapes.

"To serve is the ultimate honor," read the screen next to the kitchen. "Selfless sacrifice brings joy," declared another.

Adrian barely glanced at the familiar slogans as he took his bowl of oatmeal-flavored foodstuff from the dispenser and sat down at the table.

"You know there are other flavors of breakfast, right?" Griffith asked.

Griff was the largest Hero in their group, his wide shoulders and six-foot-five frame dwarfing most of his counterparts. His loud, abrasive personality gave him the rare reputation of being something of a bully.

Adrian shrugged. "This is what I always have. I like oatmeal."

"Yes, but what kind of oatmeal?" Melbourne asked, looking up from her virtual crossword puzzle. Although female, Mel had the typical Hero frame: muscular and wide-shouldered, with the long legs and narrow hips of a sprinter.

"What do you mean, what kind?" Nelson scoffed, stocky frame hunched over his own bowl. "There's only one kind."

"The archives say that oatmeal was never served plain. There were flavorings added, like fruit or spices."

"I had no idea," Adrian said.

"Well, now you know." There was a brief silence as Mel returned to her puzzle. "Ha! It's chlorophyll, I knew it!"

Adrian scanned the oatmeal's digital nutrition label as he ate. The main ingredient was the ubiquitous reprocessed protein that made it a filling breakfast and ensured that he met his daily nutritional requirements. There was a milk substitute, some kind of texturing agent, and a lengthy list of added vitamins and minerals; but no mention of flavoring.

"Isn't oatmeal supposed to have oats in it?" Adrian asked. "Or is it like hotdogs?"

Mel grinned, a flash of brilliant white from across the table. "It's supposed to be entirely made out of oats, actually. And you never know, maybe hotdogs are the reason there are no dogs?"

"I didn't need to hear that," Nelson muttered. "Bacon and eggs are where it's at, anyway."

"There are no dogs because pets are nothing more than a mouth on legs," Griffith retorted. "And you think that glop is supposed to be bacon and eggs? I doubt it has any more genuine ingredients than Adrian's oatmeal."

"Bacon-and-eggs flavored. At least it tastes like the real thing. Nobody really knows what genuine oatmeal is supposed to taste like."

"Are you still stuck on that stuff?" Bradley asked, emerging from his room. "You had bacon and eggs once, what was it, two years ago?"

"You did not have real bacon and eggs," Griffith scoffed. "That kind of whole protein costs more credit than you'll earn in your entire life."

"It was a thank-you gift," Nelson said. "You haven't heard about that, have you? It was before you joined us."

"Don't ask," Mel advised. "He'll go on about it for hours."

Nelson had already launched into the story of how he prevented the assassination of a private executive's son. The citizen had been so grateful that he invited Nelson to breakfast with him the next morning.

"You should have seen it. There was a whole table full of real food!"

"It's the same as what we eat," Bradley said. "Just in a different form."

"No, it was nothing like this," Nelson insisted. "It was the best food I've ever had!"

"Have you seen the news today?" Mel asked as Griffith joined the others in arguing over the merits of original-form foodstuffs.

"I haven't looked yet. What happened?"

Mel sent him an article. Adrian opened the mail icon that appeared at the bottom right of his vision and allowed the report to expand across his field of view.

"Trinity Ward's Appeal Denied," the headline read. "Company magistrates uphold ruling against Twenty-Ninth Tier's Trinity Ward. The residents have been given a deadline to improve their value or relocate to a lower-credit tier..."

"Again?" Adrian wondered aloud. "Some of those lower-credit tiers must be getting pretty crowded by now."

"You'd think so," Mel said. "There's never much on the news about them, and I can't remember the last time I was assigned a patrol down there. Not much happening on those tiers, I guess."

"Civil unrest. Infrastructure failures."

Mel grimaced. "Rumor is that the lowest tiers are going to hell in a handbasket. And now they're downgrading an entire district? If those people are already struggling to survive, downgrading them won't make them any better off."

"Don't worry," Brad said, wrapping his arm around Mel's shoulders. "I'm sure they'll be okay."

"Be thankful that can't happen to Heroes," Nelson muttered, finishing his bowl of bacon and eggs. "Lots of people losing credit and getting moved down a tier or two. It's a good time to be a Hero or an Enforcer."

"Why should they expect to keep the housing and position if they don't have the credit?" Griffith asked. "There isn't enough to go around as it is. Notice the showers this morning? They cut our hygiene ration again."

"Fourth time in six months," Brad said grimly.

Adrian finished his food and placed the bowl in the cleaning receptacle as the others began discussing the water situation. They were no strangers to water rationing; for most of their lives the per-capita ration had been gradually decreasing as the city's population grew. They were sitting on a finite resource, and the shortages had gotten so severe that the Company's Executives were discussing changing the two-child limit to a one-child limit.

"Fiftieth Tier and beyond are the problem," Griffith declared. "Always have been. They're allowed to run wild down there, eating, breeding and polluting. In the last census, the population of the Fifty-First Tier alone was more than that of Tiers Forty-Five through Fifty combined."

"Strong words coming from someone whose duty is to serve and protect," Bradley said quietly.

"Blame the Company, not the people," Mel said. "They're just trying to survive. They have little or no services. The clinics down there have all closed. How are they supposed to limit their population or stop polluting without medical services or waste management?"

"Why waste services on the creditless?" Griffith retorted. "That's just stealing from everyone who actually contributes."

"That's not necessarily true."

"Sweetheart, Fifty-First Tier and below are worthless. That's why the Company no longer bothers with them. Everyone knows that."

"Watch your tone with my partner," Brad said, his voice hardening.

"No offense," Griffith said lightly. "I'm just saying, you want to point fingers? The Over-Fifties are the problem. They need to send Enforcement down there and clean house."

"I've heard they do," Nelson said. "I always wondered what happened to the people down there then."

Griffith laughed. "What do you think happens to them?"

The door to the living area slid shut behind him, closing off the sound of the argument as Adrian joined the stream of Heroes filling the hallway outside. Some nodded or waved in greeting, and he smiled and waved back.

As a Hero who would soon pass his fifteenth year of service, he was something of a standout among his fellows. Less than thirty percent of Heroes survived into their thirties, and of those, only a quarter were fully intact and functional.

As his assignment loaded, Adrian joined the crowd taking the lift down to street level. He and twelve others would be patrolling the quiet, working-class districts of the Twenty-Ninth Tier. It seemed like the last time he'd been there, the area had been assigned more. Perhaps patrols had been reduced because nothing too exciting ever happened there.

Outside the Safety Tower, a series of colossal statues overlooked the bustling transit stop. They memorialized the entrepreneurs that had pooled their resources to form the Company, building a haven for the survivors of a region decimated by drought, famine and conflict. Tired Heroes disembarked from the shining maglev transit module, and fresh ones boarded under the watchful gaze of the city's founders.

Adrian rode the transit system around the ring of the Tenth Tier to the nearby Southern Interchange and boarded a downward-bound module. Four main avenues, one for each of the cardinal directions, descended through the city from the exclusive First Tier to the lowest, most distant outskirts. Where these avenues intersected the gently curving main street that ran down the center of each circular tier, the elevated maglev lines met at a service interchange.

From there it would be a long ride down nineteen tiers to his patrol zone. Adrian occupied himself by reading the news, safety advisories and law enforcement bulletins pertaining to the Twenty-Ninth Tier. It was not as quiet as he remembered, and Enforcement had issued a hazard bulletin for Trinity Ward. Did they expect violence from the downgraded?

As the elevated transit line descended toward the Twenty-Ninth Tier, luxurious housing towers and bustling retail areas slid past the windows. The city was built on a man-made hill, fifty tiers descending its sides like the steps of an old-fashioned layer cake. Crowned with the palatial residences of the city's chief executives, the First Tier occupied the city's peak. Tiers Fifty through Seventy-Five formed concentric circles around the base, their sprawling districts and dilapidated high-rises smothered in smog.

Over the centuries since the city's founding, most smaller buildings had been replaced with efficient high-rise towers encased in solar cells. Windows were scarce, especially on the less affluent tiers. An army of workers swarmed over the buildings each day, polishing away the film of pollutants that had accumulated during the night.

A tier could be anywhere from a few blocks wide to as many twenty, but the Twenty-Ninth measured a respectable ten blocks across. Social hierarchy was simple: the poorer a resident was, the closer they lived to street level. If the resident lost enough credit, the Company would relocate them and their dependents to a lower tier.

Vermin fled, squealing, as Adrian stepped out of the transit interchange onto the shadowy streets of the Twenty-Ninth. He kicked aside a pile of trash and more vermin scattered. The tier's maintenance workers must be on strike again, a choice that was undoubtedly damaging their credit. Adrian shook his head. Striking for better treatment was a concept that belonged to centuries past, and which never resulted in a positive outcome under the Company. After five days of absenteeism, the employees would be fired for poor attendance and replaced from the endless supply of job seekers.

A few slices of hazy white sky could be seen far above, between the towering structures and the maze of enclosed aerial walkways that connected them. Outside the comfortable air conditioning of the buildings, the air shimmered with heat.

Adrian opened his uniform's virtual control panel and activated the thermal management system. A pleasant cooling sensation began to radiate from the garment's lining, courtesy of a system of temperature sensors and conductive nano-fibers that kept the wearer comfortably cool regardless of the ambient temperature.

"Who wants which districts?" Adrian asked the other Heroes via the tier's Safety channel.

"No preference," Ramon responded from halfway around the tier.

"Okay, the district you're in now and one on either side are yours. Eddie?"

"Eh, I'll take anything but Trinity," the other Hero replied. A number of others chimed in with the same sentiment.

"Okay, Eddie, you're on the two districts to the left of Ramon's." Leadership was a role Adrian was used to filling, and he doled out assignments with brisk efficiency. "I'll take Trinity and the rest up to Ramon from the right. Any questions?"

"Sounds good to me," Ramon replied. "Sure you're up to the chaos over in Trinity?"

"You want to team up for that area? I hear bad things about that place lately," Eddie added.

"Something happen over there that I haven't heard about?"

"Not yet. But Enforcement issued that advisory. Sounds like they think the Anarchists might try something."

"I'll take my chances," Adrian replied, plotting a course toward his slice of the tier. The Twenty-Ninth was not a particularly dangerous place, and there were not enough of them to waste manpower by teaming up to patrol in twos.

The lower levels were quieter than he remembered, the hustle and buzz of human life confined within the worn walls of their tiny living spaces. The public artwork he had admired on his last visit had been painted over with layers of graffiti. The trees planted to scrub the air and provide visual value to the tier had long since died, overwhelmed by pollution and starved of light by the ever-growing housing towers.

Adrian scanned the surrounding alleys and buildings as he walked, on the lookout for signs of distress. His heat sensors detected two figures, one larger and one smaller, hidden in the shadows near an unlit service door. Both citizens' heart rates were elevated. As he paused to evaluate the situation, his augmented hearing picked up their conversation.

"I told you, I don't have any credit left," the woman said. "I won't be able to pay you until the end of the week."

"And I told you, your debt is due now. Find a way to pay!"

"Sir, please step away from her," Adrian said, moving to intervene.

"I'm not doing anything wrong!"

The perpetrator backed away, slipping the sunglasses on his forehead down over his eyes. He was a split second too slow to prevent his eyes from being scanned.

The digital identity file that popped up in Adrian's vision belonged to one Jeffrey Jensen. Forty-eight years old. Widowed under suspicious circumstances. Multiple convictions for assault, intimidation, theft, and improper use of an access device. It was surprising that the Company's magistrates hadn't revoked his citizen status and condemned him to base labor yet.

"Mr. Jensen, you are in violation of your parole," Adrian said, pulling a set of tracking restraints from his pocket and deftly slipping them around the man's right wrist. "Please report to the nearest Enforcement precinct to receive your judgment." He snagged Jensen's left wrist and locked it into the other cuff.

"Genetically engineered Company trash!" Jensen yelled.

"What are you doing?" the woman demanded. "You can't arrest him! You're not an Enforcer!"

"I am required to act when I see a violent crime in progress."

"There was no crime."

"He was threatening you."

"No, he wasn't. Uncuff him, you Company thug!"

Adrian sighed and looked into the eyes of the short, indignant older woman in front of him.

Anne Fuchs, age fifty-nine. Several convictions for shoplifting, and one for aiding and abetting a fugitive. Asthmatic. Diabetic. Divorced, with two grown children who resided in the same nearby building as she and Jensen.

"Ma'am, please," he began.

"Don't ma'am me, you monster! Get out of our neighborhood. Your kind aren't wanted here!"

Meanwhile, Jensen had slipped behind him. The grating sound of metal against gritty pavement could be heard as the man pulled a piece of old machinery pipe from the clutter.

"Heroes are here for everyone's protection, including yours," Adrian said patiently, tracking Jensen's progress as he spoke. The man raised the pipe over his head, aiming a vicious strike at the back of Adrian's skull. "We are provided by the Company to brighten everyone's lives."

"I'll brighten your life, freak," Jensen snarled, swinging the pipe. Adrian pivoted and blocked the blow with his left hand, easily absorbing the impact as he wrenched the weapon out of the man's grip.

"Please desist. Assaulting a Company employee is a class B felony."

"I hope you suffer until the day God ends your miserable existence, you walking abomination," Jensen said, then spit at Adrian's feet and walked away.

"Do you have any idea what you've done?" Fuchs yelled. "He protected us! He kept order in our building! People will be at each other's throats as soon as they hear he's been arrested."

"He's a criminal."

"You're a criminal! You're nothing but a machine, built by the criminals of the Company."

"I'm not a machine. I'm just as human as you are."

"You're nothing like me, you freak!"

Adrian sighed. "Have a nice day, ma'am."

He walked out of the alley, sending a recording of the encounter to Enforcement for use when Jensen turned himself in. If he failed to do so, a pair of Enforcers would follow the tracking chip embedded in the cuffs to the man's location.

The rusty pipe went into a recycling receptacle, the machine scanning his eyes and awarding him a few micro-credits in return for the deposit. A stream of epithets followed him as he turned the corner and took the lift to a higher level of the tier.

"Just prevented an assault and got called a walking abomination," he told the other Heroes.

"It's not pretty out here," Eddie said grimly.

"Ground level?" Ramon asked.

"You guessed it."

"I mostly stay off ground level." The speaker was a young Hero with only a few years in service. "Nobody down there wants our help anyway."

"That's not right. They deserve our protection as much as anyone else," Adrian said.

"Well, they don't want it. I don't know about you, but I'm sick of getting spit on and having trash thrown at me."

"It doesn't matter what we do or don't like," Adrian said patiently. "It's our job."

"I'd rather do my job up on the higher levels, where I'm not so likely to get ganged for it," someone else said. Several others voiced their agreement.

"Did you guys hear about what happened to Madison?" a Hero named Dover asked.

"No, must not have made the news," Eddie replied.

"He got jumped while on patrol below the Fortieth Tier. Forty-Seventh or Forty-Eighth, I think. They dumped his body in front of the tier's Enforcement precinct."

"That's messed up," Ramon said. "He was part of my home group years ago. Real solid Hero. Guy would have given his life to protect any one of those citizens."

"And they didn't just kill him," Dover continued. "They parted him down. His arms and legs were missing. His face was gone. They carved him up for his implants."

"You sure this isn't just one of those horror stories that go around?" Eddie asked.

"I saw the pictures. There's an Enforcer down there that likes to stream video and show people the really gory stuff he finds. It wasn't pretty."

Adrian left the conversation before Dover could share the aforementioned pictures with everyone on the channel.

As he crossed a covered walkway into his section, a 3D map of the tier spread across his vision. Several blocks from his location and thirty stories above, a bright red emergency marker pinpointed the location of a call for help. Pedestrian traffic parted for him as he broke into a run. Young workers and retirees with baskets of groceries hugged the walls as children and panhandlers scrambled out of his way.

"Pardon me," Adrian said, shouldering through the crowd waiting for the lift. "It's an emergency!"

His fingerprint overrode the lift's operating protocols and sent him rocketing to the fifty-eighth floor, where the lift cage stopping so abruptly that he felt momentarily weightless.

The message said that a child had found an unlocked maintenance hatch and climbed onto the outside of a covered walkway. The sender feared that she was preparing to jump. Rounding the corner from the lifts, Adrian found that a crowd had gathered to watch the scene unfold.

Locating the unsecured maintenance hatch, he stepped out onto a narrow solar cell catwalk. From there it was a short jump to the decorative bottom ledge of the pedestrian bridge. The ledge provided a scant twelve centimeters of footing, and he kept an iron grip on the decorative molding for balance.

Inside, the volume of the crowd crested as they spotted him.

People yelled encouragement and screamed obscenities, clapping and beating on the structure's clear walls. The jumper looked up in surprise from her contemplation of the space between her feet, face covered by a mop of matted brown hair. A drop of hundreds of meters yawned below them, crisscrossed with walkways. She leaned forward, preparing to jump.

"Wait!" Adrian yelled. "Why are you out here?"

"For the fall," she yelled back.

"How did you get out here?" he asked, edging closer.

"Mother found the door unlocked."

"Why did she tell you it was unlocked?" Only a few more meters. The drop swung below him, and a hot breeze ruffled his neatly clipped hair.

"So I could jump," the girl replied, as if it made perfect sense.

"Your mother told you to jump?"

"My marks aren't good enough, and I won't be able to make enough credit to support her when she's older. If I jump, she'll be able to have another child who's smarter."

"I'm sure she doesn't want you to jump," Adrian said. "Sometimes people say things they don't mean when they're angry. Let's go talk to her about it." He could almost reach the girl.

"No!" she yelled, wide-eyed beneath her mop of unkempt hair. "She'll beat me if I go back."

Marion Evony, age fourteen. Second daughter of George Anthony and Lucy Evony. No criminal record. She had mild asthma, an affliction most of the population below the Fifteenth Tier suffered from.

"You're a beautiful person with a bright mind. You have a long, happy life ahead of you," Adrian said, adding his own flair to the directions in the suicide negotiator's handbook. "Don't listen to your mother. You have too much to live for to give up now."

Marion seemed to hesitate, her eyes darting back and forth between him and the windy emptiness below.

"You don't understand," she said at last. "I don't have high enough marks to get a job. I have no credit. I have nowhere to live but with mother, and she told me not to come back."

"There are other options," Adrian said. "There's protective custody. You'll be safe."

"No." Marion shook her head violently. "I've seen what happens to the creditless. I'd rather die than wind up there." She leaned forward, hands slipping away from the molding.

Adrian lunged toward her as she dived off the walkway, catching the jumper as they both surrendered to the embrace of gravity. Tucking her safely against his chest, he rolled onto his back and prepared to meet the walkway ten meters below.

Under stress the shear thickening fluid within his uniform became solid, dispersing the force of the impact. Adrian held onto the jumper with one arm and sought to arrest their fall with the other. His fingers found no purchase on the roof's smooth, rounded surface.

No one in the city was particularly religious. But, as he slid off into thin air, Adrian considered praying. He had no idea if there was another walkway directly below them, leaving him to assume that he was facing a very long fall to the pavement below. Marion might come out of it mostly intact. His survival was less likely.

He had a few long moments to contemplate that fact before the next walkway came up underneath them. The impact added the red exclamation point of a damage report to the icon tray at the lower right of his view, but he managed to retain his grip on the girl and catch the lip of the roof as they slid off. Bringing their combined weight to a stop with one arm elicited an ugly crunch from his shoulder, and a partial dislocation was added to his list of injuries.

They dangled there for a moment, Marion screaming in panic against his chest, as he searched out footing along a lip of decorative trim. The bridge was built much like the one they'd fallen from, and he was able to inch his way to a maintenance platform.

"Are you alright?" he asked, setting Marion on her feet. "Let me bring you to a medical station."

"I guess. What about you?"

"It's not serious." Adrian unlocked the maintenance hatch and let them back inside the building. "Heroes are very durable."

Durable was something of an understatement. His survival augmentations had kicked in the moment he dived off the ledge, rendering the world in bright, sharp-edged slow motion. He barely felt the impacts as he struck each covered walkway. Adrian rotated his arm, grimacing as the joint popped back into alignment.

"It's true what they say about Heroes, isn't it?" Marion asked as they set a course for the nearest medical station.

"That would depend on what they say."

"They say you guys can survive falling a hundred stories."

Adrian laughed. "It depends on how you land, and what you hit on the way down. I suppose a Hero could, if they were lucky."

"Does it ever scare you? Are you ever afraid that you won't survive a fall?"

*Usually*, Adrian wanted to say. "We don't have a choice," he said instead. "Heroes exist to keep you safe. If you jump, we have to do everything we can to save you."

"So you're programmed to? Even if you don't want to?"

"Not programmed," Adrian said patiently. "It's how we're trained. A citizen's safety is always more important than our own."

"What if I'd jumped when you first came out of the maintenance hatch?"

"I would have had to try to save you anyway."

"Why?"

"Because every citizen's life is valuable."

"What happens if you choose not to catch a jumper?"

"The Company would see that I'd failed to do my duty, and I would lose my job."

Marion stared at the floor as they made their way through the building's crowded corridors, wild hair covering her face.

"Thank you," she said softly. "I really didn't want to jump, but mother said she'd be watching me."

At the medical station, he surrendered Marion to the custody of the receptionist and reported the incident to Enforcement. The medics didn't spare him a second glance, and he didn't bother asking for treatment. His injuries could safely wait until he returned to the Safety Tower.

"What's going to happen to me?" Marion asked as he turned to leave.

"An Enforcer will arrive to interview you. Tell him what your mother said, and be sure to tell him about her finding an unlocked maintenance hatch so you could jump. They'll probably take you in front of a magistrate, who will place you in protective custody where you'll be safe."

"Enforcers are scary." Marion wrung the hem of her faded gray shirt between her hands. "Couldn't I just talk to you instead?"

"I sent them a recording, but they have to have a statement from you as well." He knelt in front of the bench and clasped Marion's hands in his. "Don't be afraid, okay? The Enforcers may look scary, but they're here to help you just the same as I am."

"Okay," Marion whispered. "If you're sure." She looked anything but convinced.

After a medic led the jumper away, Adrian slipped out of the small clinic and resumed his patrol. He stopped a case of domestic violence in progress on the ninety-seventh floor, prevented a mugging near street level, and talked another would-be jumper into seeking a better solution for his financial problems. He rushed a man suffering a heart attack to a medical station, and gave directions to visitors seeking friends and family.

Between averting calamities, Adrian noticed that many buildings' cheerful pastel interiors had become scuffed and faded since his last visit. Splashes of graffiti, mostly harmless jokes and lovers' notes, had sprung up in the stairwells. An unauthorized mural occupied the wall above a small retail area. A group of preteens shrieked and darted through the crowd around him, absorbed in their game of tag, as he paused to examine it.

The tangled vines and gnarled branches of a verdant jungle had engulfed the remains of a crumbling cityscape. Trees scaled collapsed buildings, their roots swallowing overturned transports and burrowing through cracked pavement. More fascinating still, a host of small birds were hidden among the leaves. The more he stared, the more he found. Some stood out in bright contrast to their surroundings, while others were so well camouflaged that it took minutes for his eyes to discern them. A tawny gray creature with round dark eyes poked through the weeds in the lower right corner of the painting. Was it a fox? Adrian had never seen one outside of ancient videos that predated the founding of the city.

An artist had to pass a lengthy permitting process and gain the approval of the Company's Public Art Division before being allowed to decorate public spaces. Although the mural bore no such authorization, it did not seem subversive or indecent. Adrian chewed his lip, wondering if he should bother reporting it to the Company's Maintenance Division. Its existence was against Company policy, but it seemed a shame to obliterate such a stunning piece of art simply for lacking the proper permits.

As Adrian began filling out the digital report, a soft touch on his arm interrupted his thoughts.

"Sir? Please don't."

Nicca Perry, age thirty six. Partner of Yunna Park. Asthmatic. No criminal record. Employed as a cashier at the nearby food stand whose bright green uniform she wore.

"I know what you're doing," Nicca continued, face furrowed in distress. "Please don't. My mother painted that. Maybe you could just pretend you didn't see it?"

"You don't get many Heroes through here, do you?" Adrian asked gently. "We're supposed to report any unauthorized alteration of Company property."

Her sad brown eyes evaded him, hidden beneath a curtain of brown hair. "You don't have to if it's not hurting anyone."

"Why didn't your mother get a permit for this? I think they would have allowed it."

"They wouldn't. They labeled it protest art."

"Is it?" Adrian asked, gazing up at the mural. He was still finding new details. The painting was incredibly full of life.

"I don't know. We used to live on the Fifteenth Tier, where I grew up. When I was seventeen, the Company eliminated my mother's job. She couldn't find work, so we wound up here. I worked to support both of us."

"What did she do?"

"She was an ornithologist, a scientist who studies birds. After the last of the birds disappeared, they let all of the ornithologists go. She was always bitter about that and she blamed them for the disappearance of the last of the birds in the city."

"There were birds here?" How long ago had the events Nicca spoke of taken place? He had never seen a bird in all his years on patrol.

"Pigeons, mostly, but they've been gone for decades. But she loved birds in general. When I was little, she was always hoping the Company would send her on an expedition outside of the city. She said there might still be all kinds of wild birds out there, even with the drought and the pollution."

He was beginning to see how the Company might have viewed a mural depicting the return of a cityscape to nature as subversive. On the other hand, it had to be one of the gentlest works of protest art he had ever seen.

"All cities come to an end," Nicca continued. "All the works of man, no matter how monolithic or indestructible, eventually return to nature. One day there will be birds here again."

"Your mother was an incredibly talented artist."

"She was full of surprises. I never knew she could paint, until one night she came out and started working on this. I work in one of the shops here, and every morning people would comment on the night's progress. But no one reported it. I think everyone here enjoys it."

"There are strict penalties for subversive art. Is your mother aware of that?"

Nicca looked away. "I'm sure she was. I don't think she cared. She never stopped being angry about what they did. This was her final act of defiance, I guess. She passed away in her sleep not long after it was completed."

"I'm sorry."

"You're going to report it, aren't you?"

"No. I think I'm going to forget I was here. Have a nice day, ma'am." Adrian turned away, deleting the report as he went.

* * *

The sun was beginning to sink from the sky by time he reached the heart of Trinity Ward. Dwarfed by dreary gray towers on every side, the old brick-walled apartment complexes of the Ward rose only twenty stories above him. There were no aerial walkways in this tiny slice of the old city, increasing street traffic but providing a stunningly unobstructed view of the sky.

A few old trees had survived here, their gnarled branches stretching longingly toward the distant heavens. As Adrian paused beneath one, a small black and white vermin with upright ears and a long, furry tail peeked out of the leaves above his head. It stared down at him with round green eyes and squeaked piteously, as if calling for help.

"Annabelle! Here, kitty!" A child's voice rose above the murmur of pedestrian traffic. "Annabelle, come home!"

The child was a tiny pale thing with a blue scarf covering her bald head. Kara Mae Law, age six. The only child of Alaina Law and Victor

Marcos, she suffered from asthma and chronic myelogenous leukemia.

"Mister, have you seen my cat? She's about this big– " her hands mimed something round and roughly ten centimeters across, "–and she's black and white and soft and furry."

"Is that her?" Adrian asked, pointing up into the tree.

"Oh, no, someone must have scared her."

Before he could say anything, the girl was over the waist height railing. He followed, taking care not to snag himself on the sharp spikes that topped the enclosure.

"Please be careful," he admonished as she scrambled up the trunk of the tree and onto the narrow limb that held the cat.

"It's okay," she called back as the scarf began to come unwound from her head. "I've done this before."

Adrian positioned himself under the branch in case the child fell. The organic material under the tree felt soft under his boots, and a strangely pleasant smell wafted up around him.

"Stupid scarf," Kara muttered, relaxing her hold on the branch to adjust the garment. A startled shriek signaled that she had lost her grip.

The pale bundle that dropped into his arms was lighter than he expected, all bone and sharp angles. Adrian carefully set her on her feet.

"We still have to get Annabelle," she said. The creature stared down at them, tail flicking spasmodically.

"Let me see if I can get her."

The tree swayed under his weight as he hoisted himself up into the branches, the wood flexing worrisomely as he stretched toward the little black and white creature. The spiked fence was directly below him.

"Be careful! She's afraid of people."

The animal shrank away from his fingers, crawling farther up the narrow branch. Gritting his teeth, Adrian scooted farther from the trunk and snatched up the fuzzy vermin in one lightning quick motion. The creature wailed and sank all its pointy bits into his hand.

Careful to handle the animal gently, Adrian tucked his hand into his jacket and negotiated a dignified descent from the tree.

"Here you go," he said, returning the bundle of furry rage to its owner.

"Thank you, mister!" The girl wrapped the creature up in her scarf and cradled it in her arms. "Are you okay?"

"I'm fine," he assured her.

As the day progressed and the boost from his survival augmentations faded, the pain in his shoulder had intensified to a dull, persistent throb. The sensation had not been improved by tree climbing. He could ask his fellow Heroes to cover the rest of shift while he was seen by the Safety Division's medical staff, but in his opinion his injuries weren't serious enough to warrant it.

"What about your hand?"

The fingers of his left hand had been scraped during the fall. Another injury that wasn't serious enough to impede his function, he had simply ignored it.

"You should come with me," the child said. "Mom has a first aid kit."

It was a good excuse to speak to the child's parents about safety and keeping vermin as a pet. He followed Kara down a side street to an old white stone building carved with decorative filigree at every level, the pollution-stained artwork peeking out between rows of aging solar cells.

As Kara pressed her finger to the scanner in the entryway, an orange light flickered to life beside the lock.

"Unauthorized party detected. Please have party prove residence or exit the entryway," a tinny electronic voice announced.

"Sorry, I forgot," the girl mumbled. "It won't let me bring in guests yet."

"It's alright," Adrian said, submitting his fingerprint to the scanner. The light next to the lock turned green, and the inner door slid open to admit them. The Company granted Heroes the ability to access any building in the city.

Kara took the stairs, pausing to rest at each landing.

"I can carry you," Adrian offered. "Or we could take the lift."

"I can walk. The lift's broken, anyway."

A set of gray-clad maintenance workers carrying tool boxes passed them as they paused at the next landing. There was something odd about the men, something he couldn't quite put his finger on, but they were moving too quickly for him to scan their eyes.

Kara's parents' apartment was a tiny space at the far end of the eighth floor. Makeshift beds lined the walls of the narrow room, with less than two square meters of free space in the entire apartment. Used dishes littered the recessed kitchen, and a pile of unwashed clothing contributed a stale scent to the enclosed space. There were dents in the sky blue walls, and the doors of several of the recessed storage spaces had been torn off, revealing their cluttered gray interiors.

"I think we're interrupting something," Adrian said, indicating the young couple wrapped in blankets on a nearby cot. Neither of them seemed to notice that they were no longer alone.

"That's just my cousin, Nan, and her boyfriend. Just ignore them. That's what we all do."

Adrian settled on the edge of an empty cot, and Kara placed the scarf-wrapped vermin next to him. As she dug a medical kit out of a recessed storage bin, the black and white creature crawled out of the scarf and walked over to him, yawning. Its tiny pink mouth was full of needle sharp teeth. Finding the hand it had punctured, it hugged his wrist with warm paws and began washing the wounds with a raspy pink tongue.

"Keeping vermin as a pet is a violation of the public health code,"

Adrian said gently.

"Annabelle isn't a *vermin*," the girl said indignantly. "She's a *cat*. Mom says I'm allowed to have her because I'm sick. She's my therapy animal."

The woman on the cot across from them snorted. "It's still an illegal pet. I thought Auntie said no more bringing your friends home?"

"It's okay because he's a Hero!"

The man hastily disentangled himself from Nan's embrace and pulled his sunglasses down over his eyes, straightening his clothes as he headed for the door. "Sorry, babe. Gotta go."

"Why would you bring one of those things into our home?!" Nan demanded.

"Wait a minute," Adrian began.

"I have had it with you!"

"Nan's a bit angry," Kara said as the woman stormed out the door. "She was one of the ones that tried to form a labor union at the plant, and now no one will hire her. She says there are Company men following her. And this morning she found out she's going to get downgraded."

"I'm sorry."

"I think she's wrong about you, though," Kara said, dumping the medical kit on the cot next to him. "You don't seem scary."

Adrian debated his options as the girl sorted through bandages and rolls of gauze. Within the city, pet ownership required an expensive license and thousands of credits worth of insurance. The small furry creature next to him had no such licensing chip. Without a license, the owners could not buy the required insurance.

"Doesn't that hurt?" the girl asked, wrapping his injured fingers in gauze.

"Not really."

"How come? When I see my blood, it always hurts."

"Genetics, I guess. I have a reduced perception of pain, and survival implants that provide adrenaline, painkillers and clotting agents if I get hurt."

"Aunt Tiffany says Heroes aren't really people at all. They're just robots that leak red lubricant when they get hurt."

Adrian laughed. "That's just an urban legend. We're human beings the same as you are."

"Can Heroes get cancer?" Kara asked, putting tiny bandages over the puncture wounds on his other hand.

"Sometimes. It doesn't happen very often."

"What happens to them?"

It was not a pleasant thought. A Hero as sick as Kara would not be able to work.

"Heroes who can't work get retired," Adrian said quietly. To be more accurate, they disappeared and no one asked where they went.

The girl's eyes lit up. "Like retired for old, old people? Like where the Company pays for them to live happily ever after for the rest of their life?"

"Yes," Adrian said, disliking himself for lying but lacking the cruelty to tell her the truth. "Exactly like that."

"There aren't girl Heroes, are there?"

"Actually, there are."

"I've never seen one, so there must not be very many. Why is that?"

"I'm not sure." Heroes were vat-grown and raised by the Company. He had always heard that the fact that so few of the children were female was due to a quirk of the development process. "No one I've talked to knows."

Kara went silent. The small cat curled up against his hand and began making an oddly comforting rumbling sound.

"I always thought Heroes were robots," Kara admitted. "You all look the same. You wear the same clothes. You have the same hair and face and eyes."

"We don't look that alike, really."

"But you're different. I've never seen a Hero with silver in his hair."

Adrian laughed. "I'm glad I could help."

The door slid open, admitting a woman dressed in a food service worker's brown uniform. The girl leaped to her feet and tried to hide Adrian behind her back.

"Kara Mae Law! What have I told you about inviting people back here?"

"He was hurt!"

"Ma'am, I'd like to talk to you about your daughter's safety," Adrian said, standing up.

The heavyset woman huffed and folded her arms over her chest. Her eyes evaded him.

"Sure you do. Perfect excuse for an unauthorized search, wasn't it?"

"I didn't search anything. I'm just concerned about your daughter being outside by herself. It can be dangerous for a small child out there."

"Sure, sure. You're all concern, aren't you? Just want to make sure we're safe, while you record everything you see and send it to Enforcement!"

Nan hovered in the hallway, scowling over the other woman's shoulder.

"I recorded nothing," Adrian insisted.

"Get out of my home."

"Mom, please! Can he stay for dinner?"

"Absolutely not!"

"But–"

"I said no!" The woman turned back to him. "Get out of my home!"

He finally managed to catch a glimpse of her eyes. Alaina Katherine Law, age thirty-two. Asthmatic. Recently diagnosed HIV positive, with minor convictions ranging from petty theft to selling illegal homemade stimulants. The building supervisor had placed a lien against her credit for nonpayment of rent.

"Yes, ma'am," Adrian said, slipping past her into the hallway. "Have a good evening."

The lift was still broken. As he took the stairs back to the ground floor, he wondered why the maintenance men had not repaired it.

Almost every citizen he encountered in the building moved to the far side of the stairway, head down, muttering under their breath. Public sentiment had shifted since the city's founding and the inception of the Safety Division. In the eyes of the citizens, Heroes had become little more than a shady extension of Enforcement. In reality, they belonged to separate agencies, their missions completely different; Heroes existed to serve and protect, while Enforcers maintained order and ensured compliance with the Company's law.

Outside, the sun had sunk into the sea of pollution that shrouded the horizon. Although the upper floors of the city's highest towers still caught sunset's fading radiance, day had given way to night at street level. Safety lights bathed the pavement in a soft blue glow.

As he resumed his patrol, the same pair of maintenance personnel hurried past him. Neither was carrying a tool box this time.

"You shouldn't be here, Hero," one of the men said.

"Didn't you read the bulletin?" the other demanded.

Adrian blinked in shock, an eye scan revealing what the first man's average features had not made apparent. Martin, Enforcer 52676915. In service for seven years, three hundred and two days, seven hours. Special Investigations.

Only Special Investigations possessed Enforcers designed to blend into the civilian population. They were something of an urban legend, a bogeyman of the citizenry. It was only the second time Adrian had ever spotted one.

With a parting scowl, the pair of undercover Enforcers

disappeared into the crowd. Evening pedestrian traffic flowed around him as he puzzled over their odd warning.

The deafening roar of the explosion and its shockwave hit him at the same time, sending him sprawling. Metal and stone shrieked as the building he had just visited collapsed in on itself. Citizens picked themselves up off the ground and fled, screaming.

Sending a call for help to Emergency Services and a recording of the blast to Enforcement, Adrian rolled to his feet and sprinted toward the settling structure.

"My mother's in there!" a woman screamed as he passed.

"My children!" a man yelled.

An image hung in his mind's eye as he surveyed the wreckage, that of a child in a blue scarf cradling a black and white cat in her arms. It had been no simple structural failure. The stone walls had blown outward in the initial explosion, and lay scattered across the sidewalk and street. Scraps of metal jutted from the sides of nearby buildings and broken bodies sprawled amid personal effects and furniture. The entire twenty-story structure had pancaked in the aftermath of the explosion, and there was no telling where the eighth floor had been. Adrian felt sick to his stomach.

He spent the next several hours digging through the rubble, rescuing the trapped and injured. More Heroes joined him. Emergency Services arrived, bringing a portable medical station and more rescuers. Enforcement appeared, faceless and sinister beneath their dark gray armor and enclosed helmets.

A chaotic crowd grew around the collapsed building, and barricades were set up to keep the press from interfering with the rescuers. Survivors hugged loved ones and searched for friends, and hundreds of citizens from neighboring buildings turned out to watch and comfort the survivors. Emergency Services brought in a high-powered scanner and declared that there was no one left alive in the rubble. The crowd surged against the barricade, screaming and crying.

"I'm sorry," the head emergency responder announced. "There's no one else to rescue. It's basic cleanup and extraction at this point."

Standing off to one side, Adrian couldn't help but hear individual voices in the crowd.

"My daughter's still in there!"

"Has anyone seen my husband?"

"Where is my son?"

"I'm sorry, but there's no one else."

"Liar!"

A woman charged the barricade, screaming. A pair of Enforcers intercepted her, pressed a neutralizer to her side, and shoved her limp body back into the crowd.

"Hero," someone said at his shoulder. "Hero, we need to talk to you."

The young emergency responder motioned him over to the scanner and pointed to a dim heat signature deep in the rubble.

"There might be one more. Do you think you can get in there?"

"Are you sure they're alive?"

The responder changed settings and showed him the faint echo of a heartbeat.

"We didn't find it until we moved the machine to start packing up," the man said sheepishly. "Don't let the crowd see you go in. There'll be a riot if they think we were wrong."

"What do you guys think?" Adrian asked via the Safety channel. "Think we can get to them?"

"That's way in there," Eddie noted. "Looks like a cave-in waiting to happen."

"Our shift's up in five minutes," Ramon said. "Pass it to the next shift. They'll be here any time now."

"Mine too. I second giving it to the next shift."

"I agree! It's been a long day and we've all more than filled our quota. Let the next group have this last one."

"We can't leave this guy down there to die during shift change,"

Adrian argued.

"If he's survived this long, he can wait a few minutes more. Just call it a night," Ramon said. "At the end of the day, no matter how hard you try, you'll never save everybody."

The other Heroes were already dispersing, making their way back to the transit interchange.

"If you decide to go in anyway," Eddie said, "good luck. You're a braver Hero than I."

Broken stone crunched under his feet in the alley beside what remained of the building. The air was full of the sickly sweet smell of smoldering wiring and spilled coolant. He found a partially intact side door and descended the stairwell within, wondering how much stone and concrete he would have to move to reach the victim. The building groaned, and something deep in the wreckage settled with an ominous crash.

Turning sideways, he slipped into a partially collapsed hallway. As he grew closer he was gradually able to discern a heartbeat, drumming furiously. Scraping sounds and whimpering came to his ears as he knelt and crawled into an even smaller space.

"...crazy. You'd have to be insane..."

"How does someone like that survive to be..."

"...not me! Not worth..."

The comments of his fellow Heroes faded in and out on the Safety channel, disrupted by the ruined structure above him. The building's internal relays had undoubtedly been knocked offline by the blast.

Heavy room partitions brushed his shoulders and back as he moved, transmitting faint tremors as the building continued to shift and settle. The darkness was so absolute that not even his enhanced night vision could penetrate it. Adrian patted his pockets, hoping the light he carried had not been broken by his earlier fall.

The narrow beam of brightness illuminated a maze of broken cement, twisted beams, fallen walls, and crushed personal effects.

The survivor lay somewhere within.

"Is someone there?" It was a man's voice, weak and muffled. "Is anyone there?"

"I'm here," Adrian reassured him. "I'm coming to get you."

"Over here, behind the wall! I was in bed when the walls fell together. What happened?"

"There was an explosion and the building collapsed. You're going to be alright."

In this part of the building, the walls had fallen against each other like dominoes. The ceiling had come down on top of it all, pinning the mess below a slab of solid cement and all the floors above. This cement slab forced him to crouch, brushing his hair whenever he tried to get a better view.

As best he could tell, the victim was somewhere on the other side of the nearest wall. Adrian sighed in frustration. A rescue team with better lights, jacks to steady the ceiling, and a cutter to chew through the wall could much more safely extract the victim than he could.

"Don't give up," the man pleaded. "Don't leave me here."

"I'm not going anywhere," Adrian said, staring at the wall.

Setting the light on the floor, he put his shoulder against the ceiling and pushed. The nearest wall shifted a few centimeters toward him.

"I'm going to lift, and you're going to push the top of the wall between us toward me, then slip through between it and the ceiling. Do you think you can do that?"

"I think so," the man replied. "Are you sure it won't fall on me?"

"Yes," Adrian lied. With the way the building was settling, staying there was a death sentence. Emergency Services had already stated that they had no intention of sending more rescuers into the building.

"Ready?"

"Ready," the man replied shakily.

Adrian braced himself and lifted. The wall listed toward him, and with much straining and swearing the victim clawed his way through the narrow gap at the top. Something settled deeper in the living units beyond, and the weight on his shoulders tripled.

"Are you alright?" the man asked, crouched in front of him in the narrow space. "You don't look so good."

"Take the light and go," Adrian gasped, fighting the feeling that his spine was trying to compress in exactly the same way as the building's structural supports.

"What about you?"

"Just go! It's going to cave in any second now. Follow the hallway straight back until it widens out, then take the stairwell to the ground floor."

The man grabbed the light and scurried for safety as the nearest wall gave in to the pressure of the others behind it. It fell just shy of Adrian's knees, crushing dirty dishes and a child's stuffed toy. The weight on his shoulders increased.

Surrendering to the inevitable, Adrian slid backward and let the ceiling drop. Debris crunched and cracked all around him as the slab of concrete came to rest, leaving him lying flat on his back in a coffin-like space only a few centimeters taller than his chest. The slab was too low to even allow him to roll him onto his stomach. Taking a deep breath, Adrian began crawling back the way he'd come.

A series of violent crashes echoed through the building, each closer than the last, and Adrian scooted even more quickly. The building groaned around him as his shoulders slid into the wider space of the hallway. Something immediately above settled with a thunderous crack and the cement slab dropped, pinning his legs just above the knee.

Adrian screamed. For a moment the world lit up, bright and white, and then there was nothing.

# CHAPTER TWO

He regained consciousness, unsure of how much time had passed. The red exclamation point of his damage report flashed violently, detailing a lengthy list of new injuries.

His legs were nonfunctional. It felt like they ended a hand's width above his knees, and in the absolute darkness it took patting himself and his surrounding down to ascertain that they were still there. A thick cement slab had fallen on them, and there seemed to be more debris on top of it.

Twisting and searching out handholds in the wreckage, Adrian tried to drag himself free. Sparks and flashes of light lit up his vision, but the slab refused to release him. He collapsed onto his back, panting, and considered the possibility that he might not be able to free himself.

He had never given much thought to when or how he might die. If he had, he might have guessed it would be a jumper. They said it could be a quick and even painless way to go. At enough height, they said you wouldn't even feel the impact.

If he had to choose a death, it would not be here, entombed beneath thousands of metric tons of debris. It would not be here in the absolute darkness, listening to the building settling around him, hoping that another collapse would bring a quick end to his suffering.

Adrian wrapped his hands around a snapped structural support that jutted from the floor near his head and began to pull, determined to drag his lower body out from under the slab. Crunching and popping sounds came to his ears, combined with an awful squealing. He had heard something like it once. A vermin had been hit by a transport and lay in the street, partially crushed but still alive. Adrian clenched his jaw and kept pulling.

With one last explosive heave, he was free. The cement slab dropped with a crunch, displaced air ruffling his sweat-soaked hair as he rolled onto his stomach and began to drag himself toward the exit.

Every few minutes he tried to connect to the tier's Safety channel, getting nothing but an error each time. Eventually he realized that a communication module failure had been added to his damage report. He was disconnected from the network, unable to call for help.

As Adrian dragged himself up the stairs and out into the alleyway, a cacophony reached his ears; sirens blared while citizens screamed and cried. An Enforcer could be heard bellowing for everyone to disperse, his voice nearly drowned by the tumult.

Chaos reigned in front of the building. Enforcers with riot shields stood shoulder to shoulder along the entire barricade, holding back the crush of furious humanity on the other side. Only two emergency responders remained at the portable aid station, tending to the man Adrian had saved.

"Disperse! Disperse now, or you will all be charged with disorderly conduct and jeopardizing public safety!" screamed a nearby Enforcer.

The crowd responded by surging against the barricade, shouting obscenities and Anarchist slogans. The Enforcers electrified their riot shields, eliciting shrieks from those at the front of the crowd. Bodies convulsed, electricity crackled, and the crowd seethed in pain and rage. Those in back fought to the fore to retaliate, crushing their brethren against the electrified shields.

The new riot shields packed enough current to cause death if a body remained in contact with them. The idea was that brief contact would be so unpleasant that the attacker would immediately move back. But those at the front were trapped, crushed against the wall of Enforcers by the crowd behind them. They had nowhere to go. Despite his own injuries, Adrian felt sick to his stomach. If he could get up, if he could get everyone's attention, maybe somehow he could calm the riot.

The thought gave him the energy to drag himself across the dirty pavement toward the aid station. Neither the Enforcers nor the emergency personnel seemed to notice him, but fortunately the man he'd saved did.

"He's alive! Oh God, his legs–"

The medic who had sent him into the building gasped and pressed his hand over his mouth as if to suppress his shock.

"Calling a medical transport," the other said. "We'll stabilize him as best we can. Safety's specialists will have to deal with that."

"Okay," the young medic said shakily.

They rolled Adrian onto a stretcher and strapped him in place. He could feel the strength leaving his body, the clarity of his thoughts fading away like water running out of a punctured flask.

"Sergeant, can you tell us what happened here?" a woman asked. "Was this the work of the Anarchists?"

If they allowed her and her crew through the barricade, the woman in the sleek, dark red business suit must be a correspondent for the Company's Media Division.

"That appears to be the case. However, I can't formally comment until a full investigation has been completed," the faceless Enforcer replied.

"And how many casualties from this reprehensible act?"

"Hey, look at this Hero," a male voice said. "Camera! Get a shot of the dead Hero!"

"What happened to him?"

Adrian tried to tell them that he was alive, but found he couldn't.

He wanted to tell the reporter about what he had seen and heard in the minutes before the explosion. Instead, he continued to stare at the square of black sky far above. A speck of light glittered against the dark backdrop and he wondered if it was a star, as it was considered incredibly lucky to see one. The star accelerated and vanished behind a building, nothing more than the lights of a surveillance drone.

***

He regained consciousness in the bright, sterile white confines of the Safety Tower's medical facility. The world was hazy and distant, eclipsed by the slow, labored pounding of his heart. He could hear the staff discussing someone's injuries in cold, dispassionate tones, as if debating whether a piece of equipment should be thrown away.

"This is going to be an expensive repair job. Everything from mid-thigh down? Jesus, Hart."

"He has a good track record. One of the best. And he was running at a hundred percent during his last physical."

"Ha! At his age? It's only a matter of time till things start going. Look at the production date on his neural interface. They don't even make that model anymore! Same with most of his implants. Half of his hardware is obsolete."

"It's nothing new parts won't fix. It looks like his communication system is fried, so we'll start by giving him a new transmitter chip."

"It's all downhill from here. Not worth the time, much less the credit."

Adrian's heart slammed against his ribs as he realized they were talking about him. He wanted to plead for a little faith on their part, to assure them that he had many years of service left in him.

The doctor leaned into his field of vision, a wiry older man with black hair fading to gray at the temples. His smile was bright and reassuring.

"How are you feeling?"

Adrian shook his head. Words continued to evade him.

"Let's get you some more anesthetic. Michael, prep the bio printer. Harriet, more anesthesia please. I'm going to start cleaning him up."

An assistant appeared at his side and fitted a mask over his face, telling him to breathe deeply. She lifted his arm and added another needle to the one already there, and the world drifted farther away.

"Honestly, Hart, I don't think he's intact enough to fabricate from."

"Then do it from the scan from his last physical," the doctor said impatiently. "Saw."

Instruments clattered. The doctor leaned over his lower body, and a high pitched whine started up. It rose and fell, rose and fell, until something hit the floor with a soft splat. A muffled thump followed, and his lower body felt inexplicably lighter.

"Got his profile loaded. We're clear to print new ones as soon as he's ready."

"Fantastic. Lend me a hand over here, would you?"

***

Adrian awoke in a hospital bed. He blinked groggily at the beige curtains separating him from the other beds in the recovery bay, trying to remember how he'd come to be there. He had gone out on a typical patrol, but there were a lot of blank spaces after that.

There had been a fall with a jumper, but those were injuries he should have been treated and released for. He stretched experimentally, finding no pain in his shoulder. That was good. He checked the hand he'd damaged during the fall. A few faint scars on the pads of his fingers seemed to be all that remained of the injury.

Deciding to go in search of answers, he swung his legs over the edge of the bed and tried to stand up. His limbs felt strangely clumsy, and when his feet reached the floor they refused to hold his weight. An alarm began to blare in the distance as he crashed to the floor.

Adrian had levered himself into a sitting position, grabbed the railing of the bed, and was hauling himself to his feet when the attendants arrived.

"Hero! Please be still," the first man said quickly.

"You should not attempt to stand yet," the second man said. "Let us help you back into bed."

Adrian complied, staring in confusion at the fine strands of scar tissue that covered his skin from eight centimeters above his knees to the tips of his toes.

"What happened to me?"

"Your legs were badly crushed," the first attendant said. "The majority of your lower extremities had to be replaced."

"Will I be able to walk again?"

He felt a stab of panic at the thought of spending the rest of his life in a wheelchair. It would condemn him to spending his days performing menial tasks for the residents of the Safety Tower, until the Company finally deemed that he had outlived his usefulness.

"You'll probably be fine," the attendant said with a reassuring smile, "as long as you obey your physical therapist."

Adrian let go of the breath he'd been holding, lightheaded with relief.

"You must rest," the second attendant said. "Tomorrow you begin physical therapy. Please press the call button if you need anything."

With that, the two men slipped through the curtain and were gone.

* * *

Bradley and Melbourne came to visit him later that afternoon.

"I brought your drawing pad," Mel said, handing him the tablet.

"They said you'd be spending a lot of time resting, and we know how bored you get. Can't just relax like everyone else."

"I'd rather be learning something new, or doing something with my hands. Anything but just sitting here."

"Well, now you can be doing something," Brad said. "How are the legs? Ooh, nice scars," he added, lifting the blanket away from

Adrian's feet.

"Very impressive," Mel agreed. "What did they say?"

"I'll probably be able to walk again."

"Fully functional?"

"Hopefully." Adrian smiled. "They didn't retire me on the spot, so that's something."

"In the end, that's about the best we can all hope for," Brad said. "So, I hear you like thrilling falls?"

Adrian chuckled. "I could do with fewer, honestly."

"You have to see this video Mel shot yesterday," Brad said, grinning. "It's amazing."

As the recording began to play, Mel's perceptions overtook his own.

"Stop right there!"

The black-clad figure paused next to a maintenance hatch and glanced over his shoulder. He was adult height but on the light side of lean, with a hood, dark sunglasses and a black bandana concealing most of his face.

Mel swore as the hatch beside him popped open. She sprinted after him, her fingers scarcely missing the back of his jacket as he leaped off the edge of the catwalk outside.

Adrian gasped as Mel followed without knowing what lay below. It was a risky gamble as some citizens found death preferable to facing the Company's law.

They landed atop a covered walkway. The suspect rolled to his feet and sprinted toward the building at the far end with Mel in hot pursuit. The thief hurdled the brace for a joint in the bridge, and Mel sailed over the obstruction with equal grace, tackling him to the ground on the other side.

"Where is it?" she demanded, pinning him down with one hand while riffling his pockets with the other.

The perp swore and attempted to throw Mel off, but succeeded only in rolling them both over the edge of the walkway roof. The

Hero maintained an iron grip on the front of his jacket as they tumbled through the air.

Watching the recording, Adrian was vaguely aware that his skin was cold and slick with adrenaline-fueled perspiration. There was an incredible amount of empty space below the combatants. Meanwhile, Mel had located a compact case, no more than three centimeters long and half a centimeter thick, in one of the thief's pockets. She deftly relocated it into her own jacket as another walkway rushed up beneath them.

The thief broke her fall with a sickening crunch. The impact also knocked his sunglasses aside, revealing irises that had been modded, either through the surgical installation of lenses or the injection of a dying agent, to match the whites of his eyes. The faint outline of black-market nano-prosthetic implants could be seen through the skin of his eye sockets.

"Goddamn modders," Mel muttered.

Despite his fall, the perp still had a surprising amount of fight left in him. His left hand clamped down on Mel's right wrist with crushing force, and, in one smooth movement, he pulled a blade from his sleeve and nailed her hand to the roof of the walkway.

Adrian caught a flash of shiny blue metal between the end of the perp's sleeve and the cuff of his glove as he struggled free. This was no harmless aesthetic modder. He was a true flesh hacker, and was probably packing a fully robotic arm.

Mel examined the blade, a crude spike formed from a piece of honed scrap metal, and wrenched it free of the roof. The thief did not seem to realize that he was missing something as he scrambled away and jumped off the edge. Mel leaped after him with a reckless abandon that made Adrian wince.

"Stop! You're only making this worse!"

The perp scrambled to his feet and sprinted down the narrow maintenance catwalk, nearly sliding off the side as he skidded around a corner. The blank gray wall of an adjacent building loomed near, closing the two of them into a narrow space filled with obstacles. The thief staggered over a structural brace and dragged himself across the external housing of the building's cooling system with Mel quickly gaining on him.

The bandana came loose as he glanced back, displaying a mosaic of black-market implants and necrotic tissue. His left hand flicked in the pursuing Hero's direction and Mel ducked, lightning quick, as a honed metal spike embedded itself in the wall near where her face had been.

She lunged after him. The thief staggered and slipped off the edge of the walkway, but managed to catch himself with his augmented hand. Between his glove and the sleeve of his jacket, crude wire tendons and metal actuators surrounded the blue metal of the implant's bone structure. Mel fastened his robotic wrist to the grid of the walkway with a set of reinforced restraints.

"Give me your other hand," she said, offering her own.

The modder snarled an obscenity through blackened teeth and made a rude gesture with his biological limb.

"Reach," Mel urged, leaning farther. A fifty story drop yawned below them. "Do you really want to hang there until the Enforcers arrive? Give me your hand."

The modder released his grip on the walkway and dropped the scant four centimeters the restraint allowed, then began thrashing furiously.

"You idiot," Mel muttered, bracing herself and reaching further.

Red teardrops trickled down the modder's ruined face, but he continued to struggle. A stifled scream crept from behind his clenched teeth as his robotic arm tore loose with a sickening crunch. As his body careened down the narrow shaft between the two buildings, Mel was left staring at the naked metal limb dangling below the catwalk. The cooling system roared, venting hot air, as she scooted away from the edge and stood up.

"Holy shit, Mel," Adrian gasped as the recording came to an end.

"Couldn't you have saved him?"

"I tried to grab him. You saw. He wouldn't take my hand."

"We think he deliberately struggled until his prosthesis detached," Bradley said. "The penalty for that kind of modding is pretty severe."

"You're absolutely insane," Adrian continued, wiping his sweat-soaked palms on the blanket. "There were at least half a dozen things you did that could have gotten you killed."

"Only half a dozen?" Mel laughed. "I knew what I was doing. It was an incredible rush, but it wasn't that dangerous."

"It's not supposed to be about the rush. Protect and serve, remember?"

"I did. Didn't you see? I got it back."

Adrian frowned. The thief had made a mistake, perhaps many mistakes, but they still had a duty to protect him.

"What did he steal?"

"A prototype of a private developer's advanced neural interface. I didn't read all the lit on it, but it's supposed to support extended connectivity with external devices. It's highly experimental, and I'm not even sure if all the software has been tested yet. I don't know about you, but I wouldn't want to be the one trying that thing out. Not even if it gave me the ability to control every machine in the city."

"I guess he did," Adrian said sadly.

"Or someone he worked for did," Brad said. "According to Media, Mel's runner was part of a new branch of the Anarchists. They've embraced hardcore modding as a way to counteract what they call the unfair advantage the Company has gained by utilizing genetically modified humans."

"Us," Adrian said softly. "Someone's doing that to people to fight us?"

"Well, probably more because of the Enforcers," Mel said.

"Maybe they were willing volunteers?" Brad suggested. "Some

citizens are into that kind of thing. No accounting for taste, I guess."

"What about you?" Adrian asked. "Have you heard what they're going to do?"

Mel laughed. "You make it sound like I killed him myself. I tried my best to save his life. He made a choice."

"They let her know it had been declared an unpreventable suicide within an hour of his death," Brad said. "They even gave her a commendation for retrieving the tech he stole."

Adrian nodded. The image of the detached arm, with its bloody elbow joint and dangling wires, lingered in his mind. He wondered if it bothered Mel the same way it did him.

"How's the hand?" he asked instead. "Any lasting damage?"

"Nothing a regen cocktail and a nap couldn't fix," she replied, grinning as she displayed the small white scar on the palm of her hand. She flexed her fingers to demonstrate the lack of damage. "See, good as new!"

"I'm glad. You got lucky up there. You have a lot of people who'd miss you if you slipped or misjudged any of those crazy jumps."

Mel rolled her eyes. "Think I haven't heard that already?"

"I told her the same thing when she got back," Brad said, hugging his partner's shoulders.

Adrian was struck by how incredibly similar the two of them looked, more like twins than Company-sanctioned partners. Bradley's hair was a few shades lighter than Mel's, but their eyes were exactly the same color. They had almost the same build, and were the same width in the shoulders. Adrian bet they could even wear the same clothes. He looked away in embarrassment as Mel kissed her partner on the cheek.

"Thanks for filling me in on what I missed. I appreciate it."

"Of course! We had to know you were okay," Mel said.

"Griffith and Nelson might come down later," Brad added.

"You're going to be one hundred percent in no time," Mel declared, patting him on the shoulder. "Let us know if you need anything!"

"I will. And try to be careful out there!" Adrian called after them as the pair departed.

***

As the days passed, Adrian gradually regained his memory of the events leading up to the building collapse. An image of Kara's white stone building and the puzzle of the undercover Enforcers haunted his thoughts through the hours of grueling physical therapy.

When he was not in therapy or at the tower's gym, he mostly kept to his cot in the recovery bay. A detailed drawing began to take shape on the tablet, Kara's apartment building as he imagined it had once been. Green lawns stretched between it and the neighboring buildings, and lush trees rose toward the clear blue sky. A child sat under one of the trees, a black and white kitten cradled in her arms.

He spent hours redrawing the ornate carvings that covered the exterior walls. In this distant past, solar cells had not yet overrun the structure. Instead, there were windows, clear sheets of glass that reflected the trees and sky.

For the trees, he used the tablet's zoom feature and lost himself for hours at a time in the small, inexplicably comforting task of drawing leaves. Each was as unique as a Hero: similar, but never precisely the same. Drawing gave him a temporary sense of peace, although it could not ease his conscience for the lives he had been unable to save.

***

Three days into his physical therapy, Adrian finished the drawing of the white stone building and started drawing the river that frequented his dreams. Green water eddied around stretches of red sand, glittering in the bright sunlight. It was dark and cool beneath the overhang of the cliffs, but in the sunlight small trees and stunted bushes clung tenaciously to recesses in the stone.

The water sang, whispering over the sand and gurgling against the cliffs. It was warm to the touch in the shallows, but ran cold, fast and deep in the shadows by the canyon's far wall. Fish jumped, striking at large insects with long, thin wings that darted back and forth over the river's surface. Agile birds with dark backs and pale bellies swooped low over the water, rising to nests high in the cliff face.

When his hands cramped from hours of drawing, Adrian put the tablet away and delved into the Company's archives. The digital library was rumored to be the most extensive humankind had ever compiled. If people had ever created it, recorded it, or studied it, it was said to exist somewhere in the archives. Thousands of years of human experiences were preserved there. Every type of media, written, spoken, or video-recorded. Every type of art imaginable, every work of fiction or exposition of fact. Statistics, records, histories, observations. Every minute detail of trillions of human lives, as long as there had been someone to keep such records.

Unlimited access to the archives was one of the perks of being a Hero or an Enforcer. For everyone else, access had a price tag. Some subjects were restricted, available only to those with special security clearances. Because many citizens could not afford access, the Company and private employers often sponsored their employees' access to job-related topics.

Adrian spent countless hours searching the archives for information about the river. Over eons it had carved the canyon through which it ran, wearing a channel hundreds of meters deep and thirty meters wide through layers of sandstone, granite, limestone and shale.

The sky was never cloudy in the dream, but the archives indicated that canyons were formed by the runoff from torrential rainstorms. Nothing but weeds grew below a certain point on the stone walls, testament to the force of these periodic floods.

Above that high water mark, gray-leafed coyote willows swayed in the breeze. Iridescent trout rose to snap at green and blue dragonflies. Cliff swallows swooped and soared through the canyon, hunting tiny insects above water turned green by mats of cladophora algae.

Adrian found it miraculous that he could have such a detailed dream of a place he had never seen. Did the canyon exist, somewhere out in the unknown world beyond the exterior wall of the city? Or was it simply a figment of his imagination, a nocturnal wandering of his subconscious into a world that might have been?

****

When Adrian rejoined his fellow Heroes, he found life exactly as he had left it. The same soothing landscapes were displayed on the video screens, the same messages on the motivational posters. Nelson was seated on one of the couches, feet stretched out in front of him, watching a video show via his neural interface.

"How are the legs?" the stocky Hero asked.

"Good. They say it looks like I'm back to a hundred percent."

"That's what they said about Kenneth's shoulder too."

"Didn't we lose him to a jumper a couple of weeks ago?"

"We did. They said he slipped while trying to reach the guy, but I heard differently."

"Oh?"

"I heard that the doctor who autopsied him said his shoulder was all torn up. Same place as before. He probably fell because his shoulder blew out again."

Adrian grimaced. "Poor guy."

"Be careful with those new legs of yours." Nelson chuckled grimly. "But if it's any consolation, you made the news."

"I did?" Perhaps, Adrian thought, they had interviewed the last citizen he'd saved.

"See for yourself." Nelson forwarded him a week-old newscast.

"I'm reporting live from the scene of the latest horrific crime perpetrated by the terrorist group known as Anarchists," the reporter said as the clip began.

"Behind me, you can see where an old, substandard building in the Twenty-Ninth Tier's Trinity Ward has been destroyed. The reports I'm hearing indicate that it was still occupied. Sergeant, can you tell us what happened here?"

Adrian stared through the video, heart pounding. The pale, dark haired woman in the dark red suit scarcely came up the Enforcer's armored shoulder. Twisted rubble towered behind her. The smells of smoldering wiring and spilled coolant came to him, as sharp and vivid as if he was still there.

"Nearly a hundred have not been accounted for," the Sergeant was saying. "A formal tally will be released once the recovery and salvage phases have been completed."

"Are there any survivors present? We'd like to interview one."

"Some are in the crowd," the helmeted, faceless Sergeant said, indicating the crush of humanity seething on the other side of the wall of Enforcers. "Attempting to interview them is not recommended at this time."

The camera panned over the crowd before focusing on Adrian's unmoving form, strapped to a stretcher as the two medics worked to stabilize him. His face was deathly pale, eyes fixed on the heavens.

"Thanks," he mumbled in Nelson's direction.

"No problem."

"Hey, Adrian's back," Mel yelled as she walked in the front door. Although her uniform was smudged with blood, she seemed intact and in good spirits. Bradley was right behind her.

"It hasn't been the same without you!" Brad said.

"Hey, you don't look so good." Mel's grin faded. "You feeling okay?"

"I'm fine," Adrian said, blinking away the newscast as the reporter began interviewing the men at the aid station. "It's good to see everyone again."

"Nelson! You didn't show him that news segment, did you?"

"Why wouldn't I?"

"Nobody needs to see that! Have some decency!"

"It's fine. I dragged myself out of there. I was conscious, even if it doesn't look like it. I know what happened."

"Yes, but you still don't need to see that."

"It's great to see everyone again," Adrian said, deliberately changing the subject. "How's everyone been?"

"We've been good," Mel said.

"Survived another jumper!" Brad said proudly.

"Been nice and boring," Nelson added.

"Griffith still around?"

"Probably in the gym," Nelson said with a shrug. "You know how he is."

"You going to go see him?" Mel asked. "We may head that way soon too."

"Maybe tomorrow. I think I'm going call it an early night."

Adrian let himself into the familiar confines of his personal quarters, pulled up a video of a river, and let the sound of the rushing water drown out the memory the newscast had evoked. He imagined himself sitting on the river bank, watching the water hurry by until sleep overtook him.

***

Morning came with the same aches and pains he was used to feeling, although his knees hurt less than he'd become accustomed to. New joints had their benefits.

"You're back," Griffith said when he stepped out into the communal living area.

"I am. One hundred percent back to normal."

Griffith chuckled. "I don't doubt it. How was the vacation?"

"Could have been more comfortable." Adrian retrieved his bowl of oatmeal from the dispenser. "But it was fun. Why don't you get yourself one?"

"Ha! I'd like to survive to see retirement."

"Survive long enough for them to retire you, you mean?" Mel asked.

"Better things could happen."

Brad laughed. "Sure, man. Sure they could."

"Seen the news this morning?" Mel forwarded him an article. "It's getting ugly down there."

Riots Continue in Trinity Ward, Spread Through Twenty-Ninth Tier, the headline read.

Griffith snorted. "Twenty-Ninth Tier? Place is infested with Anarchists and freeloaders. Those idiots will riot over anything."

"Still?" Adrian asked.

Mel nodded. "Media isn't covering it, but the rumor I've been hearing is that people believe the Company was involved."

"Why would they do something like that?" Nelson asked. "Everyone knows it was the Anarchists; they destroy housing so the Company can't re-rent it after they downgrade the current tenants."

"After the evictions," Mel said. "Not before the issue is even settled."

"They're terrorists," Griffith retorted. "They don't care if people die."

"They have friends and family too, Griff. They're fighting back because the Company's policies unfairly target the weakest and poorest."

"Careful there, sunshine. You're starting to sound like a terrorist yourself."

"I think most of these so-called Anarchists are normal citizens," Bradley said. "Life is far from pleasant on some of the lower tiers. These people have exhausted all their options. They're fighting back the only way they know how, by hitting the Company where it hurts. Buildings, infrastructure, manufacturing plants–"

"Executives and their families," Nelson said.

"Some are crazier than others. These people are desperate. They want to show the Company the pain they feel from rationing, rising prices, job shortages, and the looming threat of being downgraded."

Griffith sneered. "How about you tell your Anarchist friends to get better jobs? Problem solved!"

"Have you ever had to look for a job?" Mel asked. "Right now, there are about two hundred job seekers for every one posting."

"Maybe for the unskilled ones," Griffith replied with a shrug. "Diversify. Get an education. As I said, problem solved."

"Everyone starts out unskilled, and technical schools are expensive. If they and their parents are struggling just to pay the rent, where's that money supposed to come from?"

"This disaster in Trinity Ward, though." Mel rolled her eyes as Griffith deliberately changed the subject. "The Anarchists may see that as some kind of victory, but the Company's the real winner." The big Hero leaned back and laced his hands behind his head, grinning. "That old building they blew up was full of metals and original-form construction materials. It's practically a gold mine in terms of resources."

"Once they're done hauling off all that valuable rubble, they'll put up an efficient two hundred floor building in its place," Nelson said. "More housing is good for everyone."

"They'll probably be tearing down the rest of Trinity Ward soon," Mel said sadly.

"Trust me, it's for the best."

The big Hero's words echoed in Adrian's head as he left their quarters. Remembering all the people who had perished in the explosion, he had a hard time agreeing with Griffith.

His assignment loaded as he walked to the nearest lift. He would be sharing the relatively small Sixteenth Tier with fifty other Heroes.

The ratio of Heroes to citizens on any given tier was based on the tier's credit. In the Company's estimation, more valuable tiers were worth exponentially more Heroes than lower-value tiers. Heroes, however, were taught to view all citizens as equal, regardless of their credit or status in life. A person on the Fiftieth Tier had just as much right to protection as a person on the First.

As Adrian stepped out of the transit terminal onto the Sixteenth

Tier's ground level, he was instantly bombarded with broadcasts for nearby retail spaces. Free music of a dozen different varieties assaulted his ears. Sale notifications popped up in the center of his vision, brightly colored banners scrolled across his view, and a pair of scantily clad holographic dancers beckoned him toward the nearby Entertainment District.

He rarely bought anything, so the advertising system had little information to use to tailor the content to his interests. Adverts for clothing, enhancement pills, entertainers, food and virtual games vied for his attention, all but blocking his view of the street in front of him.

Adrian launched an audio-visual projection blocker and banished the adverts with an irritated blink of his eye. Like many of the programs that made his life easier, the blocker was available for a price to the general population. Those who could not afford the filter were bombarded with adverts and any other content rogue coders managed to slip into the broadcast stream.

Even ad free, the tier was a riot of sound and color; brightly dressed citizens wandered from shop to shop, window-gazing and chatting. There were no small children to be seen, but throngs of teenagers wandered the pavement in giggling clusters or lounged against the walls, staring off into space.

Adrian watched one such boy plot an erratic course down the street, twitching violently. He grabbed the teen by the collar and hauled him back just in time to save him from walking into the path of an oncoming transport.

The boy's identity popped into his vision as he met the kid's startled stare. Kelly Baron, age fifteen. The child already had two minor convictions, one for shoplifting, one for coercion of a minor.

"What the hell, man?! I was about to beat my high score! We would've won the match!"

"You were about to walk in front of a transport," Adrian said patiently. "You won't win anything if you're in a healing coma. What are you playing?"

"Call of Justice, Extreme Prejudice Edition!"

"You're not old enough to have the license to play that."

The boy snorted. "Are you serious? There's not even any real gore in this one! You play as an Enforcer restoring the rule of law on the Fifty-Fifth Tier. The only weapons you have at the start are your armor and your riot shield."

"It's rated Mature for a reason."

"The rating's a joke. I expect some real sick stuff out of a Mature game, not just beating the piss out of some creditless trash."

"Excise that from your database," Adrian said sternly, framing a report to send to the boy's parents. "And try not to walk in front of any more transports."

The kid turned away, muttering obscenities under his breath.

"Is it just me, or are the rich kids getting more obnoxious?" Adrian asked via the tier's Safety channel. "Just saved this kid from a trip to emergency surgery, and not even a thank you. Apparently I kept him from beating his high score."

"Typical!"

"This is how you handle entitlement."

The Hero forwarded a video to everyone on the channel. The clip appeared to have been shot from an Enforcer's point of view, and opened as the officer patted down a bulky youth in a flashy red one-piece suit. The search turned up several expensive-looking pieces of jewelry.

"They're not stolen, idiot. My girlfriend gave those to me. Leave me alone!"

"Your girlfriend and her parents dispute that claim," the Enforcer said. "In fact, this is her mother's engagement ring. Present your wrists."

"Piss off!"

The Enforcer slammed the boy face first into a nearby wall, wrenched the kid's arms behind his back, and cuffed him. He could be heard laughing despite the teen's screams of pain.

"Stop resisting," the Enforcer said, placing his boot on the boy's back and lifting the kid's bound arms toward the back of his head. The teen screamed louder, eyes wide, face nearly as red as his clothing.

"Holy hell," Adrian exclaimed, stopping the video. "I hope they removed him from duty for that."

"Are you kidding? He's my hero!"

"I think we've all encountered a few citizens who deserve that treatment. Haven't you? You're lying if you say no."

"I haven't. So the kid's a thief. Let him go in front of the magistrates and receive his sentence."

"I think you're deliberately missing the larger point here."

"That the guy's a threat to public safety?"

"He's a legend. Has been ever since he crushed some rapist's skull. Haven't you heard of him?"

"Can't say that I have," Adrian replied. "Why didn't they retire him?"

"Claimed the servos in his suit malfunctioned. Guess it happens fairly often."

"I have a copy of the video, if you want to see it. Perp was hyped up on home-cooked stimulants and wouldn't stop struggling. Hardy pinned his head to the floor and applied pressure until the guy's skull popped."

"That's appalling," Adrian exclaimed. "And they believed him?"

"Like I said, apparently it happens all the time. I guess the Sergeant enjoyed his fifteen seconds of fame. He opened his own video channel not long after it blew over. Uploads under the nickname Harder Hardy."

"Enforcement's okay with that? That's a massive betrayal of the public trust."

"Not really. Most public arrests are put online by hundreds of citizens."

"Media scrubs most of those, though," a previously silent Hero pointed out. "They're rarely up for more than a few seconds, or a minute at most. What I don't understand is, why don't they scrub his stuff? Hardy's videos are incredibly popular. His channel is followed by hundreds of thousands of citizens, as well as other Enforcers and even Heroes."

"I don't know whether Enforcement condones his behavior, but he did get demoted from the Fifteenth Tier to somewhere around the Forty-Fifth."

"It wasn't a demotion. The location is a major step down, but it came with a promotion to Lieutenant."

Adrian grimaced. "Has it ever occurred to you that people like this Hardy guy are one of the reasons we have so many problems?"

"Man's just doing his job, the same as we are."

"Our oath explicitly forbids the use of excessive force. I'm pretty sure his does too."

"Hardy's not a bad guy. That's just the way Enforcers operate."

"You know what they say. You can't make an omelet without breaking a few eggs!"

"What's that got to do with anything?" someone demanded.

"The hell does that even mean?" a previously silent Hero asked. "And what's an omelet?"

Adrian shook his head and left the discussion.

The tier's buildings towered over him, two hundred floor architectural marvels glowing with multicolored signs. There was no trash to kick in frustration. Teams of sanitation personnel roamed the streets, picking up litter and scrubbing every surface until it gleamed. Adrian wondered if they had installed a program that made their job seem exciting, or if the workers simply took a triple dose of stimulants at the start of every shift.

Abstract sculptures had replaced the trees on the street, and he paused to contemplate one of the creations. Strands of red and gold composite, each as thick as his wrist, climbed nearly two stories into the air. At the top, the loosely interwoven strands spiraled together to form a sharp, multicolored point. According to the plaque at the base, the sculpture was called "The Triumph of Capitalism."

"Accurate, no?" an older man asked, stopping next to him.

"I don't think I understand."

The man grinned. Donald Simmons, age fifty six. Mild asthma. High blood pressure. Chairman of the tier's chapter of Peaceful Citizen Activists.

"The red strands represent blood. The gold ones represent money. They're entwined because you can't have one without the other." The man paused. "It's surprising that the Company permitted it, but I'm glad they did. Freedom of speech is important."

As they stood there, a distant scream reached Adrian's ears over the noise of the retail district. He glanced up just as an affluent jumper plummeted from the sky. A sculpture broke the man's fall, littering the street with razor-sharp shards of pink composite. The jumper rolled on the ground, screaming. Broken bone jutted through his metallic gold pants.

As the Hero moved to help, two Enforcers emerged from the crowd and began taking the jumper into custody.

"What are you doing?" Adrian demanded. "He needs medical attention!"

"He'll get it at the confinement facility," one of the Enforcers said.

"Damaging public property valued at over fifty thousand credits is a class C felony," the other Enforcer stated, flipping the writhing man onto his stomach and cuffing his hands behind his back. "Please cooperate, or I will be required to use appropriate force."

As the jumper continued to scream, the first Enforcer pressed the neutralizer built into his glove to the man's ribs. The jumper convulsed and went limp. The Enforcer slung the man's unconscious body over his shoulder, nodded to his partner, and stood up. A horde of custodial workers descended on the mess as the pair departed, hastily sweeping up the remains of the sculpture. More arrived with mops to sanitize the blood-streaked pavement.

"What a pity," the citizen activist said. "I really liked that one."

"You knew the victim?" Adrian asked.

"He's not a victim, he's a criminal," Simmons snapped, face hardening. "I was talking about the sculpture."

"I don't think he intended to break anything other than himself."

"Then he picked a damn careless place to jump, didn't he!"

Adrian stared at the citizen in disbelief, then shook his head and walked away.

# CHAPTER THREE

He moved at a brisk jog, following the red pinpoint of a distress signal across the roof of a two hundred floor housing high-rise. The skyscraper towered above its neighbors, its rooftop solar cells baking under the full force of the afternoon sun.

The view ahead, behind, and to his right was breathtaking. Tiers packed with light reflecting pale gray high-rise towers descended into the smog, their streets crawling with human life. A line of red lights flickered through the pall of pollution that shrouded the hill's lower reaches, marking the top of the wall that separated the Company-controlled portion of the city from the lawless tiers below. Far beyond that, shimmering like a mirage in the omnipresent heat, rose the towering sandstone cliffs that marked the city's true border.

A breath of hot wind brushed his hair, and Adrian glanced over his other shoulder. The upper reaches of the city rose to his left, a wall of pale high-rises encased in shining solar cells. The gleaming towers of the affluent stood above, stark against the white-hot sky.

The distress call had originated from the northeast corner of the building, above the Entertainment District. A wisp of human life dangled from the decorative molding below the edge of the roof, heart pounding.

"Is someone there?" the woman called as he approached. "Please help me! I don't want to die!"

It occurred to Adrian to ask her why she was hanging off the roof if she didn't want to die, but he suppressed the idea. It was not uncommon for jumpers to have second thoughts.

"I've got you," he said, leaning over the edge of the building.

The jumper was a pale, skeletally thin young woman wearing nothing but a lacy pink top and matching thong underwear. Her brown eyes were wide with panic and glassy from drug use. Ecstasia DeLorne, age twenty. Born Ann Lormer to creditless parents on the Forty-Third tier, she had changed her name at the age of sixteen. Ecstasia had most recently worked in the Entertainment District as an escort, but was now jobless.

Medical history: asthmatic. Attention Deficit Disorder. Bipolar Disorder. Schizophrenic. Fifteen minor convictions, three related to theft of goods or services, seven for causing a public disturbance, and five for assault. Treated and released for synthetic sedative addiction five times since age eighteen. Treated and released for stimulant addiction twice.

Adrian blinked, overwhelmed by the wall of text scrolling across his vision. The woman was on so many different medications that it would have taken him fifteen minutes to read them all. The last medical note was in the bold type that indicated a permanent modification; the Public Health Division had deemed her terminally unstable, and she had been sterilized.

"I changed my mind. I don't want to die! Don't let me die, don't let me die, please, please help me– " The words came out in a breathless jumble as Adrian carefully lifted her back onto the rooftop.

"You're not going to die. Everything's going to be fine," Adrian said, patting her on the back as she threw her spindly arms around him. "Why were you trying to jump?"

"My boyfriend left me and he was paying for my apartment, you know, here in this building, and they're going evict me and I can't pay, and I can't pay for my stuff anymore either–"

"Okay, slow down," Adrian said soothingly as he disengaged himself from her embrace. For someone so malnourished, the woman clung to him with surprising strength. "Everything's going to be alright. Have you put in any job applications? A new employer might help you get back on your feet."

The miasma of chemical scents that surrounded her was nearly suffocating. Beneath the synthetic pheromones in her perfume and the styling products in her short, artificially blonde hair, he detected traces of at least a dozen stimulants and sedatives. Not all of them were on her list of legally-prescribed medications.

"It's not going to be okay," she wailed, resisting his efforts to set her on her feet. "They fired me! And no one else will hire me after what they put in my record."

"Who fired you?"

"Them." She waved vaguely toward the Entertainment District. "The managers."

"What happened?" Adrian asked, finally succeeding in catching both her wrists and keeping her at arm's length despite her struggles. "Please be calm. We're going to fix this."

"It wasn't my fault. It was self-defense! What they were trying to do would have left permanent scars. I didn't sign up for that."

"I understand." He guided the jumper back toward the maintenance access. "Do you have evidence?"

"Yes, yes, I do!"

"Okay, we're going to go show your former employer that proof and see if we can get your job back. That should keep your rent paid, or we can find a cheaper unit that you can afford. Then we're going to take you to a treatment center. "

"You're going to pay my rent?" Ecstasia gasped, eyes lighting up. "I love you!" Wrenching her wrists out of his grip, she threw her arms around his neck and hugged him tightly.

The gesture might have been meant to be distracting. Adrian held his breath and once again removed the entertainer to a safe distance.

"That's not what I said," he told her firmly. "I said we're going to get your job back so you can pay your rent."

She just smiled up at him, brown eyes sparkling. Whatever she was high on, he decided, she was very high. Her eyes were almost all pupil despite the bright lighting in the maintenance lift.

"You can be my new boyfriend," she said.

"That's alright," Adrian mumbled, unsure how to respond.

On the one hand, he had absolutely no interest in such an offer. The Company strictly forbade Heroes from choosing partners from the general populace. On the other hand, he was afraid to say anything that might unsettle her further.

"It's okay, I'm not scared!"

"I'm sorry, but we aren't allowed to."

"We both know that's not true," she cajoled. "There's that really big Hero, Griffin or something. He visits us all the time! You probably know him, right? You guys all know each other." She giggled and batted her eyelashes at him.

Adrian stared. How often had Griffith been assigned to this section of the Sixteenth Tier? It couldn't possibly be often enough for anyone to know him by name.

"But you're way more handsome than he is," she continued, oblivious to his stunned silence. "And more gentle! I bet you wouldn't have accidents like he does." She leaned closer. "Why don't we go back to my place and find out?"

"What accidents?" Adrian asked, moving into the far corner of the elevator.

Her expression clouded over. "He breaks bones sometimes, in the heat of the moment, and he always leaves bruises. But it's okay!" Her smiled returned. "Then he takes me to the medical center and says that it happened during a rescue, and they fix me up for free."

"He's not supposed to be doing that," Adrian said softly, a knot of uncharacteristic anger growing in the pit of his stomach. "If any Hero or Enforcer requests your services, you need to report them."

He caught her hands as they tried to unzip his jacket and used the excuse of exiting the lift to keep her at arms' distance.

"We're going to have a talk with these managers. Do you want to go change your clothes first?" The entertainer was hardly dressed for a meeting, and only light indoor sandals protected her bare feet.

Ecstasia shook her head.

The Entertainment District was a garish sea of revelry, the crush of humanity even thicker than he last remembered it. Street stalls, licensed and illegal alike, sold intoxicants, sexual favors and novelties. Citizens were packed in shoulder to shoulder, writhing in a pheromone-addled haze to the pounding music. Entertainers worked the crowd, luring potential customers.

Nearly a third of the shop owners and entertainers he looked at ducked their heads and slunk into the crowd, a sure sign that they feared arrest if he was able to scan their eyes. He spotted three stalls on one block selling illegal, homemade stimulants. Thieves slipped through the crowd, whisking light fingers through pockets in search of poorly secured valuables. Amid the chaos, the spectacle of a Hero with a scantily-clad entertainer clinging to his arm garnered relatively little interest.

Eventually Ecstasia led him to one of the largest towers in the district. In a city where space was a precious commodity, the sheer size of the entrance was a bold statement. White marble pillars wrapped in sculpted gold vines framed a set of massive double doors, their glass etched with a scene of nudes frolicking under a waterfall.

"This is it," Ecstasia whispered.

The ceiling of the cavernous room beyond was supported by more pillars rising from a shining white marble floor. The space was empty except for a hologram of a water fountain that dominated the center of the room. An opulent white marble reception desk occupied the far wall.

As they passed the fountain, Adrian was shocked to realize it was not, in fact, a hologram. The musical tinkling of the water could be a recording, but the humidity that kissed his skin and the smell of the chemicals used to scrub the water betrayed it as the real thing. How on earth had the owners of the tower gotten the permit to use that much water?

"I'm sorry, we're not hiring," the black-suited female receptionist said as they approached.

"We need to speak to a manager," Ecstasia said nervously.

The receptionist met the entertainer's eyes, expression indifferent. "Ecstasia DeLorne, your termination was final. It is not a decision that may be appealed."

"It's a matter of the law and public safety," Adrian said. "I have evidence that a manager will be interested in seeing."

The receptionist paused for a long moment, eyes distant, as she communicated with someone via her neural interface. "Mr. Compton will see you now." She gestured toward the lift to the right of the desk.

Stepping inside, Adrian noticed that the machine had no buttons, not even a fingerprint override.

"Don't worry, they'll send us to the right floor," Ecstasia said, noticing his frown.

"That doesn't seem safe."

Ecstasia shrugged. "It's a security thing. This is the management tower for the whole district." She paused, twisting her fingers nervously. "Mr. Compton is one of the executives. I've heard bad things about him."

"I'm going to advocate for you. It will be alright, I promise."

She said nothing, only leaned against his shoulder as if he was all that was keeping her on her feet. Perhaps their next stop needed to be a medical station.

The cage rose for a long time, suggesting that their destination was the highest floor or close to it. Just as the lift came to a stop, a faint chime sounded in his inner ear and a broadcast commenced on the city-wide Safety channel. The smiling, well-cushioned face of the

Company's Executive of Safety popped into his view.

"Hello and good afternoon, good Heroes!"

Adrian banished the announcement to his inbox with an impatient blink.

The doors slid open, revealing a river of red carpet stretching across an expanse of white marble to a huge, glossy wooden desk. The high-backed chair behind the desk overflowed with a pasty-colored man in a tight charcoal gray suit. The walls to the man's right and back were floor to ceiling glass, a stunningly expensive view in terms of lost solar cell space.

"We're supposed to stay back here," Ecstasia whispered, tugging at Adrian's arm as he moved toward the desk.

"You can stay here if you want," he replied, glancing at the wooden bench at the back of the room. "I'll talk to him."

"How kind of you to visit," the man behind the desk said as he approached. "What matter of public safety can I help you with today?"

"This woman says she was fired for defending herself. Is that true?"

"I can't say as I remember," the man said, staring at his steepled fingers. "Personnel usually handles those decisions."

"Ecstasia DeLorne, citizen ID number 87446392HW. You signed off on her termination. You're not familiar with her case?"

"Ah, yes," the man purred, looking up. "The schizophrenic."

Edward Compton, age fifty-four. Chief executive of the Company-sanctioned adult entertainment industry. Partnered with Shelby Schmitt, with whom he had two children. No health problems. No arrest records.

"What does her health have to do with her employment?" Adrian asked, holding the man's blue-gray gaze. Despite the polite smile and faint expression of amusement Compton wore, there was something less than friendly about his demeanor.

"Ms. DeLorne has been warned time and again to control her

aggression and offensive outbursts. We generously paid for her to get treatment for her psychological problems. She was terminated when she continued to jeopardize the health and safety of our clients."

"They were hurting me, and security wouldn't do anything," Ecstasia yelled, leaning forward in her seat. "The client violated the agreement! And the only medication your people gave me was a prescription to drug me into a stupor."

"That's ridiculous," Compton scoffed. "As you can see, she's delusional. We've done everything we could for this girl since she came to us, a creditless sixteen-year-old with no job skills. At a considerable loss of credit, I might add. The time has come for her to find employment elsewhere."

"Do you have any proof that she did in fact harm your business?"

Compton smiled placatingly. "Don't you think this is more of a job for Enforcement, my dear Hero? As you can see, no one is in any danger here."

"She almost jumped to her death. I would call that a significant danger."

"Very well, if you insist. My assistant will see that she is placed in a position more in line with her preferences."

"Thank you." He glanced toward the back of the room just in time to see the entertainer being ushered out the door by two burly security guards.

"Don't expect miracles, though. As you may be aware, Ms. DeLorne has a rather expensive drug problem. We've tried everything to keep her clean and sober. Nothing worked, and her habit grew to the point where she was forced to find a second form of employment. Perhaps that should be your next avenue of investigation."

"It may be, after I'm done here. If I can trust that Ecstasia will be safe in your care."

"My people will do everything in their power to keep her from harm. In the meantime, how would you like a reward for the service you provide? It's on the house."

"No, thank you."

"Are you sure? Have a seat." A section of the floor slid aside, and a chair popped up behind him. A server entered from a concealed side door and placed two glasses of water in front of them. "May I offer you a glass of water?"

"Really, I can't."

"Sit, sit. Then we'll talk." The executive nodded in approval as Adrian sat and sipped his water. "Are you sure there's nothing I can do for you? Nothing at all? Perhaps I could interest you in some of our finer products."

A panel slid aside on top of the desk, revealing a holographic projector. Compton waved his hand and images of nude women danced in the air between them.

"See something you like?" Compton asked, smirking. Each girl pirouetted and did a little dance.

"No, thank you," Adrian said quickly.

"If that's not your flavor, we have men too. Whatever kind you prefer." The holographic display changed to a range of male entertainers.

"No, thank you. The only favor I want from you is her safety."

"You have my word."

"Thank you," Adrian said, rising from the chair. "And thank you for the water. Have a good day."

As he rode the lift back to the ground floor, Adrian noticed that the message icon flashing at the edge of his vision had been joined by a second one. Either the Executive of Safety was sending out a lot of announcements, or Compton had complained about him.

* * *

His patrol led him into the depths of the Entertainment District, where muted pink, red, and purple street lights lent an air of romantic privacy to the throngs of pleasure seekers. Adrian averted his eyes more than once as he spotted freelance entertainers plying their trade in alleys and dim corners of the architecture.

Seeking a public restroom, Adrian entered a sultry red building with an aging mural of an orgy splashed across the storefront. A vandal had scraped away all of the participants' faces. Faded pink neon lights hung from the floor above, flickering intermittently in the perpetual gloom.

An angular middle-aged man in a faded blue sleeveless top stood behind the front desk, greasy brown hair hanging over his eyes as he stared at the purple counter in front of him.

"Bathrooms?"

"Is that all you want?" the attendant asked, meeting Adrian's gaze. "Down the hall and to the left." A faint, defiant smirk creased his narrow face.

Adam Vermuelen, age thirty-two. Asthmatic. HIV positive. High blood pressure. Treated and released three times in the last two years for stimulant addiction. Fourteen prior convictions, eight of which were for assault. Two for coercion of a minor. Four for unauthorized distribution of controlled substances.

Adrian frowned. The man was on a work visa all the way from the Thirty-Eighth Tier. How many more convictions would it take for the Company to pull his cross-tier employment permit?

Vermuelen smiled more broadly, as if he knew exactly what Adrian was thinking.

Down the hall, there was a line at least fifteen citizens deep for the bathrooms. Adrian ducked through them, muttering an apology, and used his thumb print to unlock the small service restroom.

The light within was already on, and the air was thick with synthetic perfume. A nervous giggle reached his ears as he paused to scrub his hands with disinfectant gel. There were two pairs of feminine heels as well as a Hero's sturdy boots occupying one of the stalls. Adrian stepped back out into the hallway.

His enhanced hearing picked up more giggling, laughter, and

some banging that probably verged on damaging public property. A short time later, two scantily clad young women slipped out of the service restroom, giggling. Mathews, a Hero scarcely into his third year of service and possessing a solidly mediocre rescue count for his age, attempted to exit a moment later. Adrian caught the young Hero by his jacket and shoved him back into the bathroom, letting the door slide shut behind them.

"It's not what you think!" Mathews fumbled with his collar, trying to hide several telltale lipstick smudges.

"You know that's strictly forbidden. You could hurt someone."

"I was careful! They're fine, I swear!"

Adrian folded his arms and stared the other Hero down.

"But, you, what are you doing here? I mean, nobody takes this area unless, you know, they..." Mathews stuttered to a halt, perhaps realizing that he was only digging his hole deeper.

"We all rolled for who got which sections, and this is what I got. As it should be."

"I don't see why it's prohibited. Most of us don't hurt anyone."

"Most of you? How many others do this?"

"I'm not sure."

"Really?"

Mathews was turning red. Dishonesty was strongly discouraged during a Hero's social conditioning, and as a result they were generally poor liars.

"Look, I don't want to get anyone in trouble. But if you want to report those that are hurting people, you should start with a Hero named Griffith. They had me patrol with him when I first started and he got us this district. You want a guy who can't control his strength and doesn't care if he hurts anyone? He's your Hero."

"Why didn't you report him?"

"Have you seen him? Guy's terrifying. He can double what I lift, and that's a light day in the gym for him."

"No one said you had to tell him. You can do it anonymously."

"I'm not happy about what I saw either," the Hero said, staring at the grimy beige floor. "I didn't enjoy it. But he made it clear that if I ever got any ideas about reporting it, he would know exactly who ratted on him."

"In the future, I expect you to do the right thing. If you're afraid, come tell me about it. And stop doing this kind of thing. I won't report it this time, but this is the only leniency you're going to get. Understand?"

Mathews nodded quickly and hurried out the door.

Adrian stared at the tired-looking Hero that regarded him from the smudged mirror and grimaced. The news about his group-mate, while not entirely unexpected, still sat uneasily on his stomach. What had Griffith done that had left Mathews so cold?

The two messages in his inbox had been joined by a third. Adrian sighed in annoyance and locked himself into one of the stalls. The smell of synthetic perfume made him cough as he opened the messages.

"Hello and good afternoon, good Heroes!" the first message began. "I bear bittersweet news. Your beloved leader, the Prime Hero Marciano, passed away at oh-eight-hundred this morning." The Executive of Safety paused, expression sad. "But every end is a new beginning. The initial selection has been completed, and five potential Prime Heroes have been identified!"

So that was what all the announcements were about. He considered simply deleting them, uninterested in the process. The Prime Hero was little more than a figurehead.

The main benefit of surviving long enough and having a high enough rescue count to be selected was that the Prime Hero, unlike other Heroes, was retired in the same style that wealthy citizens were. He or she could settle down with any partner who would have them, free of the restrictions that ordinarily limited who Heroes could partner with. The Company would support them in luxury for the rest of their days.

"Three of the five are, amazingly, from the same home group," the Executive was saying. "As soon as these worthy Heroes have given their nomination speeches, we'll broadcast those speeches and let you cast your vote!"

Adrian scowled and deleted the message. He could barely remember the last time a Prime Hero had been chosen, but he recalled that the popular vote counted for little in the selection process.

The next was also from the Executive.

"Greetings, good Hero!" The singular form of his job title stopped him from deleting the message as soon as he opened it. "You have been selected! As the active Hero with the highest rescue count, you are the first nominee for the position of Prime. Please give us your thoughts on a Hero's duty, the place of Heroes in the Company, and what you would like to see from the Safety Division in the future."

Adrian's jaw dropped. It had never occurred to him to wonder what his number stood at, or if he had been in service long enough to place in the top five.

"Please proceed to the nearest communications terminal and record your nomination speech. Thank you for your service!"

As Prime, he could upgrade his aging nano-prosthetic implants. He could see the world that younger Heroes with newer visual chips saw. When he grew old and his hands succumbed to arthritis, the Safety Division's doctors would synthesize new joints for him.

The third message was from a Safety clerk, urging him submit his speech and reminding him that there was a time limit to do so. Glancing at the clock at the edge of his visual display, he realized that the deadline was a scant hour away.

Exiting the building, he set a course through the tide of Entertainment patrons to the nearest communication booth. As he passed the defaced mural, a pale, thrashing form plummeted from above. The impact made no sound, muffled by the press of bodies. Injured citizens staggered away from the impact zone, screaming in pain and shock, as Adrian called for a medical team and rushed toward the jumper.

"Everyone freeze!" he shouted, pulling an injured woman to her feet. Her arm was broken and her face was smeared with blood. It was hard to tell how much of the damage had been inflicted by the jumper, and how much by the crowd after she was knocked to the ground.

"Nobody move," he bellowed, elbowing his way to the point of impact.

Yelling for order, Adrian finally cleared enough space to see the jumper. She had traded the pale pink outfit for an even smaller blue one. Her body was still warm, but there was no heartbeat. He smoothed Ecstasia's short blonde hair and gently closed her eyes.

Turning away, Adrian put up a waypoint for the emergency responders and their phalanx of faceless protectors. The water he had gulped at the dispenser outside the bathroom sat uneasily on his stomach. This was not what was supposed to happen. He had missed something critically important, and the citizen had come to the same fate she had narrowly avoided when he first rescued her. He felt like a failure.

He slipped into the crowd as the Enforcers took charge of Ecstasia's body and cleared a space for the medics to treat the injured. Hoping that they would treat her death as a homicide, he forwarded everything she had told him, and everything Compton had said, to the investigating Enforcer. At the very least, the executive was guilty of doing an incredibly poor job of keeping his word.

Inside the communication booth, Adrian sank to his knees and leaned his head on the com console. A toxic cocktail of anger, self-recrimination and horror churned in his stomach as he considered the things he had heard in the last few hours.

They wanted a speech from him. What should he tell them? Your system is broken? Your Heroes and Enforcers have forgotten their purpose, and some do more to contribute to the misery of the citizens than to alleviate it? They would not want to hear his anger, his criticism, or his honest observations. But if he was selected, he would no longer be in a position to protect anyone.

"Hero, your immediate attention is required," the Safety clerk said. "You only have five minutes left to submit your speech. Failure to do so counts as forfeiture of your nomination."

"I'm going, I'm going," Adrian muttered, blinking away the message.

Standing up straight, he allowed the com console to verify his identity. As he pressed the record button and stared into the camera, his mind went blank. Seconds ticked by. He could almost feel the stares of the thousands of Heroes who would be viewing the video. Adrian cleared his throat and began to speak.

# CHAPTER FOUR

His mood was less than cheerful when he returned to the communal quarters.

Griffith was seated on the couch, face twisted in concentration as he played a virtual game. Nelson sat nearby, smiling faintly, only his eyes moving as he watched one of his video shows.

Adrian tossed an empty bowl into the dispenser and ordered some steak-and-potatoes-flavored foodstuff. When the dispenser beeped, he took the steaming bowl and sat down across from the larger Hero.

"Congratulations on your nomination," he said, waiting for Griffith to acknowledge him. "We need to talk."

"Huh," Griffith grunted without looking up.

"Get off your game."

"You mind?" the other Hero mumbled. "I finally got Hardy to agree to a duel. You know, Harder Hardy? I'm kind of busy."

"Get off your game. This is serious," Adrian growled.

"What's going on?" Nelson asked.

"I heard some really disturbing things today. I'd like to get his side of the story before I file my report."

Nelson's eyebrows lifted in surprise. "What'd he do now?"

"Apparently he's well-known in the Entertainment District. And what do you mean, what did he do now? What did I miss?"

The stocky Hero looked away. "It's nothing, man. Nothing major. You've probably heard the same things I have." His eyes shifted in Griffith's direction nervously.

"Heard what?"

"The hell is your problem?" the big Hero demanded, eyes focusing his surroundings. "There, I lost my match! You happy now? You made me look like an idiot in front of someone I respect."

"Nobody cares about your game," Adrian said quietly.

"It's a ranked match. People bet on these. Did someone pay you to do this?"

"I heard some disturbing things about your conduct today," Adrian said, picking an unidentifiable brown lump out of his food.

"Oh, is this your way of saying you disagree with my proposal?"

"I'm talking about your conduct in the Entertainment District."

"I thought it was entertainer I smelled when you walked in."

"That was my patrol area," Adrian said through clenched teeth. "Not all of us blithely violate our oath."

To his surprise, the other Hero laughed out loud. Nelson sat utterly still, as if trying to become part of the tan upholstery of the couch.

"Why are you telling me this?"

"Because you have a history of abusing your position of authority. Now you have two choices: you can turn yourself in, or I can file a formal report."

"You think I'm the first Company man to visit an entertainer? It's been going on for generations!"

"You did a hell of a lot more than just visit an entertainer!" Adrian shot back.

"I never heard any complaints."

Behind Griffith, Nelson rolled his eyes.

"Threatening people into silence is also a crime," Adrian hissed. "I know what you've been doing, and I have more than enough evidence to have you retired."

"Is that so?" Griffith stood up, forcing Adrian to look up to meet his eyes. "Are you absolutely sure about that?"

Adrian refused to rise to the bait. He remained seated, hands calmly clasped around his bowl.

"I'm sure. Your nomination makes a mockery of the position of Prime. You're a threat to the public and a disgrace to every Hero who's ever worn the uniform. Turn yourself in."

Griffith turned and walked away, laughing. The clatter of a bowl on the dispenser tray indicated that he was making food. Adrian poked at his cooling bowl of gray glop, appetite gone.

"You're delusional," Griffith said from across the room, "and your proposal's a joke. Updated training, more oversight, and public education campaigns? That's your big plan?"

"It would make life better for everyone."

"The city is overflowing. We have over a million citizens as of the last census! There's not enough of anything to go around. Meanwhile, the Company is wasting hundreds of thousands of credits a day on Heroes who keep those idiots from thinning themselves out. This isn't the outcome the founders envisioned when they created the Safety Division. A Hero on every street corner to protect you and your family sounds nice, but we can't afford to keep doing that."

"The founders had the right idea. Everyone has a right to protection, regardless of their social or economic status. The overcrowding situation on the lower tiers doesn't change that."

"Let me put this in terms even you might understand," Griffith sneered, returning to the couches with his food. "We live, suffer, and die at the whim of people who hate us. The Company designed us to be disposable. Some of us would like more out of life."

"Good luck with that," Adrian said, getting up.

"You gonna finish that?" Nelson asked, indicating Adrian's half-eaten bowl.

"No. You can have it if you want it."

"Thanks. You should go get cleaned up. No offense, but you reek."

Safe inside his private quarters, Adrian leaned into the warm mist of the shower and scrubbed vigorously, imagining red sand and green water. What would it feel like, to have that much water around him? He leaned his forehead against the wall of the shower and imagined walking out into the river, letting the water wash away his guilt and anger. There would be nothing but the babble of the current and the chirping of the birds as he walked out further, until his feet could no longer find the bottom and the water swept him away.

The mist ceased, his daily water allowance expended. A chime sounded in his ear and Adrian deleted the message without listening to it. He did not care who they chose as Prime. He did not want to be disturbed.

He was drying off under the blower and considering going to bed early when someone knocked on his door.

"What?" Adrian demanded, throwing on a shirt and shorts as Nelson opened the door.

"Where's Mel?"

"I don't know. Out celebrating with Brad?"

"No, she's not." There was an uncharacteristic look of panic in Nelson's eyes. "Didn't you see the broadcast?"

"No, I didn't. What happened?"

Nelson stared at him for a long moment, then shook his head. "Brad's dead. He ate it trying to save a jumper over the Twentieth Tier Southern Avenue transit interchange."

There were only a few pedestrian bridges that crossed the interchange, and only near the highest floors. They offered a long uninterrupted drop to the ground below, and the place had become a popular suicide spot.

"I'm scared for Mel. I sent her a message, but she's not answering."

"I'll try," Adrian promised.

Like Nelson's, his message also went unanswered. Sleep was no longer an option, so he returned to the communal living space and took a seat on the opposite side of the room from Griffith.

"Do you think she'd do it?" Nelson asked nervously.

"I don't know," Adrian replied, focusing on the room through the unembellished text of the archive. It was a scientific paper about the formation of canyons, and he'd been staring at the same paragraph for the last ten minutes.

"She's still not answering."

"Don't worry, I'm sure she'll be back soon." He wasn't sure he believed it. But if someone was looking to him for reassurance, he would provide it.

Thirty minutes later Mel walked in the door, face red, uniform bloody.

"I'm sorry," Nelson began.

"What happened?" Adrian asked.

"They wouldn't let me see him!"

"But, the blood," Nelson said, indicating her clothes. "Isn't that his?"

"Broke up a fight. I was fourteen tiers away when he fell," Mel said, face twisting into a grimace. "I came straight back to the medical facility, but they wouldn't let me see him. They said he was already gone. They wouldn't let me see him, not even just to see his body, not even to say goodbye!"

"They were probably trying to be kind," Nelson said. "I'm sure it was pretty bad."

"I don't care! I just wanted to tell him goodbye." Her cheeks shone wet in the bright overhead lights. Although they had belonged to the same home group for five years, it was the first time he had ever seen Mel cry.

"I'm sorry," Adrian said softly.

"Could you muzzle the drama?" Griffith yelled from the other side of the room. "I'm trying to concentrate here."

"Oh, am I bothering you?" Mel yelled back.

"Yes, you are! I'm dueling an Enforcer, and your yapping is really distracting."

"We're distracting, but the news that Brad's dead isn't?"

"Wait, Bradley's dead?" Griffith's eyes flicked toward them. "Son of a gutter licking lice infested vermin! He got me. I hope you're happy!"

"One of your fellow Heroes just died, a guy you've lived with for years, and you're angry that you lost a game?" Mel demanded.

Griffith turned to face them, grinning. "Yes. Yes, I am. Brad's dead? Great! That's one less person to annoy me while I'm trying to relax."

Mel's eyes narrowed. "Take. That. Back."

Nelson turned white. "I'm sure that came out wrong. I'm sure he didn't mean that the way it sounded."

"Oh, I meant it," Griffith retorted.

Mel marched across the room.

"Please don't," Nelson whispered.

"Get up," Mel snarled. "Show some respect for the dead!"

Griffith rolled his eyes. "Or you're going to do what, sweetheart?"

There was a crunch as Mel's fist connected with Griffith's face, and blood splattered the nearby wall. He attempted to return the favor as he came to his feet, but Mel was too quick for him.

"You had better hope that didn't break any teeth," the big Hero muttered as Nelson and Adrian moved to prevent the continuation of the fight.

"If it did, it'd serve you right," Mel shot back.

"I heard he's done a lot worse," Nelson began, but Adrian quickly silenced him.

"Let's just drop it," Adrian said. "It's been a bad day for everyone. Let's all go to our respective personal spaces and get some sleep."

Griffith snorted, mopping up blood with his sleeve. "Bad day my ass. I was having a great day until now."

"Can I get you some dinner?" Adrian asked as Mel glared at Griffith's retreating back.

"I'm not hungry, thank you. But you can come with me if you

want to know what happened."

Adrian followed her into the confined space of her room, wondering how she and Bradley put up with sharing such a small area. The personal spaces weren't designed to accommodate more than one person.

Mel sank down on the edge of the bed and held her face in her hands. Adrian sat down next to her.

"I heard it was a jumper," he said after a few minutes had gone by in silence. "That interchange has been a bad spot forever."

"It's like they don't care if people jump," Mel said. "Heroes have been saying something needs to be done for generations. Safety nets. Better locks on the maintenance accesses. Nothing changes."

Adrian nodded.

"Why are we even here?" she asked softly.

"Because people need us."

"Do they? Griffith made one good point. People don't trust us anymore. Our help is as unwelcome as the Enforcers'. What's the point?"

"People need us."

"You're something special, Adrian." Mel gave him a wan smile. "I don't know if you'll get the popular vote, but your speech was really good. If Safety wanted to change the public's perception of us, that's what they'd need to do."

"Thank you."

"Brad and I were talking about it before he got the call. He said his was just a pet peeve, a safety issue. You have real vision."

"His was important too. City infrastructure has needed effective suicide barriers for generations. More counseling options wouldn't be a bad idea, either. And making euthanasia completely free would probably lower the number of jumpers."

"Could have saved his life," Mel said sadly. "Do you want to see what happened?"

"He was recording?"

"Always. Just for each other. We liked to be able to show each other some of the funnier and more bizarre things we'd seen." She sent him the file.

Adrian played the recording with some trepidation, unsure if he wanted to experience his friend's death in the first person. His ordeal in the collapsed building was not something he would have ever wanted his friends to see.

The file began to play, and Bradley's perceptions overtook his own. A dizzying drop stretched below him, five hundred meters of empty space crossed by one other walkway. He stood outside the covered tube of a pedestrian bridge on scaffolding left behind by maintenance. A few meters away, a stylishly starved woman in a teal suit clung to the outside of the railing.

"I can see you're a wealthy citizen," Brad was saying. "You have a lot to live for. Please, let me help you."

There was a note of desperation in his voice. Brad had known that if the woman jumped, he would die.

"I have nothing left to live for." Her face was stiff and strangely emotionless. "My husband made a bad investment, and they're going to take everything to repay his debt. My private transport, my jewelry, my apartment. I'll have nothing."

"Please." He inched closer. "Just take my hand. It's going to be alright, I promise."

The woman's emotionless mask cracked, and tears crept down her angular cheeks.

"Help me," she whispered.

Bradley reached toward her, and for a moment the woman looked as if she would take his hand. Then, in one spasmodic movement, she threw herself backward off the scaffolding. The look on her face was one of confusion and terror.

Bradley vaulted over the railing after her, and Adrian's heart slammed against his ribs as the sensation of falling seized him.

Brad never managed to catch the jumper. She had too much of a lead, and there was no way to close the distance that separated them. The lower walkway rushed by, thirty meters to his left. The transit interchange, crawling with oblivious commuters, sped toward him.

He rolled onto his back and sent a short message to Mel. The impact came a few seconds later, an explosion of force that fragmented his vision. The world cracked and froze, darkness showing around the jagged edges, and the recording ended.

Adrian returned to the present to find Mel doubled over, sobbing violently. His heart was pounding and the world had gone gray. Taking a deep breath to steady himself, he put his arm around Mel and patted her on the shoulder. She hugged him back and they stayed that way for a long time, lost in their grief.

"He sent me a message," she said after a time. "He said he loved me and that he'd be watching out for me."

"That sounds like something he'd do."

"Every time I watch it, I'm yelling, 'Don't jump! Don't jump!' As if he had a choice," she said bitterly. "She basically murdered him."

"If it makes you feel any better, I'm sure she didn't survive either."

"It doesn't. But I'm glad she's dead."

They sat in silence, Adrian staring at the floor, Mel resting her head on his shoulder.

"You should probably go to bed," she said.

"I suppose I should." He didn't feel tired. He didn't feel anything. It was as if experiencing Brad's death had drained him of all capacity to feel emotion.

"Go," Mel said, standing up and pulling him to his feet. "You have to work tomorrow."

"So do you."

She shrugged. "I'm sure I'll manage."

"You promise?"

"I promise."

"Then I'll see you in the morning. Try to get some sleep, okay?"

She made a sound halfway between a laugh and a sob. "Sure."

***

Alone in his room, faced with the task of detailing everything he had recently learned about Griffith's misconduct, Adrian decided to sit down and watch the entirety of the other Hero's nomination speech. When the proposals first went live he hadn't gotten past the one minute mark before shutting it off in disgust.

"Fellow Heroes," Griffith began, grinning at his invisible audience, "I won't bore you with hollow platitudes. I won't lecture you about what you should be. Instead, I'm here to tell you what you could be.

"Our fair city is crowded. The situation grows worse every year." Griffith's face was replaced by a chart showing the upward trajectory of the city's population. "The Company's resources are stretched thin, the Company's laws flaunted and broken on nearly every level." The chart was replaced with images of rioting, subversive graffiti and property damage.

"And yet the Company still expends millions of credits a year solely to protect these people. The stupid." The video became a Hero's view of the maglev track at a transit terminal. An unwary commuter, lost in his own world, stumbled onto the track just as the inbound transit rounded the bend. The Hero shoved the commuter to safety, and Adrian winced at the audible crunch as the Company man was run over.

"The ungrateful."

As the next clip began, a Hero was confronted by an angry citizen.

"And I don't care who called you!"

"Ma'am, I–"

"I said, I don't care who called you! There's no emergency here."

"Ma'am, I have to respond to every emergency call."

The woman snorted. "You were just spying, that's what you were doing. Because the Company doesn't have enough eyes on us already, do they?"

"Ma'am, please. I'm leaving now."

The citizen shouted something which had been censored, and spit on him. Trash pelted his back as he walked away from the scene.

"And the suicidal," Griffith concluded, switching to a clip that showed a Hero sacrificing his life to save that of a jumper. Even through the electronic eye of a security cam, the footage was hard to watch.

"Three hundred million credits a year," Griffith said, staring at the camera. "All thrown away for what? So we can continue to uphold the values of a bygone era? So we can protect Anarchists and scofflaws that will go on to be a continual drain on the Company? I don't know about you, but I think a Hero's life should be worth more than that.

"When a jumper kills a Hero, it's written off as an acceptable loss. When a citizen kills an Enforcer, that citizen receives a death sentence. When New Maupin rebelled, countless Enforcers lost their lives. Have you seen New Maupin lately?" Griffith asked, staring intently at the camera. "It's a ghost town.

"Maybe you've heard the rumor. Maybe you've already come to the conclusion yourselves: we're obsolete, a waste of credit. The Safety Division's time is up. But what if it didn't have to be that way? What if we could be useful again? What if we could be as feared and respected as Enforcement?

"I'm here to tell you, it can happen! Tell the Executives to combine the Safety and Enforcement Divisions. The Company has been wasting credit on this dual law enforcement system for far too long. A vote for me is a vote to end the waste!"

Adrian ended the video, thoroughly appalled. It had never occurred to him to think of himself and his fellow Heroes as obsolete, a waste of Company credit.

Although the bravado and indifference to human suffering was all Griffith, the overall polish of the proposal, with its carefully compiled statistics and video clips, was not. Adrian scowled. Whether or not Griffith had help formulating his proposal, all evidence indicated it had been prepared far in advance.

* * *

Griffith was bruised and grumpy in the morning, kicking chairs and mumbling obscenities through his purple, swollen lips. Nelson ate his bowl of bacon and eggs in a corner, shoulders hunched as if trying to make himself as inconspicuous as possible. Adrian quietly slipped out the door and made his way down to the cafeteria at the center of the Safety Tower.

He found Mel already in line, a cup of coffee-flavored stimulant forgotten in her hand. Her expression was blank, her eyes fixed on the far side of the room.

"How are you doing?" Adrian asked, joining her. "You don't look like you got much sleep," he added, noting the black circles under her eyes.

"I didn't sleep. Did you?"

"I spent most of the night filling out a report." He hadn't been able to sleep either.

Mel nodded absentmindedly, and they continued up to the counter in silence. The hustle and buzz of the crowded room flowed around them, the oblivious current of life rushing past their island of grief.

Bowls of food in hand, they found seats next to a video screen. Rolling green hills stretched out below a range of jagged gray mountains. Purple flowers swayed in the foreground, tiny insects buzzing among their blooms.

The screens were one of the few aesthetic accents the Company allowed in the Safety Tower. Perpetually crowded, with a low ceiling that was barely ten centimeters higher than the tallest Hero, the gleaming white dining facility was a testament to the fact that even the Safety Division wasn't immune to the need to conserve space.

"That's a new one," Adrian said, gesturing at the video. "Where do you think it was taken?"

Mel shrugged and picked at her food.

"You're not even a little curious? Not even about the insects?"

"You don't know what they are, either," she guessed.

"Searching," he replied, combing the archives as he ate. "They're called honey bees."

"Never heard of them. What do they do?"

"Members of the genus Apis, primarily distinguished by the production and storage of honey and the construction of perennial, colonial nests from wax. They played a huge part in commercial agriculture. When they're gathering nectar to make into honey, they also pollinate the plant so it makes fruit."

"Sounds handy. But why is this honey stuff special? It's basically just sugar."

"It's more nutritious than sugar. At one point in ancient times, honey was considered more valuable than gold."

"How could those tiny things ever make enough honey for anyone to eat?"

"There are thousands of bees in one hive. One beekeeping business would have thousands of domestic hives."

"Do we still do that?"

"I don't think so. Domestic honey bees and most strains of wild bees are extinct." Adrian kept reading as he scraped up the last of his oatmeal. "Their extinction was partially to blame for the big food production collapse."

"But they're so tiny," Mel said, frowning. "How?"

"After the Industrial Revolution, we relied on intensive agriculture to feed the expanding population. Millions of acres of farmland owned by private businesses and tended by machines, the crops transported into cities for the masses to buy. Because there weren't enough wild bees to pollinate all our crops, we relied on domestic bees to do the job. When stress, pollution, and a colony collapse disorder killed off the domestic bees, it was a national disaster. Drought and lack of pollinators are thought to be the two largest contributing factors to the famine."

"That's tragic," Mel said, pushing away her half eaten food. "Poor little guys."

A legless Hero rolled up to their table, the tray of his wheelchair stacked high with empty bowls.

"Done with your meals?" he asked, smiling affably through a thick layer of scars.

"Thank you, Townsend," Adrian said, handing over his bowl. "How have you been?"

"Same as always," the old Hero replied, grinning. "Have to watch my back around the young ones, but that's the same old story. How about you? You're one of the ones they're considering for Prime, aren't you?"

"I am. And I think I'm getting old. The world just doesn't seem to be such a bright, shiny place anymore."

Townsend chuckled. "It's not just you. I don't know if it'll make any difference, but you've got this Hero's vote!"

"Thank you."

"And how about you? Looks like you're already having a bad day."

"My partner died yesterday," Mel said quietly.

"I'm sorry. They say that losing someone close to you is worse than death itself."

"I'd agree with them. If I could trade my life for Brad's, I would."

"He was a good Hero, one of the best."

The conversation ground to a halt, all three of them out of words. Adrian couldn't count the friends and acquaintances he'd lost to jumpers, emergency rescues gone bad, freak accidents. To his shame, he couldn't even remember all of their names. The Safety Division lost Heroes as fast as they could raise new ones. But no matter how many faces he saw come and go, it never became any easier to say goodbye.

"So what's the story behind your scars?" Mel asked. "You look like you're lucky to be alive."

Townsend grinned proudly. "It might be before your time, but do either of you remember that massive solvent spill in the industrial district on the Forty-First Tier? I was the first responder. I saved thirty-six people that day! I wound up covered in the stuff, but I kept going until I couldn't walk anymore. Burned my ear clean off!" He turned his head to show them the smooth scar tissue on the other side of his face.

"I'm proud to be able to say I met a living legend," Mel said, shaking the old Hero's hand. "You should see Adrian's new scars," she added. "A few more like that building collapse he was caught in, and he may wind up down here with you."

"Crushed and still walking?" Townsend shook his head in admiration. "Amazing what they can replace with synthesized flesh now."

"You're that guy," one of the Heroes at the next table yelled. "You're the one from the newscast!"

"That's me. I'm the dead Hero."

"You're lucky they put you back together. When I saw your legs, I thought that was it for you."

"So did I," Adrian said. "Or that I'd be down here cleaning tables with Townsend."

"Not if you get elected Prime," someone pointed out.

"I voted for you," another Hero said.

"Me too! No one's going to tell me I'm obsolete. We provide an important service, dammit!"

"Thanks, guys. I appreciate your support." Adrian stood and excused himself. "Good seeing you again, Townsend."

"You too! And watch your back. With Bradley gone, you may be carrying the popular vote."

"Be careful out there," he told Mel as they exited the cafeteria.

"What's it matter? Maybe I'll catch a jumper today too."

"Don't even joke about it. You're like a sister to me and I expect you home in one piece at the end of your shift."

"Thanks, Adrian. You take care of yourself too."

As he made his way to the Safety Tower's transit stop, he learned that he was the only Hero assigned to the Forty-Seventh Tier. Now that was some luck. Out of all the Heroes in service, he was the one who pulled that straw.

Adrian began the lengthy ride by downloading statistics, maps and advisories. It had been years since he'd last been assigned to the Forty-Seventh, and a lot had changed in that time.

As of the most recent census, roughly one hundred and fifty thousand people called the Forty-Seventh Tier home. Assigning just one Hero to such a large and densely population area was a joke. There was no conceivable way for him to patrol the whole tier, or to be available to help everyone who might need it during his shift. His was a token presence, nothing more.

Travel advisories were plentiful. First and foremost, travel to the tier was not advised. Carrying valuables on one's person was not advised. Leaving housing for anything other than work and essential business was not advised. The tier even had a curfew. Aside from shift change at nearby industrial districts and a three hour window in the afternoon, moving about the tier's public spaces could be considered a crime. There were also sections of the tier, highlighted in red on the map, which Company employees were strongly discouraged from entering for their own safety.

Since when was that a thing? Adrian wondered, zipping up his jacket and raising the protective collar. Were people rioting on the Forty-Seventh as well?

As the transit module descended through the city, a constant stream of new faces came and went past his seat. Some of the commuters smiled and nodded at him. Below the Fortieth Tier, the passengers became more unwelcoming. Conversation ceased as new commuters boarded and spotted the lone Hero seated at the back of the module. A few fixed him with icy stares, but most ignored him, their absolute silence more telling than words.

# CHAPTER FIVE

**D**rifts of trash greeted him when he walked out of the Forty-Seventh Tier's Southern Avenue transit hub. A pall of pollution hung over the street, obscuring everything above the tenth floor. He was the only person in sight.

The tier's sole Enforcement precinct, a towering two hundred floor monstrosity, stood adjacent to the transit hub. Like those around it, the building's exterior was covered in solar cells so pitted, corroded and filmed with pollution that they were virtually useless.

Row upon row of massive rectangular freight transports lurked in the lot behind the precinct, watched over by the beady black eyes of surveillance cameras. Taller than a person and nearly ten meters long, each could carry metric tons of supplies or scores of detainees. Some were still radiating heat, as if they had been recently used.

Propelled by independent maglev, a budding technology poised to make fixed maglev lines and the space they required a thing of the past, the windowless transports required no tracks and could go virtually anywhere. They could even traverse the cluttered streets of the city's lowermost tiers. So far, however, the propulsion system had proven to be prohibitively expensive for general adoption.

The rattle of armored boots against pavement snapped him out of his inspection of the containers. A group of Enforcers rounded the corner of the building, their dull charcoal armor blending into the smoggy background, their features hidden beneath enclosed helmets. They made their way along the back of the building and filed into a recessed entrance.

Adrian moved on, eyes and throat stinging in the polluted air. Down here, on the restless tiers, he could almost understand Griffith's envy of Enforcers and their armor. Especially the armor.

Made up of many small, fitted sections, the composite armor enclosed the wearer in an indestructible shell. Flexible joints, protected by overlap, allowed free range of movement. A system of mechanical amplifiers and shock absorbers allowed the wearer to hit harder, run faster, jump farther, and recover from greater falls than a genetically augmented human such as a Hero could.

Composites were the cornerstone of all Company manufacturing processes. Like the reprocessed protein and nutritional materials listed on many food labels, most items contained something referred to as composite. Once 3D printing became a viable alternative to traditional manufacturing processes, it paved the way for the Company to replace traditional materials with those synthesized from the molecular level up. The resulting substances became known as composites, printed to combine the strengths of multiple substances with different molecular properties.

Composites encompassed everything from the bulletproof, fireproof, nonconductive armor of the Enforcers to delicate artwork like that which a jumper had shattered on the Sixteenth Tier. They accounted for ninety-five percent of construction materials in most buildings, from structural supports to load-bearing walls to noise-reducing room partitions. In all but the oldest buildings they formed the electrical system, the ducts and vents that provided cooling, and the piping that delivered water and carried away waste.

Almost every living unit in the city was furnished with sturdy composite furniture. The bowls and eating utensils in the kitchen were composite, as were the bathroom fixtures. Solar cells and view screens were 3D printed, as was the faux glass of the few real windows. Even most clothing was printed rather than woven. None of the fabrics in a Hero's uniform had ever existed in nature.

Something large plummeted from above and crashed into a nearby refuse heap, interrupting his thoughts. Vermin exploded from the pile and scurried for cover as a shower of household garbage followed. Adrian waited until trash stopped raining from the sky before scaling the pile to investigate.

The first impact had been that of a human body, dead at least twelve hours. An eye scan determined that it belonged to Evan Minico, age twenty-seven. Unemployed, formerly a factory worker. Asthmatic. Habitual homemade sedative user. He had carried a number of moderately serious infectious diseases, none of which he had been treated for.

The man had a lengthy list of minor convictions, and an even longer list of liens against his credit. He had been downgraded five times, and was facing yet another eviction, this time to the Forty-Eighth Tier. Adrian closed the man's eyes and forwarded the location of the corpse to Enforcement.

Falling bodies and garbage-clogged streets were a symptom of the poverty of these tiers. The lack of funds had shuttered recycling centers, garbage collection businesses, and most of the health clinics and mortuaries. Without basic services, the citizens disposed of the by-products of life as best they could. Maintenance accesses and open walkways became de facto garbage disposals.

The number of bodies concealed beneath the layers of day to day garbage was not something Adrian cared to contemplate. The teeming vermin were probably the sole reason the streets didn't smell worse.

Tired of the smoggy silence, Adrian let himself into a housing tower. The roar of an overworked ventilation system greeted him within, doing little more than circulate the scent of unwashed bodies and rotting trash that hung in the hot air.

Half the width of the cluttered corridor was occupied by crudely constructed sleeping spaces. Each just large enough to hold a human body and bedding, they were stacked three high the length of every hallway. Garbage was piled in every corner, and the narrow corridors were crisscrossed with lines of dirty clothing hung up to air.

Activating his heat sensors and dimming his vision to black and white, Adrian's view swarmed with human life. Just on his floor and the four above it, his sensors detected hundreds of people. The residents were packed in at nearly five times the building's designed capacity.

Except for the distant murmur of conversation and the sound of doors sliding shut as he approached, the corridors were eerily quiet. Many of the living spaces lining the hallway were occupied, their cloth and scrap privacy barriers pulled shut, the occupants holding their breath in silence until he passed.

Turning up his augmented hearing, he caught snatches of conversation from nearby living spaces.

"There's one out there. Wonder what it's doing all the way down here?"

"Don't ask, man."

"But who's it here for?"

"Don't ask. We didn't see anything."

The conversation passed out of hearing range, replaced by discussions about the Company's free video shows, late rent and financial troubles.

"We got another late fee, didn't we? Are we going to get downgraded?"

"Don't worry, honey. It'll be okay, I promise." Women's voices, an adult and a child.

A man's hoarse whisper came from the stacks of sleeping spaces in the hallway.

"Though I walk through the valley of the shadow of death, I will feel no fear."

An addict, perhaps. He seemed to be speaking to no one in particular as he repeated his mantra, his tone desperate.

Adrian found most of the lifts in the tower out of service, their doors sealed off with streamers of hazard tape. He took the stairs, the sound of his boots echoing in the narrow stairwell. Layers of graffiti mocked him from the walls, decades of anger and disenfranchisement voiced by crude cartoons and notes scrawled in handmade paint.

A trio of blood-spattered enforcers looked down on him at one landing, demonic red eyes glowing through the visors of their helmets. A pile of broken bodies lay at their feet. The work had been signed by someone named Marco.

"The only good Hero is a dead Hero," read a fresh scrawl at the next floor.

After climbing stairs until his calves burned, Adrian found the higher floors only marginally less cluttered. The corridors were still lined with makeshift sleeping spaces, but these were tall enough to stand up in.

The end of curfew came and went, and people began to emerge from their living units. None of them acknowledged his presence. The corridors became packed with citizens in drab one-size-fits-all clothing, their tired faces floating above a sea of neutral colors as they hurried about their business.

Devoid of expensive pigments, worn and laundered until it matched the dull beige of the architecture, the residents' clothing was almost a form of urban camouflage. To stand out from the crowd was to declare oneself a criminal, or worse, a Company man.

Smog stung his nose as he entered a pedestrian bridge on the hundred and twentieth floor. Halfway across the span, the cloudy composite had been hacked away to form an opening large enough for a person.

With a firm grip on a structural support, Adrian leaned out of the makeshift exit and scanned the haze below. The opening yielded an unobstructed drop all the way to the ground. Pulling himself back inside, Adrian took a picture of the breach and forwarded its location to maintenance.

Informative graffiti surrounded the damage– it was not simply a hole; it was labeled a "Happy Hatch." Another message succinctly summarized the societal impact of suicide. "Less of you equals more for us."

In fact, choosing to jump could even be considered a gift. "Give your family the gift that keeps on giving: one less mouth to feed."

Perhaps exiting via the "Happy Hatch" wasn't suicide at all, but rather "Euthanasia, free of charge."

The Company had legalized euthanasia countless generations past, first for cases where the patient was terminally ill and suffering. Later, the definition of eligibility was expanded to include any legally competent adult who was willing to come before a magistrate. Now, the only barrier between a citizen and humane euthanasia was the fee the Company charged for the service. Much of the city's population was so poverty-stricken that splattering themselves on the pavement was the affordable alternative.

A tattered strip of black cloth hung above the entrance to the next building. Within, layers of graffiti covered the dirty beige walls. Corridors and stairwells ended abruptly, sealed off. Many of the living spaces had been subdivided, their inner passages so narrow that his shoulders scraped the walls.

It was a disaster waiting to happen. In the event of a fire, the clutter and unauthorized modifications would prevent the suppression system from reaching the flames. Without a clear path to the stairs, many would be unable to escape. The death toll would number in the thousands.

The hallway he was following turned a corner and narrowed to less than half a meter, forcing him to turn sideways to squeeze through. Solid composite pressed against his back and chest, and for a moment it felt as if the walls were closing in on him. Adrian forced himself to take slow, measured breaths and continue on.

"You lost, Hero?" someone jeered as he emerged, and shouts of

"You don't belong here!" trailed him as he walked away.

All of the building's interior security cams had been defaced or destroyed, preventing the Company from monitoring the corridors. The makeshift passages and choke points seemed to have been deliberately designed to keep out Company agents, especially Heroes, who tended to be taller and more muscular than the average citizen, and Enforcers, whose armor would not allow them to pass any of the gaps he had managed to squeeze through.

"You're going to die here," someone hissed at his shoulder.

Adrian spun around, but the speaker was already gone. The crowd flowed around him, glaring and muttering.

He would have to take extra care to walk softly and watch his back. Heroes, the kindly ambassadors of Company justice, were strictly forbidden to carry weapons. Their training stated that any interaction with the potential to turn deadly was a situation for Enforcement.

In reality, Company agents were frequently met with hostility or outright violence in the lower reaches of the city. It hadn't always been that way, but Heroes' training and equipment had failed to keep up with the shift in public perception.

* * *

Afternoon found him halfway around the tier, making his way through yet another fortified building. Residents packed the corridors despite the return of curfew. Children scampered through the crowd, leaving a trail of shouting in their wake. Although the oldest was no more than eight, the children had already learned the art of petty theft.

A few floors above, freelance entertainers in artfully torn clothing lounged outside their living spaces. A matching pair of brunettes in neon purple body stockings latched onto his arms, whispering offers in his ears. Adrian politely disentangled himself and kept walking. Evidently he had stumbled across a low-credit version of the Entertainment District.

"Don't waste your time," someone called to the pair he'd just shaken off. "Company man ain't interested in you, and he ain't got the credit to pay anyway."

One of those statements was untrue, but Adrian didn't bother to object. All Heroes received a monthly stipend. It was how he had bought his drawing pad, how Nelson paid for his video shows, and how Griffith afforded the subscriptions for his games. A thrifty Hero was never creditless.

Some of the residential units he passed held drug operations, their noxious chemical odors seeping into the hallway and advertising their business to a steady flow of customers. Adrian forwarded their location to Enforcement.

Homemade stimulants and sedatives might be cheaper than their Company-manufactured counterparts, but they were also far more dangerous– purity and content could differ greatly between producers. What was sold as the same product and dose might result in a safe high from one vendor, and death or disfigurement from another.

Rounding a corner, he was confronted by a chaotic scene. A dozen angry men had someone pinned against the wall, while a horde of entertainers pummeled them with fists, garbage, and anything else that came to hand. A high pitched scream of terror sliced through the angry shouts and screeches of outrage as the men wrestled with their captive.

"Break it up!" Adrian yelled, struggling to be heard over the pandemonium. "Break it up!"

He waded into the melee and began hauling clients and entertainers out of the way. At the center of the crush, a fat, stubbly middle-aged man had a woman pinned to the wall, a crude blade pressed to her throat.

"Drop your weapon!" Adrian bellowed. "Let her go!"

The man turned to him, dark brown eyes narrowed in rage. Peter Mahoney, age forty-three. Asthmatic. High blood pressure. HIV positive. Contagion warning: recombinant herpes positive, strain H5, early stage infection. Containment procedures recommended. Eighteen convictions: fifteen for assault, three for theft or improper use of Company property.

"I'm doing a public service!" Mahoney snarled.

"Release her," Adrian repeated. "Whatever your grievance is, it's not worth a death sentence."

Mahoney snorted. "I'll get base labor at most. I hear they'll give me two squares and treatment, all for ridding the world of the disease-ridden trash that gave it to me."

Adrian glanced at the victim. Her eyes were squeezed shut, tears leaking from under her lashes. The right side of her face from chin to cheekbone and both her lips were swollen with red, puss-filled sores. The sight made him grateful for his all-encompassing Company vaccinations.

"Let her go. Do all of you want to wind up infected?" he asked, indicating the throng of clients backing the attacker. The woman's outbreak looked aggressive enough to be transmitted through even the briefest skin-on-skin contact.

That statement cleared a wide space around them, leaving himself, the victim, and the man with the knife alone in the center.

"Do you want to wind up looking like her? Drop the knife and step back!"

"That's not possible, is it?" The man recoiled, a look of horror spreading across his fleshy face. "Is it?"

The woman bolted, sobbing, as Adrian disarmed the attacker and snapped him into a pair of tracking cuffs.

"Report to Enforcement," he said, forwarding a recording of the incident. "And don't try to run. You won't do yourself any favors by adding evasion of justice to your charges."

"How am I supposed to explain this to my partner?" Mahoney wailed.

"Aren't entertainers supposed to have vaccinations?" someone else demanded. "Isn't spreading disease a crime against public safety?"

"You try affording vaccinations on what we make," one of the entertainers retorted. "Once the bosses take their cut and we pay our rent, there's barely enough left for food. The first round of vaccinations alone costs more than I make in a year."

"You have a moral obligation–"

"Shove your moral obligation! You get what you pay for. If you don't like it, go to the Sixteenth Tier."

"Anyone who spreads disease should have to pay for it!"

"That is enough," Adrian yelled, positioning himself between the opposing groups. "Disperse now, or Enforcement will be called. And you will all be charged with assault," he added, directing a hard look at the group of angry clients.

The mob began to disperse, muttering darkly. The infected woman was gone, vanished into one of the nearby living units. Adrian followed the faint sound of sobbing to the correct door and knocked gently.

The entertainer that answered the door was nearly Adrian's height, wide-shouldered, and dressed in nothing put a pair of knee-length gray cargo shorts.

"Can I help you?"

"The woman you're sheltering needs to go to a medical facility. Without treatment, she's a public health hazard."

The man's warm brown eyes darkened. "I don't know what you're talking about."

Adrian wedged his boot into the gap as the door began to slide shut.

"We both know she's in here," he said, eying the crowd of entertainers blocking his view of the rear of the apartment. "I can hear her."

"Listen, it's just a flare-up, okay? She's on the regimen. We pooled our money to buy it for her."

Adrian scanned the man's features, weighing whether he should keep pushing or accept the statement.

"Look, I know you're reading my file. You can see she's my sister. I've been trying to watch out for her since we got downgraded and wound up here." He grimaced and looked away. "I know I haven't done a great job, but this wasn't supposed to happen."

Adrian scrolled through the sister's file. It did appear to be the same woman, and she was undergoing treatment. He nodded decisively.

"I'll accept that. I hope she's feeling better soon."

A quiet murmur of surprise followed him as he walked away.

* * *

Safe from the eyes of the Company, the residents of the barricaded buildings seemed to have little fear of the penalties for violating curfew. A bustling improvised food court had sprung up in the commons of one housing tower.

Most of the shops were selling street meat. Skinned vermin roasted over an improvised grill behind one counter. The workers turned away when Adrian approached, refusing to acknowledge his presence. At another shop, a smiling vendor ladled out bowls of brown soup.

"What's in it?" Adrian asked the old woman that seemed to be in charge.

"Yesterday's catch," she replied, smiling a wide, toothless smile. "Today is yesterday's catch. Tomorrow will be today's catch. Always fresh!"

"That's a violation of the public health code."

"What else are we supposed to cook? Go ahead, arrest us all. People will starve. Is that what you want?"

Adrian shook his head and walked away.

"Only fifty credits a bowl!" she called after him.

He purchased a meal packet from a nearby dispenser instead. If the Company didn't cover basic meals for Heroes, it would have set him back nearly two hundred credits. Resting his shoulders against the nearby wall, he munched tasteless dehydrated food flakes while watching the murmuring beige crowd flow by.

On the far side of the room, a group of dark-clad figures spilled out of a side corridor and spread out through the crowd. They seemed to be looking for someone. Adrian tucked the packet into his pocket and slipped down the nearest hallway. As he passed an intersecting corridor, rough hands seized his arm and spun him around.

"Where do you think you're going, Company man?"

The speaker wore a faded black hoodie and dark sunglasses. His teeth were crooked and blackened by homemade stimulant abuse.

"Don't you know your kind aren't wanted here?"

Foot traffic broke around them, grumbling at the obstacle they posed.

"I'm just here to help people. Nothing else. I'm one of the good guys."

"Sure you are. More like just doing a little spying for your masters and causing trouble."

"I'm not here to do either," Adrian said, backing out of range.

"That's not what I heard," the man yelled after him as he walked away.

The criminals trailed him at a distance, their dark shoulders bobbing through the sea of beige civilians. Adrian continued along his chosen patrol route and ignored them.

In another hallway lined with makeshift living spaces and the panhandlers that occupied them, a faint, repeated plea caught his attention.

"Water, please, can anyone spare some water?"

The voice belonged to a frail old woman tucked into a tiny gap between two sleeping spaces.

"I can take you to a water dispenser," Adrian offered.

The old woman looked up at him from under a nest of tangled

white hair with eyes so filmy he found them impossible to scan.

"I can't walk," she said. "And if I leave, I'll lose my spot."

"I could carry you."

She was silent for a long moment, then nodded decisively. Adrian knelt and gently gathered her up.

"That way." She gestured in the direction they were going.

Adrian nodded, glad not to have to return the way he had come.

Shouts of outrage trailed him as he moved through the crowd, and a glance over his shoulder revealed that the criminals were in pursuit. With his height and distinctive uniform, there was little chance of losing them in the crowd.

He rounded a corner and broke into a run. A stairwell opened to his right, and he ducked inside and descended the stairs two a time.

Stepping out into a busy hallway several floors below, Adrian followed the flow of traffic to the lobby for the tower's central elevator shaft. Of the dozen lifts, only one was still functional.

"Excuse me. Sorry. It's an emergency," Adrian said, shouldering his way to the front of the line. To his dismay, someone had broken the fingerprint reader for the manual override.

"Go to the back of the line and wait your puke sucking turn like everyone else," someone hissed. "Company scum!"

Facing a sea of angry faces, Adrian readjusted his burden and tried to plead for calm. "It's not for me, it's for her. She needs water. She can't walk."

"No excuses!"

Quick reflexes saved him from being hit in the head, and a rancid meal packet splattered the lift doors behind him.

"You can have my place in line," a young man at the front of the queue said. "Carl, we're going to the back."

"What? No way," his companion sputtered.

The unnamed altruist took his protesting friend by the arm and pulled him toward the back of the crowd as the lift arrived. Residents poured out, and Adrian was the first on board as the cage rapidly refilled. The doors slid shut just as the first of the criminals entered the lobby.

"You remind me of my son," the woman said as they rose toward their destination. "He was such a sweet, polite boy. Tall and strong, like you."

"I'm sure he was a great pride to you. Does he still live around here?"

"The Enforcers raided the shop where he worked and took him. I never heard from him again."

"I'm sorry."

"My other son doesn't visit anymore," she continued, "but I'm proud of him anyway. His marks were so good that he got into medical school. He became a doctor on the Tenth Tier."

Adrian wondered if her son worked in the Safety Tower, and if the man was anyone he knew.

"One day he'll be back for me." She nodded, as if reassuring herself. "I'm sure he's just saving up the credit to buy me a visa, and then he'll bring me to live with him."

Adrian nodded. It was not his place point out how common it was for people to work their way to higher tiers and forget about those they had left behind.

"If you're looking for water," one of the other passengers said, "this is your stop."

The lift jerked to a halt, and the doors slid open on a crowded lobby twenty floors above the one they had just left. Rough hands shoved Adrian and his charge out of the cage.

There was a working water dispenser against a nearby wall. As Adrian helped the old woman stand, he noticed a small device fastened over the machine's original fingerprint scanner. It was a highly illegal modification, amounting to both identity theft and misuse of Company resources. While the modification allowed users to access water without depleting their daily allowance, it was undoubtedly also skimming biometric data.

As he reached to remove it, a horrific screech froze him in his tracks. A small child, no more than eight years old, darted out of the crowd and thrust himself between Adrian and the dispenser. More children gathered, watching with wide, worried eyes.

"Mister, please don't," the boy said softly, shielding the machine with his body.

"That's an illegal modification."

The child shook his head, long brown hair flying.

"You'll still be able to get water. You have your daily allowance."

"My fingerprint doesn't work." The child spoke so quietly his words were almost inaudible.

"Are you sure?" Adrian asked, puzzled. "Let me see your face." The boy stubbornly continued to stare at the floor. "I won't hurt you," Adrian promised, reaching out to tilt the child's face upward. "You're not in trouble."

Terrified brown eyes met his own as a fist came down on the back of his head.

"Leave him alone. He's just a child!"

His assailant took advantage of his momentary surprise to haul the boy out of his reach. As the child's identity file popped into his view, the woman dived into the crowd and fled.

The boy's identity was flagged as potentially fraudulent. According to the file, the retina he had just scanned belonged to a twenty-year-old named Marshall Nimes who resided on the Nineteenth Tier.

The stares of the remaining children locked with his own, then darted to the dispenser, then back to his face. One by one he verified their identities, finding each similarly flagged. They were ghost children, the saddest victims of biometric identity theft. With their identities flagged as possibly fraudulent, hacked dispensers were the only places they could get food and water.

It was a common practice on the lower tiers to steal the identities of those who couldn't defend themselves. The biometrics disappeared into the city's shadowy underworld and reappeared as eye implants and fingertip prosthetics for recipients of similar stature and gender.

Adrian turned away from the dispenser. He could not bring himself to remove someone's ability to survive.

"I'm going to take you to see a doctor," he told the beggar woman.

"There's no point. I have no credit left to my name."

"They can see you on charity. It might cover enough to get you walking again."

"There's no point," the woman grumbled. But she allowed Adrian to gather her up and bring her to a medical station.

The inside of the facility was barely three meters squared, and suspicious stains marked the floor. The room contained a narrow counter, a chair, and a single gurney. A medic with thinning blonde hair and purple bags under her eyes sat behind the counter, staring off into space.

"What do you want me to do with her?" the medic asked.

"File a charity request. Provide her with a bed, meals, and whatever treatment she needs."

"Her eyes are too covered with cataracts to scan."

"Then run her fingerprints," Adrian said impatiently.

"Look, Hero, maybe you haven't been down here in a while. Maybe you're new to the higher-numbered tiers. But what you're looking at is all I have to work with. I have no spare beds. I have no credit to provide her with food and water."

"Not even on charity?" Adrian asked, appalled.

The medic sighed as if she had heard his response many times. "Not even on charity. The funding was cut a few years ago. I can examine her, and write her a prescription if that will help, but she'll have to find a way to pay for it herself."

"That's it?"

"Or..." The medic paused and looked away. "Well, she doesn't look like she has much time left. There's always euthanasia."

"Don't leave me here," the old woman exclaimed, clutching his jacket with withered hands. "I'm not ready to go yet."

"Thank you for your time," Adrian told the medic, turning away. "Where do you want me to take you? Do you have any other family left here?"

"Not anymore. Just take me back to the water dispenser."

"Are you sure?"

"Yes. I'll be fine there."

Adrian walked back to the hacked dispenser and left the old woman sitting beside it, knees drawn up to her chest, head down as if resting. As he walked away, he saw the ghost children gather around her. One of them offered her a bowl of food, so maybe she would be alright after all.

***

He was several floors below when he rounded a corner and came face to face with the group of criminals. Eight men in dark clothing blocked the corridor in front of him, grinning unpleasantly. Several had covered their faces with black rags. All concealed their eyes behind dark sunglasses.

Adrian assessed the group as beige-clad residents scurried for cover. Eight to one weren't bad odds for a competent Hero.

"Let me pass," he said calmly. "Don't make trouble where there isn't any."

"You think you're the one giving the orders down here, Hero?"

The speaker was a tall, gangly man, his skin liberally pocked with plague scars.

"Let me pass," Adrian repeated.

Pockmarks laughed, and the rest of the group joined him, moving forward menacingly.

"Where's the rest of your team? Don't you Company cowards always come down here in pairs?" Crudely etched facial tattoos peeked over the mask of the second speaker.

"My backup is on the way," Adrian said as several of the men tried to sidle past him. He moved backward to keep them in view.

"Is it now?" The leader chuckled. "That's funny, because you've been alone the whole time you've been in our building."

"Looks like the Company sent us a gift." The speaker was a stocky, broad-chested man with bad teeth. His gloved hands held a length of hefty-looking pipe. "They say a Hero's neural interface is worth a fortune. I've always wanted to come into some real credit."

"Hey," exclaimed a lean youth whose hands were crisscrossed with knife scars. "You promised you'd split it with us!"

"Don't worry, there'll be plenty for everyone," Pockmarks said soothingly.

"I don't want a cut of what's left over after Brady takes what he wants, I want an equal portion!"

"Listen, Brady knows the guy who runs the chop shop, so he gets the largest cut."

"That's not what we agreed to," someone at the back of the group shouted.

Adrian saw his chance. He grabbed the nearest man, slammed him face-first into the wall, and cuffed his hands behind his back.

A homemade blade broke against his side as he ducked the pipe aimed at his head. He grabbed the knife-wielder's arm and swung him against another attacker, sending the two men crashing into the wall.

The stocky man moved behind Adrian, slipped the pipe over his head, and pulled it tight across the Hero's throat. Blue-gray metal flashed at the attacker's wrists, indicating that he was packing not one, but two prosthetic arms. Adrian gasped and clawed at the pipe. The modder's grip was as strong as a Hero's.

Men with pipes closed in from either side, working him over as he kicked and struggled. The group clearly had practice subduing Company men.

Straining for leverage, he fought back until he was able to slip out from under the bar, turn, and smash it into the criminal's face. A second blow put the man on the floor.

Pockmarks closed with him, fists swinging. As Adrian dodged and wove around the boxer, Tattoos picked up the modder's weapon. The blow to his lower back distracted him just enough for Pockmarks to land a vicious right hook.

Adrian returned the favor. He realized it had been a mistake the second the blow connected. Something crunched, his knuckles stung, and the force traveled up through his arm as a dull ache. Pockmarks crashed to the floor.

He deflected another blow meant for his back and closed with the tattooed pipe-wielder as the remaining criminals gathered their fallen companions and fled. Tattoos fought back with panicked strength, screaming in pain as Adrian pried the pipe out of his hands and tossed it aside. With a pang of guilt, he realized he'd broken the man's arm.

Tattoos ducked out of reach and bolted before he could be cuffed, screaming obscenities. Adrian forwarded the encounter to Enforcement. The injured criminals would be apprehended as soon as they visited a medical station.

Angry shouts rose from the far end of the hallway, signaling that his attackers had returned with reinforcements. He turned and sprinted back the way he had come, scattering startled residents from his path.

Ducking into a nearby stairwell, he descended the stairs two at a time. Shouts of outrage rang out above. Word spread like fire in these crowded towers, and the story had undoubtedly already lost much of the facts in the retelling.

They were waiting for him on the ground floor. As he wove through the crowded hallway, a hulking citizen with misshapen modifications concealed beneath an ill-fitting black shirt stepped into his path. The right side of the man's face was a patchwork of artificial skin and blackened, necrotic tissue. The sickly odor of decay rolled out of his residence as Adrian ducked past him and sprinted for the exit.

Making his way out into the street, he scrambled over mounds of garbage and hurdled makeshift barricades. Shouts echoed behind him, and the sound of running feet filled the narrow avenue. Even out here, the criminals were not content to let him go.

His throat began to burn and his eyes watered as a line of bright red text scrolled across his vision.

"Health warning: atmospheric pollution exceeds safe limits for physical exertion. Cease exertion immediately or serious respiratory damage may result."

Adrian swore and dug a mask out of his jacket pocket. The thin, adhesive rubber gripped his face like a second skin, and it felt like he was trying to draw each breath through a straw. The burning in his throat began to subside.

Although he was putting distance between himself and the criminals, he could still hear them. He was already gasping like a fish out of water, and it would only be a matter of time before he was forced to stand his ground and fight. Heroes were built for short sprints, not long distance running.

Under the shadow of the corroded towers, the streets began to darken. A few battered security lights flickered to life, their glow all but smothered by the brown industrial fog. Ahead, there were no more lights. The towers that rose above the street were dark, silent, and curiously lifeless.

Adrian skirted a derelict transport, its magnetic drive train facing the darkening sky. The doors were missing, and vermin had made the interior their home. Glancing inside, he was startled by the vacant stare of a human skull. Human remains littered what had once been the ceiling of the vehicle.

Other transports had been reduced to charred shells. An Enforcer's riot shield lay abandoned in an open space, its surface gathering dust. Sooty streaks marked the sides of the buildings.

Opening the tier map, the significance of the detritus suddenly struck him. He was crossing New Maupin Ward, site of one of the worst riots in recent memory. Spurred by an avalanche of downgrades and arrests for sedition, the citizens of the Ward had risen in revolt. Barricades made of overturned transports and burning garbage had held Enforcement at bay for days.

The siege came to an abrupt end when the ventilation systems in the buildings of the Ward inexplicably shut down. Citizens streamed into the streets to surrender. Those who stayed indoors suffocated. The death toll had been in the thousands.

The memory evoked an old, long-forgotten surge of outrage. Adrian had watched the riot unfold via newscast, wondering why the Company refused to send Heroes or emergency responders into the Ward. How many lives could have been saved?

Nearly a decade later, the streets of the Ward remained as they had been when the rioting ended; empty buildings towered overhead, their power systems gone dark. In light of the housing shortage, Adrian couldn't understand why the Company hadn't cleared the buildings and re-rented them. How calamitous had the ventilation failure been, to render the entire Ward uninhabitable? Instead of rehabilitating the area, the Company had allowed New Maupin to become a no-man's land.

* * *

Night had wrapped the city up in her embrace, but no lights came on in New Maupin. Adrian paused and stared up into the polluted darkness, listening. His pursuers seemed to have given up. Gradually the pain in his sides diminished, but the taste of copper remained.

It was going to be a long walk around the curve of the tier to the next transit interchange. Adrian plotted a course that passed through one of the Company's manufacturing districts and several low-credit residential areas, determined that the entire tier would at least hear the rumor of a Hero's presence before his shift was over.

Switching on his night vision, New Maupin's ground level

became a monochrome wasteland bathed in gray-green glow. Hordes of vermin, their beady eyes glowing white, swarmed over the garbage piles and trailed him as he made his way down the street. There were rumors of vermin attacking lone citizens down here, but he credited them with little legitimacy; with garbage so plentiful, why bother with something that would fight back?

As he crossed an intersection, his musings were interrupted by an eerie howl. It might have been the protest of some massive piece of machinery in the manufacturing district, but the source seemed more immediate.

The sound racketed around the intersection, bouncing off buildings and charred transports, defying his attempts to locate its source. A deep groan that was more felt than heard, it throbbed and wavered as it rose in pitch, ending in a wail that set his teeth on edge.

Adrian cautiously scanned the piles of charred wreckage as he walked. The vermin were suddenly conspicuously absent. Jagged shapes taunted him from atop distant mounds of detritus, proving to be nothing more than discarded furniture, the shattered remains of a privacy screen, or a twisted tangle of tubing.

A dark wall loomed in front of him, the barricade demarcating the edge of New Maupin. A manufacturing district lay ahead, its security lighting seeping through the smog like the faint glow of approaching dawn.

Something crashed to the ground behind him. He glimpsed a shifting shadow atop a transport as he turned, but it was gone before he could focus on it.

The howl came again, distinctly from the same direction. It reverberated off the surrounding buildings, echoing and dividing, until the high pitched end of the wail was all around him.

The hair on the back of his neck stood on end. It was not a sensation he was familiar with, nor was the irrational panic that urged him to run, as far and as fast as he could. Adrian stood his ground and switched on his heat sensors. The streets of the Ward were empty, devoid of even vermin.

He scaled the barricade with stiff, precise movements and skidded down the far side into the street beyond. He refused to acknowledge the feeling that some unnamed menace lurked among debris of New Maupin. There was nothing in the darkness behind him. A thermal scan had confirmed it.

On the far side of the barricade, the lights of the manufacturing district bathed the street in their orange glow. The Company could afford outdoor lighting for its commercial areas, no matter what tier they were on. Adrian deactivated his night vision as he approached the district's security gates, unable to remember the last time he had been so glad to see a controlled-access area.

The gates consisted of a row of posts a meter apart that spanned the width of the street. There was nothing between them but orange hazard stripes painted on the pavement. Signs on each post stated that it was a controlled area, authorized personnel only– "Warning: entry restrictions enforced by E-Gate."

Anyone who had business in the district had the applicable permission codes written to their identity chip. Sensors embedded in the pavement detected anything with a pulse that came within a few meters of the gate, while a passive ID scanner checked the person's credentials.

The denial-of-entry system operated on a simple principle: the detection of life without the detection of the correct permission codes activated an electrical current between the nearest posts. The charge was sufficient to stun and eject most humans.

A large vermin scuttled across the street in front of him, its paws encroaching on the orange hazard stripes. Electricity crackled, and the air smelled of ozone and singed fur.

Adrian crossed the hazard markings a few meters away from the smoking lump. The pavement beyond was clean, the spaces between the buildings vacant. There was no trash, no vermin, and no graffiti on the walls.

A transit rattled by on elevated tracks, muffled by the smog. Although the general service line that circled the tier had long since been shut down, the Company still maintained maglev tracks to carry workers to and from the manufacturing district.

Brown smog swirled around the lights and caressed the solar cells with grimy fingers. Within their corroded walls, the manufacturing towers pulsed with life. Machines hummed day and night, churning out commodities for the city's retail districts. The building to his right produced clothing. The building to his left returned composites to their original forms so they could be reused.

A pair of patrolling Enforcers approached him, their dull dark gray armor soaking up the light, their boots rattling against the pavement. Adrian smiled and waved a greeting. The Enforcers' heads turned in unison, and they moved toward him with purposeful strides.

"Stop, Hero. You are wanted for questioning," the first Enforcer said, his voice deepened and distorted by the filter of his helmet.

Adrian stared at the pair in confusion. "I think you have the wrong person."

"Place your hands behind your back," the second Enforcer said, unclipping a pair of cuffs from his waist.

"Why am I wanted for questioning?"

"You are in no position to ask questions, murderer," the first Enforcer growled.

"I think there's been a mistake," he said, projecting calm into his voice and movements. "I'm a Hero, a Company agent like you. I'm not a murderer."

The Enforcer in front of him reacted so quickly that even his enhanced vision could not follow the movement. One second, he was standing an arm's length from the other man. The next, the Enforcer had him pinned against a wall by the throat.

Adrian choked and clawed at the armor-clad hand crushing his windpipe, survival instincts overtaking his better judgment. It was never a good idea to struggle with an Enforcer.

He was vaguely aware of someone unzipping his jacket, and then the Enforcer's fist slammed into his side. Prongs built into the knuckles of the armored glove pierced his undershirt, crackling as they sent thousands of volts coursing through the Hero's body. Armor protected the Enforcer from becoming a grounding point as Adrian screamed and convulsed.

His vision went dark as the Enforcer dropped him and delivered a vicious kick to his ribs. Ungentle hands flipped him onto his stomach, wrenched his arms behind his back, and secured his wrists.

# CHAPTER SIX

Consciousness returned an unknown amount of time later. The last thing he remembered was something coming down on the back of his head with crushing force as he lay with his face pressed against the pavement.

He blinked, wondering why he couldn't see. A line of text marched across the darkness.

"Neural interface experienced an unanticipated shutdown. Recovering..."

Come on, Adrian begged, boot up. Please don't be damaged.

His vision remained dark, and something hot and wet trickled down the bridge of his nose. The droplet landed in front of him with an audible plop. A few feet away, composite scraped against composite and someone coughed impatiently.

"Auditory systems online." A wall of text scrolled across his vision and a series of tones sounded in his inner ear.

A brightly lit room full of shiny gray composite appeared in front of him, upside down. He blinked frantically, and the room righted itself.

"Visual systems online." Another wall of text followed as his visual implants ran through their functionality checks.

A second drop of blood rolled down his nose and joined the first on the gray surface in front of him. A faceless Enforcer watched him from the other side of the table, the room reflected in the polished visor of his helmet.

Adrian struggled to sit up straight, grimacing as pain shot through his shoulders. His hands were still cuffed behind his back, the cuffs secured behind his chair. The weight of his upper body had been hanging against his restraints for however long he had been unconscious.

"Sensory module functionality confirmed. Connectivity to network confirmed. Submitting crash report."

He was in an interrogation room. Adrian had read about them, but never expected to see the inside of one.

The Enforcer leaned forward in his seat and rested his arms on the table.

"Good morning, murderer." The distortion of the helmet added a hard, electronic edge to the man's gravelly voice. The ugly chuckle that followed was positively unpleasant.

"I'm not a murderer," Adrian rasped, finding his voice hoarse and painful to use. "I'm a Hero. I can't kill people."

"You can, and you did. You even sent us the evidence."

Adrian stared in confusion.

"Maybe this will jog your memory."

The Enforcer sent him a video clip recorded from his own viewpoint, the moment when he punched the pockmarked boxer. The criminal's head snapped back as the blow connected, and the man crashed to the ground. He lay utterly still as Adrian turned to confront the other attackers. The Hero's heart sank.

"It was self-defense," he protested, horrified. "I was fighting for my life."

"Oh, is a Hero's life worth more than a citizen's now?"

"They were after my neural interface. It would have been a massive breach of security."

His interrogator laughed again, a hard, grating sound. "Security cleans up a breach like that almost every day. The compromised permissions are purged from the system, and new ones written to your identity chip without you ever knowing it.

"I had no idea. But I didn't hit him that hard. Is he really dead?" Adrian felt sick to his stomach.

"Your excuses are invalid," the interrogator replied, ignoring his question. "Only Enforcers are allowed to use lethal force. You aren't, even if you are a candidate to become Prime."

"That had nothing to do with it. It was an accident."

"Are you sure?" Chair legs squealed as the Enforcer stood up and walked around the table. "All your noble intentions snuffed out in an ugly, dirty place like this. The thought of that doesn't make you feel a bit... panicky?"

An armored hand clamped down on the back of his neck, forcing his eyes away from the growing puddle of blood.

"Look at me when I'm talking to you," the Enforcer grated. Adrian barely recognized the bloody face and tired eyes that stared back at him, reflected in the man's visor.

"Dying here, ending your whole pointless, miserable existence on this vermin-infested dump of a tier. That doesn't bother you?"

"You would have done the same if you were in my place."

"I have the right to use lethal force, and the intelligence to stay out of Anarchist-controlled buildings. If I had been you, I would have been a good little Hero and paid the price for my stupidity."

"Since when is doing the right thing stupid? Those people needed my help."

"The Anarchists needed your help." The Enforcer chuckled. "Is that so?"

"Laugh all you want, but did my job. I saved lives. What have you done to make people's lives better today?"

The punch that connected with the Hero's face seemed to come out of nowhere. He found himself on his back on the floor, chair and all, mouth full of blood. Adrian coughed and tried to sit up, struggling to free his cuffed hands from behind the chair.

"Attempting to escape," the Enforcer informed him with a gravelly chuckle, "is an act of hostility." He seized Adrian by the collar and lifted him upright.

Adrian coughed and spit out a mouthful of blood. His teeth felt loose.

"This is why no one likes Enforcers."

The second blow hit his chest with enough force to slam him and his chair against the wall. His arms and legs went numb, and he couldn't seem to catch his breath.

"Being an Enforcer isn't about being likeable. It's about being in control."

A certain suicidal urge drove Adrian to answer– even if he got out of the precinct alive, his injuries would ensure that the Company retired him. The possibility of becoming Prime had never felt real, and now it was gone.

"Like you're in control of all those towers the Anarchists have taken over?" He paused and gasped for breath. "Looks to me like they have half the tier. I doubt your people could even get in there to restore order if they wanted to."

The Enforcer placed his boot on Adrian's chest and pressed him against the wall. It felt like what being crushed in a building collapse might feel like, and he was not surprised when his ribs began to make ominous crunching noises. The exclamation mark in his icon tray pulsed warning red as a list of life-threatening injuries were added to the damage report.

"Aren't you glad I'm holding back?" the Enforcer asked, releasing him.

Adrian gasped for air, pain radiating from his broken ribs and blood bubbling into his mouth with each exhalation.

"Answer me. Aren't you glad I'm holding back?"

"Yes," Adrian rasped.

"Good boy." The Enforcer pulled the chair away from the wall and removed Adrian's cuffs. "Are we having fun yet?"

"No." What was going to happen next?

"I'll give you a hint," the Enforcer said, leaning close. "This is where you say yes, or I break your arms."

"Yes," Adrian mumbled.

"What?"

"Yes, I am."

"Good. Now, I'm going to need two things from you. First, you're going to broadcast this interrogation."

"I don't have a channel."

"That's fine. You're going to put it up on mine."

A message with the Enforcer's video channel and temporary login credentials appeared in Adrian's inbox. Brushing aside error messages and dire warnings from his neural interface, he logged in and scrolled through video after video detailing horrific acts of brutality. The man wasn't just careless; he was deliberately injuring citizens. And he was proud of it.

"You're Harder Hardy, aren't you?" Adrian asked as the Enforcer removed his helmet and began to shed his armor.

"Yes. I hear you're not a fan." Hardy chuckled, a deep, ugly sound even without the helmet's distortion.

"The citizens in these videos trusted you. They rely on people like us for protection. What do you think putting out these videos accomplishes?"

"It's fun. It instills fear, and fear creates compliance."

"You're violating your oath," Adrian said softly.

"I don't see your broadcast up yet."

Beginning with his arrest and return to consciousness in the interrogation room, Adrian posted his recording of the interrogation.

"Good. Now keep streaming. I want to see this entire interrogation going up in real-time."

Adrian wanted to ask why it was so important that he act as the Enforcer's videographer, but chose to keep the question to himself. The room was bright and sharp-edged, his survival augmentations straining to keep him conscious and functioning. A few more blows like those he'd already taken and it would be lights out.

There seemed to be a process to removing Enforcer armor. Starting at the throat, each section Hardy unlocked and removed revealed the catch to remove the section below. Molded pieces of composite, their undersides comfortably padded, piled up on the table. Some, especially across the chest and arms, seemed to house mechanical components.

Beneath the armor, a shiny surgical steel framework that resembled human vertebrae protected the Enforcer's spinal column. The bottom of the framework vanished into Hardy's lower-body armor, while the top disappeared into the flesh at the base of his skull.

Adrian frowned, finally grasping what he was looking at. The framework wasn't another removable piece of armor. It was an implant, a permanent part of the Enforcer's body. The rounded, polished steel segments flashed in the light, flexing with Hardy's movements. A system of tiny connectors allowed the plates that protected his back to latch directly to the implant, forming the base for the rest of the upper half of the suit to connect to.

"Why are you doing this?" Adrian asked. "What's the point?"

When Hardy turned around, the expression on his hard, angular face was as warm as the inside of a walk-in freezer. Sinewy lean muscle rolled beneath the sheer khaki fabric that protected his skin from the joints of the armor, and his thin lips curved into a smile that failed to reach his icy pale blue eyes.

Lieutenant Hardy, Enforcer 52670059. In service for twelve years, thirty-nine days, and twenty-two hours.

"Pull up your chair," Hardy said, ignoring Adrian's question. "It's time for round two."

"I'd rather not."

"You can cooperate, or I can take your badge." Hardy sent him a video of an Enforcer scraping off a suspect's facial tattoos. "Your call."

Adrian struggled to his feet, scooted the chair over to the table, and sank back into his seat. The Lieutenant pulled up a chair, moved his armor to one side of the table, and extended his hand.

"We're going to arm wrestle." He smiled that cold smile that didn't reach his eyes. "If you cooperate, I might be able to find grounds to dismiss the charges against you."

Adrian reluctantly clasped hands with the Enforcer.

"On three," Hardy said. "One. Two. Three!"

It felt as if his hand was caught in an industrial-strength vice. Despite throwing every ounce of his remaining strength into the contest, the Enforcer was easily overpowering him.

"Come on, Hero! Can't you do better than that?"

Adrian gritted his teeth. Holding up the weight of multiple floors of a collapsing building had been easier; it felt as if his arm was going to be ripped out of its socket.

Finally Hardy grew bored of the contest and slammed Adrian's hand down on the tabletop.

"Was that really the best you could do?" the Enforcer demanded. "I'm disappointed."

Adrian coughed and wiped his bloody face on his sleeve. Even with survival augmentations pumping his body full of adrenaline and painkillers, it felt like he was drowning.

"I think I'm going to need a few more things from you. Get up."

When Adrian didn't move, Hardy dragged the Hero to his feet and wrapped an arm around his shoulders to hold him upright.

"Where are we going?"

"We're going to get you fixed up," the Lieutenant said, chuckling darkly as they exited the interrogation room.

When Adrian said nothing, Hardy squeezed the Hero's shoulders until he gasped in pain.

"Say thank you," the Enforcer hissed.

"Thank you," Adrian mumbled, "for showing the world what a corrupt piece of vermin waste you are."

"Cut the insults." The Enforcer squeezed Adrian's shoulders again, and he felt bone grind against bone. The pain took his breath away.

They made their way through a maze of short gray corridors lined with unmarked doors. The more corners they turned, the more deliberately confusing the floor plan seemed, perhaps to thwart would-be escapees. Eventually Hardy shoved him into an empty washroom and cuffed him to a rail across from the entrance.

"Don't go anywhere," the Enforcer said as he walked out.

Adrian slumped to the floor, right wrist cuffed to the railing above his head, and stared at the gray composite tile. The facility was so clean he had a hard time believing it had ever seen other occupants. He coughed, spattering the floor with pink froth.

Sensing that he was stationary, his damage report opened across his vision and urged him to get help immediately. Adrian glanced up at his cuffed wrist and laughed. The sound came out as a cross between a gasp and cough.

He scrolled down, silently summarizing his injuries. At least half a dozen broken ribs. A punctured lung. Ruptured organs and internal bleeding. A fractured jaw and accompanying skull fractures. A concussion. Breaks, fractures, and torn connective tissue associated with the crushing injury to his right hand. It wouldn't matter whether he made it back to the Safety Tower alive– his body was damaged beyond the point of cost-effective repair.

Meanwhile, Hardy's broadcast was still running. In the short time it had been up, it had already garnered fifty thousand views. Comments rolled in, complimenting Hardy's physique and encouraging him to ramp up the violence. Adrian spotted scores of Enforcers among those weighing in, and plenty of citizens. Many of the suggestions were painfully graphic, including repeated calls to curb stomp the Hero.

Adrian closed the comment window and refocused on his surroundings, sick to his stomach. He had been unprepared for the bloodthirstiness of Hardy's fans and their irrational hatred of him.

The whisper of an opening door and the sound of boots on tile signaled Hardy's return. A needle bit into his neck, and his heart raced as the synthetic adrenaline coursed through his veins.

Hardy uncuffed him and dragged him over to a row of sinks under a long mirror. It took Adrian a few moments to recognize the bloody figure staring back it him from beside the hulking Enforcer.

"Feeling better?" Hardy demanded. "I have to say, I'm not feeling very charitable about your charges so far. How can someone who fought off a mob and killed a citizen suddenly be so unwilling to defend himself?"

"I feel," Adrian began, leaning on the edge of the counter, "like the Company made a horrible mistake in creating Enforcers. You may have been created from the Hero genome, but there's something missing. You're defective. You're a monster."

Hardy snorted derisively.

"Heroes couldn't keep the public's trust or convince the citizens to love their government. So the Company created Enforcers to keep the city from descending into chaos. Enforcement is the only thing standing between the ungrateful masses and the law-abiding citizens of this shining city. Heroes are just a waste of credit at this point."

"That's not true."

"And that's why Griffith is going to become the next Prime," Hardy continued, ignoring him. "The Safety Division is over, pointless, a failed experiment."

"This is what a vote for Griffith is," Adrian rasped, addressing Hardy's viewers. He knew there must be many Heroes among them, silently watching as their idol cut down one of their own. "A vote for Griffith is a vote against your own existence. A vote for Griffith is a vote for this egotistical steroid freak, and it's a vote for the torture of innocent citizens. Is a future without Heroes really the future you want?"

"Shut up!" Hardy snarled, and kicked Adrian's feet out from under him.

His head hit the edge of the counter on the way down, and the world exploded in light and stars. Then there was only darkness.

# CHAPTER SEVEN

Consciousness returned by degrees as his neural interface recovered from the crash.

"What's wrong with the Hero, Mommy?"

"It looks broken, sweetheart. Don't touch it, okay?"

"But if he's broken, why did the Enforcers leave him here? Why didn't they take him to the medical people?"

"I don't know, honey. It's not our business, okay? Just leave it alone."

"But he looks hurt."

Adrian was vaguely aware of the sensation of movement. A two tone chime sounded, and a crisp female voice announced that the transit module was approaching the Forty-Second Tier Southern Interchange. Adrian slid more tightly against the surface to his left as the module's brakes engaged. He was sprawled on the floor, in the corner between a row of seating and the bulkhead separating one module from the next.

The transit came to a stop, and the door across from him slid open. Passengers disembarked, and new ones got on.

"Jesus, what the hell happened in here?" someone asked.

"No idea. It was here when I got on."

"Some Enforcers brought him on," the young girl said helpfully.

"Shush, honey," the mother said. "We didn't see anything."

"Anyone called Emergency Services yet?"

"No."

"Uh-uh."

"I'm having no part in that!"

"Well, I'm going to. Doesn't look like he has much time left, coughing blood like that."

Adrian realized that the horrible gasping, bubbling sound he had been listening to was his own labored breathing. It felt like he was drowning.

"Whatever. It's just another Hero. It's not like you're going to get anything for it."

"Have some decency," the first man admonished. "He'd give his life for you. Why's it so hard to place a call to get him some help?"

"And have Enforcers asking me questions about how he wound up like that? Down here? Uh-uh, man! Not me!"

Murmurs of agreement joined the second speaker.

"They know how it happened," a third voice whispered. "That's the Hero from the video."

"Is it really?" Shadows passed between him and the bright overhead lights of the module, accompanied by astonished whispers. Darkness retook him as the transit began to slow for its next stop.

***

He dreamed of water. The current held him in soft hands, caressed his skin and whispered in his ears. It gurgled and sang as it carried him away from the dark, grimy towers of the city. Cold stone slipped past his fingers as he plunged over a waterfall and into utter darkness.

The rush of the water quieted, revealing the melodic plunks and gurgles of a river traversing a subterranean cavern. Dripping water provided a soft counterpoint to the sound of the stream.

Gradually his eyes became accustomed to the darkness, and he began to make out vague shapes. The impression of furtive movement plagued the corners of his eyes, sinuous shadows that crept among the spires and columns of the cave. Although he could not explain the feeling, Adrian was sure he did not want the creatures to notice him.

He felt greatly relieved when the river brought him out into the light. Colorful cliffs rose above him, layered with reds and browns and pinks, dotted with pockets of stubborn vegetation. Swallows tickled his skin with their wings as they skimmed over the surface of the river, and trout brushed against him as they rose to snap at unwary insects.

His awareness was all-encompassing. He could feel the cool stone of the canyon walls, the cold currents that hugged the depths of the riverbed, the warm, gritty kiss of the sandbars. In the process of becoming one with the water, he had left his body behind.

The realization did not bother him. The water held him, carrying him away from the pain and violence of his existence. Human lives were finite, but the river went on forever.

"I'm telling you, Doc, you're wasting your time," a vaguely familiar male voice said.

"Have a little faith, Michael. He's got a lot of life left in him."

Someone snorted derisively. "Look at the scans. He's brain dead."

"He'll come out of it. He's going to be fine."

"In all seriousness, Doctor Hart," a third voice interjected. "Look at the scans. There's nothing going on upstairs."

"Listen to Harriet, Doc. You're jeopardizing your medical license, putting this much new hardware into a breathing dead body. Just pull the plug and scrap him."

"Get to work," the doctor growled, "or I'll have you charged with insubordination."

"Fine! Don't say I didn't warn you," Michael muttered.

The river was gone. Adrian was once again aware of his body, and it hurt. He grimaced, wondering why he could neither control his limbs nor open his eyes. Something hot and wet rolled down the side of his face and dripped onto the plastic cover of the operating table.

"Harriet, I think we need some more anesthetic over here," the doctor said. "Hang in there, son. We're going to have you all patched up in no time!"

The world became a hazy, distant place. Adrian floated in and out of consciousness, trying to find his way back to the river, as the doctor discussed his injuries in gruesome detail.

* * *

He awoke some time later in a curtained space in one of the medical facility's massive recovery bays. Staring at the tan curtain that divided his bed from the others around it, he wondered why he had never noticed how crisp and well-defined the weave of the fabric was. Each stitch in the hem stood out in stark contrast, white on the rough pastel fabric. Fingerprints, made visible by age and dust, showed on the rails that held up the divider. If he concentrated, he could even make out the individual grooves and swirls of each print.

A quiet cough alerted him to Doctor Hart's presence. The older man was seated beside his bed, smiling kindly.

"Finally awake, are we? How are we feeling today, son?"

"Okay, I guess."

Adrian found it strange to be addressed as son rather than Hero. Perhaps the doctor, having rescued him from death multiples times, had taken a personal interest in his well-being.

"Let's conduct a few tests then, shall we? Take a deep breath for me."

Adrian inhaled and exhaled obediently.

"How does that feel?"

"Fine."

"Does it hurt? Does it feel tight? Does everything feel normal?"

"It feels normal. It doesn't hurt or feel tight."

"Good, good!" the doctor said, rubbing his hands together excitedly. "Heroes in the condition you came to me in are usually scrapped, but I knew you were worth saving, and I made them listen to me. You're something special!"

Adrian laughed ruefully.

"Thank you, but I'm not. Apparently I'm a murderer." The

knowledge settled onto his chest like a stone, a cold heaviness that made it difficult to breath.

"Accidents happen. And in your case, I know it was an accident." Hart smiled kindly. "You're a true hero. You stood up to Lieutenant Hardy himself, and you showed the whole city what goes on in an Enforcer precinct."

"Somehow I doubt that's going to win me any fans."

"You'd be surprised. After that video went out, almost every Hero I know voted for you. Which makes what the Company chose to do even more disappointing."

Adrian nodded. He was beginning to get the feeling that he had missed something important, something that might also explain the dozens of messages waiting in his inbox.

"Now, in the process of repairing the damaged components of your neural interface, I managed to give you some upgrades." The doctor gave him a sly wink. "You're now the owner of the latest state-of-the-art visual chip, and a brand new, nine-hundred-zettabyte memory module."

"You shouldn't have," Adrian whispered. "That's not standard, is it?"

"It isn't, but no one will ever be the wiser. I took the liberty of doing a little pre-formatting to make your memory module appear to the Company network as a standard replacement to your damaged one."

"Were you able to save what was on my old one?"

"Of course. As for the rest of your body, you'll need physical therapy to regain your lung capacity and retrain your hand. I've also given you a few physical augmentations. If the genetic tweaks are successful, you will have a greatly enhanced rate of physical regeneration. A word of caution: set any broken bones immediately; they will heal much faster than you expect."

Adrian stared at the doctor in horror.

"Don't look so fearful! Unless someone sequences your genetic code, they'll never know. And why would they? The Company already has your genetic signature on file."

"Tampering with the Hero genome is highly illegal," Adrian said softly.

Hart smiled. "The genetic signature resting in the Company's memory bank is intact. You are my first experiment."

"Why me?"

"Because you're a good Hero, one of the very best. There are bad times ahead. I know you'll use these upgrades to do the right thing. But most importantly, I want you to survive. Think you can do that for me?"

"Yes, sir."

"That's good," Hart said, smiling. "It's been a pleasure knowing you."

He stood, shook Adrian's hand, and slipped through the curtain before the Hero could think of anything else to say.

The mail icon at the edge of his vision flashed twice, indicating the arrival of another message. Adrian sighed and checked his inbox. The first was from Mel, wondering why he was late returning from patrol. She pointed out that if she had to come back in one piece at the end of the day, so did he.

The second was a broadcast from the Executive of Safety.

"Hello, good Heroes! It is my pleasure to announce that your new Prime has been selected." Adrian held his breath.

"After reviewing the results of the popular vote, it has been determined that voting was contaminated by fraud, disinformation, and Anarchist propaganda. Therefore, the vote has been discounted from the decision.

"The position of Prime now goes to the Hero with the highest rescue count, a Hero whose vision of a new direction for the Safety Division is fully supported by the Company. Good Heroes, meet your new Prime: Griffith!"

An image of the Hero's grinning face replaced the Executive's as the broadcast came a close. Adrian snorted in disgust and deleted the message. On some level he had suspected the outcome, but that didn't make the news any less unpleasant. How had Griffith pulled ahead of him in rescues, anyway?

The rest of the remaining messages were from Heroes he knew, expressing their sympathy for his defeat. The last was from Mel.

"I don't know if you're still with us, or if you'll ever get this. I just hope you're okay. If you survived what happened down there, send me a message. I just want to know you're alright."

Adrian stared at the words in confusion. She made it sound as if he'd been gone some considerable length of time. Checking the current date, he found that seven days had passed since he'd been assigned to the Forty-Seventh Tier.

"Where was I all that time?" Adrian wondered aloud.

"Probably asleep," a stocky young man in white medical scrubs replied, pulling the curtain shut behind him. "Some downtime is normal considering the severity of your injuries."

Adrian listened intently as the therapist outlined a regimen of exercises to regain the full use of his crushed hand and rehabilitate his lungs.

"You are hereby released, and may return to your quarters," the therapist concluded, handing him a stack of fresh clothing. "Your duties will resume once you have fully recovered. Good luck!"

After the therapist had departed, Adrian sat and stared at his right hand for a time. The fingers remained curled, huddled together as if seeking protection, despite his attempts to straighten them. Fine movements were out of the question.

The staff arrived with fresh sheets for the bed he'd been occupying, indicating they needed the space for someone else. Adrian dressed and made his way toward the cafeteria, composing a message to Mel as he walked.

"I'm not gone," he told her. "They just put me to sleep to heal. If everything goes well with my physical therapy, they're going to return me to duty."

The cafeteria was as packed as ever, roaring with a thousand simultaneous conversations, but the tone of the crowd was darker than he remembered.

"This is wrong!" someone proclaimed as he walked by. "Did you see what they did to Simon?"

"Yes, but it has its benefits."

"It's corruption. There's no other explanation."

"They can't do this. I have a good record!"

Adrian took his place in line and let his mind wander. He wondered if drawing would ever be possible for him again. He longed to return to his daydreaming sketches of the river and lose himself in the fine details of other places.

"So you think they're going to return you to duty? Do you know what that means now?"

Adrian turned to find Mel standing behind him, her expression somber.

"What do you mean?"

"Returning to duty means being integrated, Adrian. The Safety Division is over. If you can pass the physical and mental evaluation, they'll start conditioning you to become a Junior Enforcer."

Adrian stared at her, a cold knot of distress growing in the pit of his stomach.

"You're joking. Already?"

"They started evaluating Heroes the day after Griffith ascended to Prime."

"But people need us! Doesn't the Company understand that?"

"If they do, they don't care. Griffith may have been right, because the Executives wasted no time in declaring us obsolete."

"That self-serving sack of vermin waste," Adrian muttered.

"He is, but I doubt it had much to do with him. He just happened represented the changes they wanted to make."

The line inched forward. Life in the Safety Tower continued as it had every other day, as if their world was not quickly approaching its end. A pair of Heroes passed them, bowls in hand, searching for seating.

"I heard Enforcer food is better."

"Anything would be better than this glop," his companion said. "I'm kind of scared of the armor, though. I'm claustrophobic. I don't know if I'm going to be able to handle the helmet."

"You haven't signed up, have you?" Adrian asked.

"I passed the test the first day it was out. Aced it, actually."

"Don't go! There has to be another option."

"Not really. I've heard they'll retire you if you don't make the cut. I miss Brad, but I'm not that suicidal. And there's a rumor that a few Heroes who pass certain standards may be transferred into private service. But they're not formally offering that as an option."

"Ask about it," Adrian pressed. "You're not Enforcer material. You're not like them."

"I'm not private property material, either. I have no interest in babysitting some rich family's brats, or whatever else they might do with me."

"Nothing you're going to see in private service is as bad as what goes on inside an Enforcement precinct."

"With enough good Heroes, we could change Enforcement from the inside."

"If people like Hardy are training Junior Enforcers, I doubt it. I don't think anyone with their heart in the right place will survive."

"There'll be oversight. I'm kind of looking forward to meeting him," Mel said as he stepped up to the counter to receive his meal. "I don't think he'd stand up so well to an opponent with the same enhancements and augmentations he has. Someone who hadn't already had the stuffing beaten out of them," she added pointedly.

"I don't think there'll be enough oversight," Adrian muttered, pressing his thumb to the payment screen. "There isn't now."

"Then a little karmic justice will be good for him," Mel said as she accepted her bowl of foodstuff.

"Did you not see what he did to me?" Adrian demanded, an edge of panic creeping into his voice. "He'll do the same thing to you, or worse."

"They roughed you up first, electrocuted you, gave you a broken jaw and a concussion. You started out in cuffs while he used you for a punching bag. That's not a contest. It's target practice," Mel said, leading the way to an empty table under the view screen where they had eaten before.

"And you think they won't do that to you?" Adrian sat down and discovered that it was painfully difficult to grasp an eating utensil with his right hand. He switched to his left and picked at his food, trying and failing to find his appetite.

"Of course not. If I went up against him, it would be a training exercise. And then he'd have a training accident."

"And what if you wind up crippled? Or dead?"

Mel shrugged.

"I may never be fully functional again!" Heroes around them turned to stare.

"I'm sorry."

The silence stretched out between them, hidden beneath the roar of surrounding conversations. The bees were missing from the image on the view screen beside their table. Purple flower stalks swayed forlornly in an imaginary wind, doomed without their host of tiny pollinators.

"That's odd," Adrian murmured. "What happened to the bees?"

Mel seemed not to hear him. Her gaze was fixed on the distance, or perhaps something she saw on her visual display. A small smile creased the corners of her mouth.

"Mel?"

Her gaze turned to him, with that smile that made her face glow and her eyes sparkle. He was quite sure it was not meant for him.

"Everything alright?"

Mel laughed. "I think he'd look good on his knees, don't you?"

"Who, Hardy? I think he'd look good retired."

"That too."

She stood up, gathered her empty bowl, and patted him on the shoulder.

"Take care of yourself, Adrian. And good luck. You're going to need it." Then she was gone, the crowd closing on her retreating back as if she had never been there.

He had to admit, if anyone was going to change Enforcement from the inside, it was Mel. Assuming her moral compass survived the training process, and her twisted sense of justice didn't get her killed first.

The thought made Adrian grimace as if he had found something bitter in the bottom of his bowl.

***

"Greetings, Hero. Your presence is requested by the Executive of Safety. Please proceed to Floor Two-Fifty, Suite One."

"I know where it is," Adrian snapped, interrupting the trim, black-suited Executive's assistant. "I'll be there. Thank you," he added, embarrassed.

The assistant ended the conversation, and Adrian was left staring at the empty wall across from his bed.

Why had the Executive sent for him? It had been five days since he'd been released from the recovery bay, and he had another three before he would be reevaluated.

He stripped and stepped into the shower, letting the warm mist just dampen his skin before shutting the water off. Sometime during his time in recovery, the Heroes' water allowance had been cut yet again. He worked a drop of liquid soap into a lather between his palms, scrubbed, and turn the water back on for a quick rinse.

The face he saw in the mirror as he scraped away multiple days' worth of stubble seemed leaner and more grim. The laugh lines at the corners of his mouth were gone, replaced by a tired, stoic expression. There were new scars on his lips and cheek, but his faded insignia remained intact.

His hair was a little too long on top, but barely a centimeter of growth covered the fresh scar above his ear, where Hart had cut into his skull to repair the components of his neural interface. Adrian rubbed the scar absentmindedly, then pulled out a pair of clippers and buzzed everything down to the same length.

Donning his uniform, he stepped out into his home group's communal living space. The couches were vacant, the kitchen clean, the view screens blank to conserve power. Nelson was already gone, training to pass his entrance exams. He hadn't seen Mel in days.

Outside of the hustle and bustle of shift change, the hallways seemed unnaturally quiet. For the first time he could remember, he had the lift to himself. A wide, pristine white waiting room greeted him at the top, empty save himself and the black-clad assistant.

"Greetings, Hero." Startling green eyes focused on his face. "Please be seated. The Executive will see you shortly."

"I want to apologize for earlier. That was rude of me."

The woman nodded absentmindedly, gaze focused on something she saw on her visual display.

Adrian sat in one of the plush white armchairs that lined the walls, took a deep breath, and tried to banish the nervousness that sat like a cold stone at the bottom of his stomach. He pressed his hands together, forcing all the fingers completely straight, and held the exercise for a count of ten. Then he practiced touching each of the fingers on his right hand to the thumb, a set of movements that he found easier in theory than in practice.

He could do pull ups and other exercises that showed he had regained full strength in his hand, but regaining the fine coordination he'd once had was more of a challenge. Adrian sighed in aggravation and stared at the generic vista on the far wall, where the gleaming towers of some other city rose in front of the sharp ridges and peaks of a blue mountain range.

It was all wrong, Adrian thought. It was a fantasy landscape, combining two realities that could never exist together.

In the world that had once been, clear, cold streams would flow down out of the mountains, rushing under the boughs of a dark alpine forest. They would wind through the rocky foothills and verdant lowlands, joining together into great rivers that flowed all the way to the ocean. A flock of birds would wheel above the coastal wetlands, cavorting in the light of the golden sun.

If he drew the present-day world, a haze of pollution would obscure the mountains. He would move closer to the sprawling city, letting its teeming towers nearly touch the top of the screen, the width of the entire wall barely enough to encompass its dirty, decaying outskirts.

The old towers would be less shiny beneath their film of pollutants, the manufacturing districts flat, gray, and grim. He would draw the burned-out husks and derelict, leaning buildings of the outer districts with painstaking care, leaving out no detail of the filth and poverty he had seen there. The spires of wealth and ambition at the center of the city would rise above it all, cold, aloof and distant as the moon, backlit by the red glow of the setting sun.

"The Executive will see you now."

Adrian rose and self-consciously straightened his uniform as the Executive's door slid open. A river of powder blue carpet stretched across the white room to a pale blue armchair, a massive wooden desk, and a tall faux leather chair. The Executive's back was to the door, contemplating the view from the massive window that formed the wall behind his desk. View screens displayed a peaceful vista of rolling green hills on one side of the room, a pale beach and an expanse of calm turquoise water on the other.

Adrian paused, halfway down the strip of carpet, and cleared his throat nervously.

"Come in, come in," the Executive said, turning to face him. "Have a seat, Hero."

Unremarkable dark brown eyes met his own, framed by a round face accustomed to smiling and neatly clipped, light brown hair. Evan Kamaguchi, age forty-three. Executive of Safety. Partner of Minette Kerchner, with whom he had one child. Suffering from high blood pressure.

"Thank you, sir," Adrian said politely, taking the offered seat.

"Adrian, isn't it?"

"Yes, sir."

"Identification numbers are so clumsy, aren't they?" the man said, smiling broadly. "I much prefer names, even for Company men such as yourself."

"So do we," Adrian said, unable to shake the feeling that the comment had been a subtle reminder that Heroes weren't exactly people in the eyes of the Company.

"My condolences on your loss."

"Thank you, sir."

"How are you feeling?"

Adrian stared at the Executive in surprise. He had never expected to be asked how he felt about losing.

"A little sad, I guess."

Kamaguchi nodded, expression unreadable.

"If I may ask, sir, why have you called me here? Is it because of the charge against me?"

The Executive grinned. "There's the curiosity I expected of you! And no, it's not. The charges have been dismissed. Your actions in defense of Company property and data were commendable, and any injury your attackers received is excusable in light of the situation."

"So why was I arrested? And did that man really die?"

"Those are both good questions, but so far I've been unable to answer either of them. In light of the video you broadcast, I think that charges might be in order for several Enforcers. But the larger question I have, at the moment, is why you broadcast it at all."

Adrian swallowed and looked at the floor. "Because he ordered me to, sir."

"I saw that. When the contents of the video came to our attention, we had it removed. Unfortunately, by that point it had already been downloaded more than two hundred thousand times."

Adrian's jaw dropped.

"Astonishing, isn't it? Despite Media and Communication's best efforts to scrub it from the database and prevent it from being circulated, it's out there, and it keeps being viewed."

"I'm sorry, sir."

"I'm satisfied that your actions were not intended to damage the Company."

Adrian nodded, lightheaded with relief. Deliberately undermining the Company's authority was an act punishable by the strictest penalties. In a Hero's case, the penalty would be immediate retirement.

"I've been watching you," Kamaguchi continued, staring at his steepled fingers. "You're very scholarly, aren't you?"

"Yes, sir." He was unsure if it was the right answer. But if the Executive had investigated his use of the archives, there was little point in denying it. "I enjoy learning new things."

"So I've noticed," the Executive said, smiling. "You've always had a notable thirst for knowledge. Where most Heroes spend their free hours on trivial pursuits such as virtual games, video shows or socialization, you choose to follow your curiosity."

"I hope that's acceptable, sir."

"I think so. According to the Information Monitoring Division, your exploration of restricted subjects has always been reasonable and easily explained by circumstances. But, as you can imagine, after the incident with Enforcement your history was subject to a great deal of scrutiny. The head of Enforcement's Special Investigations unit called me and bluntly recommend that I have you retired."

"Thank you for not following that recommendation, sir."

"Oh, don't thank me. It was a simple matter of economics. You were an exemplary Hero, one of the best. You performed your duties with heart and compassion, saving lives and helping citizens with an absolute minimum amount of collateral damage. Your loyalty and dedication to your purpose were unquestionable."

"Thank you, sir," Adrian said, trying not to flinch at the repeated use of his career in the past tense.

"So, you're a scholarly Hero. And an artist. Records tell me your sole non-knowledge related pursuit is drawing."

"Yes, sir."

"How would you like to have more time to pursue your interests, Adrian?"

"If we're talking about what I would like, sir, I would like to return to my duties as a Hero."

"That's not possible. In line with the vision of the new Prime and the wishes of the majority of the Executives, the Safety Division is being integrated into Enforcement. The final generations of Heroes will be known as Junior Enforcers."

Adrian's heart sank. "Why?"

"It's a matter of economics, and of politics. As the boots on the ground, I wouldn't expect you to understand either one."

"Do you agree with it?"

Kamaguchi laughed. "It doesn't matter whether I agree with it or not, because those who are in favor of it are the ones with the most power. Now, here is my offer. You will get to keep being a Hero, in a manner of speaking. The Company is looking to cut their losses by transferring Heroes with the right temperament into private employment."

"Yes, sir," Adrian said, struggling to conceal his dismay. "What will I be doing?"

"You'll become a bodyguard for a nice, affluent family. With Anarchist attacks on the rise, bodyguards are increasingly popular. And, with your experience and skills, you'll be uniquely suited to the task."

"Will I get to keep my implants?" Adrian asked, as the implications of what the Executive was telling him began to sink in. He would no longer be a Company employee, and he might be expected to give up many of the perks that went with that status.

"Of course! That's part of the package we're selling these people—a real, live Hero to defend you and your loved ones. One of the best! I already have a family picked out for you. They live on the Fifth Tier, and they're good friends of mine. You'll like them. And you'll love your new home!"

"Thank you, sir," Adrian murmured. It was obvious he had little choice in the matter.

"Smile! It's not so bad," the Executive said, grinning. "Your new employer will send for you as soon as you've fully recovered from your injuries. Be well and enjoy the rest of your life, Adrian."

"You as well, sir," Adrian said, rising from the chair. He straightened his shoulders and walked out of the office without looking back.

"Why the long face?" the assistant asked as he entered the waiting room. "I thought you'd be happy after the news he had for you."

The woman's unnaturally brilliant green eyes told him that she was Helena Lelasdottir, age twenty-six. No health problems, no criminal record. Her cheekbones and the elegant curve of her jaw were surgically augmented. The jet black color of her hair was the result of genetic editing. Bleaching agents were the leading means of achieving a lighter skin tone among the largely medium-complexioned populace of the city, and the milky paleness of her skin undoubtedly resulted from their use.

Adrian walked over to her desk as he waited for the lift to arrive.

"I take it he told you something you didn't want to hear?"

"I just don't feel that I'll be useful to many people as a bodyguard."

"I understand," she said with a sympathetic nod. "There are

people out there who need you, and you can feel it."

"How did you know?"

"I learned about it in school. It's something you guys were genetically engineered to have. You know, like how in the old days they used to breed dogs to make loyal companions."

"Wait, what?"

"Your empathy and that constant feeling like there are people who need your help? That's a genetic trait. Way back when, some Company scientist decided Heroes needed to have that. Amazing, isn't it?"

"I guess so." The lift arrived, saving him from having to find anything else to say.

*** 

The rest of the day passed uneventfully. He visited the Safety Tower's gym, where there were no longer lines to use the equipment, and ate his dinner alone in his home group's quarters, where the whisper of air through the vents was the only sound. After dinner he retreated to his room and attempt drawing. He practiced straight lines, graceful lines, and the curve of leaves until the cramping of his hand forced him to put away the tablet for the night.

The new memory module Doctor Hart had given him beckoned. Beneath a formatted upper layer that mimicked the standard upgrade, he found a program he had never encountered before. It was represented by a single, transparent snowflake. Curious, Adrian investigated it.

"You have selected to launch Snow. This is an independently developed, self-evolving network navigation system. Please present a valid access key."

"More information."

The snowflake shimmered. "Extracting... Processing... Access granted." The icon expanded, becoming a sparkling multifaceted structure not unlike the collection of ice crystals its design was based upon.

"Snow is based on code written by Doctor Corvin Romanoff two hundred and fifty-three years ago. In order to bypass the censorship, identification and monitoring features of most communication networks, Snow is a self-aware, constantly-evolving program. This awareness allows Snow to quickly detect hostile code and implement a solution before the user or Snow's central code is affected, providing flawless security, anonymity, and freedom of access.

"Over time, Snow has embedded strands of code in virtually every program in existence. To the machines and their human programmers, even those set to monitor security, these strands of code appear to belong in their surroundings. When called upon, however, this omnipresent network provides a means of communication invisible to government watchers, as well as access to virtually any information available via the network.

"Nothing differentiates Snow users from non-users. All carry the same innocuous strands of code. If your neural interface is ever audited, you can rest easy in the knowledge that Snow is impossible to detect."

Adrian stared at the wall of information in awe. Snow was possibly the most peculiar program he had ever encountered. Self-aware and evolving? That almost sounded like sentience.

"Isn't that illegal, though?" he asked.

"Use of this program has never been proven by the Company," the program replied. "Since its inception, the Company has spent over ninety-seven trillion credits on personnel, training, and the creation of programs to unmask and block programs such as Snow. This program is the only one to retain its integrity."

Adrian sat in silence, staring at the wall across from his bed. The Company might not be taking back their proprietary implants, but he suspected that his transfer to private employment would revoke his access to much of the Company's sensitive information, including that which was contained in the archives. He could not imagine life without access to that knowledge.

"Snow, can you access the archives?"

"Access obtained. Specify desired action."

"Calculate memory needed to copy all archived information."

"Processing."

Without his new high-capacity memory module, the request would have been laughable. Even compressed, the archives contained an unimaginably massive amount of data. And yet, the more he pondered Hart's intentions, the more he had a feeling that this had been the doctor's plan. After all, why else would he ever need that much storage space?

"Calculation complete."

The final number was a roomy fifty zettabytes short of the capacity of the memory module. Adrian breathed a sigh of relief.

"Specify desired action," the program prompted.

"Download all files," Adrian whispered.

# CHAPTER EIGHT

**W**hen the time for his physical assessment arrived, the sterile hallways of the tower's medical facility were less crowded than Adrian remembered. He hoped it meant that his fellow Heroes were weathering their transition to Enforcement well.

A woman with gray-green eyes and curly brown hair greeted him at the door to the evaluation room.

"I'm Doctor Jones, and I'll be conducting your assessment today. If you have any objection to this assessment being conducted by a female, we can have you assessed by the next available male doctor."

"I don't," Adrian replied, shaking her hand.

Aliesha Jones, age thirty-two. No criminal history. A lengthy list of medical degrees rounded out her file.

"Why would anyone object?" Adrian asked as Jones led him into the suite.

"It makes some people uncomfortable."

The doctor's assistant, a lean young man with light brown hair, stood up from the equipment he had been working on as they walked in.

"Now this is some luck!" He seized Adrian's hand, brown eyes shining with excitement, and shook it vigorously. "I never imagined I'd actually get to meet the people's Prime."

Brian Sonnet, age twenty-eight. No criminal record. His medical history read like a psychology textbook, a recipe for a cocktail of stimulants, sedatives and mood altering drugs. All were perfectly legal, prescribed to him by the good psychologists of the Company.

"Thank you, but I'm not."

"Jones, do you have any idea who this is? This is the guy! The Hero from the video!"

"I'm aware of his notoriety," the doctor said with a dry chuckle. "Please try to contain your excitement at least until the evaluation is over."

"May I have a picture with you?"

"Sure, why not?" The idea of someone wanting their picture taken with him was an utterly foreign concept to Adrian. He was no celebrity.

"Can you put your arm around my shoulders like we're friends?"

"Sure, sure," Adrian replied, laughing.

He put his arm around the assistant's shoulders. Sonnet smiled, he smiled, and Jones stepped in front of them and snapped a picture. A second later the image landed in his inbox.

"This is the best thing that has ever happened to me! Thank you so much."

"You're very welcome."

"Now, if we could return to business," Jones said. "Hero, there's a curtain provided for your privacy."

Adrian stepped behind the curtain and changed into the black gym shorts he found there. Outside, Sonnet motioned him into the spherical, human height diagnostic system. The door of the see-through sphere slid shut behind him, sealing him off from the doctor and her assistant.

"You know the drill: static imaging first. Please stand still," Jones said, her words appearing as glowing text that slowly faded from his view.

Adrian obediently held his place as the faint tingle of ambient electricity crawled over his skin. He knew that if he looked down, every hair on his body would be standing on end, electrically charged.

"Very good," Jones said as his scans came through. "Your file says you tore your right rotator cuff recently. Is that an error?"

"I don't think so. I had a long fall after catching a jumper."

"I'm not seeing as much scar tissue as I'd expect from that." The doctor frowned. "That's unusual."

"Is that a bad thing?" Adrian asked, a flutter of uneasiness rising in his stomach.

"There doesn't seem to have been any lasting damage, and that's definitely a good thing. Moving on to the stress tests. Powering up the rollers in three. Two. One."

Adrian broke into a jog as the floor under him began to move. He stared at the blank white composite of the far wall as he sprinted in place, concentrating on pushing himself. The stress tests were the benchmark of his ability to do his job. If he scored too low, he would be retired.

"Very good! Slowing rollers," Jones announced. "Now, let's run some tests of your upper body strength."

Adrian was gasping and drenched in sweat by the end of the physical assessment.

"How are you feeling?" Jones asked. "Do you have any pain? Any difficulty breathing?"

"No, no. I feel fine. How do my lungs look?"

"Good as new," Jones replied, smiling. "I just wanted to make sure all your new bits and pieces are working correctly, and they seem to be. Sonnet?"

The assistant let Adrian out of the sphere.

"Did I pass?"

Jones laughed. "You ran a five minute mile, and your overall results put Heroes a decade your junior to shame. I would definitely say you passed."

Adrian grinned in relief.

"Now, let's see that hand. Crushed, correct?"

"Yes. It was an Enforcer-related incident."

"Arm wrestling." The doctor frowned. "With an Enforcer. That's not something I'd recommend doing again."

"It's not an experience I'd like to repeat."

"I can imagine. There is one other thing. Sonnet, isn't it about your break time? Why don't you go to lunch while I finish up here."

"Yes, ma'am!" Sonnet nodded happily and put away the cleaning solution he'd been sanitizing the sphere with.

"What other thing?" Adrian asked as the door slid shut.

"Your neural interface is pulling an unusually high amount of energy. Have you been feeling tired lately?"

His heart slammed against his ribs.

A person's neural interface was powered by the faint electrical current present in all living bodies. Downloading the entirety of the archives was a lengthy and energy-intensive process, although over the past few days Adrian had come to barely notice the drain. If he had remembered, he would have paused the download before the assessment.

"I'm just downloading something," Adrian mumbled.

Jones frowned at something on her visual display, then shook her head.

"Your neural interface shouldn't be pulling that much energy." The doctor's eyes focused on Adrian's face. "That must be quite some download."

"Just some high-resolution art." Adrian rubbed the back of his neck and stared at the floor.

"I'm sure Hart will be glad to hear that," the doctor said, smiling. "But if you start to feel unusually tired, contact me right away. It could indicate a malfunction, and that kind of thing can be deadly if left unattended."

"Yes, ma'am."

"I hereby declare you fit for duty. Good luck, Hero!"

Adrian shook her hand, grinning in relief, and ducked behind the curtain to change back into his uniform.

***

He returned to find his home group's living quarters in disarray. Broken furniture and shards of shattered composite littered the floor. View screens hung crooked in their brackets. Deep dents marred the walls.

As Adrian stepped inside, a chair crashed into the screen next to the door. Sparks and a tendril of acrid black smoke rose from its ruptured surface. Adrian quickly opened the room's virtual control panel and shut off power to everything nonessential.

Nelson stood on the far side of the room, naked except for his uniform pants. He screamed an obscenity and hurled another chair.

"How is it possible that I don't pass after all this?" He waved his arms wildly, seeming to indicate himself as well as the destroyed room. "How? Why?!"

"Nelson," Adrian said calmly, "why don't you tell me what happened."

"I hate this," the Hero roared, punching the kitchen table. "I took all the garbage they take, all the pills and injections. I spend eight hours a day in the gym! And I let them do this to me." He turned around, uncharacteristic tears streaming down his face as he indicated the smooth metal attached to his spine from the base of his skull to somewhere below the waist of his pants.

Nelson was much bigger than the last time Adrian had seen him. In the course of only a week, his chest, arms and shoulders had grown to the point that he might have been bigger than Griffith. His pants barely fit over the new muscle in his legs, and red stretch marks covered the Hero's pale flesh like the tracks of healing scars.

"Calm down," Adrian repeated. "Take a deep breath. Have a seat." He righted an overturned couch and sat down. "Relax for a few minutes."

"You don't understand. I can't calm down! It's like I'm stuck or something."

"Sit down and tell me about it."

Nelson snarled in aggravation and swatted the kitchen table out of his way, sending it skidding across the room. He dropped onto the couch with enough force to make the springs groan in protest and nearly toss Adrian onto the floor.

"I just want to tear this thing off," he muttered, struggling to reach the spinal implant. Too musclebound to reach the center of his back, Nelson settled for clawing at the section that protected the vertebrae of his neck. "It's ached since they put it on, and now it itches too. I'd give anything to be able to go back and just say no!"

"I don't think any of us had a choice," Adrian said, eying the metal framework and the red, puffy skin that surrounded it. "Have you seen a doctor about that?"

"What good will it do?"

Adrian ran his fingers over the skin around the implant. It was hot to the touch, as was the metal itself.

"Scratch harder," Nelson demanded.

"I wasn't–"

"Scratch harder!"

"Okay, okay. Calm down." Clear fluid oozed up where the puffy skin met the smooth metal as he rubbed his way down Nelson's spine. "You need to go see a doctor. I think you're having some kind of allergic reaction."

"Oh, God." Nelson hunched forward, holding his face in his hands. "I'm dead!"

"They'll make it stop itching," Adrian promised. "They can give you something to stop the reaction, and you can take the test again. You'll probably pass if your body isn't fighting your new implant."

"It's not that simple. I'm out of chances. If my body's rejecting the spinal implant, this is it for me."

For once, he couldn't think of anything to say.

Nelson snarled in aggravation and began clawing at his neck again.

"Stop. Stop! You're going to hurt yourself," Adrian said, catching the other man's hands and holding them still. "You have to go to the doctor. If you're not cut out to be an Enforcer, there are other options. Ask them to transfer you to private custody as a bodyguard. That's what they're doing with me."

"There's no point."

"You're going to be okay." Adrian pulled the other Hero to his feet and helped him put on a shirt. "Go to the medical facility," he said, steering Nelson toward the door. "Don't make me walk you there."

"I'm going, I'm going," Nelson muttered.

The dented door slid shut, leaving Adrian alone in the trashed communal living area. He made himself a bowl of foodstuff he had no appetite for, retreated to the tidiness of his room, and tuned in to Media's hourly newscast. Seated behind a desk in a shining white newsroom, the pair of well-dressed newscasters appeared comfortably removed from the story they were covering.

"As we've covered before, the reservoirs are direly low. The Division of Public Services is saying that if no rain falls in the next week, the water crisis will reach a state of emergency."

"Is there any rain in the forecast, Kim?"

"Not at this time, Dave. Meteorology is telling us that a stubborn high pressure ridge is parked over the mountains, blocking any precipitation from coming within a few hundred kilometers of the city."

"That's not good, Kim. How about the condensation project? I know the Company has invested millions of credits into a system to capture and condense airborne moisture. Are we seeing any significant benefit from that?"

"Not really, Dave. The condensation system just doesn't yield enough water to make an appreciable difference to a city this size."

"That's unfortunate. What can we expect if the Division of Public Services is forced to enact a state of emergency?"

"Much of the city will be facing a new form of water rationing. Water access will be provided solely through public dispensers, where Enforcers will be stationed to diligently check the credentials of anyone requesting water."

"Won't that be a hardship for some?"

"Yes, but it's nothing compared to the hardship we'll all be facing if the city's reservoirs run dry. According to Public Services, two of the largest reservoirs are already empty. Three more are so low there's little left in the bottom but particulate sludge. The remaining five are critically low."

"It has been documented that there are a lot of people finding ways to exceed their water allowances, especially on the lower tiers. If Public Services feels these measures will extend the life of the reservoirs, I'm all for it."

"Good point, Kim. Now let's hear from our man on the street, Brandon Nicholas. How are things on the Twenty-Ninth Tier, Brandon?"

The view of the newsroom was replaced with that of a disheveled reporter standing in an enclosed walkway a few floors above street level. A seething crowd could be seen through the clear composite behind him.

"It's chaos down here, Dave, utter chaos! At this point, Enforcement has placed most of the tier under martial law, but they have had little success in quelling the unrest that began fifteen days ago. Protests and rioting have spread all the way around the tier, from Aberdeen Ward to Keating Business Park."

"Now, Brandon," Kim interjected, "that doesn't mesh with what I'm hearing from Enforcement. They're saying they have the Anarchist rioters contained to small pockets of resistance, and otherwise the residents are free to carry on business as usual in the tier."

"As you can see, Kim, that's not the case." His videographer dutifully panned over the scene outside the walkway. "I've seen it firsthand. It's like this all the way around the tier."

The street below was wall to wall with protesters, a seething tide that surged against the line of Enforcers struggling to keep them out of the transit interchange. Flickers of light illuminated the street-level gloom as bodies were crushed against electrified riot shields. Pillars of black smoke roiled up from piles of burning debris and ground-level storefronts.

"Sounds like it's time to check the view from our eye in the sky over Trinity Ward!" Kim smiled brightly as the street reporter was replaced by an aerial view of the city. "What are we seeing here, Dave?"

"Well, it looks like the Anarchists have set fires inside several buildings, Kim," the male newscaster said. "This is actually very close to Brandon's location, within one of the pockets of Anarchist activity you were talking about."

"That's right, Dave. And I'm hearing a report now, Enforcement has issued a statement that they're working to restore order here as well so that Emergency Services can move in and begin putting out those fires."

"Good to hear! Now it's time to go to Candi at the Home Sense Desk, who has a few tips on water conservation."

"That's right, Dave! And after that, the Lifestyles Report! Who's wearing what, and who wore it best? After this brief message from Home Sense."

Adrian shut off the report and held his head in his hands.

"Greetings, Hero!" Adrian blinked the message to the center of his field of vision.

"You have passed your post-duty physical assessment, and are hereby reassigned. Your Company-ordered duty is to protect the private citizen known as Jeremiah Williams, citizen ID number 87251839-PX579."

Adrian raised an eyebrow in surprise. He should have known he would not be sold to just any wealthy citizen. The PX designation denoted a private executive, the owner or co-owner of one of the private corporations that provided services for the Company. Five-hundred series corporations were food producers.

"You will follow citizen Williams' orders in every detail, so long as they do not run counter to the interests of the Company. You will have the sub-task of protecting his family members, but Mr. Williams' safety is your first priority.

"A private transport will arrive in fifty-eight minutes to relocate you to Mr. Williams' residence. Have a good day."

The day he had been dreading since he spoke to the Executive of Safety had finally arrived. With a sinking feeling, Adrian pulled a duffle bag from the storage area under his bed. It easily held his spare uniforms and the few possessions he had to his name.

Bag over his shoulder, he left his room for the last time. The air in the wreckage of the communal living space smelled of unwashed dishes and stale sweat. Adrian located several abandoned bowls and placed them in the cleaning receptacle on his way to the door.

The residential floors of the tower were silent as he made his way to the lift and descended to ground level. A few Junior Enforcers passed him as he walked to the exit that interfaced with the private transport tracks. None of them acknowledged him.

Outside, Adrian set the duffle bag on the ground and leaned against the tower's smooth, dove gray outer wall. The street was silent except for the distant hum of life on nearby tiers and the occasional passing transport. The air shimmered with heat. Adrian sighed and stared at the pavement.

A utilitarian white transport slid to a stop in front of the building with a hiss of well-maintained brakes, releasing a phalanx of blank-faced Junior Enforcers. The men wore plain gray trainees' overalls, devoid of markings except for identification numbers stenciled over the right breast and across the upper back of their clothing. Flashes of bright metal could be seen between their suit collars and the base of their skulls. There was a patch of white scar tissue on each trainee's cheek where their Safety insignia had once been.

They did not talk among themselves. They did not joke or laugh.

They stared straight ahead, blue eyes cold and dead, as they marched into the building.

One of the Junior Enforcers at the end of the line caught his attention. That serial number was familiar. It belonged to Mason, another long-lived Hero. They had been in the same home group once, years ago. They had been friends.

"Mason!" Adrian said, stepping away from the wall. "How have you been? How are Jody and Dev? I haven't heard from them in ages."

The Junior Enforcer passed him without so much as glancing in his direction.

As the last of the trainees filed into the building, Adrian leaned against the wall and resumed his contemplation of the pavement. His chest hurt, a directionless ache that made it hard to breathe, and he was suddenly very angry. Angry at the Company, angry at the Executives, angry at the Enforcers and whatever they had done to his fellow Heroes.

His thoughts were interrupted by the emergency alert that flashed across his vision. Nelson's face and serial number accompanied the broadcast.

"All available personnel: Class Five Security Breach in Sub-Level Fifteen, Sector D." People had already been critically injured or killed, and there was the potential for further loss of life. "Aggressor is highly unstable. Caution is advised. Lethal force is authorized."

Adrian blinked the alert out of view, relegating it to audio-only as he picked up his duffle bag and turned toward the entrance.

"Aggressor is confirmed in Lift Seven, ascending."

He didn't even hear the private transport pull up behind him, silent on its magnetic propulsion system.

"Where are you going, Hero?" The voice was calm and even, with the faint accent of expensive schooling that marked residents of uppermost tiers. Adrian turned to find a bearded, middle-aged man in a conservatively cut blue suit standing next to a sleek black private transport.

"There's an emergency alert."

"But you're not a Safety employee anymore," the man replied, smiling. "It's not your problem."

"People have been hurt. More people could be injured."

"But it's not your problem," the man repeated, stepping forward and extending his hand.

Shrewd brown eyes regarded him from a face that was more accustomed to frowning than smiling. The man's receding brown hair was as neatly clipped as his beard, despite a stubborn cowlick above his right temple. Jeremiah Williams, chief executive of Nutrition Recovery Inc. Forty-two years old. Partner of Amira Murrette, with whom he had one child. Suffering from high blood pressure.

Adrian shook Williams' hand as the emergency alert continued.

"Aggressor has disembarked on Floor Seventy-Five, Quadrant B. Lifts have been stopped per emergency containment protocol.

"Aggressor has entered Stairwell Sixteen B at Floor Seventy-Five, moving upward."

He wondered how long it would be before someone stopped Nelson. Were the Junior Enforcers responding to the situation?

"What a pleasure it is to add you to my household," Williams was saying. "After all, it's not every day a citizen has the opportunity to add a Hero to his staff."

"Assault with injuries in Stairwell Sixteen B at Floor Eighty-Seven. Nearest available medical personnel, please respond."

"I'm sorry," Adrian said, "but may I have fifteen minutes? There's a friend that's involved."

Williams frowned. "I was told you would be ready at this time. I have an appointment to keep."

"This is the only time I will ever ask for a favor. Give me your address, and I'll take a transport there as soon as I'm done. I know your time is valuable, and I don't want to hold up your business."

"It is, and you're not going to. Get in the transport. That is an order," Williams added, scowling.

"Assault with injury in Stairwell Sixteen B, at Floor One-Oh-Five. Casualty in Corridor Fifty-Seven F on Floor One-Oh-Five. Available medical personnel, please respond."

Adrian stared at the citizen in front of him and wondered what would happen if he walked away.

"Are you hearing me?" Williams demanded, waving his hand in front of Adrian's face.

"Security breach at maintenance access 105-36B."

"Don't do it," he told Nelson via private message, finally realizing where the Hero was headed. "You can still turn back. You can fix this! Just stop."

"If you don't get in the transport right now, I am filing a complaint!"

He received no response. The time to have done something was when Nelson was still near the ground floor, when he could have caught up to the Hero and talked some sense into him. There was nothing he could do now. Adjusting the duffle bag on his shoulder, he moved toward the transport.

"Aggressor has chosen to self-neutralize. Neutralization complete in five. Four."

Against his better judgment, he looked up. A flash of silver caught his eye, Nelson's spinal implant catching the light as he rolled onto his back and plummeted toward the pavement. The wet crunch came a moment later. He was glad the Hero had hit the ground behind the transport, where he could not see.

Williams glanced in the direction of the sound before joining Adrian inside the vehicle.

"I didn't know the Safety Division had jumpers," he said casually. "Or was that a victim of your emergency alert?"

"Both."

"What a pity. Waste of perfectly good material," Williams said, staring out the window as the transport slid away from the building.

"What?"

"Biological material. Protein. Liquid. Minerals like the calcium in bone and the iron in blood. They can all be recovered and recycled. Due to the trauma of impact, jumpers are quite wasteful."

Adrian nodded absentmindedly, comforting himself with the knowledge that Nelson could not have suffered much.

The ride to Williams' residence passed in silence, shining towers sliding past the tinted windows as they climbed toward the Fifth Tier. The man across from him said nothing, completely motionless except for the occasional frown at whatever he was viewing.

The transport slowed and disembarked from the cross-tier tracks, slipping down a wide avenue lined with gleaming retail towers. Well-dressed pedestrians flowed around them, trailed by domestic assistants laden with bags of purchases. Towering trees, their leaves green and healthy, rose on either side of the street. Solar-spectrum lighting kept the trees alive and thriving despite the perpetual shade of street level.

After a handful of turns, the transport entered a smaller avenue called Cherry Lane. The trees lining the street were like nothing Adrian had ever seen. Instead of leaves, the branches were covered in a multitude of tiny pink petals that drifted to the ground in showers as they passed. Turning to look behind them, he saw a storm of fallen petals dancing in their wake.

The transport slipped through a security gate and entered an enclosed courtyard surrounded by more flowering trees. A shining silver building rose above them, gold where the sun struck its south and west sides, pale silver in the shade. A few artfully placed solar cells broke the mirror-like surface of the building, forming geometric patterns that seemed more artistic than functional.

The transport came to a stop under the arched roof that extended from the entryway. Adrian hesitated respectfully, waiting for the executive disembark.

"You first," Williams said impatiently.

Framed by composite in a muted pinkish-tan that complimented the flowering trees, the front doors of the building were even wider than the main entrance of the Safety Tower. Massive sheets of clear glass embellished with slender gold vines slid aside to admit them.

The theme was repeated within, where a glass console stood in front of a massive video screen. It depicted a world where brightly colored fish shimmered beneath the surface of a stream lined with flowering trees. A field of lush grass and colorful flowers stretch away into the distance, swaying gently in an imaginary breeze.

The directionless female voice nearly made Adrian jump.

"Welcome to Elysian Fields, Mr. Williams and guest. How may I assist you today?"

"I would like to register an addition to my personal staff. He is to have the highest level of domestic security clearance."

"Registering," the sterile, unaccented female voice said. "Please submit your biometrics."

"This is Valkyr," Williams explained as Adrian stepped up to the console and submitted his hand print and an eye scan. "Valkyr is the security and management system for the Elysian Fields housing tower. The security clearance I'm giving you will allow you unrestricted access for the purpose of performing your duties."

"Successfully registered," Valkyr intoned. "Do you have a common name by which you wish to be addressed?"

"Adrian."

"Registered. Will there be anything else?"

"That is all," Williams said.

"Thank you. Please enjoy your stay at Elysian Fields."

Adrian would have liked a moment more to examine the scene on the view screen, but Williams was already walking away.

"You don't know the first thing about being a bodyguard, do you?" Williams demanded as they stepped out into a massive, park-like common area.

"Just that I'm supposed to protect you."

The air was soft with humidity, evaporation from the live plants that lined the quiet walkways and shady nooks of the indoor park. The floor was smooth and clear, shielding an enclosed ecosystem of lush green moss, dark stones and trickling water.

"Get over here," Williams growled, snapping his fingers impatiently and pointing at the spot beside him.

"My apologies," Adrian said as he joined the executive in one of the lifts beside the entrance.

The walls of the lift were clear, offering a view of the two floors the indoor park occupied. Next they passed several floors filled with shops and restaurants. Beyond that the lift shaft closed around them, decorative murals sliding past the clear walls.

"I want you to read these manuals." Williams forwarded him each title as he announced it. "Etiquette for Domestics, The Fundamentals of Protective Service, and Security 101. You do read, don't you?"

"Of course."

"Good."

The lift rose for a long time, and when they finally disembarked he realized why. Outside there was no hallway, only a room with a single door on the far side. The sign beside it read, "Williams, Suite 200-1."

"I have the entire floor," Williams said, using his thumb print to open the door. "It is the highest suite in Elysian Fields, and comes with a private rooftop garden."

The communal living space eclipsed even the largest family rooms Adrian had seen. A high ceiling with decorative wooden rafters stretched above a cavernous open space dotted with islands of seating and art displays. Glass walls on either side of the room added to the feeling of infinite space.

"One of the domestics will show you around. I expect you to spend the rest of the afternoon learning your place in the household."

As Williams spoke, two women entered the room. The first was tall and lean, with blonde hair and gray eyes. She wore a hot pink suit with strategically placed cutouts that accentuated her toned arms and slender waist. The second woman was more conservatively dressed in a loose-fitting sleeveless white jumpsuit, cinched at the waist with an ornate black and silver belt. Light brown hair fell over her softly rounded face, concealing her eyes.

"This is my partner, Amira," Williams said, "and my daughter, Yulia."

The woman in pink was Amira Murrette, CEO of Murrette Industries, one of the city's largest food suppliers. A polite smile touched her lips as she shook his hand, but her body language remained disinterested.

"Pleased to meet you," Adrian said politely. "And you," he added, extending his hand to the younger woman.

Yulia Murrette-Williams' gray gaze remained unfocused, no doubt occupied with something on her neural interface.

"Yulia! Stop playing your game and shake the man's hand," Williams snapped.

The young woman sighed. "I'm trying to finish the test for one of my programming courses. These are timed, remember?"

A faint frown creased her face as she clasped Adrian's hand. "You look familiar."

"You may have seen me out on patrol."

"No, it's something else."

"You wouldn't have trouble remembering faces if you didn't spend all your time in virtual reality," Williams muttered.

"Better than being here."

"Go to your room!"

"That's where I was until you dragged me out here to meet the new help," Yulia retorted.

"Watch your tone, young lady," Amira said. "I'm still paying for those courses, as well as the licenses for your games. All of which can be revoked."

Yulia was already gone, a pale figure vanishing down the dimly lit hallway at the back of the room.

"I wish you hadn't bought her either one," Williams muttered. "Programming? Really? She's not programmer material, and it's not a suitable job for someone of her station anyway. And kids from all over the city play those games. I don't think she needs to be exposed to that element."

"Actually, she's shown quite an aptitude for programming. And she needed friends."

"Might I remind you that she was dating some dirty twenty-three-year-old from the Twentieth Tier before I grounded her?"

"I'm sure it would have turned out alright. She's just going through a phase."

"He was taking her out to the Entertainment District!"

"She is legally an adult, dear. Please try to remember that."

"She doesn't need to be associating with the unwashed masses."

Adrian examined the ornately carved beams that supported the lofty ceiling and pretended he was not witnessing a private family disagreement.

"You would do well to remember that if I hadn't associated with the unwashed masses, as you so nicely put it, I would never have partnered with you. And if I hadn't, you would not be where you are now."

With that Amira turned on her heel and walked away, hot pink boots clicking smartly on the polished floor.

"And that's my family," the man concluded, tone contemptuous.

An inconspicuous side door slid open, and a compact young woman in a black-trimmed fawn uniform entered the room. Short black hair in a business-like bob brushed her cheeks. Her dark brown eyes did not meet his.

"Anna Chung, this is my new bodyguard, Adrian." The woman

bowed, unobtrusively smoothing her uniform. "Anna will show around. Tomorrow you will begin accompanying me. Do you have any questions?"

"No, sir."

"Good. Anna, I will be out on business until six. Inform the kitchen staff that dinner is to be served at seven."

"Yes, sir. Should I inform Amira and Yulia as well?"

"I'm sure they'll figure it out."

"Pleased to meet you," Adrian said, holding out his hand. "I look forward to working with you."

The woman's handshake was cool and brief, as if she was somehow affronted by his courtesy. "You as well, Hero."

"Technically, I'm not a Hero anymore. You can call me Adrian."

"You have the look, the badge, and the uniform. You will always be a Hero," Anna said icily. "Please follow me."

The family's massive central living space with its vaulted ceiling, priceless artworks, and empty couches occupied less than a third of the suite. An equally oversized and richly decorated dining room opened off the far side of the main space, dominated by a long, genuine wood dining table.

"This way, please." Anna motioned him through a set of doors at the back of the room. "This is the kitchen. You're welcome to come here for food outside of scheduled meals, but please stay out of the way of the staff."

"Where are they?" The gleaming white counters were empty, the food preparation devices lining the walls dark and silent.

"The kitchen staff arrive in the early morning to prepare breakfast, and again later in the afternoon to prepare dinner. If you desire lunch or a snack, there is food in the refrigerators on the far wall."

"Actually, I don't really know how to cook."

Anna gave him an exasperated look. "There's also a dispenser for the domestics. You're welcome to use it."

The tour continued into the suite's central hallway. The corridor, paneled in satiny dark wood, was wide enough for three people to walk side by side. A soft, footstep-muffling burgundy carpet ran its length.

Anna pointed out Mr. Williams' room, Amira's room, and Yulia's.

"Mr. Williams and Ms. Murrette sleep in different rooms?"

"That's none of our business." Anna paused in front of the door between Yulia and Amira's rooms. "This was Yulia's nurse's room when she was a baby, and her tutor's when she was a child. Now it's yours. Have a nice evening."

"Thank you." Adrian stared after her retreating back, wondering what he could have done to offend the domestic assistant.

Beyond the door, he discovered a micro-suite more spacious than his entire home group's living quarters. The main room was dominated by a wall-to-wall window that delivered a stunning view of the Fifth Tier and the tiers geographically above it. An intricate watercolor painting covered the wall to his right. To the left there were two doors, a watercolor of dancing birds hanging between them.

The first door opened into the bathroom. The second led to a spacious bedroom, one wall of which was also a window. A sliding screen could be drawn across it to block the light.

One third of the room was occupied by a massive bed, its burgundy sheets and black cover complimenting the dark red carpet. Adrian put down his bag and wondered what he was supposed to do with that much sleeping space. The bed was the width of at least three of the bunks in his old quarters.

There was an armchair, turned toward the window, and an old-fashioned dresser made of satiny dark wood with real metal handles. It might even be an antique, an heirloom passed down from a time long before the city's founding. A framed picture of a forest scene hung above the head of the bed, its jade leaves and mossy stones providing a pleasant counterpoint to the burgundy theme.

One of the doors on the left led into the bathroom, the other into a walk-in closet roomier than his entire personal space in the Safety Tower. After he had hung up his spare uniforms and stacked everything else on the shelves, the closet still looked empty.

It was a strange concept for the facilities to have their own space. The counters, walls and floor were composite fabricated to mimic pale granite, their surfaces sparkling with crystalline black and pale gray flecks.

There was a toilet and a sink against the wall the bathroom shared with the hallway. A floor-length mirror hung beside the bedroom door, and a clear cube occupied the back of the room, its walls real glass rather than opaque composite. The door slid open at his touch. Adrian immediately recognized the shower, but he had never seen anything like the deep basin next to it. Turning one of the polished metal knobs sent steaming water cascading into the bowl. Adrian winced, wondering if he had just expended his entire water allowance.

He returned to the main room and examined the larger painting. Jagged blue-gray peaks rose above a row of blooming cherry trees, their boughs arching over a placid river. Like the shady forest path in the bedroom, the pale pinks and muted blues of the picture complimented the plum-colored carpet.

A round table made from planks of dark genuine wood sat in the center of the room, and a matching desk rested against the wall under the watercolor. A pair of comfortable-looking gray armchairs huddled together in front of the window, as if conspiring against the rest of the furniture. Their color exactly matched the painted mountains. He settled into one of the armchairs and began reading the material Williams had given him.

As part of the domestic staff, he was not to look at or speak to Williams or his family unless spoken to. He was to perform his duties in the least obtrusive manner possible. Failure to do so, the manual stressed, could lead to the immediate termination of his employment.

The Protection and Security 101 manuals were just as dull. He must remain alert and vigilant for threats at all times, especially when accompanying his employer. Upon exiting any building or transport, it was his duty to precede his employer in order to identify and neutralize potential threats. The rest of the time it was his place to walk unobtrusively behind, one step back and to the left.

Snow's search window opened across his vision. The phrase "one step behind and to the left" appeared to define the query. The results were all related to companion animal training. One of the videos opened of its own accord, showing a four-legged, knee-height brown animal trotting dutifully a step behind its human handler. When the human stopped, the animal promptly sat down on its haunches. The video was titled, "A dog obeying the heel command."

Adrian chuckled and dismissed the video. How had he accidentally triggered the program's search function?

Some time later, his studies were interrupted by a soft tap on the door.

"Come in."

The door slid open to reveal an angular wisp of a young woman in a drab fawn domestic assistant's uniform. From her amber eyes to her light brown hair to her faintly tanned skin, everything about her seemed slightly faded, as if she, like her uniform, had been through the laundry too many times.

Bridget May, age twenty-two, youngest child of Edith May and Tony Dunn. She possessed mild asthma, as well as several surprising convictions for violations of privacy pertaining to the illicit recording of citizens.

"Can I help you?" Adrian asked. His augmented hearing picked up the panicked drumming of her heart from across the room. "Is everything alright?"

"Yes, everything's fine," the young woman said quickly. "My name is Bridget. I handle the laundry. Do you have anything you'd like me to take?"

"No, thank you. All my clothes are clean."

"Thank you, sir. Please place anything you would like laundered in the hamper in your closet, and I will collect it tomorrow morning."

"I will, thank you." It was strange to have someone collect his laundry.

Before he could say anything else, the young woman bowed quickly and fled.

The next intrusion came at six thirty, when Anna announced herself with a sharp knock. She did not wait for his response before opening the door.

"Mr. Williams has indicated that you are to dine with him. Your presence is required in the dining room at six forty-five. Please prepare yourself."

"Wait, I have a question."

"Yes?" A glint of annoyance flashed in her dark eyes.

"What is the big sink-like thing next to the shower?"

Anna shot him a look of disbelief. "It's a bathtub. Do you mean to tell me you've never seen one before?"

"I haven't. What's it for?"

Anna muttered something and walked into the bathroom.

"This closes the drain," she said, pointing to a switch under the faucet. "That knob brings hot water, the other brings cold. Close the drain, adjust the water to the temperature you want, and let it run until you fill the tub. If you overfill it, the water will escape through that backup drain." She pointed to a small hole high up on the side of the basin. "Please refrain from burning or drowning yourself."

"I don't think my water allowance will let me fill that." He doubted his entire daily hygiene allowance would cover the bottom of the tub.

"When you joined the household, your water allowance was increased. You could probably take four baths a day if you wanted to."

"But the whole city is about to be under emergency water restrictions!"

"Anyone with enough credit can buy more water, and the Murrette-Williams household can certainly afford the cost."

"The reservoirs are running dry. They're saying there may not be enough water to go around, soon."

Anna looked up and met his gaze, her expression flat. He had assumed that her avoidance of his eyes meant she was hiding something, but an eye scan revealed nothing out of the ordinary. She was a law-abiding citizen on a work visa from the Twenty-Fifth Tier.

"You're going to have to wrap your head around a different kind of reality, Hero. Rules like rationing and curfew don't apply to the people who live up here."

"That's just wrong."

"And that will get you fired," Anna retorted. "Keep your subversive comments to yourself or you'll find yourself on the receiving end of some of that justice you Company thugs are so fond of dishing out." She accompanied the statement with a brief, icy smile. "Mr. Williams looks forward to your presence at dinner. Good evening."

"I wasn't even that kind of Hero!" Adrian protested, but the domestic assistant was already gone.

* * *

"Glad you could join us. Have a seat," Williams said, pointing out a chair midway down the length of the massive table.

Amira lounged at the end of the table to his right, chin on her palm, a black shawl around her angular shoulders. Her stare was vacant, focused on something only she could see. Williams sat rigidly upright at the opposite end, to Adrian's left, stare similarly empty. Yulia fidgeted in her seat, fingers running back and forth over the shiny metal eating implements on the napkin in front of her. Her lips moved now and then, as if she had never quite mastered the art of having a virtual chat without speaking out loud.

Curious, Adrian watched her lips. She was not, in fact, talking to someone. She was singing along to a pop song.

Adrian considered starting a conversation to break the silence, then thought better of it. He was not their equal. He was not supposed to talk to them.

The minutes ticked by, and Adrian wondered why Williams bothered assembling the family fifteen minutes before dinner was served. They didn't spend the time sharing news or socializing. Did the family derived comfort simply from sitting in the same room together? Bored, he tuned in to Media's hourly newscast.

"I'm told we have some very good news tonight, Dave."

"Indeed we do, Kim. According to Enforcement, the Anarchist activity on the Twenty-Ninth Tier has been completely contained."

"That's fantastic! And as you can see from our eyes over the tier, life is back to normal."

The view screen behind the newscasters came to life with images of a tier seemingly untouched by fire, riots or looting. The streets and covered walkways were crowded with pedestrian traffic.

"I'm hearing that the fires have been extinguished, and almost all of the damage has been repaired. Meanwhile, Enforcement is conducting a thorough investigation. I'm told they've already arrested seventy-nine riot inciters, and are tracing evidence that may lead to the arrest of nearly a hundred more."

"Incredible work on the part of our heroic Enforcers!"

The double doors at the back of the dining room swung open, admitting a line of kitchen staff in crisp white uniforms. Adrian dismissed the newscast and looked up a formal etiquette guide. Looking at the array of small, carefully arranged dishes the staff were setting out in front of each person, as well as the row of unfamiliar eating implements that accompanied his napkin, he knew he would need it.

The clink of utensils on plates and bowls replaced the silence as Adrian, Amira and Williams began eating. Yulia continued staring into space.

"Yulia!" Williams barked, looking up from his plate. "Stop playing and eat your food!"

Yulia let out an exaggerated sigh and began picking at her food using her bare fingers.

"And use your fork like a civilized person," her mother added.

Adrian stared at his plate and concentrated on processing the strange, startling flavors and textures of the meal. As someone who had lived on processed dispenser cuisine his entire life, the bright, crisp vegetables, flavorful soups and chewy meats were difficult to associate with food.

"How do you like it?" Williams asked.

"It's different. But very good," he added quickly.

"If you like it so much, you can have mine," Yulia said, pushing her mostly untouched meal toward him.

"Yulia, finish your dinner!"

"Seriously?"

"Finish your dinner, or you're not leaving this table," Williams warned.

Yulia huffed, rested her elbows on the table, and stared at her plate.

"Tomorrow I have business at a facility on the Forty-Ninth Tier," his employer said. "I expect you to accompany me."

"I look forward to being of service."

"Aren't you a good Company man," Amira said, laughing. "Maybe you can keep him out of trouble. Make sure he comes home without any unauthorized detours."

"How many times do I have to tell you? That was a one-time thing."

"She seemed pretty certain it was something more," Amira said, folding her napkin and placing it on her plate.

"Can I be excused?" Yulia asked.

"Yes. Go to your room," Williams said, waving the girl away.

"And how's the other one?" Amira continued. "Tiffany, wasn't it? The one you keep buying shoes for. How is she?"

"That's nothing inappropriate. She's my assistant." Williams was beginning to turn red, and his hands shook as he put his eating utensils down.

"Three hundred and seventy-five thousand credits in shoes," Amira said with a faint smile. "That's, what, three times her salary in gifts? What a valuable assistant she must be."

"We are not having this discussion!"

"Can I be excused?" Adrian asked quietly, eyes fixed on his plate. He was excruciatingly uncomfortable.

Williams shot him an annoyed look. "Of course."

"Thank you. Have a good evening."

"You as well," Amira said with a warm smile. Her sudden friendliness made him even more uncomfortable.

"So, you were telling me," she continued as he walked away, "how this assistant of yours is worth almost four hundred thousand credits in gifts."

"I will not explain myself to you."

"Our prenuptial agreement says you will. Your carelessness with my family's money is grounds for divorce."

The dining room doors closed behind him, and Adrian let out a breath he hadn't realized he'd been holding. He'd never cared for mediating family disagreements, but it was even worse to sit in the middle of one, unable to do anything.

The carpet swallowed his footsteps as he walked back to his room. Darkness waited within, broken only by the warm golden glow spilling from the windows of the nearby housing towers. The city stretched away into the haze below their feet, aglow with a million tiny lights.

He had spent most of his adult life patrolling those streets, watching the city grow and change as the months and years went by. Although it came with danger and sadness, it was a job he enjoyed.

He had been created for helping people. With the Safety Division gone, it was a purpose he would no longer be able to fulfill.

Adrian sank into a chair and stared out the window at the brightly lit towers that seemed to float above the luminous smog. Suddenly, he felt very tired.

# CHAPTER NINE

The hazy glow of approaching dawn slowly invaded the room, pulling him from a tangle of nightmares. Adrian found it incredibly strange to have real daylight in his living space. He lay in bed, staring at the decorative rafters, until the first rays of the rising sun struck the upper reaches of the city. Shedding his shirt and shorts, he padded across the cold composite to the shower.

He had never been allowed so much water. Adrian scrubbed and rinsed, watching steam fog the surrounding glass. As he closed his eyes and ducked to rinse his hair, Snow's search window opened.

There were no search parameters, no word or phrase that defined the stream of images that filled his vision. There were rivers, waterfalls, pools where water lapped against smooth, round rocks covered with green moss. There was a sea of milky green water that eddied around the trunks of massive trees, their exposed roots contorted like the limbs of some ancient swamp creature. Tiny, round-leafed water weeds drifted past them, caught in the gentle current that wound its way through the forest.

The forest ocean was replaced by a green valley shrouded in mist. A murky swamp so choked with lily pads and weeds that the water itself was invisible. A steaming, rocky pool surrounded by snow. A gray ocean where waves crashed against jagged rocks, spray flying against the darkened sky.

"Stop," Adrian commanded as the torrent of images continued.

The dried mud of an exposed lake bed surrounded sparse pools of stagnant water. The surface of a depleted reservoir reflected a cloudless sky, its walls showing the marks of water levels hundreds of meters higher. Rivers, straight and narrow as only human intervention could make them, reduced to shallow trickles within their steep concrete banks.

"Stop search. Close program," Adrian repeated. He was beginning to think that Snow's search function was broken or had been hijacked by a virus.

As the seconds ticked by, the images deviated further and further from their original theme. The program showed him a drought map of nations that had not existed in hundreds of years, their agricultural regions and population centers showing the oranges and reds of decades of extreme drought. Snippets of old newscasts joined the stream, delivering dire news.

"Today, it is confirmed that the Colorado River has stopped flowing. With water levels in major reservoirs low and falling rapidly, the water crisis has reached a state of emergency..."

"...threatening military action if the agreed-upon amount of water does not flow across the border..."

"With municipal wells and even new deep wells running dry across the Southwest..."

"...entering the third week of rioting, as strict water rationing is extended to a larger swath of the United States. Meanwhile, the spread of disease has become a concern..."

"Initial estimates indicate that the combined death toll has already surpassed five million..."

"...a declaration of war, based on the coalition's failure to provide the water and food assistance the treaty hinged upon. However, analysts doubt the nation's ability to carry out that threat..."

A cascade of images accompanied the newscasts. Dusty irrigation ditches snaked through barren fields, baking under a white-hot sky. Desiccated bodies sprawled under the tatters of a relief station awning. A hand-painted notice hung from a faded green road sign, bearing the words "Go home. We're dry too." A pall of blowing dust settled over the empty streets and derelict buildings of an abandoned town.

Adrian leaned against the wall of the shower cube, pressed the thumb and forefinger of his right hand to the bridge of his nose, and squeezed. The pressure triggered the manual reset of his neural interface, and the world went dark.

Directionless flashes of light exploded in his vision, his optical nerves trying to connect to the bio-electronic interface of his optical implants and failing. There was popping and crackling like a shorted electrical connection in his ears. His balance and sense of touch went haywire.

Adrian curled into a ball and retched as vertigo overtook him. Ideally, a reboot should only take place while the user was asleep or unconscious.

His senses began to return, starting up one by one as they rolled through their functionality tests. He was curled on his side on the floor of the shower cube, the water no longer running. A cold draft flowed over his wet skin as an anxious domestic shook him.

"I'm going to alert the medical station, okay? Just hang on." It was Bridget, the woman who had come to collect his laundry the day before.

"No, no, I'm fine," Adrian mumbled. "My interface just glitched."

Rough fabric slid across his skin as he sat up, and he realized the young woman had covered him with her uniform jacket.

"That looked serious."

"It's not serious," he insisted. "It looked worse than it was."

His neural interface had not appreciated the hard reset, and his vision was beset with error windows. The more he closed, the more they seemed to multiply. A quiver of panic fluttered in his stomach as he considered the possibility that he'd downloaded some kind of virus.

An error window pointed out that the reset had interrupted his query, and asked if he would like to resume. He quickly denied the request.

"Are you sure you're going to be okay? I can stay."

"I'll be alright. I wouldn't want to delay you from your duties." Adrian attempted to hand the jacket back to her and started edging toward the wall-mounted drying unit. It was too cold in the air-conditioned room to stand around soaking wet.

"No one will notice if I'm here for a few extra minutes. And you can keep that," she added, turning red. "Just leave it in the laundry bin."

"No one will notice? Don't the terms of your conviction stipulate that you be supervised in situations where you have access to citizens' personal space?"

"How do you know about that?" Bridget demanded.

"I still have access to the criminal records database."

"Damn. I kind of hoped you wouldn't know."

"Everyone makes mistakes."

"It wasn't a mistake, it was a misunderstanding. The Enforcers wouldn't listen."

"I understand. But I'm cold and I'd really like to dry off, so unless you'd like to stay and chat while I do that..."

"I'm so sorry. Have a nice day!"

"You too," he replied, but she was already gone.

Dropping the damp garment on the floor, Adrian stepped under the blower and basked in the jet of warm air. He stayed there for a long time, trying to warm away the cold, queasy feeling from the reset.

* * *

By time he was warm, dressed, and presentable, he was late for breakfast. Williams, wearing an identical copy of the conservative blue suit he had worn the day before, didn't look up from his plate when Adrian walked in. Amira, radiant in a sleek, form-hugging white suit, greeted him with a wide smile.

"How nice of you to join us! Why don't you sit next to me?"

Adrian complied, unsure what else to do. A glance in Williams' direction gave him no cues. The man glowered at his plate while angrily sawing off a bite-sized piece of toast.

"It's so nice to have someone to chat with over meals," Amira continued.

"You wouldn't have to chat with the help if your daughter could be bothered to join us," Williams grumbled.

"*Our* daughter, dear," Amira said. "And leave the poor girl alone. You and I both know teenagers aren't morning people."

Williams snorted. "She's hardly a child anymore, *dear*. The least she could do is be respectful and join us for meals."

"And why should she respect you, when you insult her and her friends?"

"I deserve the respect of my family. It's my right!" Williams banged his fist on the table, rattling the dishes arrayed in front of him.

"Respect is a privilege, not a right," Amira replied primly.

Adrian tuned out the argument as his breakfast arrived. The dishes the kitchen staff placed in front of him contained another confusing assortment of unfamiliar foods. He recognized the bowl of fruit from pictures, and there was a bowl containing a pale, gooey substance that reminded him of oatmeal-flavored dispenser food. It was warm, grainy, and faintly sweet.

The three white ovals in another dish puzzled him, their appearance like nothing he had ever seen. He poked one experimentally with his spoon. Its surface was hard and rattled against the edge of the bowl. He picked it up and examined it, hoping he was not committing a major breach of dining etiquette. It was smooth, weighty, and cool to the touch, but yielded no clue as to what he was supposed to do with it.

"Ready to admit defeat?" Amira asked.

"What are they?"

"Boiled eggs. You have to shell them first."

"Oh. How do you do that?"

"Here." She leaned against his arm, slipped the egg out of his hand, and smacked the end of the oval against the table. A network of cracks appeared in the pale outer coating, and she used these to deftly shuck the shell off the white inner surface of the egg.

"Thank you," Adrian said as she handed it back to him.

The inside of the boiled egg was cold, soft, and faintly slippery. Although he did not particularly care for its taste or texture, its digital nutrition label indicated that it was a valuable source of protein and other nutrients.

Yulia quietly joined the table as Amira explained the different types of fruit and how to eat them.

"You're so tense!" Amira exclaimed. "Relax a little!"

"It's just my uniform."

"Well, then you should take it off."

Across the table, Yulia rolled her eyes.

"Yes, ma'am." Adrain shrugged off the jacket and hung it on the back of his chair.

"That's much better. You're safe here. You don't need to wear that in this house."

"Yes, ma'am." He bit into a peach, hoping his silence would encourage her to converse with someone else.

"What is this, anyway?" Amira continued, tugging at the sleeve of his white undershirt. "Don't you have any nice clothes?"

"These are my nice clothes."

"As far as I'm concerned, you should take this and have it recycled. It doesn't suit you. Let me take you shopping. I'm sure Jeremiah won't mind if I borrow you for the afternoon."

"No, you may not borrow him. I have an inspection to do," Williams snapped.

"Oh, that's no fun. Seriously though, what do you think?" She took his hand and placed it on her shoulder, sliding his fingers across the fabric of her suit. "It's silk. How would you like something like that?"

The fabric was thin and incredibly soft, and he could feel the warmth of her skin through it. Adrian quickly pulled his hand away.

"It's very nice, but I don't think I should."

Yulia caught his eye and shot him a sympathetic look.

"Damn it, Amira!" Williams yelled. "He's my bodyguard, not your toy!"

"I don't see why I shouldn't get some enjoyment out of him as well."

"Why? He's not your investment. I own him."

"And whose money did you buy him with?"

"You may have given me a little startup money when we were newly partnered, but that does not mean you own everything I've earned since then."

Adrian pushed his plate away and looked for an avenue of escape. He hadn't intended to start a fight.

"The least you could do is show a little gratitude."

"I wish I'd never accepted that loan. How's that for gratitude?"

"Then you'd still be working some menial desk job on the Fifteenth Tier. A middle manager, at most."

"I can tell you where I wouldn't be. I wouldn't be watching my wife flirt with my property at my own table!"

"Let's go," Yulia said, rising from her seat. "They'll be at this for a while."

"They won't mind if we leave?"

"They won't even notice." And indeed, neither of the heads of the household seemed to.

"I'm sorry," Adrian said as they settled into a pair of overstuffed chairs near the family room's south-facing windows. "Does that happen a lot?"

Yulia shrugged. "You'll get used to it after a while."

Adrian stared out the window and stretched his fingers. The

thumb and ring finger of his right hand still did not want to connect with each other. Outside, muted sunlight sparkled on the windows and solar cells of the surrounding towers. Swarms of workers emerged to polish away the film of pollution that had coated them during the night.

"What's eating you?" the executive's daughter asked. "You miss your old job? Your friends? Do Heroes have friends?"

"We do. Most of my friends are dead."

"I'm sorry."

"I guess I should be used to it by now."

"You could make new friends."

"The domestics don't seem to care for me much, and I'm closer in status to them than anyone else in this tower."

"I'll be your friend. And there's Bridget, the laundry domestic. I think she'd like to be your friend too."

"I think she feels a bit uncomfortable around me."

"That's only because she's shy and she thinks you're hot."

"What's with the suit?" Adrian asked, looking for a way to change the subject. The stiff gray jumpsuit with her citizen identifier stenciled across the right breast pocket was a far cry from the stylish piece she had worn the day before.

"If they're going to treat me like a prisoner, I might as well look like one," Yulia replied with a grin. "Like it?"

"Sure, but I wouldn't wear your identification number out in public. Everyone who knows the modifiers will know you're the heir to a five-hundred series corporation. It could make you a target."

"Oh, I wouldn't be caught dead out in public like this. I'm just letting them know how I feel about being held under house arrest. I ordered a whole bunch of these last night, and Bridget helped draw my number on all of them."

"Nothing wrong with a silent protest, I guess. How did your parents take it?"

Yulia sighed. "I'm a little disappointed. They haven't said

anything yet."

"Aren't you worried?"

"Not really. What are they going to do? It's not like they can restrict my movements any more than they already have."

"They could suspend your game subscriptions."

Yulia snorted. "They've never put a lock on my network access that I couldn't decrypt or find a way around."

"What if they just cancel them altogether?"

"Then I'll just start paying for them out of my own account."

Adrian was about to respond when Williams stormed out of the dining room.

"Hero! Get off your ass! We're leaving now."

"Have a good day," Adrian said, standing up.

"Good luck," Yulia called after him.

The ride down to the ground floor passed in icy silence. Adrian stood by the door, hands folded calmly in front of him, while Williams scowled angrily from the back of the lift. As the display counted down the last ten floors, the executive took a deep breath and adjusted his suit.

Without other commuters to watch, the ride down to the Forty-Ninth Tier was rather dull. Adrian initiated a virus scan of his neural interface and the new memory module, then tuned in to Media's latest newscast to pass the time. The Twenty-Ninth Tier's unrest was completely contained. Meanwhile, Enforcement had taken "literally thousands of Anarchists" into custody. Outside the windows, the buildings they passed became more and more run-down.

He downloaded travel advisories and safety bulletins for the Forty-Ninth Tier, grimacing at the wall of bold red text. Residents were not to leave quarters without a valid affidavit of need, and travel at street level was strictly forbidden. Vermin infestation in seven districts had reached critical levels, whatever that meant, and there was a pollution alert in effect. Under no circumstances should unfiltered outdoor air be breathed or allowed to enter buildings.

As they approached the Fortieth Tier, the haze began to thicken. Derelict billboards loomed just above the elevated maglev tracks, their screens dull and dark. The few that were still operational displayed adverts for products no one on these tiers could afford.

Beyond the Forty-Fifth Tier, the murk deepened, enveloping them in a dense brown fog. Dilapidated buildings ghosted past his window, their walls coated with a furry layer of pollution. The burned-out skeleton of a tower jutted out of the smog, blackened beams reaching toward the tracks as if pleading for repair.

"Look alive, Hero!" Williams barked as their transport diverged from the main line. "There are Anarchists everywhere down here."

"They're all indoors. There's a pollution alert. No one's going to come out in this murk."

Williams snorted. "Have you ever seen what they do to the towers down here? It's like a vermin nest, so packed with bodies they have to crawl over each other to get to the door."

"I've patrolled down here. It's bad, but not that bad."

"They're lawless animals. They eat each other. They sell their own children. The best solution would be to pump the whole place full of carbon monoxide and gas them like the vermin they are."

Adrian stared at the executive, speechless.

"Oh, don't look so horrified. It's a painless death."

The transport slowed and descended to street level, gliding it over the empty pavement of the factory district. A transport-sized door appeared out of the murk in front of them, Williams' name stenciled across it in bold black letters.

The bay door rolled shut behind them and the haze of pollution diminished, sucked away by the ventilation system. When the light on the wall changed from red to green, Adrian stepped out and held the door for his employer.

The air within the building smelled of heavy filtration and some kind of biological decay, a combination that left an unpleasant taste in the back of his throat. The farther they walked, the stronger the stench grew. Adrian gagged quietly and coughed into the shoulder of his jacket.

"Enjoying the atmosphere?" Williams asked. "Be thankful we're not going out onto the floor.

"What exactly is that smell?"

"Death," Williams replied with a grim smile.

An empty corridor led from the private parking stalls to a reserved lift. The walls and floor were a pale brown that had gone out of style decades ago, the interior of the lift a utilitarian gray. They rose several floors and exited into a wider corridor that seemed to have been hastily scrubbed in anticipation of Williams' visit. The stained composite was still damp.

Several turns later, Williams entered an unmarked door that led to a narrow observation room. Beyond the windows, a massive enclosed conveyor system dominated the multi-story factory. The elevated walkways that provided access to the belt were lined with workers, faceless and featureless beneath their protective white hazmat suits. They leaned against the clear composite, arms buried past the elbow in the thick plastic gloves built into holes in the clear cover.

Black fluid oozed from a joint beneath a large piece of machinery, dripping into the shadows behind a network of service walkways. A persistent drip kept time beside a walkway that passed under the housing, and another leak had stained the dirty composite at the far end of the room.

"Do they know about the leaks?" Adrian asked.

"What leaks?"

Adrian dutifully pointed them out.

"Heads will roll for this. If we were inspected right now, we could be shut down."

The door at the end of the room slid open, admitting a breathless middle-aged man in a well-worn gray suit.

"Can I help you, sir?" the man gasped.

"It's about time you got here, Stanford."

"I'm sorry, sir. The message said you wouldn't be here until ten, and I was wrapping up some interviews."

"Interviews? I thought I instituted a hiring freeze."

"We've lost a lot of workers lately, sir. It's beginning to affect productivity," Stanford said, wringing his hands.

"Apparently it's affecting maintenance, too."

"Sir?"

"What's being done about those leaks?"

The plant manager turned a horrified gaze to the room in front of them.

"Unacceptable," he muttered. "This will be dealt with."

A stocky worker, silver hair tucked under the hood of his protective suit, joined them a few minutes later.

"How can I help you?" he asked, glancing nervously between Williams, Stanford, and Adrian. "Is there a problem?"

"What's being done about the leaks?" Stanford asked.

The man turned to the window and frowned intently at the glass.

"Oh, no," he sighed, shoulders slumping. "They're back."

"Back?" Williams demanded. "You mean to tell me this is a reoccurring problem?"

"There have been a few problems with certain sections of housing," the plant manager said carefully. "As you know, this whole system was slated for retirement last year. We've kept it running as best we could, but the seals are failing and the underside of the housing is badly corroded."

"Then fix it!"

Stanford flinched and the older man paled.

"That would require stopping this entire line. We've been working double shifts to keep up with the increase in material. In light of the waste it would cause, shutting down to conduct repairs did not seem like a feasible option." Stanford paused and swallowed nervously. "Sir."

Williams sneered. "So this was your solution? To just wait until an inspection team comes in and fines us out of business?"

"I ordered patches and sealant applied to the leaking sections," Stanford said. "Hargrave is in charge of the sorting floor, and he oversaw the repairs."

"They were sound and held through my shift yesterday," Hargrave said quickly. "I just came in. I'll need to speak to the night supervisor to find out when they began leaking and why nothing has been done to contain them."

"I've heard enough excuses," Williams said. "Fire the night supervisor. Fire the workers who performed this sub-par repair job. And fire him, too," he added, gesturing toward Hargrave.

The sorting floor supervisor gasped in shock. "Please, sir! This isn't my fault."

"Get out of my sight or I'll have you charged with criminal negligence."

"I've worked here for twenty-five years! I have an excellent record!"

"Adrian, escort this man to the front and turn him over to Enforcement."

The order didn't sit well with him. He did not see the necessity in firing the man at all, much less turning him over to Enforcement on charges. And wouldn't he be derelict in his duty to protect Williams if he was elsewhere in the building?

"Are you sure that's necessary?" he asked.

Williams' eyes narrowed. "That is an order."

"I really don't think this is the right thing to do."

"Now, Adrian."

"I'll go quietly," Hargrave mumbled.

They walked in silence, Adrian monitoring their route against a virtual floor plan of the building, Hargrave staring at the floor.

"You're that Hero," the sorting floor supervisor said at last. It was more of a statement than a question. "The one from the video."

"So I'm told."

"The video the Company doesn't want anyone to see," Hargrave continued, a hint of bitterness in his voice. "Because if it can happen to a Hero, it can happen to anyone."

Adrian decided to remain silent. It was undoubtedly something the Company would not want him to talk about.

"Is this your punishment?"

"Of course not." But even as he said it, the idea suddenly made a certain kind of sense.

"They sold you," Hargrave said sadly. "An easy solution for an ugly problem. I bet it earned them a nice bundle of credit, too."

"I wouldn't know."

"They're building shrines to you," the sorting floor supervisor said as they stepped into the lift. "They're building monuments to the last Hero. They think you were killed. You're, what do they call it? A martyr."

The doors of the lift opened and let them out onto the ground floor.

"If people knew you were still alive, they would follow you."

"I don't want power. I don't want to be a leader. I just want to help people."

"You could still help people! I have a wife and children. None of them have been able to get work. This job kept us from starving."

"I'm sorry."

"They'll downgrade us. I've heard what happens to the downgraded when they arrive on Tier Fifty. I can't let that happen to my wife and daughters."

"It's not my choice."

"It could be."

"I can't get your job back."

"You don't have to turn me over to the Enforcers," Hargrave said, a note of desperation creeping into his voice.

"I don't have a choice. I have to do what Williams says."

"You swore an oath to protect people!" The last set of doors slid open. A pair of Enforcers waited on the other side, faceless and sinister beneath their mirrored helmets.

"That's not my job anymore," Adrian said. He couldn't bring himself to meet the man's eyes.

Hargrave shot him one last pleading look as his hands were cuffed behind his back, and then the Enforcers led him away.

Adrian made his way back to the observation room with a hollow, queasy feeling gnawing at his stomach. He found Williams and the plant manager quibbling over the extent of the firings. The processing system continued to drip on the factory floor below.

Eventually the executive and the plant manager moved on, Adrian trailing behind them as they navigated more brown corridors and entered another observation room. An array of machinery ran in front of the window, an automated process that separated chunks of bloody meat onto separate enclosed conveyor belts.

"How's the new sterilization system working?" Williams asked.

"Much better than the old one, sir. We haven't had a single sample fail testing since it was installed."

"Good. We can't afford another scandal like the Hepatitis B outbreak."

"The vendors should have been held responsible. If they were cooking the product according to the health code, no one would have gotten sick," Stanford said.

"Yes, but of course they're not going to own up to their mistakes. When the infection was traced back to certain food vendors, the first thing they did was claim we sold them tainted product.

"We ate the fines, we installed an expensive new decontamination system, and we passed the cost along to everyone who buys our product. Especially the whole protein buyers," Williams added with a smile of satisfaction. "In the end, they're the ones paying for it."

Adrian wanted to point out that it was not, in fact, the merchants who would be paying the price of the fines and upgrades. It would be the hungry citizens at the end of the chain, because the merchants would pass along the cost increase just as Williams had.

"What kind of meat is it?" he asked.

Both men gave him an odd look, as if the furniture had spoken.

"It's pork," Williams said, grinning. "At least, that's what they tell me it tastes like." Stanford chuckled darkly.

# CHAPTER TEN

As the transport climbed back toward the apex of the city, Adrian entertained himself by researching the Company's meat production system. Livestock, like the vegetables of the subterranean hydroponic gardens, were raised in farms tucked away deep beneath the streets of the city. Farm worker positions were filled by citizens condemned to base labor, the Company's way of helping the convicts repay their debts.

Beyond that, information was scarce. How was the Company able to produce meat in the quantities Williams' plant was processing? The entire hill must be honeycombed with farms in order to supply the demand.

They diverged from the transit track and came to a stop in front of an upscale housing tower. Stepping out of the transport, Adrian found the bright daylight of the Twelfth Tier a startling contrast to the smoggy gloom of the district they had recently visited. Reflected sunlight sparkled off the building's polished glass doors and played on the leaves of the trees flanking the entrance as he held the door for his employer.

"Do you consider yourself Amira's man? Or mine?" Williams asked as they walked into the building.

"I don't understand."

"Would you report to her, if she asked?"

"Is there some reason why I shouldn't?"

"I paid for you."

"Yes, sir." He grew to dislike being referred to as property more with every mention of it. "I won't."

"Good."

A second set of doors opened into a wide foyer decorated in shades of turquoise and teal. Williams joined a group of wealthy young women waiting for the next lift, ogling assets showcased by sleek skintight suits as the residents laughed and chatted among themselves.

Although the lift was already crowded, Williams squeezed in after them. Adrian was forced to follow.

One of the young women, an augmented redhead in a dark green suit with daring asymmetrical cutouts, gasped softly and began elbowing her neighbor in the ribs. The other women followed her gaze, staring at Adrian and whispering among themselves.

"Is it a real Hero?" the redhead asked.

"One hundred percent authentic," Williams replied, grinning.

"I thought they were all gone," the redhead exclaimed. "Can I touch it?"

"Yeah, can we?" one of the other young women asked, giggling. Her elaborately styled blonde hair kept falling across her eyes.

"Of course," Williams responded, smiling more widely. "Do anything you want to him."

Adrian found himself surrounded by giggling women. Fingers brushed his hair and traced the curve of his lower lip. Hands unfastened his jacket, sliding it back over his shoulders, and began pulling his shirt free of the waist of his pants.

"Ladies," Adrian gasped, choking on a cloud of clashing perfumes. "Personal space, please. I'm working."

"Don't mind him," Williams said. The lift purred to a stop, caught between floors. His employer had triggered the emergency shutoff.

"You should think about wearing cologne," the redhead murmured next to his ear, and he shivered as her lips brushed his neck.

Someone's hands were under his shirt, cold against his skin.

"How much time do they have to spend in the gym to get body like that?"

"They don't, silly. They're genetically perfect. They don't have to work out or anything."

"You'd think they'd do something about the scars."

Cold fingers traced the ridge of scar tissue that crossed his stomach, the souvenir of an ugly fall in his early twenties.

This was probably something he was supposed to be enjoying, but he felt overwhelmed. Leaning against the opposite wall with a smirk on his face, Williams seemed to be enjoying the scene.

A tangle of slender arms held him tight as another woman joined the redhead in kissing his neck. His skin tingled and his pulse raced, and someone giggled in delight.

"They do react!"

Adrian barely caught his pants in time to prevent them from being pulled down. This triggered a struggle for control of the pants, and amid the wave of giggling and Williams' deeper chuckles, Adrian opened the lift's virtual control panel and overrode the manual controls. The executive swatted the emergency stop button in annoyance as the cage began to move, but a Hero's control codes took precedence.

"Please stop," Adrian said.

Amid the press of overly-perfumed bodies and groping hands, he felt like he was drowning. No matter how many he brushed away, more fought with him as he struggled to straighten his shirt and button his pants.

The door slid open. A collective gasp of shock rose from those waiting for the lift as Williams and Adrian exited, the latter red in the face and still straightening his clothing. Disapproving murmurs accompanied their passage through the crowd.

"What the hell is wrong with you?" Williams demanded.

"I would appreciate it if you didn't do that."

"I don't give a vermin's ass. I was having fun, and you should respect that. I know you overrode the emergency stop."

"Holding up a lift for non-emergency purposes is a crime."

Williams snorted derisively. "So? Who's going to report me? You?"

"No, sir."

"Good boy. Don't do that again."

The hallways of the tower were carpeted in deep blue, the walls a frosty bluish white. There was little art to be seen, but the cleanliness and simple elegance of the color scheme hinted at the affluence of the residents. Turning down a side hallway, they stopped at the last door on the left. The flowery filigree nameplate read "Tabitha Plathe, Suite One-Seventy-Five." Williams let them both in without bothering to knock.

The interior was a sharp contrast to the minimally decorated corridors. Silky pillows in bright colors accented a black couch shaped like a stretching cat. White chairs so minimal they were more of a suggestion of seating than the actual thing surrounded a matching table inlaid with a black spiral pattern. A teal vase served as a centerpiece. More bright vases and impressionist statuary occupied the corners of the room, sparkling against the pristine white walls.

"Oh, Tabby," Williams called softly, walking toward the hallway at the back of the suite's main room.

A pale woman in a black and gold bathrobe walked out of the hallway, drying her dark hair. She shrieked in surprise when she saw Williams, and the executive laughed.

"Surprised to see me, sweetheart?"

"Don't you ever knock?!" the woman demanded, clutching her robe to her chest. "And who's this?"

"This is my new bodyguard. Adrian, say hello to the lovely lady."

"Pleased to meet you, ma'am," Adrian said politely, extending his hand. He was acutely aware that he was still red in the face and disheveled.

The woman's full red lips switched downward in distaste as she clasped his hand. Tabitha Plathe, age twenty-nine. Employed by Nutrition Recovery Inc, personal assistant to Mr. Williams. No medical conditions. One minor conviction, nearly a decade old, for extortion.

Tabitha withdrew her hand and wiped it on her robe.

"So you're back," she said flatly.

"Was there any doubt I would be?"

"It's been two weeks. I was beginning to wonder."

"Wonder about what, sweet thing? Don't you trust me?"

"Two weeks," Tabitha repeated. "No communication. My rent hasn't been paid. Nothing. I was beginning to think I'd been fired." She laughed bitterly. "And then you just show up here. Without knocking, as usual."

"You haven't been fired," the executive said, moving toward her. "I've been busy. Why don't you grab us some drinks and have a seat? I'll tell you all about it."

"I'm not sure I want to, at this point. I think I've moved on."

"Adrian, go get cleaned up," Williams said, waving him toward the hallway. "You're covered in lipstick."

"Yes, sir."

"Sweetheart, don't be like that," Williams continued as he walked away. "Tell me what's bothering you."

Tabitha's sparkling white bathroom was so brightly lit it made his eyes burn. Cleaning bots swarmed around a massive sunken tub, sucking up the spilled water from the bath the woman had just taken.

Across from the door, a large mirror hung above a wide counter filled with makeup products. Adrian grimaced as he caught sight of his reflection. There were at least three shades of lipstick on his neck and collar. Locating a clean cloth, he began scrubbing.

"I just want to know!" Tabitha's voice rose from the other room.

"You keep saying it's almost over, but it never happens."

"Divorces take time."

"Not this much time."

"I have to orchestrate it very carefully. If she suspects something, she'll take me to the cleaners. That's money I could be spending on you, dear."

"I'm tired of waiting! Excuse me."

The rustle of bare feet on the hallway carpet announced Tabitha's presence. She walked past him, face wet, and retrieved a tissue.

"That stuff doesn't just come off," she said. "You'll scrub your skin off trying." She wetted a clean cloth with makeup remover and handed it to him. "Use this instead."

"Thank you."

"Everything okay in here," Williams demanded, appearing at the door.

"No, everything is not okay," Tabitha retorted. "We've been doing this for how many years now? Three? Four? And you're still giving me empty promises. I'm beginning to think you're leading me on."

"Tabby, sweet thing, beautiful. How would you like to go shopping? It's on me."

"I don't want more shoes, Jerry. I want you to keep your word!"

"You know I hate that nickname."

Tabitha's reply was muffled as the pair moved deeper into the apartment. Adrian made one last check for makeup, then dropped the washcloth into the laundry bin. The argument continued as he straightened his uniform and made his way back to the main room.

He had rather not be witness to Williams' extramarital affairs. It was a sad, ugly thing, a relationship built on lies, and he could not see it going anywhere good. He felt sorry for Amira and Yulia.

What had compelled Ms. Murrette to partner with Williams in the first place? He could see Williams' angle; Amira was beautiful, as well as CEO of one of the largest corporations in the city. The man had partnered himself into wealth and used it to buy his own business. What had Amira gotten out of it? It was a question he might never be able to answer. Whatever spark had originally drawn them to each other was clearly long gone.

His train of thought was broken by the sound of someone being slapped, followed by an outraged screech. Tabitha stormed out of the hallway a second later, clutching her face. Williams was right behind her.

"Where do you think you're going?" he demanded. "This discussion is not over."

"You and I are over! Get out of my apartment."

"You mean my apartment," Williams said, an ugly smile spreading across his face.

"It's my name on the rental agreement, Jerry!"

"And I pay the rent. Even in the Entertainment District you won't be making enough to pay for all this."

"I have other options," Tabitha said icily.

"Good. Maybe your other options will pay to replace this." Williams picked up the teal vase from the table and hurled it against the far wall, where it shattered with a spectacular crash. Tabitha shrieked in outrage.

"And this," Williams continued, grabbing a small dark red vase shot with fine streaks of gold from a nearby shelf.

"Stop! That was made by a friend."

"And I bought it!" Williams roared back. "I can do whatever I want with my property."

Adrian intervened as Williams flung the second vase, snatching it out of the air and setting it on the table.

"Stop. This won't end well for anyone," he said, stepping between the dueling parties.

"Get out of my way," Williams growled.

Adrian opened a private chat channel with his employer. "This doesn't look good. What if the neighbors report the noise? Having Enforcement called isn't going to make anything better."

"Out of the way," Williams repeated. "That is an order."

"I can't stop the Enforcers from arresting you for causing a domestic disturbance. Do you really want to have to explain this to Amira?"

"You're right. She's not worth it. I'm done here." The executive turned on his heel and walked out the door.

A message from Williams appeared a second later.

"Why don't you stay and make sure Tabby doesn't have an accident? I imagine she's going to take this rather hard, once it starts to sink in that her financial support is gone. It would be a pity if she decided to take a flying leap off her balcony."

"I don't think you need to worry about that," Adrian sent back. "And I would be derelict in my duty if I stayed here."

"I can take care of myself, thank you. Physical protection is not the only reason I hired a bodyguard. As you pointed out, it would be unfortunate if Amira were to hear about this. I expect you to protect my interests as well as my person."

"You made this mess," Adrian replied, perplexed. "There's nothing I can do to fix it."

"This is your job now. My problems are your problems. I don't think I need to remind you what will happen if you fail to perform your duty." He could almost hear Williams' annoyance. "The balcony is probably the tidiest way to do it. Take the transit system home when you're done." His employer ended the conversation.

"Why are you still here?" Tabitha asked. "Aren't you supposed to go with him?"

"Does this apartment have a balcony?"

"Yes, it opens off my bedroom. Wait, why?" She began to back away from him. "Williams wouldn't tell you to do that, would he? You're a Hero. You can't hurt people. Right?"

It finally dawned on Adrian what his employer had been insinuating.

"I'm not going to do that," he said, and saw himself out.

***

When he returned to the residence, neither Williams nor Amira were home. The artificially cooled air was icy, the lights turned low to conserve energy.

Adrian padded down the hallway to his room, stripped out of uniform, and stepped into the shower. As the hot water cascaded down his back, Snow's search window opened and images from the mega drought filled his vision. Dusty fields baking under a white-hot sky. Starving cattle pawing the dried mud of a watering hole. Abandoned towns. Cities suffocating under blowing dust.

Adrian shut the program down, opened his security module, and queued a series of in-depth threat scans. Those he had run earlier in the day had not turned up anything, but something was interfering with Snow's proper function.

The offending program did not attempt to launch itself again. Scrubbed and clean, he stepped out of the shower and dried off, shivering in the cool air. Wrapping a fluffy white towel around his waist, Adrian paused to examine his reflection in the mirror above the counter.

There were still a few smudges of lipstick on his collarbone. Even after a shower, the color showed no sign of coming off.

A soft knock alerted him to a presence at the door. How long had Bridget been standing in the doorway, quietly watching him? As if realizing his train of thought, the laundry domestic turned a deep shade of red.

"Just dropping off your clean laundry. Is there anything else you'd like me to take?"

"Just what's in the hamper, thank you." He had no intention of giving up the towel.

"Have a nice evening," Bridget said, and disappeared from the door.

"Wait! Could you do me a favor?"

"Certainly." The brown eyes that peeked around the door frame were bright with interest.

"I need makeup remover."

She returned a few minutes later with a bottle and a bag of fabric puffs.

"Make it quick," she said, handing over the supplies. "These have to go back in Amira's room before she gets home."

"You won't get in trouble for this, will you?" Adrian asked as he wetted a fabric puff and turned to the mirror.

"Doubt it. I have a lot of practice at borrowing things."

"But you always return them, right?"

"Of course. Can't have you trying to arrest me."

"I can't arrest anyone anymore."

"Good to know. So, you have a girlfriend? Or a partner?"

"Neither. Heroes aren't supposed to get overly familiar with the general population."

"Ah, the whole no mingling thing. Doesn't that get kind of lonely?"

"I'm used to it."

"So what happened? If you don't mind my asking."

"Williams' idea of fun. I didn't have much say in it."

"At least where he is now, he has to pay for it."

"You know where he is?" Adrian asked, glancing up in surprise.

"Everyone knows. He's either with his assistant or in the Entertainment District."

"Even Amira?"

"Probably. Has anyone ever told you that you have a nice back?"

"I don't think so. But thank you anyway."

"You're welcome."

She wore a bright smile when he turned to hand the makeup remover back to her.

"Have a nice evening," she said, then hurried out the door.

Adrian dressed and made his way back out to the suite's central living space.

In his absence, Amira had arrived home with a group of smartly dressed business people. It took Adrian a moment to recognize her. The conservatively cut black business suit downplayed her assets, while her long blonde hair had been swept up into a sleek curl fit for a boardroom rather than a night out. The CEO of Murrette Industries was entertaining business guests, and Adrian resolved to stay out of their way.

He slipped into an inconspicuous seat by the north-facing windows and let the murmur of conversation flow around him as he sifted through the archives. The more angles he approached the subject of meat production from, the more the information he sought eluded him. It was almost as if the subject had been scrubbed, excised from the archives like a citizen's recording of Enforcer brutality.

While he was puzzling over the lack of information, he noticed Amira watching him with keen interest while conversing with her guests. Was she wondering where her partner was, or simply wondering why his bodyguard was not with him? Adrian rose from his seat and quietly retreated down the hallway.

What he had assumed to be a wall at the rear of the hallway had been moved slightly to one side. Closer inspection revealed an elegant, clear-walled lift hidden behind the screen. Pulling the partition closed behind him, Adrian stepped inside.

The lift rose into a sunlit world dressed in shades of verdant green. Like the lift shaft, the walls and ceiling of the rooftop oasis were made of clear composite. Exotic shrubs and trees flourished in the humid air of the enclosed garden, their gnarled branches, stiff fans of leaves and delicate fronds forming an impenetrable wall of greenery. A cool breeze kissed Adrian's skin as he stepped out of the lift.

The path wound away from the entrance, branching in various directions before disappearing into a jungle of untrimmed foliage. Streamers of pale gray-green lichen and curtains of vines occupied the gaps, swaying gently in the breeze from the vents. Emerald green moss formed velvety mounds on either side of the stepping stones, giving off a strange, earthy scent whenever he left the path.

Adrian chose the least overgrown walkway. As he ducked under low branches and parted curtains of trailing plants, the faint tinkle of falling water lured him onward. Large insects took flight at his approach, their wide, colorful wings propelling them toward the ceiling.

Roughly a hundred meters from the lift, the path came out into a circular open space dominated by a mound of black stone dotted with islands of moss, miniature stands of bamboo, and tiny saplings. Water sparkled down the dark rock and trickled into a large pond lined with moss-covered stones. The water was green with algae, the surface dotted with lily pads and white flowers. Flashes of color moved in the depths.

As Adrian approached, colorful fish rose to the surface as if to greet him. Pale gold, dark orange, white with a red spot on its forehead, they ranged from the length of his hand to the length of his forearm. It was the first time he had ever seen real fish, and they seemed similarly interested in his presence. They rose up and kissed the surface of the water, blowing bubbles.

"They're hoping you'll feed them."

Adrian turned to find Yulia sitting on a wooden bench tucked back under the boughs of the forest. She was once again dressed in a baggy gray jumpsuit.

"What are they?"

"Koi. See the big white one with the red sun on his forehead? His name is Tanaka."

"Do the others have names?"

"Sure. The one that's all gold is Sunshine. The white one with the orange stripes is called Hope. I've forgotten some, but you could ask Valkyr. She knows all their names."

"Valkyr? The tower's security AI?" Adrian asked, watching the koi swim in circles and brush the surface of the water.

"She's not just security; Valkyr manages the whole tower. She's the one who asked me to feed them. They've been here since the tower was built, but I've only been coming up here since I was four or five."

"I had no idea fish could live that long."

"Koi can live for hundreds of years. They're supposed to be very wise. Sometimes I tell them my problems. They never answer, but they're good at listening."

"I think being a good listener is an important part of being wise."

They sat in silence for a few minutes, listening to the falling water and watching the koi.

"How do you like working here?" Yulia asked.

"I'm beginning to wish I knew how to keep my mouth shut."

"Father's last bodyguard never said much."

"He had another bodyguard?"

"He's had several. None of them lasted long."

"That's interesting."

"The last guy got into a big argument with father. He was yelling that something wasn't even in his job description. Father called him insubordinate. He yelled, 'I quit!' And father yelled back, 'No, you're fired!' That was the last I ever heard of him."

"I wonder what that was all about."

Yulia shrugged. "No idea. I hope he keeps you, though. You're easier to talk to than any of the others were."

"Thank you. I hope he keeps me too."

***

Later, alone in his room, Adrian ate a meal of dispenser food and searched for his employer. In response to his query, Snow produced a map of the Entertainment District. Williams' location was pinpointed on one of the uppermost floors of a tower in the classiest part of the district. Adrian sighed and scraped the last of the food out of his bowl.

Outside the windows, the lights of the Fifth Tier twinkled through a pall of evening smog. The air pollution had aspirations of upward mobility much like the residents of the districts it hailed from, visiting the wealthier tiers by night to see the sights and wipe its grimy fingers on the walls.

The citizens up here likened them to vermin. They claimed that residents of the lower tiers used forged travel visas to journey up through the city by night, defacing public property with Anarchist slogans. These human vermin were blamed for everything from disease to burglaries to mysterious kidnappings. Amira's wealthy business guests had been discussing the subject while they waited for dinner.

When it began to get late, he wandered into the bedroom. The forest depicted above the head of the bed seemed like a sleepy place, with its trailing branches, deep shadows, and pillows of moss. The archives told him that in a forest bird songs might be heard, or wind sighing in the trees.

Adrian stretched out on the bed and searched for recordings of forest sounds. There was one called *Wind in Mountain Pines* that he especially liked, although he had no idea what pines were. The archives defined them as conifers. He yawned and saved the subject for later investigation.

The wind did make a sort of sighing sound in the trees. It was like the sound of someone breathing very slowly, as if the world itself had been on the edge of falling asleep.

****

Adrian clawed his way out of a tangle of nightmares early the next morning, the red orb of the sun still hidden below the smoggy horizon. Some of the nightmares had been about the sorting floor manager and his family. So much misery could have been averted if he had simply kept his mouth shut about the leaking equipment.

He rolled out of bed, straightened the blankets, and took a shower. For once, Snow did not try to launch a water-related slideshow. The scans he had begun the night before were still running. Clean and dressed, he walked out to the main room and took a seat by the south-facing windows.

A short time later Amira walked by in a fluffy pink bathrobe, hair up in a matching towel, headed toward the kitchen and the bustle of early morning meal preparation. She returned a few moments later, trailed by a domestic with two cups of a hot beverage. The domestic handed them each a drink as Amira took a seat on a nearby couch.

Coffee-flavored stimulant, Adrian realized as soon as he lifted it to his lips. Bitter and hot enough to scald, he had never understood why people drank the stuff. He pretended to take a polite sip, and warmed his hands on the expensive genuine ceramic mug while Amira sipped hers.

"You're here," she noted, "and my husband is not. Is he tired of you already?"

"I'm not sure. He might be angry at me."

"Oh, and why would he be angry at you?"

"I disobeyed one of his orders."

Amira raised a curious eyebrow and sipped her drink.

"It was an illegal order."

"An illegal order?"

Adrian stared down into his cup. He had done an excellent job of cornering himself.

"Mr. Williams ordered me to deal with somebody, to help them commit suicide. I can't do that."

"And?" Amira asked softly.

"And I haven't seen him since. He told me to return here when I was finished."

She nodded, a trace of a smile curving her lips. "I think it's time for him to get over his little fit of pique and come home, don't you?"

"Yes. It's not the safest place for him to be without a bodyguard." He regretted the words the moment they were out of his mouth.

"You know where he is." Amira smiled warmly. "Good. Perhaps, after breakfast, you would be so kind as to go collect my wayward partner and bring him home."

"Yes, ma'am." Adrian began to get up.

"Don't go yet. Breakfast will be ready soon. You should eat first."

He sat back down.

"While we're waiting for breakfast, why don't you tell me about yourself?"

# CHAPTER ELEVEN

Breakfasted and ready to face the day, Adrian boarded a downward-bound transit. The module he entered was packed, wealthy locals doing their best to ignore the drab laborers and domestics commuting to work around them. Adrian claimed an empty handhold and stood, watching shining buildings and public artwork slide past the windows.

A message popped up, signaling that the scans he had begun the day before were complete. The red-edged text detailed a laundry list of programs acquired during his download of Company data. They primarily originated from two specific locations on the Company network, a secure.net and a hive.net. Surprisingly, both domains were considered safe and legitimate. Secure.net belonged to the Enforcement Division, and hive.net was an innocuous library maintained by the Company's programmers.

As Adrian selected a program and attempted to analyze it, his vision flashed red and an error window appeared.

"Warning! Budworm may compromise the security of communication systems. Do you still want to remove this program from quarantine? This action is not advised." The end of the message held the flickering snowflake he had come to associate with Snow.

Examining the quarantine list more closely, he realized that it held Snow's watermark rather than that of his Company-provided security module. Why didn't his state-of-the-art Company antivirus consider these a threat?

He chose a harmless-looking program called Marionette and tentatively examined it. Another error window appeared, pulsating violent red.

"Removal of Marionette from quarantine is not advised," the bold text read. "This program is known to cause loss of control of motor functions, loss of access to communication networks, and loss of augmented systems including sight, hearing, smell and touch."

The warning was absolutely right; he did not want to open Marionette. As he pondered why such a program existed, and why was it stored in the Company programmers' database, the transit began to brake toward the Sixteenth Tier interchange.

Adrian disembarked among a flood of passengers, stepped out of the flow of pedestrian traffic, and pulled up the tier map. He found himself smiling as he plotted a course toward the Entertainment District. It almost felt like going out on patrol.

It was not until he felt a gentle tug on his sleeve that Adrian realized someone was trying to get his attention. He turned to find a nervous young man in a domestic's beige uniform standing beside him.

"You're that Hero," the domestic said, voice nearly drowned by the roar of the interchange. "The Hero who stood up to Hardy."

It wasn't the question he'd been expecting, and he wasn't sure it was one he should answer.

"Sorry to bother you," the young man continued. "I just wanted to say thank you."

"You're welcome."

"Can I ask you something?"

"Depends on what you want to ask."

"Just your name. Everyone knows you as that Hero from the video, but I want to know who you are."

"It's Adrian."

"Pleased to meet you, sir. I'm Victor."

He scanned the man's dark brown eyes as they shook hands.

Victor Hull, age nineteen. A resident of the Thirty-Eighth Tier with a work visa, he possessed no criminal record.

"People will be glad to know you're alive," the young man continued, smiling. "What was going through your head when you faced Hardy? What made you say what you did?"

The question reminded him of smoggy streets and gritty pavement, the taste of blood and the grating sound of Hardy's voice. It reminded him of pain, confusion and helplessness. He knew he should not answer, but he did anyway.

"I was confused at first. I thought it was a mistake." He felt strangely short of breath. "If I had done what they said I did, there's a procedure for that. Pull me out of service. Let me be judged for what I've done." He paused, heart pounding. It was as if he was back there, seated in Hardy's interrogation room. "What they did to me was wrong. I didn't deserve that. I offered no resistance at all."

"Wrong for you as a Hero?"

"Just wrong. It's something that shouldn't ever happen. But it happens every day on our streets, in our homes and places of business, in Enforcement precincts all over the city."

"Why did you speak out? That was either incredibly brave, or crazy."

Adrian laughed ruefully. "I was angry, I guess. I was sure I was going to die there. I just told him what I thought of his behavior. This is not what any of us Company men were created to be. Enforcement treats the city like a war zone, where everyone below Tier Ten or Twenty is the enemy."

"I think a lot of people out there would agree with you."

Adrian nodded.

"What would you say if I told you that the man you were charged with killing is still alive?"

"Really?"

"There's proof. What would you say to that?"

"I'm glad. I hope he's alright."

"Thank you for answering my questions. Stay safe out there."

"Wait, you said you had proof. Can you show me?" But it was too late; the domestic had already disappeared into the crowd.

Adrian exited the interchange into a retail district bustling with activity. A tide of pushing, jostling shoppers flowed around him, overwhelmingly loud and bright. He nearly jumped when a pair of citizens asked him for directions.

His heart rate gradually returned to normal as he made his way around the tier. The recollection of his encounter with Hardy faded more slowly. He broke up a domestic dispute, and provided more directions. A few minutes later he stopped a pickpocket and gave the man a stern warning.

Eventually the Entertainment District came into sight, the entrance plastered with signs declaring it restricted to citizens under sixteen. A pair of faceless Enforcers patrolled the street outside, their heads turning in unison as he passed. A shiver of apprehension crawled up his spine. Did he still show up as a criminal in their database, or was it simply curiosity?

The Enforcers trailed him as he entered the dimly illuminated district, and the same tide of intoxicated humanity that he had fought his way through on his last visit now worked in his favor. He slipped past entertainers is barely-there costumes and elbowed his way through the line for a refreshment stand.

A pack of ravers with hair in shades of florescent pink, purple and green closed around him, thrashing to a beat only they could hear. The impromptu rave surged through the crowd and spit him out on the far side of the intersection, farther ahead of the Enforcers than he had been.

Finding a path between the wall of a building and the edge of the crowd, Adrian ducked his head and walked faster, heart hammering against his ribs. If the Enforcers ordered him to stop, he would. In the meantime, he was going to put as much distance between himself and them as he could.

Snow's search window opened and a music video began to play, blasting through the public speaker system as well as his own audio interface. A pair of entertainers latched onto his arms as the crowd surged to the music. The press of bodies dragged them away from the wall, nearly drowning him in thrashing limbs and a tide of pheromone-laced perfume.

The music video retreated to the edge of his vision, replaced by a surveillance camera's view of the street. His figure was highlighted in green, the pair of Enforcers in red. They seemed to have lost track of him in the crush of revelers.

A chat window opened, and a cold hand squeezed his chest as Adrian recognized the Enforcement logo at the top. If they ordered him to surrender, he would have no choice but to comply.

"It's a madhouse in here. Looks like someone just started a rave. Wall to wall thrashers."

"You lost it?"

"Temporarily. I see there's an eye over the far side of the district. Can someone send it over?"

"Sent. Low-altitude protocol. You're going to need all the help you can get in that crowd."

The conversation was taking place on the tier's Enforcement channel. Although it did not mention him by name, Adrian could not shake the feeling that they were searching for him.

One of the entertainers leaned close and slipped an arm around his shoulders.

"Follow," she said into his ear. Tiny green jewels sparkled on her eyelashes and in her long, dark hair.

"No, thank you."

"Trust us," the other woman said, a statuesque blonde whose golden hair was liberally streaked with neon pink highlights.

"And keep your head down," the first woman added with a smile. She was yelling, but he could barely hear her.

With an entertainer on either arm, Adrian allowed himself to be guided through the crowd. The women leaned on him, their hair spilling over his shoulders and occasionally into his face, but their hands did not stray from his shoulders.

On camera view, the outlines of the Enforcers had been joined by a pulsating red dot. The surveillance drone's path spiraled outward from the intersection where they had lost him. Was it hunting him? Or had he just stumbled into the middle of an unrelated investigation?

"In here," the brunette said, nudging him toward a dim alley nearly as crowded as the street.

His first reaction was to resist; he did not want what they were leading him toward. But, alone in the crowd, the drone would almost certainly spot him. Adrian allowed himself to be steered into the near-darkness between the sultry vermillion walls of a pair of commercial towers.

A pattern of concentric circles appeared on the security camera view, centered over his outline. They extended ten meters from his body, rippling gently, representing the broadcast signal of his identity chip. Fear gripped him as the drone circled closer. Low altitude protocol meant that it was scanning chips as well as faces.

The entertainers pulled him deeper into the alley, elbowing their way down a narrow corridor that led into one of the buildings. Most of the security lighting had failed, and the hallway was packed with couples seeking a private place.

The women pressed him against the wall a few meters from the building's lighted entry. They were just far enough from the main alley that the signal from his chip would not reach the drone unless it entered the corridor.

"Don't move. Don't make a sound," the brunette whispered. The blonde plastered herself against his chest, and together they formed a human screen between him and the alley outside.

Warm arms wrapped around his neck as the drone entered the alley. Its lights illuminated the press of bodies outside their hiding place, eliciting shouts and curses from the crowd.

His heart pounded and cold sweat beaded on his skin as the lights grew brighter. Enforcer drones were nasty customers, packing an assortment of crowd control tools. The shock the arresting Enforcer had given had been unpleasant, but it was nothing compared to what a drone could dish out. Or its operator might simply pop a canister of gas into the confines of the corridor and let the boots on the ground sort out the mess.

Sweat trickled down his ribs as the spotlight flashed down the corridor. The light vanished, returning just as he began to draw a breath of relief. It flickered over the crowd and bathed the wall he leaned against in brilliant white as his self-defense augmentations kicked into overdrive. It knew he was there. The Enforcers were coming for him.

"Calm," the entertainers whispered in unison. "Relax." Warm hands held him tight, preventing him from giving in to the urge to run.

The light vanished, the drone retreating from the alley as it continued its search.

"Thank you," Adrian mumbled.

"It's nothing," the blonde said with a smile. In the light of building entrance, her eyes were a startling sky blue.

Angel Devine, age twenty-two. No criminal record. Originally from the Twenty-Seventh Tier, she now called the Entertainment District home. Her birth name had been Tiffany Mickel, but the note in her virtual file said she no longer used it. Her medical history indicated mild asthma and a list of cosmetic augmentations too long to read.

"A favor for a friend," the brunette added with a sly wink.

Her eyes were the dark green of emeralds. Ivy Rose, age twenty-four. Like Angel, she had abandoned her birth name and now called the Sixteenth Tier home. Her list of cosmetic augmentations was only slightly shorter.

These were no street-level entertainers. Their augmentations alone were worth hundreds of thousands of credits. They worked on an upper floor of one of the district's most posh towers, safe behind security doors and an extensive client vetting process.

Ivy swept her hair away from her collar bone, revealing a beautiful digitally modulated tattoo of shimmering silver stars. They flickered and dimmed, fading back into invisibility as the color of the ink changed to match her skin. Only one remained, not a star but a shimmering, pale blue snowflake.

"Why don't you come with us," she suggested, letting her hair fall back over the tattoo. "You were going this way anyway, weren't you?"

Pulling up the map, Adrian was surprised to find himself directly under the tower Williams was visiting. One hundred and forty-five floors above them and fifty meters to the right, his employer was probably doing something he shouldn't be.

The entertainers let him into the building, listing him as a guest despite his protests.

"In case they're watching," Ivy said with a wink before they left him.

Locating a service lift, Adrian rode it up to Williams' level. As the lift cage rose, he smoothed his hair and mentally prepared himself to face his employer's wrath.

He stepped out into shimmering ruby hallways lined with footstep-muffling gold carpet. The corridors were mostly empty, their silence broken only by the occasional sound of distant laughter. He located Williams' suite and knocked.

There was no response. Adrian knocked more loudly, then pressed his thumb to the lock and let himself in.

Williams' suit jacket lay across a cream colored couch in the main room, next to a few scraps of fabric that might have been an entertainer's uniform. A painting of a naked woman hung crooked on one wall.

The bathroom door was closed, the murmur of women's voices

audible within. Williams was passed out in the bedroom. He did not stir when Adrian switched on the lights.

The room smelled of stale sweat and perfume, sex, and the alcohol slowly evaporating from a glass on the bedside table. A decorative gold lamp lay next to the table, broken. Someone had cut themselves on it, leaving red stains on the carpet.

Averting his eyes from the bed, Adrian lifted a sheet from the floor and pulled it over his employer.

"Mr. Williams."

No response.

"Mr. Williams!"

Still nothing. Adrian sighed and gave his employer's shoulder a firm shake.

"Shove off," the man mumbled.

"You need to go home. People are looking for you."

"Don't you people ever do what you're told?" Williams rolled onto his back, blinking in the bright light. "What the hell are you doing here?"

"Your family is worried about you."

"Sure they are."

"This is not a safe place for you to be without a bodyguard."

"Took you long enough to come to that conclusion."

He returned to the main room, gathered the man's clothing, and dumped the pile on the bed.

"Get dressed. We're going home."

"What are you, my mother?"

Adrian folded his arms and waited.

Williams staggered to his feet, mumbling under his breath. A rustle at the door announced the entrance of a pair of towel-clad entertainers.

"Oh, you're–"

"His bodyguard," Adrian finished for her. "Your client is going home now."

The woman nodded.

"Thank you," the other entertainer said. The pair gathered their clothing and departed.

Having succeeded in getting his employer dressed, Adrian steered the man out the door. Williams was having difficulty walking a straight line, and he leaned heavily on Adrian's shoulder even while grumbling about insubordination and interference. A striking woman in a form-fitting emerald one-piece suit swayed past them, artificially red hair cascading down her back.

"Hey, baby! Why don't you and I get to know each other?"

"No," Adrian said firmly as the woman hurried away.

"Bring her back here! It's rude to walk away when someone's talking to you."

Adrian ignored him.

"You not interested in women or something? Why am I not surprised." His employer broke into grating drunken laughter as Adrian maneuvered him into the lift.

The building's red and gold motif was repeated in the opulent lobby below. Through a crowd of clients and a wide, gilded entryway, Williams' transport waited. Adrian helped his employer down the steps and into the vehicle, then scooted into his own seat. The man groaned and massaged his temples as the transport pulled out into the crowded street.

"You didn't tell Amira where I was, did you?"

"I didn't have to. She already knew."

Williams swore.

The transport slowly made its way out of the Entertainment District and into the nearby retail area. Shiny storefronts glittered in the sun, the roar of free music and throngs of shoppers all but indiscernible within the transport's noise-proof shell. The interior was so quiet that Adrian could hear the panicked drumming of his employer's heart.

"Sir? Are you feeling unwell?"

"Do I look like I'm feeling well?" Williams growled.

"Not really." His employer looked like a man who was going to have a nasty hangover in a few hours.

"Did you at least tell her I was called away to urgent business at the plant, or a last minute Company meeting?"

"No. Why would I?"

"Jesus," Williams muttered, clutching his chest.

"She already knew. She told me to look for you here. Your secret's out."

Williams stared at the floor, face gone deathly pale.

"Sir?" As he checked the man's vital signs, Williams made a choking sound and slumped from his seat.

Instructing the transport to head for the nearest emergency clinic, Adrian began performing chest compressions. His employer's medical monitoring system indicated that he was having a heart attack.

The short trip to the clinic seemed to pass in slow motion as Adrian struggled to revive his employer. He did not want to imagine what would happen to him, unemployed and unwanted by the Company.

The transport slid to a stop, and he moved out of the way as a trio of medics lifted Williams onto a gurney and rushed him into the clinic.

***

"Friend? Family? Domestic assistant?"

The question snapped Adrian out of his contemplation of the waiting room's pristine white flooring.

"I'm his bodyguard."

"Excellent," the young man in the physician's white suit said. "Why don't you come on back? He's been asking for you."

"He's going to be fine, right?" Adrian asked as he followed the doctor into the back of the emergency clinic.

"More or less. We've applied a stent, put him on anti-clotting agents, and given him something to reduce his blood pressure. The antidote seems to have also been a success; we haven't detected any loss of mental function so far. He should be cleared to go home in under twenty-four hours."

"What antidote?"

"Someone slipped him a poison which causes neurological decay over time. I won't bore you with the toxicology report, which we've already forwarded to Enforcement, but I will say that the most likely vector was a meal consumed in the last twelve hours. If I were you, I'd remind him to be extremely cautious of any food not prepared by his own kitchen staff."

"I'll do that. Did the poison cause the heart attack?"

"Probably not. It looks like high blood pressure and some lurking arterial clogs conspired with a stressful event to cause that. He's actually exceedingly lucky it happened. Without it, it's unlikely that anyone would have noticed that he'd been poisoned until the damage was already done."

"I see."

"Of course, you don't have to tell him that," the doctor added with a chuckle. "Unless you think it'll help him be more cautious in the future." He opened the door to a private recovery room, and ushered Adrian inside.

A gauzy white privacy curtain separated a few chairs near the door from a gurney on the far side.

"Mr. Williams?"

"Who else do you think it would be?"

"I'm glad you're going to recover," Adrian said, coming around the end of the curtain. "I hope you'll consider staying away from the Entertainment District in the future."

Williams made a disdainful noise. Pale and haggard under his white smock and tangle of tubes and monitoring equipment, he looked like a shadow of the man Adrian had met a few days before.

"I bet you're glad," his employer muttered.

"I think you should be a little more appreciative," the doctor said, joining Adrian beside the gurney. "If it wasn't for your man, you probably would have died in your transport. He saved your life."

"Huh," Williams grunted.

"Now, I see you have a physician. Has he talked to you about diet and exercise?"

Adrian took a seat in one of the pale blue chairs by the door as the doctor began to go over Williams' prognosis.

* * *

The whisper of the door opening woke him in the early hours of the morning. Adrian remaining motionless, head on his arms, as a shadow moved across the room and entered the curtain. He was about to intervene and verify the intruder's identity when Williams spoke.

"Took you long enough to get here," his employer muttered.

"You want me to just waltz in here during the day shift? How about you just announce to everyone that I'm working for you?"

"Keep your voice down."

Adrian sat up, curious about Williams' visitor. The man was not, as he had first assumed, one of the medical staff.

"What do you mean you can't find her?" Williams hissed.

"Your man must have spooked her. She's gone. Probably bought herself new biometrics and split. It's going to be like looking for a needle in a haystack now."

"Damn. How much?"

"I don't think you understand. Even if I tap into the Company database, I may not be able to find her. Do you really need this done?"

"She was my assistant for years. She knows far too much."

"Then you probably should have called me before giving the job to a Hero. What were you thinking?"

Williams' response was inaudible.

Adrian pretended to sleep when the man departed a few minutes later, then found a more comfortable position in the chair and considered his options. With a deep sigh, he gathered the recordings of Williams' visit to Tabitha's apartment and Williams' conversation with the hit man, and forwarded them to Enforcement.

It was not something he took much satisfaction in doing, considering his tenuous hold on employment, but Williams had demonstrated a credible intent to harm the woman. He could not continue to turn a blind eye lest someone actually get hurt.

After most of an hour had passed, he gave up on sleep and checked the news.

"Exposed! Anarchist identity theft ring running out of the Entertainment District. What locations and services to avoid in order to protect your biometrics, coming up right after this message from Home Sense!"

Adrian stared through the newscast, wondering what would happen to him when Williams realized what he'd done.

# CHAPTER TWELVE

Williams was released to return home later that morning. The family's suite was cool and quiet when they arrived, and it struck Adrian as a little sad that the man's family did not seem to have missed him, accustomed as they were to his unexplained absences.

Safe in his own room, Adrian stripped off clothing that reeked of synthetic perfume and the heavily sterilized atmosphere of the clinic. The shower cube beckoned.

He leaned into the spray, imagining a canyon that had not appeared in his dreams for some time. The river rushed by as gray-green coyote willows swayed in the breeze. Bird shadows flitted over the water.

His thoughts were interrupted by a newscast displaying images of the geographically lowest tiers. Enforcers guarded public water dispensers, herding thirsty citizens into orderly lines. Some residents were turned away altogether. Some seemed so weak they could barely walk. There were parents with infants and children, adults supporting elderly relatives.

"Shocking images to be sure, Kim, but this was expected. There's been a lot of illicit water use down there in the past."

"And it was high time that changed. The images we're seeing are from tiers Forty through Fifty, where an unprecedented number of Enforcers have been deployed to maintain order."

"The effort is paying off, however. Early reports show that water use is down twenty-seven percent on those tiers."

Adrian shut off the newscast and stepped out of the shower, sick to his stomach.

"Are you trying to tell me something?" he demanded of Snow.

The program responded with a barrage of images. Green lawns. Swimming pools. Deserts irrigated into lush crop lands. Falling reservoirs. Dry riverbeds. Sprawling parks and golf courses, watered nightly, sizzling under a desert sky. Drought maps. Receding water tables. Depleted aquifers.

"That's old news." So old, in fact, that all of the images predated the city.

Snow showed him water distribution charts, engineering reports, and geological surveys.

"Wait, wait, go back," Adrian exclaimed, pausing the flood of information.

Artesian springs bubbled up through the bedrock below the city, refilling the reservoirs the Company relied on. A hundred years past, the upwelling of water had slowed to a trickle, then dried up altogether. Rain remained as scarce as ever.

Snow produced more information, mostly Media headlines. The onset of water rationing. The argument that water was a human right, to which the Company responded that every citizen had a right to the minimum daily intake of drinking water. Simultaneously, they announced that more water could be had– for a price.

The commencement of bitter arguing over whether insufficient rationing or overpopulation was to blame for the shortages. Eventually, the two-child limit was enacted. Meanwhile, water allowances continued to decrease.

"If you had a problem with how much water I was using, you could have been less ambiguous about it."

Snow's search window went dark.

Adrian shook his head. The definition of insanity should be

updated to include trying to have a conversation with a malfunctioning information retrieval program.

* * *

Late afternoon found him in the rooftop garden, sketching the koi pond and its lush surroundings. His coordination was slowly improving, although he still found some shapes difficult. He had redrawn one of the fish eight times, and was hoping his ninth attempt would turn out better, when Yulia appeared. She looked surprised to see him.

"I'll leave if I'm intruding on your quiet thinking spot," Adrian offered.

"I don't mind. It's just that no one else has ever taken much interest in this place."

"It's a bit fascinating. The whole rooftop is a giant terrarium. With the exception of people coming and going via the lift and feeding the fish, it's a completely closed system."

"That explains why the air always seems fresher up here," Yulia said, sitting down next to him. "Drawing anything interesting?"

"Just practicing." Adrian showed her the sketch. "I haven't gotten the hang of koi yet."

"That's not bad. Is that why you do that weird thing with your hands?"

"It's just a physical therapy thing. My right hand was crushed awhile back."

"That's awful, especially for someone who draws."

"A bit. This is my happy place– it's what I do to relax." It occurred to him that Yulia was the first person who had shown any sympathy for what the injury had taken from him.

"There are a lot of really sick people out there," Yulia said, selecting a fallen twig from under the bench. "I follow the unofficial news from the lower tiers, and I finally figured out where I recognize you from."

"I'm nobody, just another Hero. There are thousands more just like me."

Yulia laughed quietly, twirling the twig in her fingers. "No, you're not. You're the Hero from that video. The guy who told Harder Hardy off to his face."

"I think you're mistaking me for someone else."

"Do you think he did it on purpose?"

"What?"

"Your hand." She paused and bent the twig until it snapped, a dry, brittle sound. "I think he did."

Adrian stared at the fine detritus of fallen twigs and dead leaves beneath his feet. The possibility had not occurred to him until Yulia suggested it.

"Who can trust an entity that enables Enforcers like him?" Yulia asked. "What was done to you in that interrogation room was the catalyst, the proverbial last straw, for a society that's watched the Company commit abuse after abuse."

"I find that hard to believe. Heroes aren't much more welcome than Enforcers on most tiers."

"You'd be surprised. Heroes still hold something of a special place in the collective consciousness. You can't get much more selfless than giving your life to save a jumper, or to pull one more person out of a burning building.

"When an Enforcer brutalizes a civilian, there's a lot of outrage. But there's also arguing. People say 'he shouldn't have been there,' or 'he shouldn't have been doing that,' or 'he should have put his hands up more quickly.'

"But nobody can make that argument about you. As a Hero, you were the epitome of innocence. You had broken no laws. You had violated no curfew, entered no restricted area. You followed all of their orders calmly and quietly. And everyone knows that Heroes don't go around killing people.

"When proof surfaced that the man you'd been accused of killing was alive, it demonstrated that the Company was not above fabricating charges, even against one of their own. And when Hardy continued uploading videos and announced that he'd been promoted to some kind of special task force, it showed that the Company not only knew what he'd done– they approved."

"He's still uploading?" Adrian asked numbly. Somehow he had imagined that Hardy had paid for his crimes, and that there was no chance they would ever cross paths again.

"Most recent one went up six hours ago. Want to see?"

"No, thank you." He continued to stare at the ground. The world had gone gray and distant, drowned under a dull roar.

"Hey, you okay?"

"I'm fine."

"Have you gotten checked out for that? Post-traumatic stress is serious stuff."

"I'm fine. It's nothing."

"Okay then. What do you want to talk about?"

When he tried to think of a topic, his mind remained stubbornly blank. There was only the here and now: bright greenery and earthy smells, the moment to moment act of breathing, the musical tones of water trickling into the pond. He was so hyper-aware of his surroundings that his senses felt raw.

They sat in silence for a long time. Yulia gathered a handful of dry twigs from under the bench and wove them into a lattice. The sun slid a little farther toward the hazy horizon, and water continued to trickle into the pond.

"What got you into programming?" Adrian asked at last.

"I've always had a quiet fascination with how and why things work. Did you know that more than half the city's infrastructure exists in virtual reality? Everything's automated. Water flow, cooling systems, energy conservation. The entire transit system. And don't forget MADDE."

"Who's Maddy?"

"Monitoring and Disorder Detection Entity. It's a surveillance system that encompasses millions of cameras, microphones, chip readers and biometric scanners throughout the city."

"I've never heard of it."

"Most people haven't. When MADDE was first rolled out, the biggest push-back wasn't because every word and movement was being monitored by the Company; it was because an AI would be doing the monitoring. So the Company just put the system under the Enforcement Division rather than rolling it out as a stand-alone program."

"How did you find that out?"

"I've dredged up a lot of interesting things during my research. There are an incredible number of programs helping the Company monitor and control their people. Programs are more accurate and massively cheaper than human labor. They're immune to bribery and personal prejudice, and they never talk about what they've seen. Best of all, programs don't feel guilt or have consciences. And whoever writes those programs essentially controls the city."

"I suppose so. There are safeguards in place to ensure nobody hacks those systems, though."

"Oh, I wasn't talking about anything like that. With mother's backing, I could become a Company programmer."

"I was wondering, since you have some training in the field, if you would be willing to give me a professional opinion on something I turned up during a scan?"

"Sure. You have it quarantined, right? Send me the scan results, and I'll have a look."

Adrian copied the file and sent it. The silence stretched out between them.

"It's really bad, isn't it?" he finally asked.

"Well, it could have been. Where did you get this program? It's like an urban legend."

"What program?"

Yulia laughed. "Nevermind."

"What do you mean, it could have been? Is there any way to get rid of them?"

"Probably. You'll be fine if you just leave them in quarantine. I'll work on finding a way to get rid of them later." Yulia stood and brushed off her hands. "Mother's calling me. She sounds a bit peeved."

A large insect settled on his wrist as Yulia walked away. Its brilliant blue wings, each bordered with velvety black, were larger than the palm of his hand. Spindly black legs propelled it across his skin as a tube-like appendage unrolled from its mouth area and sampled his palm.

Soon more blue butterflies joined the first one, covering him in a rustling sea of iridescent blue.

***

"You okay?"

Yulia's voice pulled him out of the melancholy meditative state he had been floating in. Adrian opened his eyes and sat up, sending a cloud of blue butterflies fluttering toward the ceiling. It had gotten late while he rested, and the sunlight filtering through the garden was dull and red.

"I'm surprised you're still up here."

"Williams hasn't needed me." He didn't want to admit that he was intentionally staying out of sight of both the man and his partner. "How was your chat with your mother?"

"Oh, she's pissed." Yulia laughed and sat down on the bench next to him. "I'm supposed to be in my room changing my clothes for dinner."

"I take it she didn't like your prison suit protest?"

"Not one bit. She would have gone on about it a lot longer if Enforcement hadn't shown up."

"Really? When?"

"A little while ago. Don't worry, they're just here to talk to father. It's probably nothing."

All the calm and sense of security he had spent the last hour building vanished, replaced by an inexplicable sense of panic.

"I see you've made friends with the butterflies," Yulia continued. "I've never seen so many on someone's face at once."

"According to the archives, it's called puddling. They're attracted to the minerals in sweat."

"Tears, too. I used to come up here to hide when I was little."

"Yes, that too."

"The domestic who fed the fish told me they were kissing away my tears." Yulia laughed sadly. "I miss her."

Darkness had begun to fall. Tiny lights sprang to life on the floor, lighting the way back to the lift.

"Aren't you supposed to be going to dinner soon?"

"It's not until eight. And I'm not going, anyway. I think I'll go out to eat instead."

"By yourself?"

"What? I'm an adult. Or are you referring to the fact that my parents have me under house arrest?"

"It might not be safe."

"You're welcome to come too."

"I don't think I should. Williams might need me."

"Father's not going anywhere tonight. He'll never even notice you're gone."

"Won't they notice us leaving?" he asked ask they made their way back toward the lift.

"If we don't go out the front door, no one will even know we're gone."

"I had no idea there was more than one way out of this suite." The floor plan did not indicate that there was.

"Of course there is. How do you think the domestics come and go without disturbing anyone?"

Downstairs, Yulia led the way to her room. Bridget waited within, arms full of clothing. Her smile widened into a grin when she saw

Adrian.

"Did you tell him about his new clothes?"

"I had Bridget pick out some new clothes for you," Yulia called over her shoulder as she disappeared into the bathroom. "Why don't you try them on?"

"That's going to be a negative."

"You can't sneak out dressed as a Hero," Bridget pointed out.

"New clothes won't cover up my badge."

"Yulia already thought of that. Now, which of these do you like better?"

Adrian chose the black suit with the dark purple accents at the cuffs and collar over the pale blue one. Neither was really to his taste, and both were made of lighter fabric than he was used to wearing. Pausing in front of the mirror in his room, he straightened the collar and wondered what he was getting himself into.

When he returned, Yulia had traded in her gray jumpsuit for knee-high purple boots, pale green shorts, and a dark purple sleeveless top. Gaps in the weave revealed a neon green undershirt.

"You look like a raver," Adrian remarked. "If anyone needs to worry about attracting too much attention, I think it's you."

"Oh, don't worry about me. Now, about your badge." Yulia motioned him into the bathroom. "Have a seat so I can get that covered up."

"I'd rather not," he said, eyeing the slender case in her hands.

"Relax! Everyone up here wears makeup, even father. Otherwise he'd look a lot worse than he does." She chuckled. "You won't even be able to tell it's there, and neither will anyone else."

She dabbed something cool and damp across his cheek, blowing on the liquid to dry it. When she turned him back toward the mirror, the shield badge he had worn most of his life was gone. The concealing substance mimicked the color and texture of his skin flawlessly.

"That's pretty good," Adrian admitted.

"Told you so! Now it's time to make our escape."

At the back of the Yulia's walk-in closet, hidden behind more brightly-colored clothing than he had seen in some shops, was a nondescript wood-paneled wall. A section of the paneling slid aside as they approached, becoming a narrow doorway.

The passage beyond was dimly lit and scarcely wider than his shoulders. Neither the floor nor the walls had been painted, lending the corridor an unfinished feeling. It was as if this part of the building was not meant to be seen.

"What is this, exactly?" Adrian asked.

"Domestics' access. We're between the walls, so walk softly and keep your voice down."

The corridor twisted and turned, finally coming out into a narrow antechamber that held a utilitarian lift. The cage was already at their floor.

"Don't look so serious. This will be fun," Yulia said, smiling, as the lift descended.

"I'm a little concerned about what will happen when you miss dinner."

"I'm sure they'll be too busy arguing to even notice."

Adrian adjusted the sleeves of his new suit and said nothing, hoping he had not just condemned himself by participating in Yulia's escape.

# CHAPTER THIRTEEN

Their destination was not on the Fifth Tier, but the Sixteenth. The last of the sun's red light had faded from the reflective skin of the towers by time they arrived. Drones passed high overhead, their flashing lights filling in for stars against the darkened sky.

"How do you feel about spicy food?" Yulia asked as they made their way through the crowd streets of the retail district. "There's a really good place around the corner."

"I'm willing to try it."

The shop she led him to was small and noisy, the smell of heavy spices as loud as the volume of the customers. Someone took their order and tucked them into a booth at the back of the shop to wait. Yulia seemed lost in thought, so Adrian checked the newscast.

There had been a ventilation failure in an overcrowded tower on the Forty-Ninth Tier. The death toll was five hundred and growing. On the Forty-Fifth and Forty-Seventh Tiers, Enforcement had made a record number of arrests amid the growing discontent.

The subject changed to the lawmaking process of the Company's Executives. The two-child policy that had stood for decades had just been replaced with a one-child limit. Those currently pregnant or already possessing two children would be given a waiver.

The Executive of Enforcement proposed assigning even more Enforcers to Tiers Forty through Fifty, setting up additional checkpoints, and restricting all public movement on those tiers. The Executive of Public Services raised an alternate motion to move the wall, the city's formal boundary, upward and inward ten tiers. Bitter argument ensued as the Executive of Commerce suggested that moving the wall was tantamount to abandoning the city's manufacturing districts, most of which resided below the Fortieth Tier.

It was after eight when their food finally arrived, two bowls filled with noodles, broth, and chunks of meat. The soup was hot enough to scald, seasoned with something that made his lips burn and his nose run like crowd control gas. He choked and coughed, finally calling for a glass of water.

"It's not that spicy!" Yulia exclaimed, laughing.

"What do they put in this? They could use this stuff as a crowd control weapon."

"If you don't like it, order something else. It's on me."

"This is not an admission of defeat," Adrian said between gulps of water.

Despite the burning, the soup was surprisingly good. Perhaps he could ask the kitchen staff at home to make something like it, only with less spice.

When they left the shop some time later, Yulia headed in the opposite direction from the nearby transit interchange.

"We're not going home?" Adrian asked.

"Hair salon! There's a place just down the way that does really good dyes."

He took up a post outside the entrance and watched the flow of pedestrian traffic. The crowd had become rowdier, full of intoxicated party-goers fresh from the Entertainment District. An impromptu mosh pit formed in a nearby public rest area, dancers in neon green writhing to an inaudible beat atop the decorative benches. Ravers, the rebellious, party-loving children of the affluent.

A pair of Enforcers arrived and began breaking up the dance party with surprising restraint.

"Aw, looks like we missed the fun," Yulia said, appearing beside him.

"Good lord, what is that?" Her hair had been dyed black and streaked with iridescent green, blue and purple, the rainbow of an oil slick.

"Isn't it amazing? It's a retro classic."

"Amira isn't going to like that."

"She won't care if she doesn't see it," Yulia said, laughing. Then she was gone, weaving away from him through the crowd. Adrian swore under his breath and followed.

They passed the bright warnings at the entrance to the Entertainment District as Adrian jogged to catch up. By night, the district's street level was a dim, sweaty, dangerously overcrowded place. Yulia made a sharp left and shouldered her way down a narrow street illuminated only by the muffled glow of neon signs and seedy storefronts. Freelance entertainers lined the walls, as sad and tired-looking as their surroundings.

They entered an alley, the walls splashed with phosphorescent paint that provided just enough illumination to prevent people from running into each other. A pair of entertainers detached from the wall and moved toward them, the taller of the two latching onto Yulia's arm.

"What brings you here, pretty lady?"

"Just out to have a little fun."

"It's free if it's your first time," the man offered, leaning close. His friend put his arm around Adrian's shoulders.

"Your boyfriend can come too," the second entertainer said. "Two for the price of one."

"No, thank you," Adrian said firmly.

Yulia laughed. "He's not my boyfriend."

"Offer still stands," the taller entertainer replied, smiling. "If everybody's having fun, we're having fun."

"Don't you want to unwind, tough guy?" the other man asked, squeezing Adrian's shoulders. "You don't look like a guy who gets to have much fun."

"No, thanks," Adrian repeated.

"Sorry guys, gotta go."

"Come back if you change your mind!" the taller entertainer called after them.

Yulia ducked into a darkened alcove and knocked sharply.

A series of knocks sounded from inside the door. Yulia answered with a complex pattern of her own, and the door swung open to reveal a hulking form in dark clothing.

"Who's the new guy?" the shadow demanded.

"Protection. A had somebody tail me all the way back to the interchange last time."

The shadow grunted and stepped back just enough to let them squeeze past.

"Nice mods," the man rumbled as Adrian went by.

"What?"

"Your eyes," the shadow said, grinning. Metal flashed where his teeth should have been. "Takes balls to get modded eyes like a Company man."

He was about to reply when Yulia pulled him through a second set of doors.

The room beyond was lit with black lights that pulsed to the beat of music so loud it was more of a roar than distinct sounds. From the entrance, steps led down into a writhing sea of bodies.

The lights illuminated neon clothing and turned skin dark, casting the ravers in negative. Many wore elaborate phosphorescent makeup that gave off an ethereal glow. Others sported ultraviolet tattoos. Slender pale blue spirals wound around Yulia's bare arms and legs as she made her way down onto the dance floor.

Adrian lost sight of her almost immediately, caught in the press of thrashing bodies. He attempted to pull up the establishment's security camera feed, only to find that there was none. There were no accessible systems in the club at all.

Frowning, Adrian pulled up the floor plan. The space was listed as nothing more than basement storage for the building above. There was no club. The place was an illicit operation, a speakeasy.

Several pairs of arms encircled him as he struggled across the crowded floor, their skin warm and sticky with sweat.

"Nice eyes." The dark purple text of the message pulsed gently until he dismissed it. "You're new here, aren't you?"

"Yes. I'm looking for someone."

"I'm Antoinette."

A raver in a bright purple sleeveless top pressed herself against his chest. Her teeth were blindingly white, her irises an unnatural florescent green.

"I'm Adrian," he replied, attempting to disentangle himself from the women. "Excuse me."

"Looking for your friend? She went to the VIP lounge."

"Don't worry, we'll take care of you." The message was from a different sender, the text pink. "I'm Portia." There were hands on his shoulders, hands in his hair. Someone, perhaps Portia, was kissing the back of his neck.

"No, thank you. I have to go."

"Then we'll go with you."

The group of women guided him toward the back of the club. None of them seemed to mind being crushed against him.

They stumbled up a set of steps, hidden in the darkness and the press of bodies. More ravers lined the railing at the top, swaying in time to the pounding beat. The air swirled with chemical intoxicants, the club's inhabitants so high that the chemicals seeped from their skin and rolled out on their breath.

A pair of massive bouncers stepped aside to allow Antoinette and her party into the back room of the club, an area only marginally less crowded than the dance floor. Clusters of white couches and floor cushions provided seating. Bodies writhed under the black lights, teeth, eyes and augmentations flashing bright in the dimness.

Yulia's distinctive tattoos were nowhere to be seen.

"This way," Antoinette said, steering him toward the back of the room.

"The woman I came in with, have any of you seen her? Where did she go?"

"Relax," Portia said, pushing him toward an empty space on one of the couches. "You're here to have fun, right?"

They had accumulated quite a group. He tripped over someone's legs and they all went down in a tangle, at least six women who giggled hysterically as he tried to extricate himself.

"Oh, there you are," Yulia said in a message. "Isn't this place fun?"

Adrian looked up and found her seated next to a moderately fit man whose naked torso was wrapped in glowing purple tribal tattoos. Long, artificially blonde hair cascaded down his back. His arm was around her shoulders.

"Why are we here?" Adrian asked, giving up on removing himself from the couch. Several of the women were sitting on his legs, as if afraid he might escape.

"I need to talk to some people. This is Tony, by the way." She nodded toward her companion.

The man's augmented electric blue gaze turned to him. "Pleased to meet you, Mr?"

"Adrian."

"Welcome to my club, Mr. Adrian."

Anthony Milton, age twenty-four. Resident of the Fifteenth Tier. His medical history was mostly clean, but his criminal record was another story. Coercion. Distribution of counterfeit mood-altering substances. Felony disregard for the revocation of consent. Adrian grimaced. Enforcement had issued an arrest-on-sight bulletin for the man. If convicted, he could look forward to spending the rest of his life condemned to base labor.

"Something the matter?" Tony asked.

"What's the maximum occupancy for a space this size? There are an awful lot of people on your dance floor. I doubt they'd all get out if there was a fire."

"There's never been a fire in this building," the man said, smiling.

"That's not what I asked."

"My, your friend asks some odd questions."

"Don't mind him," Yulia said quickly. "He's one of us."

"He has eyes like a Company man."

Yulia laughed. "It's just a mod."

"What else do you have modded? I'll show you mine if you show me yours." Tony was grinning, and Adrian couldn't quite tell if the statement was a joke or an offer.

"I'd rather not."

A raver appeared with a tray bearing three glasses of water.

"Water's on the house," Tony said.

Adrian reluctantly accepted a glass. There was something about the man's smile that did not sit well with him.

"Relax," Antoinette whispered in his ear.

"I am relaxed, thanks."

"Shhh." Portia kissed him. Someone else was undoing the buttons on his suit.

Brushing hands away, he took a gulp of water and contemplated how to extricate Yulia from the club.

The water had been a mistake; the drug cocktail might have been flavorless to anyone else, but his augmented sense of taste detected exotic additives. Analyzing the flavor, he concluded that it was laced with a strong muscle relaxant, an antidepressant known to cause disassociation and euphoria, and a mild sedative.

The drugs began to take effect almost immediately, and Adrian wondered just how heavy a dose he'd been given. The room seemed to pulsate to the beat of the music. He was immobilized, floating in a peculiar state of euphoria, hyper-aware of the velvety feel of the couch cushions and the warmth of the bodies around him.

The hand holding the glass of water sagged. One of the women cupped his hand and helped him drink, and he finished most of the water before he remembered why he shouldn't. Antoinette and her friends laughed as he spluttered and struggled to push the drink away.

Someone took the glass from him. The weight of his body seemed to triple and the room wavered, a blur of glowing eyes and teeth and augmentations. Hands struggled to lift him and pull the suit off his shoulders. Others worked on his shirt.

Portia snuggled against his side and draped his arm around her. He stared at it, wondering why his limbs were being so familiar with people he didn't know. The group had gotten his shirt off. They were going to have him naked soon, and although he was aware that he should be excruciatingly embarrassed, he felt strangely unconcerned.

"What's with all the scars?"

He glanced down and realized that the marks glowed faintly under the black lights, a constellation of close calls.

"He looks like a torture victim," Portia exclaimed, pulling away. "I mean, the ones on his face aren't so bad, you know? They provide character. But this is just gross."

"I wouldn't have pulled him back here if I'd known. Are you creditless or something?" Antoinette demanded.

"Of course not," he mumbled, deeply offended.

"My friend got run over by a transport, and he doesn't look nearly this bad! You can't even see his scars," Portia said. "This is just nasty."

"They're not that bad," Adrian protested.

Among most of the citizen population, remaining unblemished throughout life was seen as a sign of beauty and affluence. In order to sell costly reconstructive surgery and cosmetic augmentations, the Company had been marketing scars, cellulite and the signs of aging as shameful for generations.

"Cover him up," Antoinette ordered. "If I wanted to look at that,

I'd go to a butcher shop."

Someone tossed his shirt at him. If he could have moved, he would have put it on. This was not the reaction he had anticipated, and for some reason it hurt his pride that these people did not share his respect for the marks of a lifetime of service.

"Those places are fun though. At least you get to watch them scream."

"Do you think we could make him scream?" Portia asked, giggling.

The room began to come back into focus as someone passed her a razor blade. Yulia was sprawled on a nearby couch. Tony was nowhere to be seen.

His survival augmentations kicked in as the blade bit into his chest, a queasy combination of sedation and adrenaline. Something hot and wet ran down his skin.

"Please stop," he said, struggling to push away the hand with the knife.

"Why should we?"

"I have to– have to– " He knew exactly what he needed to do, but the words evaded him.

The women laughed at his clumsy efforts and held him down. More spectators gathered, turning their little group into a crowd.

"Cut him deeper!" someone yelled.

Portia leaned in, grinning. A small woman with hot pink hair and an artfully shredded lavender minidress, she wouldn't have seemed threatening if not for his inability to defend himself.

The metal left a trail of fire across his skin. There was a lot of blood running down his chest, dark under the lights. The crowd cheered.

Adrian finally found the strength to shake off his attackers and stagger to his feet. The crowd scrambled out of reach as he fumbled with his shirt and gathered Yulia up from her couch. Her skin was cold, her breathing slow and shallow.

All but a few of the spectators had dispersed; those that remained shoved at him playfully, trying to knock him off balance. He shrugged them off and made his way toward the doorway at the rear of the VIP area.

The room pulsated in time to the music, and he had to concentrate to keep his balance as he threaded his way through the maze of couches and reclining bodies. Fighting his way back through the crowd of thrashers on the dance floor was out of the question. The pounding music and the labored rasp of his breathing sounded far away, as if at the end of a long tunnel.

The door led to a short, unlit stairway. At the top, a corridor extended in either direction. To the left, light spilled from an open door. To the right, a maintenance access led to the main floor of the tower. Adrian adjusted his grip on his unconscious charge and turned right.

***

Sitting next to Yulia's gurney, lulled by the electronic whisper of the monitoring equipment, Adrian fought to keep his eyes open. Outside the door, someone began yelling and was quickly silenced. They appeared to be entering the busiest time of night for the emergency clinic.

"You look tired," Yulia said.

"I am tired."

She nodded slowly. "I feel like shit."

"I can imagine. I don't feel too good either."

Yulia sighed. "That's not how that was supposed to go. Tony's usually a really good source of information."

"He's wanted by Enforcement on a bunch of really nasty charges."

"Explains why he got spooked." She grimaced. "What happened to you?"

"I think I was someone's entertainment."

"I'm sorry. You didn't deserve that." She sat up and swung her legs off the side of the bed. "How bad is it?"

He undid a button and looked down his bloodstained shirt. The wounds didn't sting, and what blood remained seemed to have dried. Perhaps he had not been cut very deeply after all.

"I don't think it's serious. Don't you think you should rest until you're feeling better?"

"They gave me something to counteract whatever Tony roofied us with. You got a shot too, right?"

"No. It's already mostly worn off. Heroes are pretty hard to drug."

"I guess that's something," Yulia said. "If you hadn't been able to shake it off, we might have been in trouble. I owe you one for that." She stood up and smoothed her clothing. "You need to be a little more discreet, though. Nothing screams 'Company man' quite like demanding to know why a place is over the occupancy limit."

"I'm sorry. I really think you should stay until you're released, though."

"Until my parents come looking for me? I don't think so." Yulia moved toward the door. Adrian levered himself out of the chair and followed.

* * *

The flow of leisure-seeking citizens at its lowest during the early morning hours, and the transit ride back to the Fifth Tier was less crowded than the ride down had been. Yulia dozed in her seat, slumped against his shoulder.

Elysian Fields was quiet, the lifts mostly empty except for a few returning revelers. Adrian breathed a sigh of relief when he found no one waiting for them. He padded down the hall to his room, trailing a hand down the cool wood paneling to steady himself.

A hot shower beckoned, but he was fighting a losing battle with gravity. He fell into bed without bothering to take off his clothes.

The carved rafters rippled, shadows crawling between them. For Bridget's sake, he debated dragging himself back out of bed to undress and clean up. Before he could make up his mind, the darkness rose up and dragged him down into unconsciousness.

***

The sensation of someone frantically shaking his shoulder dragged him back to awareness. Bridget's face came into focus as he blinked in confusion.

"I'm sorry about the blood," he mumbled. "I'll turn in my laundry later, okay?"

"No, you have to wake up. You need to leave right now."

The domestic's voice was breathless, panicked.

"What's going on?"

"I did a bad thing for you," Bridget said. "He's planning to sell you."

He had not seen that coming.

Adrian sat up and swung his legs off the edge of the bed. The room was no longer moving. The sensation had been replaced by a dull, hollow feeling and a piercing headache.

"How do you know?"

"See for yourself." She forwarded him a video clip.

The woman's perceptions overtook his own as the recording began to play, and he found himself standing in the darkened hallway outside Williams' rooms. The sliding door had stopped a centimeter short of closing, a feat that must have taken a low level hack to accomplish. A sliver of light slipped through the gap from the dimly lit room within.

"He's in excellent condition, as far as I know," Williams said.

"Yes, but good enough to be worth what you're asking?" A second voice, deeper, belonging to a man perhaps Williams' age or a little older.

"Here's the data from his last physical assessment. Take a look."

"Very nice," the unidentified man said after a few moments. "He'll certainly do. Surprisingly well-preserved specimen for his age. Lots of new hardware, too."

"Cost a pretty bundle of credit," Williams muttered. "He's been nothing but trouble. Keep him out of sight, they said. He's good at following orders, they said." His employer laughed bitterly. "First thing he does is bungle a simple job that's going to cost a small fortune to clean up. Next day he takes off on a misguided quest to rescue me, and gives some wannabe reporter an exclusive interview along the way.

"Next thing I know, I get a message from the Executive of Safety. This Hero is supposed to be dead. Why is his face all over the network? And that's not even the end of it! Somehow he got nosy, eavesdropped half a conversation, and decided to report it to Enforcement. Completely innocuous business, of course. No laws were broken. But I don't need that kind of stress right now."

The other man chuckled. "Let this be the end of your troubles, then. You have yourself a buyer."

"You have no idea what a relief that is. Now, how do you want to set this up? It might be best if he's not aware he's being transferred."

The view shifted as Bridget peered through the gap in the door. More of the room came into focus, shadows and dark paneling broken by old-fashioned bookcases and the bulky outlines of black armchairs. The unidentified man sat in one, his back to the only light source in the room. Williams sat nearby, behind a massive wooden desk.

Try as he might, Adrian could gather few details about his prospective buyer. The man's face was hidden in shadow. An eye scan was completely out of the question, and even his facial recognition software was unable to get a good read between the low light and the angle.

"Just send him to me for a checkup," the buyer was saying. "Tell him it's routine for household staff. I'll handle the rest."

"Be careful." Williams chuckled. "He's entirely too perceptive for his own good. You'll have Enforcement at your doorstep if he catches on."

"I'll make up a reason to have him sedated. He'll never see it coming. As far as he's concerned, it'll just be a routine operation until he never wakes up from it."

The two men were silent for a few minutes, sipping their drinks.

"You expect to get more than parts out of him, yes?" Williams asked.

"Oh, yes. I wouldn't be expending this kind of credit for just his neural interface and nano-prosthetic implants. With the dissolution of the Safety Division, we're seeing the end of an opportunity as well as the end of an era. It would be a tragedy to see the Hero genetic profile permanently locked away in some Company database."

"I had no idea you were such a fan of the Company's old genome modification program."

"Their geneticists put a lot of time and effort into tailoring the Hero genome. Heroes don't develop cancer. They don't suffer from asthma, diabetes or heart disease. Their DNA harbors no genetic disorders. They're immune or resistant to a wide range of human pathogens."

Williams grunted skeptically. "They're also insanely strong. Cripplingly compassionate. And disturbingly shortsighted when it comes to how a little human suffering can benefit the greater good."

"Once I've sequenced the Hero genome, I'll be able to pick and choose which of those genetic edits I make available to the public." The buyer smiled, teeth glowing white in the dimness. "For a price, of course."

"Of course." Williams chuckled.

Bridget turned away from the door, ending the recording.

Adrian sat on the edge of the bed and stared into space as the news sank in. He felt numb, empty. The inevitability of his fate settled over his shoulders like a lead vest, pinning him in place. It was pointless to run– no matter where he went, the Company would find him.

"Get up," Bridget hissed, shaking his shoulder. "The sooner you leave, the more of a head start you'll have before he realizes you're gone."

"There's no point," Adrian mumbled, holding his aching head.

"Yes, there is! Get up. I already found you a disguise." She sent him a file, the contents of which requested to edit the registry files of his identification chip.

"Is that what I think it is?"

"Yes. The Company has ID scanners everywhere, so you're going to overwrite your identity chip."

"Who does the new one belong to?"

Bridget shrugged. "No idea. It's not really important, is it? It'll help keep them from tracking you."

"Yes, it's important. Is he still alive? Does he know it's been stolen?"

"I have no idea. Put these on."

"Bridget, no. I can't run. I'm a Company man, and Company men do what they're told."

The young woman snorted. "That attitude is going to get you killed."

"When Heroes graduate training, we swear an oath to obey the Company."

"And to serve and protect. To help people. If you get out of here, you can keep doing that. If you stay and follow Mr. Williams' orders, you're going to die."

"I can't break my oath."

"Then don't think of it as the Company telling you to go with that man," Bridget said in exasperation. "I find your insistence on upholding your oath ironic, considering the fact that the Company already threw you away."

"I don't–"

"Listen, why don't you go get changed and think it through? I need to finish gathering everyone's laundry, but I'll see you again before I go."

Adrian reluctantly accepted the bundle of dark gray clothing and took it into the bathroom. Stripping off his bloodstained shirt, he was surprised to find nothing but the faint white lines of healed scars beneath. The injuries he had sustained a few hours before were gone.

He stared at his reflection in the floor length mirror. There were dark circles under his eyes, and a layer of stubble covered his jaw. Yulia's makeup had survived the night, still rendering his badge invisible.

He owed his existence to the Company. Designed solely to serve and protect, he was human but not quite a citizen. All of the Safety Division's propaganda served to emphasize a Hero's place in the world, but that world was changing. While the city's founders might have been egalitarians, the present-day Executives only represented the city's elite.

The Company's policies were no longer in line with the values he had sworn to uphold. If he obeyed orders that ran counter to the public good, he would be breaking his oath to protect and serve all citizens equally. The choice to protect the innocent over the interests of the elite was one he had already unwittingly made when he refused to follow Williams' orders regarding Tabitha.

Adrian nodded decisively, wincing as his headache intensified in response, and began putting on his new clothing. The pants and long-sleeved top were lightweight and loose-fitting, subtly altering the shape of his silhouette. The dark gray fabric rendered him unremarkable, ready to blend into the shadows of the city's architecture.

Shivering in the artificially chill air, Adrian retrieved his bag and packed it with spare clothing and a few personal items.

"That's a good look for you," Bridget said when she returned. "If you keep the hood up and wear sunglasses, you shouldn't have much trouble with facial recognition scans. Although you might want to stay out of well-lit areas, just to be safe." She handed him a pair of dark glasses. "Did you activate the ID?"

Adrian sighed. He did not relish the thought of losing all the privileges and access codes tied to his Hero identity. Nevertheless, he opened the file and allowed it to make its registry edits.

His neural interface went dark, all five senses shutting off as it rebooted. A moment later awareness of his surroundings returned. Bridget was tucked under his arm, holding him up.

"Did it work?" she asked.

"I think so."

Gathering his duffle bag, he allowed Bridget to lead him through the maze of narrow domestics' corridors to the service lift.

"Do you know where you're going?" she asked as they descended.

Adrian shook his head.

"You need to go somewhere they'd never think to look for you. You remember Victor, right? The guy who interviewed you? He's been working to crack the information blackout around the subterranean farms. What he found was a lot worse than anyone expected."

"Worse than what?" Adrian asked, puzzled.

Bridget shrugged. "There's a big announcement coming, and then everyone will know. Just be advised that things may get a lot worse before they get better."

"Thanks, I guess."

"I'm sure you know the city like the back of your hand. Find a good hiding spot, and stay out of sight."

He had never devoted much thought to what he would do if he had to go into hiding. There was virtually nowhere the Company couldn't hear or see. Marketing and payment devices read identity chips and captured eye scans. Surveillance cams streamed footage of nearly every square meter of the city, combined with facial recognition software that could pick a target out of a crowd of thousands. And then there were the citizens themselves, whose neural interfaces could easily be tapped to search for someone who was hiding from the eyes of the Company.

"I'm not sure that's really possible. The Company sees

everything."

"What about outside the wall?" Bridget asked as they stepped out of the lift. "There's no Company presence down there."

Adrian hadn't even considered the forsaken tiers. Rumor called them the realm of Anarchists, hackers, and thieves, where a citizen was as likely to wind up parted down for their neural interface and implants as to succumb to the many diseases that abounded beyond the reach of Company medical services.

It was also the final home of the downgraded. There were plenty of horror stories about what lay beyond the wall, but he had no idea how many of them were true. As a Company man, he had never been there.

"I hadn't thought of it," Adrian admitted.

Hot night air settled over them as they walked outside, a shock after the artificial chill of the building. A blanket of pollution lay over the streets, muffling the lights as if to threaten that this tier, too, would one day be as grimy and neglected as the places the smog hailed from.

"I'll miss you," Bridget said, looking at the ground.

"I'll miss you too. Thanks for everything."

Before he could turn away, the laundry domestic hugged him tightly. For a moment his headache and the weight of all his problems disappeared. There was nothing but the early morning quiet, the smell of smog and blooming cherry trees.

"Keep your head down and stay away from people," she said, patting him on the back. "Be safe." Then she was gone.

The street outside Elysium Fields was dusted with pink petals. More drifted down as he passed, just another shadow beneath the sleeping trees. Lights glowed in the surrounding housing towers, the wealthy residents living it up late into the night, but there was little traffic at ground level.

Adrian investigated his new identity as he walked. The ID belonged to Larry Allan Lasange, a resident of the Forty-Fifth Tier with an extensive criminal history. Assault. Theft. Distribution of illegal homemade stimulants. Non-payment of various fees.

The man had no travel visas. In fact, it seemed he had not been seen on any tier in several years. Adrian pulled his hood farther forward, painfully aware that the citizen's unexplained appearance on the Fifth Tier would seem more than a little suspicious. Thanks to his poverty and criminal background, the man would be less than welcome in many parts of the city.

Up ahead, Western Avenue descended from the Fifth Tier to the Sixth. Half a dozen Enforcers manned the checkpoint there, ensuring that no one without a residency permit, visitor pass or work visa moved up in the city. Such control points separated each tier from the one below, preventing citizens from accessing the tiers above without authorization.

Adrian ducked down a side street, searching for a gap between the towers that lined the Fifth Tier's border with the Sixth. He found what he was looking for behind a row of recycling receptacles at the back of a narrow alley. Nothing but a shoulder-height fence separated him from the twenty meter drop that divided each tier from the one below.

The beady eye of a surveillance cam peered down at him as he hoisted himself over the railing, but the monitoring system was unlikely to take special note of his passage. Enforcement only cared if people circumvented the checkpoints to move up in the city.

He dropped down onto the maintenance catwalk of an adjacent building and carefully lowered himself onto the structure's solar cell scaffolding. When the scaffolding ran out he dropped the last five meters to the ground, readjusted his bag, and hurried onward.

***

By time he reached the Tenth Tier he had begun to feel tired. The towers that housed the city's lawmakers and all their clerks and staff rose around him, sleek and forbidding. Enforcers stood guard at the entrances, a new development since he had last visited. Adrian left the main avenue and utilized alleys and side streets that kept him out of their sight as he crossed the tier.

Adverts plagued him as he passed through retail districts on the tiers below. Without the ad blocker that had been registered to his old identity, he was experiencing the city as the majority of the citizens did: beset by virtual hucksters and blinded by pop-up ads.

Most of the adverts offered to extend credit at exorbitant rates or championed low cost samples of their main product, a nod to Larry's extremely poor credit. Virtual banners for enhancers, stimulants, and cosmetic augmentations splashed the walls. Back alley food stalls beckoned, their savory smells tantalizing, but Larry was flat broke. Even if he had the credit to purchase food, transactions also required a thumb print, and his would not match his new identity.

The late night bustle of the retail areas were a welcome sight after the silent streets of the Tenth Tier. He kept his head down, and to his relief no one seemed to give him a second look. Groups of neon-clad ravers drifted from store to store, whooping and laughing. Amid the gaudy chaos, he was little more than a passing shadow.

The bulk of the adverts changed to sexual services as he passed the Entertainment District. The rest were for chemical refreshments, the performance enhancers, stimulants and sedatives that powered many of the district's transactions. Adrian scowled and suppressed the urge to swat at the swarm of advertisements.

A virtual entertainer materialized in front of him, a tiny, knobby-kneed waif in a minuscule pink skirt and tube top. Adrian detoured around her, deeply disturbed. The entertainer looked like a child of scarcely more than ten.

"Hey, daddy," the advert called after him. "Don't you want to come visit me?"

Adrian walked faster.

Advertisements were based on the purchasing habits of the viewer. If there were no prior purchases in that category of services the adverts were more generic, appealing to a wide range of tastes to lure new customers. All of the adverts generated from Larry's preferences contained entertainers so young he had a hard time believing they were of legal age. He found himself developing a strong dislike for the donor of his new ID.

***

His eyes and throat were burning by time he reached the Twentieth Tier's Western Avenue transit interchange. There was little Enforcement presence there, perhaps occupied with the unrest elsewhere in the city. If he did not want to walk all the way to the Fiftieth Tier, this was the best place to board the transit system.

As he made his way through the crowded interchange, Adrian contemplated the fact that it was likely the last cross-city trip he would make. Transit service was completely free and anyone could board a downward-bound transit, but only those who lived on the upper tiers or possessed a cross-tier visa could return.

No one gave him a second look as he joined the flow of boarding commuters. As the transit left the interchange, he made his way to an empty seat at the back of the module and sank into it with a sigh of relief. Leaning against the wall, lulled by the motion of the transit, he was asleep in minutes.

# CHAPTER FOURTEEN

drian slept so soundly that he missed the transit's passage through the Twenty-Ninth Tier, the tint of the windows darkening to obscure the plumes of sooty smoke that rolled from the sides of the buildings. Working class citizens came and went. Some stole glances in his direction, nudged their companions, and whispered excitedly. A few left food packets and flasks of water in his lap as they departed.

He awoke some time later and discovered the haphazard pile, utterly confused.

"Whose are these?" he asked of the citizens on the other side of the isle.

The nearest commuter shrugged. "People have been leaving you those since I got on. They say you're the Hero that stood up to the Enforcers."

"I'm not," Adrian said, pulling his hood farther forward.

"Maybe you're not, but people do these things as much for themselves as for you."

"There's a shrine to that Hero in my district," the worker in front of him said, turning to look back over her seat. "He was something special, but I'm pretty sure he's dead. You do look a bit like him, though."

"It's just a coincidence." He was immensely glad for the dark sunglasses that covered the telltale pale blue of his eyes and the makeup that concealed his badge.

The transit slowed, braking toward the Forty-Third Tier's Western Interchange. Many of the passengers disembarked, more boarded, and the transit continued its descent. Adrian ate a meal packet and sipped some water, watching the pollution swirl past the windows.

Two tiers later a chime sounded, followed by the announcement that general service was discontinued below the FortyFifth Tier. Passengers commuting to factory jobs were advised to transfer to modules providing service to their district of employment.

Tucking the last of the packets and flasks into his bag, Adrian exited the transit module. Outside, the stench of toxic manufacturing processes and rotting garbage had overwhelmed the air purification system of the interchange. Adrian dug his filtration mask out of his bag and put it on.

He scarcely looked out of place among the press of commuters. Cheap, disposable white masks abounded, many showing signs of extended use. Those who could not afford masks wrapped clothing around their faces. The crowd flowed around him, heads down, never giving him a second glance.

Snow's map spread across his vision, constantly up-dated with information collected from the neural interfaces of residents and commuters. It displayed the locations of posted and patrolling Enforcers, and highlighted a safe path he might follow across the tier.

It was the Enforcers that concerned him. According to Snow's real-time map, there was a pair posted at every street level exit. They were fewer in the higher levels of the multi-floor interchange, where factory workers queued for transits with direct service to the manufacturing districts. There were also a few unguarded walkways connecting the upper levels of the interchange to nearby towers.

Adrian took the stairs to the next level, listening to the insufferably cheerful public service announcement that seemed to be on a never-ending loop in the interchange.

"In line with the enactment of a one-child per couple reproduction limit, all reproduction prevention services are now free! And if you reside between Tiers Forty and Fifty, you are eligible for a payout of twenty thousand credits in exchange for undergoing permanent sterilization."

Adrian shook his head. Twenty thousand credits was not a lot, but to the residents of these tiers it might be enough to stave off starvation or keep from being downgraded for another month. It was certainly enough to convince the city's poorest residents to submit to a procedure they might not otherwise consent to.

As he stepped out onto the next level, a new announcement began to play.

"Have you ever wondered where your food comes from?" a male voice intoned. "Don't you think you should?"

The broadcast was accompanied by images that obscured the crowded open spaces and blank beige walls of the interchange. Bloody chunks of flesh rolled down an enclosed conveyor belt, familiar shapes and contours covered in pale skin. A rib cage. An arm. Half of a thigh. He was no stranger to blood and gore, but there was something unspeakably sickening about human parts being treated like meat in a packing plant.

"Have you ever wondered what happens to those downgraded from the lowest tiers? Have you ever wondered what happens to the condemned? Perhaps you should."

The broadcast showed Enforcers herding the residents of a housing tower into freight transports like those he had seen on his most recent visit to the Forty-Seventh Tier. The scene changed. The residents, stripped of their possessions, were herded into a long white room. Another white room held line after line of convicts.

The image went dark; when the lights came back up, bodies lay sprawled atop one another as if they had fallen where they stood. Workers in white hazmat suits, each bearing the cheek barcode of those condemned to base labor for life, entered and began clearing away the dead.

"For the Company, we present a twofold problem," the narrator continued. "It is impossible to raise enough livestock to feed all of us. And when we fail, we expire in debt. To the Executives, the one is the solution to the other."

The entire transit interchange had come to a standstill. Commuters stood transfixed in shock and horror, hands over their mouths. Adults held their children close. In the distance, someone could be heard screaming.

"I have some news for you: no matter how you die, you will end up here."

Row upon row of naked human bodies, hung like meat in a slaughter house, slowly advanced toward the gleaming blades of automated butchers.

"And if you think you've never consumed human flesh because you can't afford original form foodstuffs, think again."

The view changed to tidy silver containers of processed food. Bagged snacks. Cases of dispenser powder. Portable meal packets. The image displayed the ingredient list of each. Certain contents, like protein, calcium and iron, were highlighted in red. So was the source, generally listed as reprocessed nutritional material.

The meal packet, which had already been sitting uneasily on his stomach, did a queasy flip. Frantically peeling off his mask, Adrian staggered to the nearest recycling bin and threw up. The bin snapped its lid shut and attempted to fine him for depositing biological material in the wrong receptacle.

Around him, other commuters were having a similar reaction. Some had been sick, or were struggling not to be. Some covered their faces and sank to the floor, sobbing. Scattered shouts of anger rose from the crowd.

"Are you outraged?" the presenter demanded. "Sickened? Angry? Well, you should be."

The scene changed to a luxury apartment not unlike Williams

and Amira's. Real food was being prepared in the gleaming kitchen.

"On Tiers One through Nine, they can afford the exorbitant price of authentic foodstuffs. No one makes them wait in line and verify their identity to access water. In fact, they're allowed to purchase as much water as they want."

The shouts of outrage were gaining volume.

"Up there, they're not like us," the presenter continued, voice rising. "They've never had to want for anything. They've never seen their brothers and sisters carried away by Enforcement. They've never had to face the threat of being downgraded.

"To the Executives and their pawns, we are nothing more than a consumable commodity. They reap the profits of our labor while feeding us nothing but the recycled bodies of our dead."

The interchange roared.

"But the day has come when they will be downgraded. Rise up, and take back what was built with the proceeds of your suffering!"

Images of tree-lined streets, gleaming housing towers and indoor gardens sparkled in front of his eyes.

"This has been a city-wide broadcast. Citizens everywhere are with you!" The message ended abruptly, replaced by an overly chipper voice explaining birth control options.

Screams and shouts echoed from the walls, a deafening cacophony of outrage. Knots of young people stood together, their fists raised in defiance. Chants of "Eat the rich!" and "Kill the Company bastards!" rolled through the interchange.

Adrian moved with the flow of traffic toward the walkway that connected the interchange to a nearby housing tower. Stacks of makeshift sleeping spaces lined the corridor beyond. He was bombarded with advertisements for credit-saving services and discounted household items. The garish virtual banners cluttered his view to the point that he had difficulty finding his way through the crush of angry citizens.

By elbowing his way down a side corridor, Adrian was able to escape the frenzied mob. Trash crunched underfoot as he ducked under laundry hung to air out. The residents seemed mostly concerned with the announcement and paid him little attention. There were none of the closing doors and hushed whispers that had accompanied his passage when he had been dressed as a Hero.

"What's in the bag, man?" someone shouted as he passed. Adrian ignored the citizen and kept walking. The man's crazed laughter faded as he entered a stairwell and began to descend.

At the landing below, an intricate drawing depicted an Enforcer's armor. It lay on dirty pavement, fragments of a skeleton still inside. Vermin had made the abandoned suit their home. The words "the only good Enforcer" were written on the wall below.

The next landing held a series of drawings of a striking young woman, the quirk of her smile and the sparkle in her eyes portrayed by an artist of considerable talent. The muse smiled down on passersby with warmth and benevolence. People had left a small shrine of personal effects and knickknacks below the images.

The series ended with a riot, the chaos of beige-clad citizens and dark Enforcer armor depicted in chilling detail. There were citizens on the floor, trampled underfoot. People fighting to free their friends. Broken limbs and fallen bodies, citizens in cuffs and Enforcers wielding their riot shields as weapons.

The woman struggled with a pair of Enforcers, arms twisted behind her. The look on her face was one of pain and terror. It was apparent that the scene was burned into the artist's memory.

On the adjacent wall someone far less skilled had drawn a lone figure, head down, gazing out of a gap in a covered walkway. Scattered paint cans and pens lay at his feet. In the next frame the hatch was empty, the forlorn figure gone. The artist's tools remained.

"RIP Marco," someone had written in block letters below. Others had added their own messages.

"Hope you're with Rain now."

"Best the Forty-Seventh ever had."

"Inspired."

"Wish you'd stayed."

When Adrian exited the stairwell at the ground floor, the stream of pedestrian traffic immediately swallowed him. He was dragged along by the roaring, jostling crowd until the hallway opened out into a common area.

A handful of smaller residential hallways converged there, next to broken dispensers and lifts hung with streamers of caution tape. The food dispenser was awaiting repair. The water dispenser was closed by order of the Division of Public Services. "All requests for water must be made at the controlled dispenser on Floor Seventy-Five," its digital signage read.

A group of gaunt creditless huddled against the wall next to the defunct machines. Some held each other; others hugged their knees and rocked back and forth. There were mothers with children, orphaned siblings, and an elderly couple. Adrian quietly handed out meal packets and flasks of water. His charity was greeted with murmurs of surprise and spontaneous hugs. Supplies exhausted, he slipped back into the crowd and set a course for the nearest exit.

On the Fifth Tier, the sun would be bathing the tops of the towers in rosy morning light. On the Forty-Fifth, dense smog enclosed the streets in artificial darkness. Adrian switched to night vision as he stepped out onto Western Avenue. Vermin rustled among the mounds of trash, beady eyes glowing.

The heat settled over him like a blanket as he walked, sending beads of sweat rolling down his skin. Traveling through the surrounding towers and their network of enclosed walkways would be cooler, but out here there were fewer prying eyes. Disguised, he was just another citizen to the Company's surveillance systems.

Of course, he was also utterly exposed. If Enforcement was coming for him, he would have little warning. The thought filled him with a worry that verged on panic. He hurried toward the wall, bag bouncing on his shoulder, lungs burning.

***

A pack of vermin trailed him as he jogged down the empty steps between the Forty-Fifth Tier and the Forty-Sixth. The nearby security checkpoint sat abandoned, its windows smashed, its walls covered in faded graffiti.

Although the vermin maintained a respectful distance, their presence as well as his fear of pursuit kept him from pausing to rest. He found himself looking up and over his shoulder often, scanning the smoggy dimness for anything that might signal the presence of Enforcement's drones or independent maglev transports.

As noon approached, a murky twilight came to street level. The vermin took little notice of the growing light, going about their business with the same boldness as before. Adrian rounded a corner to find them feasting on a body in the center of an intersection. The corpse lay atop a midden of debris, heaved from an enclosed walkway tens of floors above.

His first impulse was to identify the body and report it, but an eye scan was out of the question. The scavengers had been at it for a while, and there was little left of the victim's face. The vermin chittered and hissed as he approached, threatening to fight for their meal until he turned away.

There was only a five meter drop between the Forty-Sixth Tier and the Forty-Seventh, and the checkpoint was just as unmanned as the one before it had been. Below the steps, the trash cluttering Western Avenue grew deeper. Occasionally Adrian thought he heard someone following him, but it might have been nothing more than garbage falling from above. The events of his last visit to the tier crossed his mind more than once, adding to his unease.

The air pollution grew thicker as the day wore on, a stifling brown haze that held the acrid tang of burning housing material. Tuning in to Media's broadcast, he didn't have to wait long for news about its origin.

"With air quality across the city plummeting, I'm going to ask what we're all wondering. Kim, what's the word on the fires?"

"Emergency Services are on scene, and Enforcement is attempting to restore order. Evacuation orders still stand for residents of the affected buildings, but all other movement in those districts is forbidden. There is to be absolutely no leaving housing for any reason until order is fully restored."

"Sounds reasonable, Kim. In the wake of the latest Anarchist smear campaign, we're seeing a lot of destructive activity out there. Enforcement has their hands full, and they don't have time to separate regular commuters from Anarchists. If you're caught outside your living space in one of the affected zones, you will be treated as a lawbreaker."

"That's right. And here's that list, from the top down."

Adrian grimaced and sipped his water as the newscaster detailed a lengthy list of districts under lockdown. Nearly every tier below the Tenth was affected. The outrage sparked by the rogue broadcast was on track to paralyze the city.

* * *

Ruined buildings rose around him as he descended to the Forty-Eighth Tier, the twisted, burned-out structures marking the site of some great calamity. The streets were littered with trash and charred transports, quietly corroding under layers of toxic dust.

The district was eerily silent, not even vermin stirring among the mounds of scorched waste. Even the intact towers were deserted, their composite skins sloughing solar cells as the corrosive pollution ate through the mounting brackets.

Adrian paused and peered up into the smog at one such tower. Aside from a lack of electricity, little seemed wrong with it. With the state of overcrowding in the lower reaches of the city, why hadn't the Company rebuilt the damaged towers and restored service to those without power?

Darkness fell, a dusky curtain that crept toward him through the smog. It had been several days since he had gotten a real night's sleep. Each step became a struggle, the bag growing progressively heavier on his shoulder. The threat of pursuit was the only thing that kept him moving.

Something crashed to the pavement a few blocks away. Switching on his night vision, Adrian peered back the way he had come. Although nothing moved in the smoggy darkness, the skin between his shoulders prickled with unease.

Entering an open space, he noticed that the trash had been cleared away and charred human femurs had been lined up end to end, their lines radiating outward from the center of the intersection. At the focal point of the design, human skulls ringed a blackened transport.

Adrian cautiously approached the center, an intricate pattern of small bones crunching under his feet. The transport itself was topped with a strange collection of shiny odds and ends. Jewelry. A broken mirror. Polished bits of metal. Scraps of cloth covered in glittery sequins.

The display was like nothing he had ever seen, and he could not imagine what would drive someone to collect human remains and arrange them in such a way. He glanced over his shoulder, skin crawling. The darkness behind him held nothing but tendrils of smog and lifeless towers. Adrian lifted his bag higher on his shoulder and hurried onward.

Pulling up the map and looking ahead down Western Avenue into the Forty-Ninth tier, his heart sank. All travel was prohibited. Enforcers patrolled the streets as well as the corridors of the towers.

"There's no way I'm going to make it through that," he muttered.

Snow's map reset to his location and a path appeared to his right, marked in florescent green.

"Where does that go?"

Snow responded with a jumble of images: a building, a maintenance hatch, a tunnel of some kind. The inside of another maintenance hatch, followed by a street as deserted as the one where he stood. All of the images were stale, pulled from the archives. It occurred to him that in the absence of residents and functioning surveillance cams, Snow had no eyes on the district but his own.

"Are you sure it's safe? Where does that tunnel come out?"

The map shifted sideways and zoomed out, a point on the Fifty-First Tier marked in green. A straight line connected it to a building several blocks around the Forty-Eighth Tier from his location. Adrian took this to mean that the tunnel led under the wall and surfaced a few blocks from Western Avenue on the far side.

Burned out buildings loomed overhead as he turned down the gently curving street to his right. Abandoned storefronts crawled past, their contents long since burned or looted. His footsteps seemed painfully loud in the silence.

The building Snow had led him to stood intact but lifeless beneath its jacket of corroded solar cells. Its doors were furry with pollution, untouched in years. He spent thirty minutes sifting through trash piles before he found a rusted section of pipe to serve as a pry bar. It took another fifteen minutes of sweating and straining to overpower the lock.

The stale air that flowed from the dark opening was hot and fetid even by the standards of street level. Adrian dug out his flashlight and peered inside. A lifeless hallway greeted him, the floor thick with dust. Snow's map zoomed in on the interior of the building as if urging him forward, displaying a short path to what he assumed was the tunnel entrance.

Within, makeshift sleeping spaces lay toppled across the hallway. Many of the doors to the original living spaces had been torn off their tracks. There was no sign of the occupants. It was as if they had vanished into thin air, leaving all their worldly possessions behind.

The farther he traveled into the building, the more impure the air became. A warning popped up, reminding him that low oxygen environments could cause brain damage or death, and sagely advising him to return with an oxygen pack. Adrian blinked the warning away and walked faster.

Beyond another maintenance access, the door of which was already broken, a set of narrow stairs descended into the bowels of the building. An Enforcer's riot shield lay at the bottom, covered in dust.

Impending suffocation made the room feel claustrophobically small. Pipes and skeins of wiring, the guts of the building's utilities, covered the walls and ceiling. A bank of control panels dominated one side of the room, their old-fashioned interactive faces dark and lifeless. Had the riot shield's owner been attempting to restore power?

At the back of the room, tucked between banks of silent electronics, Snow highlighted another locked maintenance access. Adrian stared at his makeshift pry bar and took a few deep breaths.

A splitting headache came on as he struggled with the door. He had a sudden recollection of Williams' sneering comment about pumping overcrowded towers full of carbon monoxide. If he was forced to turn back, would he be able to get out of the building in time?

The lock gave way with a deafening crack and air rushed through the gap, stirring the dust. He took a deep, grateful breath of the draft from the utility corridor, shouldered the broken door aside, and peered into the tunnel. Thick conduits for wiring, water, and sewage ran along the ceiling. Dust and darkness waited between the narrow walls.

Adrian turned back and grabbed his bag, nearly forgotten in his haste to escape the building. The breeze continued to whisper past his ears as he stepped into the utilidor. Somewhere at the far end, there was open air. If he could have, he would have run toward it. The weight of the building seemed to settle on his shoulders, attempting to pin him in place. Steps unsteady, he pressed onward.

***

The utilidor sloped gently downward and seemed to go on forever. When he opened Snow's map to track his progress, he found that he was passing beneath the Forty-Ninth Tier.

Exhaustion weighed on him. Shadowy figures plagued the edges of his vision, begging for help, before melting back into the stained gray walls. Snow presented him with an article about insomnia-induced hallucinations, and highlighted the passage that suggested that the best cure was sleep. Apparently the program felt the utilidor was as good a place as any to take a nap.

Here and there side corridors joined the tunnel, their echoing reaches home to nothing but dust and shadows. No one seemed to have ventured into this part of the utilidor network in years. A lonely place, its silence broken only by his dragging footsteps, it seemed the safest of all the places he had passed through.

A three-sided nook beckoned, home to a row of darkened control panels. The alcove provided a quiet spot, sheltered from the whispering breeze, where he might lean his shoulders against the wall and catch a few moments of rest. He promised himself that he wouldn't even close his eyes. He just needed to gather his strength.

The world went dark.

* * *

Pain woke him. The surface under his body was cold and hard, the darkness full of rustling and chittering. Sharp teeth bit into his hand as he sat up and began to search for his light. Adrian screamed and scrambled to his feet, shaking off vermin. They squealed in indignation and mobbed him, biting and clawing.

The flashlight, he realized, was still connected to his wrist by its safety strap. It must have shut off when he passed out and fell over. Who knows how long he had lain unconscious in the darkness, but it had been long enough for the vermin to find him.

The light wouldn't come on, so, swearing in frustration, he smacked it against his leg until the contacts realigned with the battery and granted him a dim beam of illumination. It revealed an utilidor packed with vermin, beady black eyes glittering. They were not deterred by his shouts, his flailing, or his dim light. They latched onto his legs with razor teeth and fought to climb his clothing, biting higher. For each one he sent flying, two more took its place.

Snow popped up an article at the edge of his visual display, an old one judging by the obsolete font. He blinked it away in annoyance.

The piece reopened, obscuring his entire field of view. It was an article on the Safety Division's new crowd control device. The contents had been briefly covered during his training. Although it had been deemed obsolete, older Heroes were still equipped with the destructively loud defensive augmentation.

"You have it, but you shouldn't use it," his instructor had said. "Citizens will get hurt, and you probably will too." Crowd control was best left to the professionals.

Drowning in a furry tide of biting, clawing vermin, Adrian took a deep breath and screamed.

The sound quickly surpassed the decibel level of human vocalizations. His ears popped and the skull-splitting headache returned with a vengeance. Vermin writhed, squealing in pain and terror, and ran into the walls. Adrian recalled that the things were mostly blind, relying on smell, hearing and touch to find their way, and he almost felt sorry for them.

Out of breath, the enhanced scream died in his throat. His ears rang. The vermin had bitten through his clothes everywhere they could reach, covering him in bloody, stinging bites.

Some of the rodents fled. Others milled, bumping into each other and fighting in their confusion. Adrian did not wait for them to come to their senses. He gathered his bag and jogged down the tunnel, hoping the smell of blood would not attract more.

* * *

The bites had ceased to sting. His head and ears continued to ache, and aside from the roar of his own pulse, the world had gone mute. He could not hear his own footsteps, the rasp of his breathing, or the whisper of the breeze.

When he ran his fingers over his ears, they came back crusted with blood. Had he ruptured his eardrums? It was small solace to think that, without the crowd control weapon, he might have been eaten alive. A Hero without hearing was not good for much.

With that grim thought for company, Adrian finally reached the Fifty-First Tier. A narrow side tunnel led to a broken maintenance hatch and a utility room. Although the space was cluttered with bedding and personal effects, only vermin tracks marred the dust. No one had lived there in a long time.

Nothing remained of the building above but a tangle of listing support beams, the original structure long since demolished by fire. Although night had fallen at street level, the smoggy darkness seemed bright after the utter lightlessness of the utilidor. He turned off the flashlight and switched on his night vision.

The streets of the Fifty-First Tier slept under a blanket of pollution, the surrounding towers dark and lifeless. A few ancient solar cells still clung to their faces, the architecture of a bygone era slowly crumbling from air pollution and toxic rain. Faded graffiti splashed the walls, monochrome in the darkness.

Adrian turned in a circle, searching for some sign of life. A faint glow seeped through the smog back the way he had come, topped by a row of blinking red beacons. He was looking at the wall, the official border of the Company-controlled city. Ten stories of impenetrable gray composite bristling with surveillance cams and spotlights, the wall encircled the outer edge of the Fiftieth Tier, cutting the city above off from the forsaken tiers below. Enforcers patrolled along the top and around the base, concealed by the smoggy darkness.

Where were the teeming multitudes of lawless citizens that were supposed to inhabit the tiers outside the wall? The downgraded, the Anarchists and criminals? If these tiers were the reason there was never enough of anything to go around, where was everyone?

His stomach growled, and he wished he'd saved some of the meal packets. As disgusting as the concept of eating processed human flesh was, it was better than starving. Adrian sighed and leaned against the side of a nearby building to think.

He had expected to find people here. He had planned to find those who needed help and trade his services for food and water. Now, staring down the deserted avenue into the darkness of the forsaken tiers, he wondered what would happen to him.

# CHAPTER FIFTEEN

As the hours ticked by, eerily deserted districts fell behind him. A drop of only a meter or two separated each tier from the next, and there was no sign of the security checkpoints that divided the tiers of the city above. Had the citizens once been free to move about the city as they wished?

On the Fifty-Fourth Tier he found signs of more recent habitation. Makeshift shelters leaned between vacant buildings, the residents' possessions still inside. A child's plush toy lay at the entrance to one, spilling stuffing. Clothing had been hung from beams and wires to air out, as if someone planned to return for it. Where had these people gone, leaving all their worldly possessions behind?

Morning came and went. As noon approached, a murky brown twilight gradually came to street level. A handmade wall marked the boundary between the Fifty-Fourth Tier and the Fifty-Fifth, and although Adrian walked along it for several blocks in either direction, he could find no point of entry.

The lower floors of nearby buildings had been stripped down to their internal supports to form the barrier, an impressive edifice that rose to nearly twice Adrian's height. The word "quarantine" and a series of grim pictorial warnings faced those coming down Western Avenue. What had its creators been trying to contain?

Adrian paused to consider his options. His Company vaccinations and genetic resistance to disease left him with little fear of sickness. His sensors detected no more life beyond the barrier than in the streets behind him.

After building a ramp out of debris and scraps left over from the creation of the barricade, he was able to pull himself up and over the structure. The avenue on the far side lay deserted under its pall of brown smog.

The stink of rot and human waste grew as he crossed the tier, and he began to see groups of starving, sickly vermin. Some of the creatures carried rough, scaly growths that hindered their ability to move. Those that died appeared to have been cannibalized by their own kind.

Ramshackle hovels crowded many of the side streets. Even through his mask, the stench within the shantytown was nearly overpowering. Deformed vermin fled his footsteps. Someone had scrawled the phrase "heaven help us" on a nearby wall.

Peering into one of the shacks, he was confronted with a strange sight. A rough, lumpy, gray-brown object lay atop a pile of filthy bedding. Its stubby appendages reminded him of the gnarled limbs of some deformed tree.

Nudging the thing with his boot, he found it weighty, but not as massive as it appeared. The scabrous surface cracked under his touch, revealing more gray material beneath the initial topography of dark brown peaks and ridges. A vermin popped out of the side and fled, beady eyes bulging in terror.

The more he stared at the thing, the more the feeling of wrongness gnawed at him. There was something unspeakably horrific about the jagged, scabrous lump, yet he could not define why it affected him so.

Adrian ducked out of the shack, skin crawling, and performed a cursory search of the rest of the shantytown. He found many more of the scabrous lumps, but of the human residents, there was no sign.

*** 

Another haphazard barrier separated the Fifty-Fifth Tier from the Fifty-Sixth. Piles of charred debris choked the street beyond, covered in sooty dust. It reminded him of ancient photographs of war zones.

Some of the buildings had fallen, their ruined bulk spilling across the pavement in a tangle of beams and twisted composite. Others leaned drunkenly, awaiting the right catalyst to give in to the effects of gravity. Charred trees lined the avenue, their bare branches stretching toward the sky like skeletal hands.

In the monochrome darkness of evening, he once again lost track of time. Sleep beckoned, stealing snatches of his consciousness as he walked, retreating each time he stumbled or mistook some piece of trash for a threat. Abandoned districts plodded by, muffled under a layer of pollution.

In his exhausted state, he almost missed the shantytown. A patchwork wall blocked the entrance, its exterior covered in threatening pictorial warnings. Flickering orange light glowed on the other side. Adrian's heart leaped at the sight.

He paused outside the entrance and skimmed through his library of Company programs, searching for something that would allow him to communicate with the residents. There was a sign language interpreter, but he found it unlikely that anyone down here knew sign language. He also had a lipreading program, but it was an inaccurate science, easily hindered by poor lighting and speech impediments.

As he stood lost in thought, a rough hand grabbed his shoulder. Adrian twisted away, surprised to find a handful of people behind him. One of the smaller men stepped forward and put his hands up, palms out. He appeared to be speaking. Adrian launched the lipreading program and crossed his fingers.

The pale-haired representative, meanwhile, had begun to look concerned. Glancing down the darkened street, he tapped the Hero's arm and gestured urgently toward the gated shantytown. Adrian allowed the group to steer him through the barricade, noting that two of their companions quickly blocked the opening with a thick piece of composite.

One of the larger men leaned into Adrian's face, expression hostile.

"Where are you from?" he demanded. "How did you get here? Answer me!" The words appeared as white text at the bottom of Adrian's view.

"I came from above the wall," Adrian replied calmly. "I was going to be downgraded, so I ran."

The smaller man was speaking at the same time, but the program only caught an unintelligible jumble of words.

"What?"

"How'd you get across the wall?" the sandy-haired man repeated with exaggerated care. "We haven't gotten any new downgraded in years."

One of the others grabbed Adrian's arm and forced the Hero to face him.

"Why come here?" The speaker was a wide shouldered man with a pronounced hump. His body language was blatantly hostile. "How'd you find this place? You're a long way from home, boy."

"I just found a tunnel that led under the wall and ran. I had no idea this place was here until I saw the lights."

The hunchback sneered and muttered something to his companions.

Meanwhile, the pale-haired man gave Adrian a sympathetic nod. "That's a long walk," he said. "You must be tired."

Adrian eyed the men warily. The rest of the group seemed to be speaking among themselves, and their body language was less than welcoming. The hunchback and several others closed around the pale-haired man, gesturing angrily at Adrian. He could imagine what they might be saying. People down here undoubtedly didn't need another mouth to feed.

"I can help," he offered. "I can work. I'm not looking for charity."

The group continued conferring among themselves. Finally the group's pale representative turned back to him and nodded.

"You can stay if you're not carrying crawlers."

"What?"

"Crawlers. Maggots," the hunchback snapped, leaning into Adrian's face. "You know, those worms as make the itchy threads in your skin?"

"I don't have anything like that."

"Good. We kill anything that shows signs of them."

"You're safe here," the representative said, turning Adrian away from the hunchback. "Come with us."

The town consisted of a maze of ramshackle structures that filled the dead-end alley from wall to wall. Having outgrown the space at hand, haphazard stacks of residences climbed the tower walls on every side. Makeshift lamps dangled overhead, strung from wires that crisscrossed the open space above. Little more than tightly wadded balls of rags and trash, they produced plumes of sooty black smoke and were the source of the wavering orange light he had seen from the street.

The group led him toward the large structure that occupied the rear of the alley. Light and shifting shadows spilled through the many gaps in its walls.

A tattered blanket formed the door. The interior was smoky and sweltering. Nearly two dozen people sat at tables made of composite slabs resting on salvaged furniture, or at the old-fashioned bar that occupied the back of the room. Noting the glossy genuine wood, Adrian guessed it had been looted from someplace that had once been much more posh.

The group's representative tapped him on the shoulder and waved a hand in front of his face. He realized that the man had been talking to him for some time. What he had thought was blonde hair in the darkness was in fact a mop of greasy gray curls.

"Nice mask you have there," the man was saying. "You mind taking that off? You're making people uncomfortable."

Adrian peeled off the filtration mask and tucked it into his bag. Without it, the stench of unwashed bodies was nearly overpowering.

"You deaf, man?" the hunchback demanded, moving in front of him. "You don't listen so good."

"I am," Adrian admitted. "I lipread. I can't tell what you're saying unless I'm looking at your face."

"Huh. Nice bag you have there."

"What you got in the bag?" one of the hunchback's friends asked, peering over the other man's shoulder.

"Nothing good. Just junk." He was acutely aware that it contained valuables and a very recognizable uniform.

"Hand it over," the hunchback demanded, reaching for the shoulder strap.

"Hands off," Adrian retorted, taking a step back.

A wiry man with an impressive collection of pockmarks joined the group, trapping Adrian between a wall of bodies and the bar. His lower lip was lopsided and misshapen, and his left eye was covered with a white film of scar tissue.

"He's gonna be trouble, I can already tell," the wiry man said. "What did you do up there on the Company tiers, tough guy?"

"Street cleaner. Garbage man," Adrian said, thinking quickly. He did not have the physique of an average citizen, and he picked one of the most physically intensive jobs he could think of to justify it.

"You gonna pick up our garbage, garbage man?" The hunchback sneered. "Gonna sort and recycle all that trash out there?"

"If that's what you need me to do."

The gray-haired representative elbowed his way into the group, pushing the others back.

"I'm Andy. What do you go by?"

"Adrian."

The hunchback sneered. "Ooh, an upscale name. We got

ourselves a fancy one here."

Andy turned to argue with the hunchback, and after a moment the group backed off and settled farther down the bar.

"Don't mind Neal and his boys," Andy said, turning back to Adrian. "They're good guys."

Adrian nodded.

"I know they have rough edges, but we need them," Andy insisted, as if sensing that Adrian's silence hid disagreement. "They keep the peace. Without them, people would be at each other's throats."

"I see."

"If you want to join us, there are a few rules you'll have to follow. Can you do that?"

"Depends on what they are."

"Just reasonable things," the man said, smiling reassuringly. "No picking fights or starting trouble. No stealing. Anything that someone else is already using is theirs."

Adrian nodded. The room behind his host swam, the crude lamps casting jittery shadows. Many of the residents were still staring at him.

"You're responsible for making your water allowance last until the next distribution, understand?" the representative concluded. Adrian realized he had lost track of the conversation when he looked away.

"I'm familiar with how water rationing works."

"Very good. You'll start out as a scavenger. You bring back everything you find, understand? Neal deals with those who horde for themselves."

The hunchback leaned over Andy's shoulder and grinned unpleasantly, showing off teeth blackened by decay.

"Sounds fair enough."

"Welcome to the Free Men's Society. Work for the best of the group and don't break the rules, and maybe one day you'll earn a promotion!"

Adrian nodded, too tired to ask what he might be promoted to.

"Someone tell Lindy to get the new man some food," his host said.

One of Neal's group disappeared through a curtain behind the bar, and a few minutes later a smaller person came out, draped from head to toe in grimy brown cloth. The hooded figure carried a plate.

It was not until the citizen set the plate in front of him that Adrian realize it was a young woman. Nervous brown eyes met his for a split second from under a fringe of matted dark hair. One side of her face was dark and swollen with bruising.

Lindy Enstrom, formerly a resident of the Fiftieth Tier. The word "evicted" had been digitally stamped across her residency file in glowing red letters. She was only seventeen, and had little in the way of medical history or convictions. Her only crime had been the circumstance of being born to creditless parents. She had been downgraded at age thirteen.

The young woman ducked her head and hurried away, flinching out of reach as someone at the bar grabbed at her. Adrian continued staring even after she disappeared into the curtain at the back of the room, skin prickling. All of the signs pointed to abuse. Was that how new members of the group were treated?

Neal seized his shoulder and spun him around.

"Don't stare! She belongs to someone else."

"Who?"

"That's not important," Andy said quickly. "You'll get one of your own if you pull your weight. For now, how about some food?" He gestured at the plate the young woman had left on the bar.

The dish held a small pile of steaming gray chunks in watery sauce and an old-fashioned metal fork. Adrian picked up the fork, speared one of the chunks, and cautiously tasted it. The meat was bitter and bordering on rancid.

"What is it?" he asked, glancing at his host.

"Rat. It's the most plentiful thing down here, and it keeps the little bastards from overrunning us."

Adrian speared another piece of meat and tried not to gag as he choked it down. After watching him for a few moments, Andy tapped him on the shoulder.

"Something wrong with the food?"

Adrian shook his head. He might have turned the meal down, but he was ravenous and it didn't seem likely that he would get anything else anytime soon.

By time he finished eating, the others had turned to talking among themselves. Adrian pulled his bag into his lap, laid his head on the lacquered wood of the bar, and promptly passed out.

* * *

He was awakened by someone tugging at his bag. Opening his eyes, he found a gaunt young man trying to get into its pockets. Adrian yanked it back, scowling. The teen put his hands up and backed away.

Nearly four hours had passed while he slept. Andy was gone, but the bar was not much emptier. Neal and his group were gathered a few stools down, watching a dancer use the top of the bar as a stage.

The dancer's face was concealed under a gray scarf that hid everything but the faint sparkle of dark eyes. Below that, she wore a simple dress sewn from a single piece of delicate ivory cloth. There was not enough fabric to meet at the sides or form sleeves, leaving her shoulders, ribs, and the sides of her legs bare.

Slender and graceful, her movements had an almost hypnotic quality as she swayed down the bar toward him. The garment shifted to reveal flashes of pale skin without leaving her completely exposed. Adrian tried in vain to catch a glimpse of her eyes. What was her name, and what had brought her to this place?

A heavy hand fell on his shoulder. Turning around, he saw unmistakable jealousy in the hunchback's eyes. Neal's friends moved in, grinning unpleasantly, as the dancer began to back away.

"Marissa, why don't you show our new boy your face?" Neal said.

The hunchback grabbed the hem of the dancer's dress and pulled, sending her crashing to the ground in a tangle of delicate limbs and fabric. There were stark, black bruises on her thighs and stomach. The group dragged her to her feet as Neal ripped her scarf off. Grabbing a fistful of tangled brown hair, he forced her to look up and meet Adrian's eyes.

The woman's face was grotesquely lumpy, swollen with oversized pustules oozing yellowish fluid. An eye scan revealed that her name was Marissa Thomas. Her last known residence was on the Sixteenth Tier, where she had worked in the Entertainment District. Her medical files were stamped "Quarantine." Her identity file had been marked "Missing, presumed dead."

"Why don't you give him a kiss, sweetheart?" Neal shoved Marissa toward him.

"The hell is wrong with you people?" Adrian demanded.

"Aw, you'll hurt her feelings." Neal grinned mockingly. There were real tears running from the woman's eyes. "She's diseased, obviously, but it's only contagious if you touch the sores. We took pity and decided not to throw her out with the vermin. She has to dance and put out for food. And she'll do anything for water, so save part of your ration if you want some."

The world slowed to a crawl as Adrian struggled to contain his outrage.

"What's the matter? Can't believe your good luck?" The hunchback laughed.

His self-control slipped. He grabbed Neal by the throat, pinning the bully against the bar. The white-hot rage controlled him. What had been intended to be one punch turned into a succession of blows, bone shattering under his knuckles.

Overcoming their shock, the group converged on him. Neal slumped to the floor as Adrian blocked a punch meant for his head. He grabbed the offending limb and twisted until the man's arm snapped, then elbowed another attacker in the face as the man tried to grapple him from behind. The shantytown's self-proclaimed peacekeepers fell back, leaving him and the dancer alone in the center of the room.

Adrian lifted the woman's scarf with shaking hands, dusted it off, and handed it back to her. He did not think he had ever been so angry in his life. The room was blurry, his heart was racing, and everyone was still moving in slow motion.

Marissa bolted for the exit. As he followed, something struck him in the ribs with nearly enough force to knock him off his feet.

His attacker was the wiry man with the deformed face, and his features contorted with hate as he pulled back the table leg for another swing. Adrian sidestepped the attack, grabbed the man by his stained shirt and matted brown hair, and tossed him into the crowd. He took out several of his comrades before slamming into the wall.

The lights outside had burned low, and the shantytown was full of moving shadows. Something large and dark flowed up the wall to his left as he stepped outside, but when Adrian turned to look, it was already gone.

Marissa's pale form was just disappearing into the maze of shacks. Adrian sprinted after her, struggled to catch up. She was surprisingly fast despite her bare feet. Meanwhile, Neal's friends were beginning to spill out of the bar and pale faces peered from the surrounding hovels. Soon the whole shantytown would be after them.

Turning toward a dead end, Marissa slipped into the gap between two leaning shanties and was off like a shot, pale dress streaming behind her. Even if he turned sideways, the space was too narrow for a Hero's shoulders. Adrian swore and resigned himself to finding another way around.

Rounding a corner, he nearly ran into Andy.

"What have you done?!" the older man exclaimed, eyes wide with horror.

"Did you know what your bully squad was doing to Marissa?"

"Not mine," the man mumbled, glancing away.

"What?" Adrian barked, suppressing the urge to force Andy to face him so he could read what the man was saying.

"We're a free collective," Andy said, meeting his gaze. "Each man is responsible only to himself. I'm not responsible for them."

"What about Lindy and Marissa?"

"That's just the way it is. It's the natural order of things."

"What did you say?" Adrian hissed. He could feel the rage rising up again, threatening to take him over.

Andy cringed. "I don't make the rules. I just try to keep the peace!"

"But you didn't try to stop them, did you?"

"You can take Neal's place," Andy said suddenly, grabbing Adrian's arm.

Adrian stared at the man in disbelief.

"You can't leave us without protection," Andy continued, desperation written across his features. "You crippled our best men. They told me what you did in there. I don't know what you are, but if you stay, you can have anything you want. Anything!"

"I don't want anything to do with you people."

"You can't make it on your own out there. You need us."

Adrian walked away. He hoped Marissa was making her way toward the gate. If her treatment was any indication, how many more were being held captive? Might he be able to rescue them? Adrian wiped his face on his sleeve and glanced back the way he had come.

His thoughts were cut short by the appearance of the mob from the bar, grown from a few dozen men to fifty or more crowded into the narrow avenue that served as the town's main street. Andy was at the front, and he no longer looked desperate. His face contorted in rage as he leveled a shaking finger in Adrian's direction.

The mob surged forward, and makeshift missiles began to rattle against the walls and pavement around him. They were not going to rush him. Having realized the futility of engaging him in hand to hand combat, they were utilizing projectile weapons.

A chunk of cement hit him in the chest, knocking him back, and an expertly hurled metal bar clipped the side of his skull. His sight flickered, and for a moment he saw double. Error windows beset his vision.

Adrian turned and sprinted for the gate, chunks of debris pelting his back and shoulders. The panel that served as a door had already been shifted aside. Choosing a direction at random, he set about putting a healthy distance between himself and the shantytown.

Eventually he paused, adjusted his bag, and took a few sips of his dwindling water supply. There seemed to be no one pursuing him. Adrian sat town on an overturned trash bin and contemplated his options. Marissa's fate, as well as that of Lindy and anyone else the so-called Free Men might be keeping prisoner, weighed heavily on his mind. He tucked the flask back into his bag and headed back the way he had come.

* * *

He found no sign that anyone had ventured out of the shantytown in pursuit of him. Perhaps they had been content to run him out, as if that in itself conveyed a death sentence. Or perhaps they were too afraid of roaming vermin and whatever else the darkness might hold to brave the streets before daylight.

An ominous glow lit up the smog as he grew closer to the shantytown's location. He rounded a corner and the alley came into sight, drowned in a blaze of light that made his eyes burn even as he switched off his night vision. After staring at the ground and waiting for the afterimages to fade, he looked back at the mouth of the alley. The entire shantytown was on fire.

Hot air scoured his skin as he moved closer. Embers rained from the sky. Instinct urged him to push forward and search for survivors, but the rational side of his mind told him there were unlikely to be any. The barricade collapsed with a crash, revealing an inferno where the shantytown had been.

If anyone had escaped, they seemed to be long gone. The surrounding streets were empty except for a few bodies that lay outside the gate. One of them was Andy's. A rough metal spike protruded from his right eye socket.

Even a handful of meters from the entrance, the heat was intense enough to be painful. After taking one last look at the conflagration, Adrian gave up and turned away.

The night seemed cooler and exceptionally dark after the inferno in the alley. His night vision and heat sensors cast the Fifty-Seventh Tier in lifeless monochrome gray. Occasionally he caught furtive movement at the edges of his vision, but there was never anything there. He thought of the eerie wail he had heard in New Maupin, and the peculiar collection of human remains on the Forty-Eighth Tier, and shivered.

Exhaustion played tricks on his eyes as he descended onto the Fifty-Eighth. Shadows flickered across his path, melting into the drifts of trash, or crawled across the walls. There was no light to cast them. Menacing shapes seemed to stalk him through the ruined high-rises, becoming nothing more than broken furniture and fallen walls under closer examination.

A toppled building emerged out of the smog, completely blocking the avenue ahead. Adrian was about to turn down a side street and search for a way around when he spotted a narrow passage leading into the wreckage. The trash had been cleared away from the entrance, and support beams had been wedged inside to hold up the ceiling. He could detect no vermin or other signs of life within. Taking a deep breath, he crawled into the opening.

The passage quickly narrowed, and he found himself breaking out in a cold sweat as jagged pieces of broken composite scraped his shoulders. His bag snagged on a support beam, and he spent minutes carefully working it free. If the tunnel collapsed, no one would be able to hear his screams. There were no functioning network relays nearby to pick up his calls for help. There would be no rescue.

It seemed to take an eternity to crawl the few hundred meters to the other side of the building. At the far end, Adrian dragged himself out of the tunnel under the overhang of a precariously tilted wall. Fallen debris had mostly buried the exit. A white plush toy blocked the narrow gap that remained, suspended by a thin strand of wire. Red paint had been used to give the bear's adorably round face an angry expression. Its fur was matted with dried blood.

As he examined it, the resistance on the suspension wire briefly increased before giving way. The debris around him seemed to shift, and a breath of air brushed his sweat-soaked hair. Adrian dived into the street as the face of the building came down, burying the spot where he had stood in rubble.

He moved out from under the shadow of the unstable building and brushed himself off. The plush toy glowered up at him from the edge of the ruin, its pale fur luminescent in the darkness. It was beginning to seem as if the city itself was out to get him.

Adrian sat down on a wayward piece of debris and opened Snow's map. The program was still telling him to continue down Western Avenue toward the outermost edge of the city. What did it think he would find there?

In the claustrophobic silence of his world, the feeling of unseen menace continued to plague him. A feather-soft touch brushed the back of his neck. He leaped to his feet and spun to confront the threat, finding nothing there but the swirling smog.

Adrian turned in a slow circle, scanning the lifeless streets and empty buildings as his pulse roared in his ears. Finally he shouldered his bag and continued on, unable to shake the feeling that someone or something was following him.

***

Sometime in the early hours of the morning, he spotted the glow of lights through the smog. Adrian approached the settlement with caution, debating whether he wanted to test the friendliness of the occupants.

The illumination came from the center of what had once been a retail area. Makeshift lamps glowed from within empty storefronts, their glass windows long since reduced to jagged shards that sparkled amid drifts of shiny plasfoil cups and wrappers.

"Hello? Anyone here?" Adrian called, poking his head into an empty shop.

Broken mannequins and overturned display racks littered the floor, their clothing long since looted. Despite the profusion of lights, the place was eerily deserted and probably had been for a long time. Real glass was a safety hazard, and plasfoil packaging hadn't been used in over a hundred years.

Adrian investigated each of the vacant storefronts, growing more and more curious. Except for tiny lamps made out of glass jars and twists of cloth dipped in some kind of oil, he could find no sign of human life.

He was exiting another shop when he sensed movement behind him. The shadowy figure jumped back as Adrian spun around, its hands raised in surrender. Greasy black hair fell across the man's face, hiding all but the dark glitter of brown eyes. His wide smile showcased crooked yellow teeth.

The words that appeared at the bottom of Adrian's view lagged a fraction of a second behind the movement of the stranger's lips.

"Easy, man. No harm!"

Adrian forced himself to relax and nod in acknowledgment.

"You don't hear so good, do you?"

Adrian shook his head.

"No worries, man. I didn't think you did. I called out to you and you didn't answer."

"I'm sorry. It's been a long night."

"I'm sure it has. Not good to stop moving at night, not safe. I'm

Moe, by the way."

"Adrian." They shook hands. "Why isn't it safe to stop at night?"

"Creepers, man. They don't like the light, so we got lots of light. Come back to the safe house. No need to stand around out here." Moe turned and disappeared through a set of glass doors webbed with sparkling cracks before the Hero could reply.

Whatever waited in the safe house, it couldn't be worse than the Free Men's Society. Adrian stepped through the broken doors and followed Moe down a dimly lit hallway.

The suite beyond might have once housed a restaurant. Lamps burned on the tables, illuminating a black and white checkered tile floor and warm red walls covered with vintage movie posters. Their flickering light sparkled on the glass cases and counters that lined the back of the room.

The air was thick with the smell of home-brewed alcohol, and the men seated around the large table in the center of the room waved at him with drunken cheer. Adrian felt himself relax a little. The group seemed too inebriated to be dangerous. He found an empty seat and sat down.

The blonde hair and blue eyes of the man on his right were almost certainly cosmetically augmented, a strange sight in a place like this.

"Was you from?" the blonde asked.

"Other side of the wall. I was downgraded."

The man on the far side of the blonde leaned around his companion, grinning with inebriated enthusiasm. Most of his teeth were missing.

"You a mother too?" the second man asked.

"A what?" Adrian suspected that the men were slurring their speech, causing the lipreading program to misinterpret certain words.

"Mother. Like your body. A flesh hacker."

"I guess?"

"Nice," the blonde said, grinning. His teeth were very white. "Mine cost a fortune. Got me downgraded, though." He seemed to laugh, but his expression was rueful.

"I'm sorry to hear that."

Moe reappeared from the back of the safe house and waved to get Adrian's attention.

"Chef's got some dinner left. Want some?" his host asked.

"No thanks, I'm– " Adrian's stomach growled. "Well, if there's extra. I can't pay for it, though. I'm creditless."

"Aren't we all?" Moe said with a wink.

He returned a few moments later with a plain white bowl full of pale chunks in mystery sauce. Probably more stewed street meat, Adrian decided as he accepted the food. The chunks were far less bitter than the cooked vermin he'd had in the shantytown, for which he was grateful.

"Like?" his neighbor asked, poking him in the shoulder to get his attention.

"Yes. It's very good."

The blonde turned and yelled something at Moe, who disappeared into the back a third time. He returned with a glass of homemade alcohol and set it in front of Adrian.

The blonde grinned and lifted his glass. The rest of table joined in, and Adrian reluctantly followed suit. Remembering the incident at the club, he only pretended to drink.

The dark haired man to his left elbowed him in the ribs. "Drink up. Unless you just want to be thirsty."

"I have water," Adrian said, pulling a flask out of his bag and taking a sip. The food was extremely salty.

"Suit yourself." The dark haired man swiped Adrian's glass and emptied it in one gulp.

An argument broke out. Moe and the dark haired man seemed to be yelling at each other.

"Don't fight, guys. I don't mind," Adrian said quickly.

"Awful nice for such a scary looking guy," Moe's neighbor said. "Got them creepy Hero eyes and the personality to match."

Adrian tugged his hood forward, wishing he'd remembered to pull the dark glasses down over his eyes when he came inside. The blonde elbowed him and pointed across the table at his host.

"I said, you're not a Company man, are you?" Moe asked.

"If I was, do you think I would have gotten downgraded?"

"I didn't think so," his host said, smiling. "Never seen one of those down here, and never expect to."

Adrian nodded and scraped up the rest of his meal. The salty chunks of meat had the same metallic tang the air pollution did, but he had grown so used to tasting it in the back of his throat that he couldn't even be sure it came from the food. Suddenly he felt very tired. He blinked and his head sagged. Moe had come around to his side of the table and was clearing away his bowl.

"How you feeling?" his host asked, leaning into his field of vision. "Was the food good?"

"Just tired. It was really good. Thank you."

"Chef will be glad to hear that."

His host disappeared as Adrian laid his head on the tabletop.

"Lightweight," the blonde said, grinning. "Why you so tired?"

"Don't mock the bad man," the blonde's companion retorted, leaning around his friend to peer at Adrian. "Just look at them creepy eyes. That's a man you don't mess with."

The blonde seemed to laugh in response. Many of others were grinning. Before he could ask what the joke was, his eyes slid shut and the world went away.

*　*　*

The river closed around him and Adrian sank like a stone, heavy and immobile. The bottom was cool and dark, the mud silky soft against his skin. He settled, watching darker shadows dart through the dimness. Although the setting was as tranquil as ever, he could not shake the feeling that they were stalking him.

He awoke to find the tiled floor cold and hard under his shoulders. Apparently he had passed out and fallen out of his chair.

Moe, the blonde, and a large man were standing over him, talking amongst themselves. The newcomer seemed huge from his vantage point, a mountain of stomach, wide shoulders and beefy arms in a stained white uniform. Adrian noted with a faint sensation of alarm that the newcomer carried a gleaming cleaver in his right hand.

"Seems out cold," Moe said as he looked down at Adrian. "What you think, Chef?"

The larger man nodded. Chef's face was covered with thick scars, and he appeared to be missing an eye.

"Nice mods," the blonde said, staring down at the Hero. "A real catch, this bad man." He grinned.

"He's not so bad," Moe said, leaning down to shake Adrian's shoulder. "Are you? Can you hear me, tough guy?"

Adrian tried to respond and discovered that he couldn't even twitch the tips of his fingers.

"His eyes are open," the blonde noted.

"With that stuff," Chef said, looking down at him, "eyes open don't mean nothing."

Moe nodded, standing up.

"I like them eyes, though," Chef said, grinning. Most of his teeth were missing. He knelt and peered at Adrian's face, nodding in approval as he tilted the Hero's head from side to side.

"He's got parts. Probably new ones. That's a fresh scar," he added, tapping the side of Adrian's skull.

"He got fancy optics hooked to them creepy blue eyes?" the blonde asked.

"Only one way to find out." Chef grinned. "Bring him." The rest of his words were lost as he turned away.

Adrian was in deep trouble. The knowledge hit him with the weight of a collapsing building, all the more crushing for the fact that he had not seen it coming. These people were not nearly as friendly as they seemed.

The blonde grabbed his boots, Moe took his arms, and together the men struggled to drag him toward the back of the store. The effort ended when the blonde tripped over his own feet and sprawled on the tile.

"Some help here?!" Moe demanded of the group at the table.

A few glanced in his direction, but they all seemed too far into their drinks to provide assistance. Chef returned, cleaverless, and lifted Adrian's shoulders.

Try as he might, he still could not move. A flutter of panic rose in his chest as the men dragged him through a set of swinging doors and down a dimly lit hallway marked with suspicious stains.

After rounding several corners, they entered a wide room lined with counters and cabinets. It had probably been a kitchen and prep area. Now it was dark and dirty, the source of the odor of decay he had been smelling ever since he entered the safe house.

The men lifted him onto a cold metal prep table. Moe said something about light and moved out of his field of view.

"What's the point?" Chef grumbled. "Only got the one eye anyways."

Rough hands patted him down. Moe returned with more lamps, revealing blood stains on the walls and ceiling. There was a pair of human hands sitting on a nearby table. Chef had begun to unbutton Adrian's shirt.

"Let's get him strapped down first," Moe suggested, expression worried. "I got suspicions about this one. Don't know how long he'll stay out for."

Chef snorted. "I gave him triple. He's not getting up."

"They say he's got Hero eyes. Who gets modded like that? And look at this, where he hit his face on the floor." Moe poured something toxic-smelling on a crusty rag and scrubbed the side of Adrian's face. "That ain't no normal tat. That's a Company property stamp. These guys are insane tough, man."

"Fine. Have it your way."

Stiff straps were drawn over his body and pulled tight, securing him snugly to the table and putting an end to any hope of escape. He could not even move his eyes, condemning him to stare at whatever was in his field of view.

Chef rolled Adrian's head from side to side, examining his ears and the scars over his neuroprosthetic implants. The movement gave him a wider view of the room as Moe laid out tools on a nearby table. He saw several bone saws, a pair of pliers, a scalpel, and an assortment of knives. His head was rolled in the other direction, and he caught a glimpse of dismembered human bodies hung up like sides of meat in the next room.

Panic rose, thick and suffocating. His survival augmentations could not overcome whatever they'd drugged him with. He was going to die. After everything he had gone through to escape likely death at the hands of a new owner, he had stumbled into almost exactly the same situation. The irony was not lost on him.

"Where to start, where to start," Chef said, leaning over him. He seemed to be mostly talking to himself.

"Skull," Moe replied. "Do a neat one on his neural interface, and we can trade it to the modders. And take his face apart careful-like. I bet he's got all kinds of fancy nano-prosthetic implants."

Chef grinned, a truly appalling contortion of thick scars, and put down the bone saw in favor of a scalpel. It flashed in the lamplight as he moved it over Adrian's face.

Adrian wanted to scream, but no sound came out. He wanted to beg for mercy, to promise that he was much more valuable alive, but the time for that had come and gone. He was furious at himself for not seeing the opportunity, or the threat in the friendly gathering out front.

He sent a desperate message to both of his captors, hoping one of them would read it before they began cutting. The one for Chef bounced back immediately.

"No recipient ID or compatible neural interface found," said the blinking red text.

The message for Moe returned a moment later. "Recipient's communication module has been disconnected," Snow told him.

"What was that?" Moe asked, glancing toward the front of the building.

"Probably just another fight," Chef said with an indifferent shrug. Moe put down the tools he had been arranging and hurried out of the room.

Adrian was coming to the realization that there was little left he could do. He did, however, have a faint network connection. Somewhere out there, just barely in range, there was a functional relay station. There was no chance of rescue arriving in time to do him any good, but he could at least send a farewell message.

"Mel," he began, "I just want to say I'm sorry. I may not understand why you chose the path you chose, but I hope you're still alive to get this. I hope you have a long and successful career as an Enforcer. I wish you the best of luck with changing the system from the inside."

Chef tilted his head, shifting his view to the far side of the room and the meat locker beyond.

"I won't say that your choice was the wrong one. Maybe mine was. Private service wasn't what I thought it would be."

He was staring at the ceiling again. Chef had released his skull and was looking toward the front of the building. The scalpel hovered above his face, forgotten.

"I had to run. The guy they sold me to was going to sell me off to some shady gene hacker. I'm glad you didn't choose the path I took."

Chef traded the scalpel for the cleaver and moved toward the door.

"I just want to say thank you for everything. You're the closest thing I have to family. Keep yourself safe. And whatever you do, don't come looking for me. If you're getting this, I'm done. I'm gone."

Adrian signed the message and sent it as two flashes of light lit up the hallway. Out of the corner of his eye, he saw Chef jerk and stagger as if he had been punched by an invisible hand. An inky shadow moved into the doorway as the room went black.

# CHAPTER SIXTEEN

Someone was dragging him. The motion encompassed his entire perception of the world. Drag, pause. Drag, pause. Drag, drag, pause.

Occasionally debris became caught under his body, but even when the going was smooth, his captor seemed to be having some difficulty.

Drag, pause. Drag, pause.

The pattern repeated itself until he ceased to notice the motion. He could not hear or see. White text flickered to life in the darkness, his visual implants running through their startup processes. The launch came to a certain point, failed, and restarted.

Fear gripped him. Had they taken his eyes? How many of his implants were missing?

If the butcher had done a careful job, he could have survived the operation. It was theoretically possible for a person to survive losing the neuroprosthetic augmentations that had helped them define their world since early childhood. The brain could grow new connections to replace those it had lost. After an adjustment period, some people went on to make a full recovery. Others lost some or all of their senses. Some simply went insane.

He tried to lift his hands to his face, but could do no more than struggle weakly. The person dragging him released his arms and removed a piece of debris that had become wedged under his upper body. A warm hand checked his pulse and squeezed his shoulder.

Eventually he noticed that the startup process was failing at the line that queried whether the user was conscious.

"Override."

His sight finally returned, showing him a desolate avenue suffused with the hazy light of late morning. Deserted housing towers rose into a ceiling of brown smog, their walls buttressed by drifts of trash and stained with faded graffiti.

A shadowy figure wrapped in a billowing black poncho was crouched beside him, Adrian's duffle bag slung over its shoulder. A long black beak protruded from the garment's generous hood. Round black eyes, seemingly all pupil, reflected a glimmer of light from under a tangle of dark hair that more closely resembled braids of wire than human locks.

He had seen some bizarre mods over the years, but this was unlike anything he had ever encountered. Adrian struggled to his elbows and scrambled backward, a primal sense of self-preservation urging him to put as much distance as he could between himself and the creature. The thing settled amid its pool of dark fabric and watched him drag himself out of reach.

His shoulders hit a pile of garbage, sending plasfoil wrappers raining down around him as the creature rolled his bag off onto the ground. Gloved hands lifted back the hood, and in the light its face had the gloss of man-made material rather than skin. The eyes were the round, black lenses of a pair of goggles, the beak an addition to an old filtration mask. A faint movement of the person's head made him think they were speaking.

"I can't hear," Adrian said, touching his ears. "I lipread. I'm sorry."

The figure unbuckled the mask and slid it off. The face beneath was that of a woman, with high cheekbones, a strong jaw, and the deepest tan he had ever seen. Her bright hazel eyes were flecked with gold, her hair plaited into a multitude of tiny braids that gave her the silhouette of Medusa, the fearsome Greek monster who could turn men to stone.

"Think you can stand?" she asked, the words appearing in the lipreading program's familiar plain white font.

He braced himself against the trash pile and tried to lever himself to his feet, but his legs weren't cooperating.

"Chill." The woman scooted closer and patted him on the shoulder. "We can rest here for a few minutes. We just don't want to be here when your friends come looking for you."

"They aren't my friends."

"I'll say. They were about to carve you up when I walked in."

"I shouldn't have trusted them."

"They drugged you."

He couldn't tell if it was a question or not, so he just nodded.

"Don't feel bad. You're not the first one. They've got a whole meat locker full of people who fell for their friendly act." She pulled out a dented flask and offered it to him. "Water?"

"Thank you, but I think I have some."

He pulled the bag to his side and rummaged through the pockets until he found his flask. Nothing seemed to have been removed while it was out of his possession. Perhaps the group had been too inebriated to think of robbing him.

The woman took a sip of her water and looked at him thoughtfully as the smog swirled around them.

"What's with the tattoo?"

"It's my badge." Perhaps, like Moe and his friends, she wanted to know if he was really a Company man.

Her lips twisted into something that could have either been a small smile or an expression of mild annoyance.

"I've never seen someone with one. What does it mean?"

"It means I'm a Hero. Or I was, anyway."

"I thought Heroes were an urban legend."

"How?" he asked, perplexed.

"I've lived below the wall my entire life, and the only Company men we get down here are Enforcers. I assume Heroes are something different?"

"Yes. We're not like them."

"What do Heroes do, then?"

Adrian took a deep breath and prepared to begin his cheerful explanation of a Hero's purpose, but it came out as a sigh.

"We're created to serve and protect. We do our best to keep people safe, even if it costs us our lives. We perform our duty from the day we graduate academy until the day we die."

"What do you mean, created?"

"Heroes are lab-created human beings." He found himself looking at his hands rather than at his rescuer, despite the lipreading program's protests. "We're people, but in the eyes of the Company, we're less. We're not citizens. Until the Company decided we were obsolete, there were thousands of us."

"That's appalling," she said when he looked up. "I'm surprised they let you go."

"They didn't. Some of us were sold to private citizens. Some of us were given to Enforcement. And some of us..." He recalled Nelson's plunge from an upper floor of the Safety Tower. "Some of us died.

"Eventually I ran. I thought I might be safe down here. I thought there were a lot of people on this side of the wall, and I could make a living by helping those in need." He laughed ruefully and gestured toward the empty streets around them. "I had no idea it was like this."

"There are people, if you know where to look. We're just good at keeping to ourselves." She extended her hand. "People call me Vey." Her grip was warm and strong.

"Adrian."

Vey stood and helped him to his feet.

"Think you can walk now?"

Whatever the butcher had laced his food with, it was incredibly slow to wear off. His knees were weak, his legs felt like they were made of lead, and the foggy feeling that had plagued him since he regained consciousness seemed to also interfere with his balance.

"I don't think I'm going anywhere yet. You can leave me here. I'll be alright."

"I'm not going to leave you after I went to all that trouble to save you." Vey slung his bag over her shoulder and put her arm around his waist. "Lean on me and you'll be fine."

***

As the afternoon wore on, Adrian gradually regained the ability to walk on his own. The metallic taste of the tainted food lingered in the back of his throat, and he found himself taking extra sips of his water in an attempt to wash it away.

"You're going to run out of water if you keep that up," Vey said when they paused to rest.

"I can still taste that stuff they fed me."

"Human flesh does have a unique taste."

"That's what that was?" He was appalled.

"Vermin can be hard to catch if you're not clever. Some people have a moral objection to eating other people, and I think it's unhealthy. Your most recent hosts had no such objections. And they were lazy."

Adrian put down his flask and staggered to his feet. He barely made it as far as the nearest trash pile before his stomach attempted to turn itself inside out, and he spent a few minutes dry heaving before he managed to recover his composure.

"Try not to do that," Vey said when he returned. "Waste of good water."

Adrian wiped his mouth and eyed his own flask. It was getting low.

"Where do you get water down here?" he asked. "Are there dispensers?"

"None that are working. We collect rainwater and use condensers to capture water vapor out of the air. Occasionally you can find unopened flasks if you know where to look."

Adrian nodded and resolved to ration his dwindling supply more carefully.

****

Vey paused in front of a dilapidated housing tower and removed her mask.

"How are you with heights?" she asked.

"Good, I guess." He didn't enjoy the feeling of facing a drop of hundreds of meters, but he felt that it was something he handled well.

"That's good, because we're going up."

"Here?"

Support beams showed through building's broken walls like the protruding bones of an emaciated behemoth. Frayed wiring hung in the gaps, swaying gently in the breeze. The structure seemed anything but stable.

"Last chance to say if you're afraid of heights."

Adrian shook his head. Vey fitted the mask back over her face and led him into the building.

Smoggy daylight filtered into the structure through broken windows and gaping holes. The lifts were inoperable, and many of the staircases seemed to have been deliberately demolished. The living spaces were completely empty beneath their film of grime, as if the place had been deserted long before calamity struck. Only a few personal items remained. At an intersection of hallways, a brown stuffed bear sat on a chair as if keeping watch, its black button eyes filmy with dust.

Fifteen floors above the street, Vey led him to a gap that framed brown smog and dangling wires. A single, naked beam stretched out into the murk. His rescuer moved out onto the beam with confident steps, as if it were no more dangerous than a bridge with handrails. Adrian swallowed a wave of vertigo and followed.

The pollution stretched out below his feet, soft and insubstantial. He kept his eyes on the beam and reminded himself that he had crossed many such narrow walkways. When he glanced back the building behind them had vanished, swallowed by the smog.

The beam ended not at a gap, but at a marginally wider beam suspended against the side of a building. The second support shifted as they stepped onto it, and Adrian eyed the cables that held it up with misgiving. Vey flashed him a thumbs-up, as if to say that the movement was normal.

They continued to ascend as they crossed the Seventieth Tier, the buildings around them as deserted as the streets below. Peering down from another narrow beam, his sensors calculated the drop at a little more than two hundred meters.

Eventually they came to a rooftop where hooded ventilation ducts stood like hunchbacked shadows beneath a thick coating of pollution. A breeze ruffled his hair, and high above he could see a patch of hazy sky.

Vey led him into the forest of corroded vents and pried up one of the roofing tiles, revealing a rusty metal disk. Pulling a hook from her belt, she pried open the cover. Warm, stale air flowed out to greet them.

She removed her mask and gestured toward the hole. "Hop in."

"What's down there?"

"A safe place. There are facilities, and probably even some water and food packets."

"What about air flow?"

"There's a backup ventilation system. Go ahead, have a look."

Adrian knelt and peered into the hole. The aperture provided little illumination, and the room below remained muffled in shadows. He patted his pockets, searching for his light. Before he could locate it, Vey pulled him off balance and kicked his feet out from under him.

He landed flat on his back in what had probably once been the penthouse suit of the tower. A table and several chairs lurked in the dimness to his right. Darkened doorways led to the other rooms of the suite.

"Not nice!" Adrian yelled, climbing to his feet.

Vey slid though the opening feet first, paused to pull the lid shut, and dropped to the floor next to him.

As the stuffy darkness closed around them, Adrian detected a faint glow from one of the doorways. The room beyond held a wall of windows concealed behind a privacy screen. Outside, the smoggy afternoon was fading into early evening darkness.

There was a bare mattress against one wall, and a strange assortment of machinery in the opposite corner. Wires connected a modified stationary bicycle to a metal box, which was wired to a set of portable power cells.

Vey cranked one of the stationary cycle's pedals hard enough to set the wheel spinning. The lights in the suite flickered to life, and a breath of air flowed through the room. A scattering of red lights came to life atop the battery bank.

"Keep that spinning so we have light and air. I'll see what we have for food and water."

Adrian mounted the bike and pedaled furiously. The equipment was angled so that he could see most of the suite's main room, and he watched as Vey pulled off her poncho and stuffed it into a containment bag.

She wore a loose sleeveless shirt and cargo pants tucked into the tops of well-worn black work boots. Both garments were faded to a deep charcoal gray. A utility belt with many pouches and pockets circled her waist, and there was a small pack on her back.

"Impressive," Vey said when she returned. Ten minutes of effort had brought the power level of the first cell up to green. "That'll be fine for now. Fully charged, they'll last a week without intervention."

She slid the screen back across the window and turned back to him. "Make sure all the windows are covered before it starts to get dark. You don't want anyone to see lights in here."

"Do other people use that path?"

"Sometimes. The high paths were here before I was born, same as this hidey-hole. I'm probably one of the only ones with a key now, but you don't want to take chances."

She moved out into the main the room and motioned for him to follow.

"The facilities. You'll notice this door has been switched to open into the bathroom rather than out, and the lock is on this side. This is why it stays locked." Vey unlocked the door and pointed to where the exterior wall of the bathroom had been cut away to form a narrow opening. "The power system only runs two things: the lights and ventilation. There's no water or sewer service."

Adrian was mildly appalled. Although the platform outside the handmade doorway was a meter wide with safety rails, it flexed and swayed under his weight. He hated to think of the state of the street below.

"The bad news is, we're out of food," Vey said when he returned. "Rainwater collection system's dry too. We're still trying to set up a condensation system that won't be visible up top."

"I don't have much water, and I'm out of food."

"I'll bring you some. I'm not going to leave you to starve," she said, flashing him a reassuring smile.

"I'd rather go with you than stay here. I can be useful."

"You have to pass quarantine first."

"I'm vaccinated against pretty much everything," Adrian argued.

"There are things down here I doubt the Company ever developed a vaccine for. If nothing else, you probably picked up some crawlers."

"Someone else mentioned those too. What are crawlers?"

"Parasites," Vey said with a grimace. "They're called crawlers because some people say they can feel the things burrowing under their skin."

Adrian shuddered. "That sounds... unpleasant. Is there a cure?"

"In a manner of speaking. You're not going to like it, though." Vey shrugged off her pack, shook the contents out onto the table, and offered him an empty containment bag. "Put your shirt in this."

A bundle of padded foam unrolled to reveal a med kit. Vey selected a small ultraviolet lamp and dimmed the lights.

"If you catch them early you can kill them off or cut them out. It's not pleasant, but it's better than the alternative." She pulled on a pair of disposable gloves and held the lamp close to him. "Under UV light, their burrows will look like little white threads under your skin. Like right there." She pointed to his right wrist, where a handful of fine white lines zigzagged across the back of his hand and up his arm.

"What's the alternative?"

"They'll keep multiplying and spread to the rest of your body. As the infestation kills the upper layers of your skin, the parasites will burrow deeper. This cycle builds up layers of dead tissue that can become many centimeters thick. If left untreated, an infestation leads to loss of movement, secondary infections, and eventually death. It's not a nice way to go."

"Am I contagious?" Adrian asked, thinking of all the things he had touched in the suite.

"Depends. How long ago did you cross the wall?"

"About thirty-six hours, I think."

Vey's expression betrayed a hint of surprise. "You got down here fast."

"I'm used to doing a lot of walking."

"That's good, though. It takes forty-eight to seventy-two hours for the next generation to start hatching. Until then, nothing short of surgery will detach them from their host. Once the outer layer of your skin starts dying off, you'll shed crawler eggs. That's why areas that have suffered infestations are strictly quarantined."

Adrian shivered, remembering the handmade walls with their grim warnings. The strange objects had been infested human bodies, decaying where they lay.

Vey tapped his shoulder to get his attention. "There are a few more here," she said, indicating his left shoulder blade. "Pants off, please."

Adrian stripped off the rest of his clothing and placed it in the containment bag. He stared at the ceiling as she ran the light over his legs, hoping that she wouldn't notice that he was turning red.

"They're trying to start a nest on the back of your leg," she said when she had finished. "It's not nearly as bad as it could be though, considering where you've been."

He twisted to look and found a tangle of threads on the back of his right calf, glowing faintly under the UV light.

"How do you know where I've been?" he asked, curious.

"The group I belong to watches over the abandoned tiers. We try to keep exploitative organizations like the so-called Free Men's Society in check."

"I didn't know what they were when I joined them. When I found out, I lost my temper. I'm ashamed of that."

Vey grinned. "There's no shame in saving a life. And if I thought you were the same as them, I wouldn't have bothered saving you."

"I doubt I saved anyone's life. I should have stood my ground."

"Running was probably the best idea at that point. The only thing they respect is violence, and they would have killed you if you'd stayed."

"There was a woman named Marissa, a dancer. And a young woman they were keeping in the kitchen looked like she was being abused. There were probably others."

"We freed the innocent. Most of them were kidnapped from other communities. We helped them return home."

The news left him immensely relieved, as if a boulder had been lifted from his chest.

"Now comes the part you won't like," Vey said, pulling a pen-like device from the medical kit. "This is a handheld heating element. It kills parasites and eggs on contact."

She disinfected the back of his calf, then added the wipe to the containment bag.

"This will hurt a lot. Let me know if you need to lie down."

The first touch only stung. The sensation rapidly intensified until it felt like she was holding a white-hot slab of metal to his skin. Adrian gritted his teeth and stared at the wall until his survival augmentations kicked in, relegating to the pain to a distant throb.

"So you're a doctor?" he asked when she was finished.

"Not formally. My gran worked in one of the clinics, back before they moved the wall. She taught me how to handle most of the things we see down here."

"Where do you get your supplies?" The medical kit, as well as the packages of sterile wipes and dressings, all carried Company manufacturing logos.

Her lips twisted in a wry smile. "The Company left these tiers in a hurry. All the clinics and medical stations were abandoned as they were."

The back of his calf had become a tangle of erratic red lines. Vey dabbed ointment over the burns and applied a sterile dressing.

"Let's do your shoulder next. You can sit for this one."

He settled into a chair, and she wiped down his shoulder blade with disinfectant.

"Do you have any family down here besides your grandmother?"

"My gran passed away when I was ten. My parents disappeared when I was thirteen. My little group of watchers and misfits are my family now."

"I'm sorry." He was getting a crick in his neck from twisting to watch her face while she worked on his back, but the conversation made him feel a little less awkward.

"That's the way it is down here. What about you? Do you have family waiting for you above the wall?"

"No. Heroes don't have families."

"None at all? You can't tell me you don't at least have a girlfriend."

Adrian chuckled. "We're not allowed to fraternize with citizens. I could have partnered with another Hero, but they're more like brothers and sisters to me. I guess you could say they were my family, but they're gone now."

"And now you're down here fraternizing with non-Heroes. Shame on you." The lipreading program's white lettering was as emotionless as ever, but Adrian guessed by her smile that the comment had been meant jokingly. "You have an admirable tolerance for pain," she added as she began bandaging his shoulder.

"I've been through worse."

"I can imagine. Those are some impressive marks you have."

"So are yours." Her arms were crisscrossed with thick white scars. "What happened?"

"Crazies with knives. Unlucky falls." Vey shrugged. "I had a rough childhood after my parents disappeared." She finished bandaging his wrist and peeled off her gloves.

"I'm going to lend you a UV light. You should check yourself over for new trails every day. And have some wet wipes," she added, handing him a flat packet the size of his palm. "Get cleaned up and put some clothes on. I'm going to go check for crawlers. You're strongly advised to stay out of the bedroom until I'm done."

After ducking into the modified bathroom to shave and scrub off the worst of the grime, Adrian pulled on a clean uniform and sank into one of hard chairs that surrounded the table. Scrubbed and cocooned in cooling fabric, he felt reasonably comfortable for the first time in days.

Vey returned a short time later. She dug a meal packet out of her pack, split the contents onto two plates, and handed him one.

"You have beautiful eyes," she said after they had eaten in silence for a time. "Are they modded?"

"No, I was born with them."

"Amazing. They're very pretty."

"So are yours," Adrian said, and she smiled the most beautiful smile he had ever seen.

He scanned her eyes, feeling strangely guilty for using the

Company database to hunt up more information about her. Almost instantly, his view was beset by error windows.

"Invalid data. Initiating alternative identification procedures."

Images blurred past his eyes as the program ran her likeness through its facial recognition system, comparing her features to every set of biometrics the Company database.

"This may take a few moments. Please be patient."

That was an understatement. He blinked the display to edge of his vision and refocused on the room around him.

"You alright?" Vey asked.

"Just a little tired."

"Those look like fresh surgical scars on the side of your head. What happened?"

"Just routine surgery to upgrade my neural interface."

"Oh, you have one of those? What's that like?"

Adrian stared at her, puzzled. "Do you mean you don't?"

She laughed. "Most of us down here don't, especially if we were born here."

"I'm sorry. That's just... that's really sad."

Vey shrugged. "Not really. If I wanted one that badly, I could have bought one from the flesh hackers. But I don't. The fact that my gran was too poor to buy my mother an interface was what saved her when this part of the city was walled off. Gran never talked about it much, but I think she barely escaped. Most of the people down here didn't."

"Escaped what?"

"Does the Company not teach people about what happened when they put up the new wall?"

"We were taught that it was a matter of credit. The Executives deemed that this part of the city was too poor to be worth providing services to anymore."

"That's only a fraction of the story. Did you ever stop to wonder why every clinic down here has these?" She held up the UV lamp.

"Think about it."

"They knew about the parasites?"

"They put up the wall because they had an infestation they didn't know how to fight. They had a lot of infected creditless people down here, and the Executives decided it would be easier to wall off the problem than find a cure."

"That's horrible."

"It gets worse. As soon as the wall was in place, they sent in Enforcers to round everyone up. Herded them into giant transport containers. No one ever heard from them again."

Adrian stared at the table. He felt sick, yet somehow the news was strangely unsurprising.

"I'm descended from the people who managed to escape the purge," Vey continued when he looked up. "There weren't many of us to begin with and there are fewer now, even with those that join us from above the wall."

"I'm sorry."

"What's it like up there? Do people have it better on that side?"

"Well, it depends." He thought of the crowding, the brutality of Enforcement, and the announcement he had seen on his way to the wall. "It is if you have enough credit. Otherwise, not so much."

Vey nodded. "When I was a kid, I heard there were parks with fountains and live plants. Are there still places like that?"

"There are a few on the highest tiers. Mostly indoors, in the homes of the wealthy."

"What are they like?"

"They're... very green. And there are butterflies."

Vey frowned. "What are butterflies?"

"Hold on, I think I can show you." Adrian dug the tablet out of his bag and turned it on. His memory of the rooftop garden and the swarm of blue butterflies played across the screen.

"That can't be real," Vey exclaimed as he held the tablet out to her.

They talked long into the night, sharing experiences from their respective sides of the wall.

* * *

Adrian awoke in darkness. The lights had gone out, but a faint, murky glow came from behind the screen, signaling the arrival of morning. He stretched, opened the screen, and investigated the battery bank. Red lights flashed atop the power cells. He climbed onto the stationary bike and pedaled until several had regained their charge.

The UV lamp and heat pen were on the table, as well as a stack of food packets and flasks of water. An old-fashioned paper note lay nearby.

"I'll be back." The words were followed by a gracefully illegible signature.

Adrian broke open a food packet and stared at it. The contents taunted him, both the solution to his hunger and a reminder of one of the Company's most unpleasant secrets. He could either think of it as the same tasteless, nutritionally valuable food he had always eaten, or starve.

As he glumly munched dehydrated food and followed it with gulps of water, he investigated the results of the previous evening's facial scan. The program had been unable to find any record of his host. Her likeness was awaiting addition to the Company's database of unregistered citizens. Adrian deleted it.

After breakfast, he conducted a thorough inspection of the suite. The walls in all of the rooms had been painted a cheerful golden yellow, perhaps by the original residents. The paint was peeling in the corners and had worn away around some of the door frames. The white flooring was patterned with blue vines and bell-shaped flowers, and the window screens were a dusty emerald green.

Eventually he located what must have been the front door of the suite. The entryway had been walled off with a sheet of darker yellow composite, and try as he might he could not find a way to pry it loose.

If he jumped, he could catch the lip of the ceiling panel and pull himself up into the narrow crawl space between the drop ceiling and the roof of the building. From there he determined that the metal cover was not going to budge no matter how much he strained at it. Either it was locked, or Vey had placed something heavy on it when she left.

Out on the shaky platform that served as a bathroom, Adrian stared up at the lip of the roof. At a meter and a half above his head, jumping for it was out of the question. He returned to the suite, locking the bathroom door behind him, and searched for another way out.

Most of the ventilation ducts were in the ceiling, but there was one set high in the wall in the unused bedroom. He carefully unscrewed the cover and set it on the floor. Poking his head into the dusty space, he was greeted by still air and darkness. This duct was not connected to the same system as the others. Finding out where it led, however, was out of the question. The opening was narrower than his shoulders. Adrian screwed the cover back into place, defeated.

He spent the morning and afternoon exercising his damaged hand, breaking only to charge up the battery bank and eat a little dehydrated food. Evening came, drawing darkness down around the pollution-filmed windows.

Beneath the bandages, there was nothing but threads of scar tissue where Vey had burned out the parasites. He could find no further signs of infestation. Deeply relieved, Adrian dressed, stretched out on the bare mattress, and listened to a recording of a river to lull himself to sleep.

***

He did not dream of the river. Darkness held him, and in that darkness things rustled and chittered. He woke up screaming.

Faint gray light filtered past the screen. Adrian cleared his throat, tasting copper. The suite was empty. The vermin had been nothing but a nightmare.

After breakfast, he seated himself in front of a window and stared out at the smog. Regrets and failures haunted him. Ecstasia, and her fall from an Entertainment District rooftop. Nelson's breakdown and subsequent suicide.

The ability to save a life often lay in a simple choice. The choice to walk a jumper home or to a clinic rather than releasing them after a rescue. The choice to question a suspicious individual rather than letting them go. Perhaps he had become too trusting as the years went by, too willing to live and let live.

When he had finally stood up for what he believed in, it hadn't gone well. How would the contest for the position of Prime have gone if he'd just told the Company what they wanted to hear?

In some ways, he had always been a little too outspoken. If he had contained his outrage, perhaps he could have won the position of Prime and saved his fellow Heroes. If he had kept his mouth shut in Williams' factory, he could have kept a handful of people from losing their jobs, and saved at least one family from being downgraded. Adrian scowled at the floor, disgusted with himself.

After a time, he pulled out his tablet and began to sketch the scenes that haunted his thoughts. Morning and afternoon crept past.

As evening approached, he drew a Hero seated in an interrogation room. His thoughts often slipped back to that place, his mind gravitating toward the memory like dirty water circling a drain.

He remembered how the precinct had smelled, a mix of fear and industrial-strength cleaner. He remembered the hard angles of the chair, how the restraints had dug into his wrists, and how every sound had seemed disturbingly loud yet muffled beneath the roar of his pulse.

He kept drawing. It was easier not to think of it as himself. He was sketching someone else's life, someone else's brush with death.

The nameless Hero slumped forward, hanging against the restraints that secured his arms behind the chair. Under his unzipped jacket, his shirt was stained red.

He had lost something there, and in the weeks thereafter. He had considered himself a good Hero, exceptional at his job, essential to the Company. He had thought that he and the Company's Executives held the same values. In the space of a few short weeks, all of those beliefs had been shattered.

Outside the windows, darkness began to fall.

***

The days crept by in a dull gray haze. Each morning brought a reprieve from the nightmares, if little else. A thick layer of smog muffled the windows as thoroughly as exterior blinds, walling him off from the world outside. He desperately missed having people to talk to and the freedom to walk the city's streets. Heroes were not meant to sit idle, and the inescapable suite had begun to feel like a prison.

He took to spending hours out on the narrow platform, legs dangling off the end that had not been used as the facilities. When he came inside from one such break, he found Vey seated at the table next to his tablet.

"Everything alright?" she asked, glancing up.

Adrian nodded.

"How are you feeling? Have you noticed more parasite trails, or anything else out of the ordinary?"

"No. I don't think I picked up anything besides the parasites, and those seem to be gone."

"That's good." She lifted her pack onto the table and began pulling out tightly covered dishes. "I brought food."

"What is it?" The plate she handed him smelled even better than the food from Williams' kitchen.

"Aged spam in a seasoned sauce, served over rice. This is fine cuisine compared to vermin, so I hope you like it. We have an excellent cook."

"What's spam?"

"Salted meat preserved in a tin. It's so old that the main ingredient is listed as pork rather than reprocessed material. Apparently the stuff never goes bad."

"Thank you for sharing," Adrian said, and dug in. The meal tasted as good as it smelled.

"You're a very talented artist," Vey remarked later, indicating the tablet.

"Thank you."

"If I may ask, what happened?"

"I was arrested for something I didn't do."

"You can tell me about it if you want."

Adrian stared at his hands for a long moment.

"I think I'd like that," he said.

***

When he woke up in the morning, Vey was gone. There was a new stack of food packets and water flasks on the table.

Later in the afternoon, a stealthy movement in the main room caught his attention. Adrian left the tablet on the bed and turned up the lights, revealing a furry gray blob on the table. The creature froze and stared at him with one round, yellow eye.

It was not, as he had originally feared, a vermin. The cat's dark gray fur was matted, its ears were badly scarred, and half of its tail was missing. It also seemed to have lost an eye.

"Here kitty, kitty," Adrian called, holding out his hand.

The cat leaped off the table and bolted into the unused bedroom. Adrian rounded the corner just in time to see it wiggle under the cover and up into the wall vent. There were fresh claw marks on the yellow paint below.

Later, as he prepared for bed, he turned around to find the cat watching him from the doorway.

"Here kitty, kitty," he said softly.

The cat blinked at him.

He sat down on the bed and picked up the tablet. The cat left the doorway and made a cautious circuit of the bedroom. It sniffed his boots, then hopped onto the bed and stared at him until he returned to drawing.

***

The cat was nestled against his side when he woke in the morning. It watched him eat breakfast and accepted a few bites of dry food, seeming to have lost its fear of him. When he lifted the flask of water, the cat stood up on its hind legs and gently pulled on his hand with its front paws. He poured a little water into a dish, and the cat quickly lapped it up.

He spent the morning combing the tangles out of the cat's fur, a project that the animal seemed to enjoy. It stretched out beside him on the bed afterward, its remaining eye closed, and looked for all the world as if it was smiling.

Returning to the tablet, he set aside his sketches of the Forty-Seventh Tier and started a drawing of Elysian Fields' rooftop garden.

A solitary Hero occupied one side of the bench overlooking the koi pond. Head down, the man was thoroughly occupied with his tablet. The slant of his shoulders looked sad, defeated by the hand life had dealt him. Adrian frowned at the drawing.

He erased some details and changed others, adding Vey to the other side of the bench. She leaned over and the Hero tilted his tablet, showing her what he was working on. The image made him smile.

Making another copy, he erased part of the image and redrew the pair on the bench. She was leaning against him, and his arm was around her. The tablet sat beside them, forgotten.

***

Vey reappeared midmorning on the twelfth day. When he came inside he found her seated in one of the wooden chairs, feet up on the table, smiling at something on his tablet.

"These places you draw are so detailed, it's like they're real," she said, looking up.

"Some of them are, and some of them might be."

"How about this one?"

She showed him the drawing he had finished the day before. Sun-soaked red cliffs towered above them as they stood at the edge of the water. Cliff swallows dived past their shoulders, fearless, as the sun shone down from a clear blue sky.

"It's somewhere I used to dream about. I don't know if it's real, but I know places like it existed. I thought that if I ever found it, I would want you to see it too."

"I'd like that. I see you've made a friend," she added as the gray cat hopped onto the table.

"It found a way in through a ventilation duct, but it seems friendly."

"Old Tom's a bit ratty, but don't let that fool you. He's a sweetheart."

"He belongs to you?"

"He's one of many that live with us, but they don't really belong to anyone. We share our living space with them, and they keep the vermin away." She paused and stroked the old cat's ears. "Are you ready for your final inspection?"

Adrian nodded.

"You're turning red again," she noted as he undressed. "If I make you uncomfortable, I can bring one of the guys down to do this instead."

"It's fine," Adrian mumbled. It was no different than having one of the Safety Division's doctors look him over.

"Looks like you're clean," Vey said some time later. "Ready to leave?"

"Absolutely."

He tucked the tablet into his duffle bag, made a quick sweep of the suite, and followed Vey out onto the platform. After locking the door behind them, she produced a cable with a hook on one end and tossed it over the lip of the roof above. After pulling themselves up, they donned their filtration masks and set off over the rooftops.

# CHAPTER SEVENTEEN

A breeze ruffled his hair and tugged at his clothing as they made their way across dusty high-rise rooftops and the yawning chasms between. As they neared the end of another single-beam walkway, a handmade wall loomed out of the smog ahead. Cobbled together from rusted beams, pollution-stained composite and spirals of corroded razor wire, it rose to nearly twice Adrian's height.

Little more than a loop of cable held the end of the beam below the face of the wall. If the residents did not want to welcome visitors, they would only have to release the cable to be permanently rid of their guests.

The gate rolled aside as they approached, revealing a wiry young adult whose face and arms were streaked with blue-gray paint. A wrapping of dark rags, secured with knots and pins, covered the guard's torso and muscular shoulders. A pair of tattered black cargo pants, patched so many times there was little original fabric left, were tucked into the tops of scuffed work boots.

Hair shaved down to stubble and a hard, angular face left Adrian in the dark as to whether the guard was male or female. Intense dark eyes held his gaze until he nodded deferentially and looked away.

The guard's identity file was slightly more illuminating. Jessie Park, age nineteen. Born to creditless former factory workers on the Fiftieth Tier, she had been downgraded when she was just seven.

The guard rolled the gate shut behind them, barring it with a thick steel beam. The area behind the wall was enclosed in a tent of translucent fabric that allowed light to enter, but not smog. A ladder ascended to a trap door and a walkway near the top of the gate, providing a view of anyone approaching.

"This is Demon," Vey said, pulling off her mask.

Adrian held out his hand. The gate guard backed away, expression wary.

"Shaking hands isn't really a thing down here," Vey explained. "A lot of people are shy of getting that close to someone they don't know."

Adrian nodded. "Pleased to meet you."

"You as well." Demon's body language remained distrustful, and Adrian noted that she kept her hand near the long sheath buckled to her leg.

"What's in the sheath?" he asked.

She drew the weapon and brandished it in his direction. The blade was nearly as long as his forearm.

"Meet the Pig Sticker. Not even Enforcer armor is a match for this, if you hit the right spot." She grinned. "Nice tattoo, by the way."

"Demon is a bit antisocial," Vey noted as the guard returned to her post above the gate. "But she's an excellent fighter and an outstanding second-in-command."

Adrian nodded. Considering what her childhood must have been like, he found her distrust of people unsurprising.

Filtered air flowed through the network of tents and tunnels, ruffling their hair as they made their through the community. Everyone they encountered seemed happy to see Vey, and she made introductions as they passed.

"This is Gibbs, and his brother, Jack." She pointed out two dark-haired young men seated against the wall of a tent, honing pieces of scrap metal into crude blades. They glanced up, grinned and waved at the mention of their names.

Vey led him into a low tent that smelled of mouth-watering food.

"Gran, our esteemed cook."

The old woman left her stove and shuffled over to give Vey a hug. Although her back was hunched and her hair had long since turned silver, there was a lively sparkle in her brown eyes.

"Veyra! Loki and Lyla are looking for you."

"What did they do this time?"

Gran smiled. "For once, it's not bad news."

"Your name is Veyra?" Adrian asked as they moved on.

"That's the name I was born with, but I don't use it much anymore."

They left the kitchen tent and passed into a larger area that was surprisingly cool.

"There's air conditioning?"

Vey grinned. "It's a side effect of the water collection system. These are condensation machines, powered by the wind turbines and solar cells above. All our roofs also slope toward the middle and drain into holding tanks, so we can take advantage of any rain that falls."

They passed row after row of neatly-wired battery banks.

"Energy is stored here for lulls in the wind, although that rarely happens. We picked this spot because there's almost always a breeze. In addition to the condensation machines, we produce enough energy to power Gran's kitchen, light the community at night, and run Libby's grow lights."

"Grow lights?"

"Oh, you're really going to like that! Have you ever been inside a greenhouse?"

"What's a greenhouse?"

Vey's grin widened, and she motioned for him to follow.

They crossed a shaky suspension footbridge, passed through an entryway made of multiple curtains of translucent fabric, and stepped into a massive tent.

"So this is why it's called a greenhouse," Adrian murmured in awe.

The rooftop was filled with row after row of shelves covered with plants, their thick foliage completely obscuring their containers. Rampant vines dangled from suspended pots, festooned with red and green fruit. The network of metal posts and suspension cables that held up the roof also supported the hanging containers and a plethora of solar-spectrum lights. The air was sticky with humidity and full of the smell of growing things.

"Tomatoes," Vey said, handing him a red fruit. "The red ones are ripe. The green ones aren't ready to pick yet."

The plant had a strange crisp, prickly smell, both aromatic and pleasant, and the round fruit were sweet, tart and savory at the same time.

"They're very good."

"We never had a garden until Libby joined us. She was one of the Company's most successful botanists, and when she left she took the seeds she helped create with her. Their loss was our gain."

While she spoke, a short, stout woman had walked up behind her. The woman's gray eyes flashed angrily as she turned to say something the lipreading program didn't catch.

"Adrian, this is the infamous Libby Lordes," Vey said.

The gray eyed woman looked little different from the other greenhouse workers he had glimpsed through the orderly rows of planting racks. Her brown hair was tied back under a black bandana, and the sleeves of her khaki shirt were rolled up the shoulder. As Adrian held out his hand, she fixed him with a fierce scowl.

"Why would you bring one of them here?" she demanded. "That's a Company man, Vey."

"He isn't anymore. Like I explained to everyone last night–"

"The electronics in their head are impossible to turn off. They're always recording, just like a surveillance camera."

"Is that true?" Vey asked.

"I can choose what I record and who I send it too. And even if the Company wanted to tap into my neural interface, they have no communication with me down here. There are no relays in range. I couldn't send anything to anyone even if I wanted to."

Vey looked shocked. "They can do that?"

Libby continued before Adrian could muster an explanation. "The thing about a neural interface is that it's always connected to the network, and always accessible by the Company. The wearer is just a host. That's why I had mine removed."

"I have no network connection down here," Adrian repeated.

"He's a refugee the same as you are," Vey said. "We need all the able-bodied people we can get."

Libby tucked her hands into the pockets of her faded brown pants and scowled at him. "I don't approve. But I'll save my argument for the meeting."

Adrian couldn't blame her for her concern. An award-winning botanist, she was responsible for tailoring hundreds of crops to the Company's food production needs. In older records, she was hailed as the mother of modern subterranean farming.

She had also lobbied the Company to expand food production to areas outside the city, arguing that existing production methods rendered fresh food too scarce and too expensive for much of the population. Shot down at every turn, she had fought on until the Executives banned her from testifying at agricultural planning meetings.

The final entries in her file painted her as a terrorist who sabotaged Company operations and looted an entire seed bank, causing millions of credits of damage. Information leading to her capture was worth an astounding amount of credit.

Vey paused and turned to him after they exited the greenhouse. "Some of us are a little distrustful of newcomers with ties to the Company. Try not to take it personally. I think they'll warm up to you once they get to know you."

As the tour of the tent-covered rooftops continued, he began to notice that many of the residents were wanted by Enforcement.

Partners Manx and Mandi were responsible for many of the systems used by the community. The pair of self-taught inventors were also wanted for on a staggering two hundred and twenty-seven counts of destruction of Company property. They were thought to have sabotaged everything from manufacturing facilities to the maglev lines that served Company industrial districts.

The young woman he met next was pale and slender. Her thick brown hair fell over her face as she sat on an overturned crate, cradling a brown stuffed bear with glossy black button eyes. Adrian guessed she was somewhere between fourteen and eighteen years old.

"I'm Wisp," the young woman said before Vey could introduce her. "Vey says you're one of the mythical good Heroes."

"I try to be."

The young woman seemed to laugh as she brushed the hair out of her eyes. They were a warm brown not unlike the color of the plush bear she was holding.

Eva Martin, age twenty-one. Like many of the other residents, her identity file had been stamped with a blazing red order to arrest on sight. Immediate detention required. Lethal force authorized. Beneath, the woman's file was loaded with hacking and sedition-related charges. An orphan, she had escaped the Company's custody and gone feral on the crowded lower tiers. She had been condemned to base labor by the age of twelve, deemed a threat to order and public safety by fourteen, and sentenced to death by sixteen.

As her smile gave way to a worried expression, Adrian realized he had let his dismay reach his face.

"Something bothering you, Hero?"

Watching Wisp hug her bear, he wanted to ask what she could have done to earn a death sentence.

"What do you do down here?" he asked instead.

"I hide. What do you do?"

"I try to help people."

"Wisp is our communications specialist," Vey said. "She also collects teddies that have survived the children they were given to."

Wisp smiled nervously and stroked the bear. "Loki and Lyla are looking for you," she said, nodding toward Vey. "They found Mittens."

"Is she alright?"

"Yes. Go see them. They have a surprise."

"Loki and Lyla are the youngest ones here," Vey explained as they moved on. "Mentally, they're pretty mature most of the time. But they still manage to get into a fair amount of trouble."

Warm white lights sprang to life as they made their way back through the rooftop community, and a stripy orange cat strolled past as they entered a covered isle between larger tents.

"Does that one have a name?" Adrian asked.

"That's Trigger. There are quite a few of them, although most are staying out of sight for now. They'll probably come out to meet you once word gets around that you're not dangerous."

"Once word gets around?" he asked, amused.

"I'm pretty sure cats talk among themselves," Vey said as she motioned him toward a long, low tent. "They're intelligent creatures."

The interior of the tent was filled with stacks of crates, boxes and cans, leaving only a narrow isle down the center. Two youths were crouched over something in a dim back corner.

The young woman leaped up and waved at Vey excitedly as they approached.

"This is Lyla," Vey said, "and the other one is Loki. They're not siblings, but they came to us as a pair, and they've been inseparable ever since."

"Besties!" Loki said, stepping forward. He held out his hand, grinning, and Adrian shook it.

Both youths were brown-eyed and medium complexioned. Aside from the fact that his hair was brown and hers was black, they almost looked like twins in their faded gray factory workers' uniforms. Even their haircuts matched, trimmed close on the sides and left long on top.

The young man's identity did not exist in the database. The woman's file identified her as Samanthra Santhrum, adopted third child of Francesca Santhrum and Dubois Markham, residents of the Fourth Tier. A ghost child, her identity had been stolen at birth to allow an affluent couple to conceal an illegal third pregnancy.

As Vey and the youths shared news, a sinuous black form with a white face emerged from the overturned box at their feet and wound itself around Adrian's ankles. The cat had a mask of pale fur, round yellow eyes, and white socks.

"Mittens likes you, so you must be alright," Lyla observed. "Maybe, when they get a bit older, she'll let you pet her kittens."

In the shadows of the overturned box, nestled among scraps of fabric, were half a dozen tiny black and white cats. With one last brush against his legs, Mittens returned to the box and curled up with her squirming offspring.

When Adrian looked up, he realized Loki had been talking to him.

"–keep track of small things," the youth was saying. "We look after the cats, put away the supplies the foragers bring back, and keep inventory. And we carry messages."

"Everybody here helps in their own way," Vey explained. "Come on, it's almost time for dinner."

* * *

Soon the community came together for a communal meal in the wide tent outside Gran's kitchen. The steaming bowls that Loki handed out smelled faintly of cooked vermin, but the taste was overwhelmed by a medley of vegetables and herbs. For street meat, it was surprisingly good.

When everyone had finished eating, Vey led him to the front of the group. He turned slightly to the side so that he could read her lips while still mostly facing the assembly.

"For those of you who haven't met him yet, this is Adrian." A sea of solemn faces turned toward him as Vey spoke. "He was once a Company man, but he no longer works for them."

Libby stood and folded her arms. "How do you know he wasn't followed?"

"I wasn't," Adrian said. "I'm sure."

"He could be lying. They send infiltrators, Vey."

There was a commotion off to one side of the tent as Wisp pushed to the front, cradling a red stuffed bear.

"He can't be an informant," she said. "There are no functional relays near here. They can't talk to him and he can't send anything back."

"Why would they send a deaf informant?" Vey asked. "It doesn't follow. But if you have something to say, raise your hand. He's a part of this meeting and he has a right to be able to see what you're saying about him."

Seated on a nearby crate, Manx raised his hand. "He could still collect plenty of information. He could even be faking it, and there are relays closer to the wall. Are we going to keep him under guard to be sure he doesn't go report in?"

"He's not an infiltrator and I know for a fact that he's not lying," Vey said. "He can be trusted."

"So what are we going to do with him?" The speaker was one of the men he had seen working in Libby's greenhouse. "If he can't leave the community, what's he going to do to pitch in? Work the greenhouses?"

Libby quickly raised her hand. "He's not coming anywhere near my plants. The greenhouses are something he shouldn't have seen at all."

"He's not one of them anymore," Vey repeated. "I followed him for days after he crossed the new wall. He was completely on his own. He's a little crazy, but it's the kind of crazy that will risk its life to protect others. He belongs here."

"The hell he does," Libby said, rising to her feet. "Heroes are wired up with so many neuroprosthetics, they're more machine than human. That whole respect for human life thing? That's just how they're programmed to act. Trust me, he may say he doesn't work for them anymore, but there is no such thing as a former Company man."

"That's not true," Adrian protested. "The Safety Division has been dismantled. The Company sold me. I made the choice to run rather than wind up dead."

"I doubt it was really your choice. But even if it was, you didn't escape. They allowed you to come here."

"They don't care. They recouped their loss by selling me. As far as they're concerned, I'm dead."

"We heard about the end of the Safety Division. But they didn't just sell you off, did they? They integrated the remaining Heroes into Enforcement." Libby smiled. "Isn't that right, Wisp?"

The young woman shrugged. "That's what the newscast said."

"And some Enforcers are disguised as citizens," Libby continued. "Special Investigations, it's called. Why not one disguised as a Hero?"

Vey folded her arms and frowned at everyone.

"I swear I'm not! I'm nothing like them!"

"Let me ask you all," Libby continued, "how many of you noticed something odd when you met him? How many of you noticed him make direct eye contact, then seem to focus on something else while looking at you?" Her hand went up. Slowly many others raised their hands as well.

"He was scanning eyes and pulling up identity files. Why would he have any reason to do that if he isn't working for the Company anymore?"

"Is that true?" Vey asked.

"Yes. It's just habit. I couldn't do anything with that information even if I wanted to."

"It doesn't matter whether he says he wants to or not," Libby said. "He's taking inventory for them. Who's here. How many of us are there. What kind of protection do we have. I bet he'll make every excuse to stay by your side, since you're one of the only ones with a firearm. And as soon as the shit hits the fan he'll thoughtfully relieve you of it. Just to be sure no one gets hurt, of course."

"Wait, what?" Adrian exclaimed. "You have a firearm?"

Vey shot him a skeptical look. "You're telling me you never noticed this?"

She unclipped the holster on her belt and flashed the grip of a semi-automatic pistol.

"I hadn't. I've honestly never seen one before."

Firearms were banned in the city. Those that still existed dated all the way back to the founding, when citizens had smuggled them in from outside. Over the years, few had escaped confiscation.

He recalled the flashes of light in the hallway outside Chef's kitchen, and it suddenly occurred to him how she must have dealt with the butcher and the rest of Moe's group. Snow popped up a series of helpful images to fill in what he had not seen: exploded flesh, shattered bone and pools of blood. A corpse resting against a wall, brain matter splattered across the background. While the Company's weapons were intended to be humanely nonlethal, a gunshot was instant and permanent.

The entire gathering had gone still, everyone watching him as if they had found a venomous snake in their midst. His skin prickled under the weight of so many distrustful stares.

Demon rose from her seat at the back of the tent and raised her hand.

"I say we boot him. You can't trust a Company thug."

"Please don't," Adrian pleaded. "I'm not gathering information. I'm not a threat to anyone. I'm just trying to survive, and I'll help with anything I can if you let me stay."

Libby seemed to laugh. "We have enough help. We don't need

extra bodies badly enough to welcome an undercover Enforcer."

"I swear I'm not."

Vey was still frowning at him. That, more than anyone else's reaction, hurt.

Wisp raised her hand. "Ask him for maps," she said. "Schematics. Records. Ask him for information."

"I sincerely doubt he can get us anything you can't," Demon retorted. "I wouldn't trust my safety to his information, anyway."

"Snow says he's reliable," Wisp insisted, stroking her stuffed bear.

Vey shot him an assessing look. "What kind of information do you have without access to the network?"

"Almost anything, actually. What would you like to know?"

"He's just stringing us along," Demon argued. "He'll say whatever he thinks we want to hear."

"If I asked you for a map of this tier, could you show us on your tablet?" Vey asked.

Adrian removed the tablet from an inner pocket of his jacket and held it out to her.

"We're here." He zoomed in on their location.

"That's a useful little device," Mandi said. "How do you keep it charged?"

"It works the same way nanoprosthetics do, by tapping a small amount of the electrical current of the person holding it. The screen can also act as a solar cell."

"Fascinating. Can you get the schematics for that system?"

After a brief search, Adrian located the manufacturer's patented design.

Manx leaned in as his partner scrolled through the information.

Meanwhile, people had risen from their seats and gathered around. Adrian soon found himself inundated with requests.

"One at a time," Vey reminded them. "And remember that he lipreads. If you're asking the back of his head, he can't hear you."

"Do you have videos?" Lyla asked. "Like of horses?"

"Like this?" Adrian found a video of a galloping black stallion.

"That's from before the city!" Loki exclaimed. "Do you have more stuff from back then?"

"Do you have pictures of outside?" one of Libby's helpers asked.

Adrian pulled up some of the images of canyons he had found during his research.

"Is that a real place?" Lyla asked. "Is it near here?"

"Actually, it might be," Libby said. "Do you still have that map?"

"Sure we do," Loki replied. "Be right back."

He returned a few minutes later with a roll of yellowed antique paper. A detailed map was inscribed inside, the ink faded with age but still mostly readable.

"We're here, give or take a bit," Libby said, tapping the lower left quadrant of the map. "Of course, this map was created before they hollowed out the plateau to form the city, so it's inaccurate. But the surrounding areas should still be more or less the same."

"A topographical map," Adrian mused. "It was published more than a hundred years before the city was founded."

"Do you have anything newer?" Vey asked.

The most recent topographical map he could find was still hundreds of years old. Adrian sent it to the tablet for everyone to see.

"This is the newest one in the database. We're over here in this corner."

He pointed out the remnants of a plateau, hollowed out to hold the city. The original bedrock formed the hill which the tiers circled. The remains of the plateau formed the walls that bordered the outer edge of the city.

"How did people get in and out?" Jack asked. "Were there gates, or a road?"

"And are they still there?" Gibbs added.

"Sky cranes," Adrian said after several moments of research. "The original citizens were brought in with heli-transports." As he spoke, he forwarded the images to the tablet.

"Aw, so there's no way out then?"

Adrian frowned, skimming through classified documents dating all the way back to the city's founding.

"Actually, there may have been. There's mention of smugglers. And something about a cavern network."

"The Company has always tried to control who could come and go from the city," Libby noted. "Restriction of movement is not a new concept to them."

"How do you have all this restricted information?" Mandi asked.

"Heroes can access pretty much anything in the archives."

"But you'd still have to have access to the network."

"I don't. Before I left, I downloaded it all."

Expressions of shock and worry greeted his admission.

"Do they know?" Mandi asked, expression fearful.

"I don't think so. Why?"

"Stealing Company secrets is an automatic death sentence," Wisp said. "Of course, I'm sure you knew that."

"Of course," Adrian mumbled. In all honesty, he had not had any idea.

# CHAPTER EIGHTEEN

He awoke the next morning to full daylight shining through the fabric of the tent walls. Old Tom was curled up beside him, and two other cats had settled lower on the blanket. They all looked so comfortable that Adrian felt bad for waking them.

He found Vey in front of Gran's kitchen, eating leftover stew.

"I'm going to have to leave, aren't I?" he asked, taking a seat nearby. He suspected that the community had reconvened to discuss his status after he had gone to bed.

"Not yet," she said, handing him a bowl. "I convinced them to give you a chance. I think that if Enforcement knew where you were, they would have come for you by now. They're not known for being slow to retaliate."

"That's good, I guess."

"It is," she said, flashing him a warm smile. "Since Libby refuses to let you work in the greenhouses, you can work with Manx and Mandi. They're excited to have access to all the schematics in the archive. They're referring to it as a treasure trove, and a once-in-a-lifetime opportunity."

"I'm glad to be able to help. I really like it here."

Her smile seemed to light up the whole morning. Combined with the news that he would be able to stay, he felt as if he was floating.

Then Vey's eyes focused on something behind him, and the smile disappeared. Adrian turned and found Loki standing near the entrance to the tent, pale and breathless.

"There's someone at the gate. They say they're looking for him." The boy's eyes indicated Adrian.

"Stay here," Vey said, but Adrian followed anyway.

When they reached the space behind the gate, he could hardly contain his surprise. The intruder's back was turned, wide shoulders relaxed, hands in the pockets of a familiar gray uniform. A black duffle bag rested at their feet.

When the figure turned around, her wide smile was reflected in the sparkle of her pale blue eyes. There was an expanse of white scar tissue where her Safety badge had been.

"Melbourne?!" Adrian exclaimed. "What are you doing here?"

"Adrian! I was beginning to think you'd crawled off into some hole down here and died. I've been looking for you for weeks!" She grabbed him and hugged him so tightly that he couldn't breathe.

"Ease up," Adrian gasped. "No need to break my ribs." In the time since he had seen her last, she had put on nearly as much muscle as Nelson.

"I thought you were going to be an Enforcer. Why are you here?"

She said something he couldn't interpret, and Adrian stepped back so that he could see her face.

"What's wrong?"

"I'm deaf."

She grimaced. "I'm sorry. What happened?"

"Vermin caught me sleeping. Do you remember that crowd control weapon they taught us about? The one they instructor said never to use? Well, he was right."

"Live and learn, I guess." Her smile vanished. "I'm sorry, though. That sucks."

"Vey, this is Melbourne. Mel, meet Vey. She rescued me."

"*You* needed to be rescued?" Mel asked.

"I saved him from being someone's dinner."

"Sounds like you've had a rough time down here."

Demon, who had been watching the entire conversation from the shadows under the gate, said something Adrian could not make out.

"No," Vey replied, "I don't think that's necessary yet."

"Yes, I would appreciate it if you don't attempt to shank me," Mel said. "It probably won't kill me, but it will make me angry."

"Why are you here?" Adrian asked.

"I don't know if you've heard, but things have gone to shit above the wall. Even with every precinct mobilized, Enforcement doesn't have enough bodies to hold down the unrest. Mobs have taken over most of the transit hubs below the Twenty-Fifth Tier. Transit service is shut off below Twentieth. Entire tiers are burning. It was a good time to split."

"They just let you go?" Adrian asked, a tingle of alarm crawling up his spine.

"I had help. Do you remember Dr. Hart? He said he'd worked on you. The last time I saw him, he told me that we were brother and sister now, you and I. He struck me as a little odd, but he did good work."

Vey was still watching them, arms folded. "How do you two know each other?"

"We were Heroes," Mel said. "We worked together."

"Mel was part of my home group," Adrian explained. "Heroes don't have blood family, so a home group is the closest thing to it. Mel is like my sister."

"You do look like siblings. But you're a long, long way from where you belong. How did you find this place?"

"Adrian's neural interface connected to the relays below the wall while he was in range. Once I reached the last one he'd used, I circled outward, looking for clues. I spotted some scavengers and followed them back here, hoping to ask if they'd seen him."

"You tracked me even though I overwrote my ID chip? How?"

"Hart gave me a program that helped. Being an Enforcer also has its perks." She smiled. "I checked out that tower where you were living. The night you disappeared, the security system recorded a strange person being escorted out of the building by the domestic staff. There was no record of how he had arrived on that tier or gotten into the building. In fact, that particular citizen had been missing for years."

"Oh, no," Adrian whispered.

"Oh, yes," Mel replied, grinning. "It was pretty obvious what had happened. Speaking of which, is it true?"

"Is what true?"

"Enforcement has a warrant for you, on a number of counts of aiding in the creation and dissemination of Anarchist propaganda."

"Seriously? You know me, Mel. I wouldn't do anything like that."

"I know. If it's any consolation, I think they have their hands too full to worry about it right now. The city's gone to hell in a handbasket." Mel paused and scratched the back of her neck vigorously. "I don't suppose you have shower facilities down here, do you? It's been ages since I've been able to get cleaned up, and I itch like crazy."

"You need to go into quarantine," Vey said.

"I don't think I have anything. There are some pretty sickly people down here, but I stayed away from them."

"Did you see the husk-like things?" Adrian asked. "The shells? Those were people, Mel. We can get the parasite that causes that."

"That's not good."

"You can either go into quarantine, or we'll escort you to a community that takes in the infected," Vey repeated. "You can't stay here."

A roar so low-pitched it was felt rather than heard cut off further conversation. It reverberated through Adrian's body, stealing his breath and scrambling his thoughts. Vey stared upward, expression horrified.

"Get everyone to cover," Mel said barked. "It's a crowd control weapon!"

"Here?" Adrian yelled back.

"The independent maglev transports are fitted with them. We need to get everyone out of here right now. Is there another exit from this place?"

The fabric of the roof sagged and rippled under the sound waves, and the air itself seemed heavier. Adrian could only imagine how much worse it must be for those with hearing.

Vey led them through the tent community, gathering up residents as she went. In the open area outside Gran's kitchen, several crates and a rug had been shoved aside to reveal a round metal cover. Residents were already scrambling down the narrow ladder into the building below. Vey motioned him toward the hole, scowling impatiently.

"What about the others?" Adrian shouted. He knew there were faces he had not seen go down the hatch, although his thoughts were too scrambled to put names to them. The roar deepened, and suddenly he could not seem to catch his breath.

Vey slammed the cover shut and shoved the crates back into place as the tent exploded, knocking them to the ground. Enforcers dropped from the sky, their mechanically augmented suits absorbing the impact. The roar of the crowd control weapon ceased.

"Put your hands up!" The Enforcer's words appearing as glowing red text across Adrian's vision. "Do it now!"

The mode of communication meant that Enforcement had deployed a short-range relay beacon. They would be able to locate Wisp, and anyone else with a functional neural interface. They were also undoubtedly scanning ID chips.

Adrian and Mel reluctantly put their hands in the air. Vey began to back away. One of the Enforcers moved to stop her, and was immediately brought up short as Demon popped out of a ruined tent and impaled him on her pig sticker. As the women fled with a pair of Enforcers in pursuit, Adrian felt a surge of grudging admiration. It took an incredibly skilled saboteur to disable an armored Enforcer.

"I said, freeze," the leader repeated, the glowing red text

pulsating angrily. "What a pleasant surprise, to find so many Anarchists in once place. Murderers. Hackers. Thieves. And you," the foremost Enforcer's helmet swiveled to fix Adrian with what he assumed was a glare. "A traitor to the very institution he owes his existence to."

"I did what was right," Adrian retorted. "I doubt you can say the same."

"Such a nice little group you've found, Enforcer Melbourne."

"I always was good at finding people." Mel's reply came across in the same red font as the Enforcer's. She was smiling.

"You abandoned your post. You have been charged with dereliction of duty."

"What, no reward for finding these people? I expected better of you, Hardy. You couldn't have done it without me."

Adrian's blood went cold. He did not want to believe what he was reading.

"Thank you, Enforcer Melbourne."

The remaining Enforcers split up and moved off into the surrounding tents. If Vey and Demon had not been captured yet, they were about to have bigger problems.

"I can't dismiss your charges. But I will give you a commendation for locating these criminals."

"That's it? I'm a bit disappointed."

"I'm just doing my job." Hardy glanced over his shoulder, then unlocked his helmet from the rest of his armor and pulled it off. "If the charges are dismissed, I trust this won't affect things between us?"

"Of course not."

Mel stepped forward and pulled the Enforcer into a kiss. A flash of metal caught Adrian's eye as her hands wrapped around the back of Hardy's neck; there was a slender metal spike tucked against her right palm.

The Enforcer wrapped his arms around Mel, trapping her in an armored embrace. As he lost himself in the kiss, Mel aimed the spike at the back of his skull and drove it home.

Hardy slammed his forehead into Mel's face, crushed her to his chest, and began punching her in the ribs. Adrian seized a fallen tent support and broke it over the Enforcer's back.

Hardy didn't even pause. Adrian lifted a beam nearly as long as he was tall and slammed it down across the back of Hardy's head. The Enforcer staggered, giving Mel the opportunity to escape. Adrian followed the first blow with a second one, and he thought he felt something give as the steel beam connected with the Enforcer's skull.

Hardy collapsed, blood running from his mouth. The entire palm-length blade was gone. The Enforcer's body convulsed, his face frozen in an expression of shock.

"Are you alright?" Adrian asked. Mel's face was smeared with blood, but it was hard to tell how much of it was actually hers.

She nodded, grinning, as a pair of Enforcers burst out of the tunnel that led to the greenhouse.

Adrian swung the beam at the first Enforcer's helmet. The blow sent him reeling through the remains of the tent wall and off the edge of the roof into the smog beyond. It was a lethally long drop to the street below.

"Run!" The word popped up at the bottom of his view in bold red letters as Mel grappled with the second attacker.

There were more Enforcers coming. Snow showed him a map of the rooftop, where hostile red dots were rapidly converging on their location. The Enforcer had succeeded in taking Mel to the ground, and as he watched they rolled dangerously close to the edge of the roof. Before he could shout a warning, the combatants tumbled over the lip and were gone.

Stifling his shock, Adrian ducked into the remains of a nearby tent. Shreds of fabric littered the floor of what had once been someone's living space.

"Snow, where are the others?"

The map added green dots for the citizens with connectivity, and purple dots for those without. The location of the latter seemed hazy and uncertain. If an Enforcer could not see an unconnected citizen, their dot flickered out on the map. Off to his right, on the far corner of the roof, two purple dots and two red ones seemed to dance.

Tangled tent fabric and tins of food littered the opposite end of the rooftop. Demon had felled one of the pursuers, and was pounding on the back of his helmet with a length of steel pipe. The remaining Enforcer had succeeded in cornering Vey against the edge of the roof. Then came the scene the Hero had watched hundreds of times before: the Enforcer grabbed Vey, applied his neutralizer to her ribs, and wrenched her arms behind her back.

Adrian tackled the Enforcer as he prepared to cuff Vey, slamming him to the ground. They rolled, and the Enforcer quickly came out on top, oblivious to the blue-hued figure approaching his back with a steel pipe raised menacingly over her shoulder.

The blow sent Adrian's opponent sprawling. Before the Enforcer could regain his feet, Demon swung again. He was thrown backward, the mirrored visor of his helmet webbed with white cracks. Demon advanced, face contorted in a snarl, eyes showing white all the way around the brown irises. Berserker, Snow informed him. Insane and dangerous.

As Demon bludgeoned her opponent into submission, Adrian scrambled over to Vey and pulled her to her feet. Her clothing seemed to have protected her from the worst of the shock. Meanwhile, the remaining Enforcers had converged on their position, trapping them between a wall of armor and the edge of the rooftop.

Vey grabbed his shoulder and motioned for him to follow, then stepped off the edge. As he launched himself after her, Demon raised her weapon and charged the line of Enforcers.

He caught Vey's arm, pulled her to his chest, and rolled onto his back as the smog enfolded them. She fought him, struggling in panic, and he hugged her tighter. He was certain it was not a fall he would survive, but he was determined that she would.

It was a long way down, and he had ample time to consider the fact that this was not how he had expected things to turn out. In his search for a better life, he had brought disaster down everyone who had trusted him. With their self-sufficient settlement in ruins, what did these people have left?

His back connected with something that gave at the impact, sinking and then breaking under their combined weight. They landed on a sloped surface, skidded down a debris-studded chute, and shot out into thin air. Adrian's arm and back broke their fall at the bottom, and his shoulder collapsed with a crunch that he felt rather than heard.

Vey struggled out of his grip and scrambled to her feet. The toppled wall of a fallen building loomed above them as she helped him up.

"Are you alright?" Adrian asked.

She swore and stared up into the sky as cinders rained down around them.

"Vey? I'm sorry. I am so, so sorry."

"How bad is it?" she asked, indicating his shoulder.

"I think it's broken. Are you hurt?"

"Just a little bruised. That's what the net's for, but it can't hold that much weight in one place."

"I had no idea there was a net."

"So that thing where you tried to cushion my fall– why would you do that if you didn't think there was anything between us and the pavement?"

"So you'd live."

Vey swore again and hugged him tightly, and Adrian returned the embrace with his good arm. Out of all the jumpers he had caught, she was the one he was most glad to have saved.

Fine debris rained down on them, making them both glance up into the smog. There was no sign of the Enforcer transport, yet. A whiff of crowd control gas stung his nose and made his eyes water.

"We need to get back up there," Adrian said. "Demon and the others are still trapped."

"They'll be alright."

"We can't just leave them."

"We're not going to give the Enforcers another chance. The others know how to take care of themselves. There's a safe meeting place near here, and I have a feeling we'll find most of our people there."

They donned their masks and headed down the street as ashes and tatters of white fabric continued to rain down behind them.

****

The first stray droplets stung his face as they threaded their way through a debris-clogged side street, spattering on his jacket and raising soft puffs of dust from the pavement. Vey grabbed his good arm and steered him under the awning of a boarded-up shop.

"Of all the days for it to finally rain." She grimaced and wiped the droplets off her arms. "Jesus, that stuff stings. Wish I'd been able to grab my cloak. It was waterproof."

The rain always stung. The public health hazard it posed was balanced by the fact that rain storms were exceedingly rare, and any additional water was a godsend for the city's depleted reservoirs.

"If I'd had any idea, I would have never let you bring me there," Adrian said.

"If I'd known what kind of friends you had, I probably wouldn't have either. You're bleeding," she added, indicating the back of his head.

"I don't think it's serious." The dull throb of a headache was eclipsed by the stabbing pain in his shoulder.

"You've got a nasty cut and a lot of swelling, but the good news is that the bleeding has stopped. Let's see your eyes."

Adrian fished the flashlight out of his jacket pocket and handed it to her.

"Your pupils are equal, so it's probably not a concussion. Let's have a look at your arm, since we're stuck here anyway."

The soft rainfall had become a downpour, and a curtain of water streamed off the edge of the awning as Vey helped him remove his jacket.

"That's not just broken. That's completely dislocated."

Adrian nodded. He had suspected as much.

"I'm not going to be able to set that myself," she concluded after a bit of moderately painful poking and prodding. "There'll be help once we get to the safe house." She tied his shirt into a crude sling and used it to support his damaged arm.

They sat down against the wall and watched the gutter become a murky, trash-clogged river. The air was heavy with humidity, the pavement steaming. Nevertheless, the rain had brought a cold draft to street level that made them both shiver.

Adrian used his good arm to drape his jacket over Vey's shoulders, and she responded by scooting closer and maneuvering the jacket over both of them. They stayed that way for a long time, watching the falling rain.

***

It was getting dark by time the storm ceased. They moved on through ruined streets temporarily washed clean by the rainfall. The narrow beam of the flashlight reflected crazily off puddles, its refracted light dancing on the graffiti-stained walls and drifts of debris.

Elsewhere, the wet pavement soaked up the light like a black hole. Water still dripped from roofs and awnings. Vey seemed on edge, her hand never far from her weapon.

She motioned for him to stop as they entered an intersection, and a moment later he realized why. Pale bones had been arranged into a circle four meters across in the center of the street. In the middle, a discarded table was surrounded with even more remains. The tabletop was covered with items that sparkled in the light.

Vey carefully probed the shadows before proceeding across the intersection. Less than a block later she came to an abrupt stop and began checking the shadows around them again.

Adrian made a questioning motion. She responded by touching her ear and then sweeping an arm out toward the surrounding buildings. There was a sound, perhaps without a firm direction. Then she held a finger to the front of her mask in the gesture for silence.

As they continued on, Adrian scanned the surrounding streets and buildings for heat signatures. He found no signs of life, not even vermin.

# CHAPTER NINETEEN

The safe house was an ancient utility room, hidden behind a rusted metal door in the sub-basement of a partially collapsed tower. Loki and Jack were already there, as were Manx and Mandi and a handful of other residents.

Someone had lit a pair of lamps, and their flickering flames were reflected on dusty glass gauges that had shown no readings in at least a hundred years. Although a faint breeze flowed from screened vents high in the walls, the confined space smelled of crowd control gas, stale sweat, and sadness.

"Did Gibbs and Lyla make it out?" Vey asked. "And Gran? Has anyone seen Demon? Wisp? Libby?"

Many of the assembled group shook their heads.

"They had us trapped," Loki said. "Gran tried to protect us. They hit her, and she fell down and didn't get back up."

"Gibbs tried to distract them," Jack added. "I took Loki and Lyla, and ran. But at some point Lyla split with us, and we couldn't find her."

"I think she went back to look for Mittens," Loki said, looking miserable. "I'm scared for her."

"I would have gone back," Jack said, "but they put up gas. We couldn't breathe, even with masks."

A dejected stillness fell over the group.

"I'm sorry, everyone," Adrian said. "I am so, so sorry."

"They came looking for Libby and the others as much as you," Vey replied.

Remembering what Mel had said about deserving a reward for finding him, he felt anything but innocent.

* * *

An hour or so later, as the group ate a solemn meal from rusted food tins, a sharp knock sounded on the door. Everyone jumped.

Vey got up and said something he couldn't make out to the person outside. After a brief pause the door was unbarred and Lyla squeezed through the gap, a bag slung over her shoulder. Her clothes and hair were singed, but she appeared mostly unharmed. Loki leaped to his feet and hugged her tightly.

Mandi stepped forward, frowning. "Why is your bag mewling?" she asked.

"I tried to save the kittens." Lyla placed the bag on the floor, and a small black face popped out of the top. "I also grabbed some food and clothing."

"What about Mittens?"

"I couldn't find her anywhere. One of her kittens is missing too."

"They're too young," Manx said, examining the wriggling bundle. "They need their mother to feed them."

"I couldn't just leave them there. The tent was on fire."

Vey nodded and handed Lyla a tin of food.

More survivors trickled in as the night wore on. Libby showed up, trailed by a cadre of greenhouse workers. All of them were weighed down with packs and bags.

The botanist swore when she spotted Adrian.

"After all that, you brought him here?"

"We are not going to argue this again," Vey said. "How much were you able to salvage?"

"Seeds, mostly. There wasn't time or space to save most of the plants, although I rescued a few tomatoes." She carefully placed the tiny seedling containers on a makeshift table. "There's some food in there too. Medical supplies. Waterproof fabric. There wasn't time to gather anything that wasn't immediately at hand."

Demon appeared next, soot-smudged, bruised and bloody. Everyone cheered when she walked in.

"How bad is it?" Libby asked, indicating the gash above the berserker's left temple.

Demon touched her head and frowned at the blood.

"Can't tell. It doesn't hurt."

Vey wiped the area clean with a disinfectant cloth, then closed the cut with butterfly bandages and covered it with a fresh dressing.

"Can you help me with his shoulder?" Vey asked.

Demon looked up from her contemplation of the floor, eyes unfocused.

"You've set a dislocated shoulder before, haven't you?"

Demon nodded. "On myself. Not on someone else."

"We need to give it a shot. The longer it's out of the socket, the longer it will take to heal."

The women seated him on a crate, and Demon lifted his arm out to the side.

"This is going to hurt," she said.

"A lot," Vey added.

Demon gripped his wrist and pulled his arm straight away from his body, while Vey manipulated his shoulder. The room went blurry, and Adrian gritted his teeth to keep from gasping in pain. Finally he felt something in his shoulder crunch and settle, and Demon carefully lowered his arm back to his side.

"Thank you both," he said as Vey fashioned him a new sling from spare strips of cloth.

With his arm safely bound in place, he sat down against the wall and was soon asleep.

***

He woke in the small hours of the new day. One of the lamps had burned out, and the other was flickering fitfully in the draft from the vents. As he blinked away his neural interface's loading symbol, he noticed that a few of the other refugees were stirring as well.

Loki was seated on a crate, rubbing his eyes. Demon was sitting up in the corner where she had passed out almost as soon as his arm was fixed, hand on the metal pipe that lay beside her.

"Do you hear it too?" Loki mouthed. "The tapping?"

Adrian shook his head.

Demon climbed to her feet and threaded her way through the sleeping refugees. After communicating with someone outside, she unbarred the door and admitted Wisp. Mittens darted in the door on the hacker's heels, a kitten dangling from her mouth.

More refugees awoke as Demon shoved the door shut and barred it. Vey stirred and sat up.

"Are you alright?" Adrian asked. "Are you badly burned?"

"It's not as bad as it looks. I scooted down into the reservoir and hid in the back of the water tank through the worst of it. By the way, did you know Enforcers can walk through fire? I didn't know that."

"Their armor's fireproof up to a certain temperature."

"Vey, I managed to save your coat and your travel pack. Sorry if they're a bit soggy." She removed a small, singed red bear from the pack before handing it over.

"I'm sure everything in there will survive," Vey said. "Thank you. Are you sure you're alright?"

Wisp paused and stared down at her scorched clothing, then shrugged.

"I think I'll be fine. By the way, did anyone else see the flesh hackers?"

"They know better than to be on this side of the tier," Demon said, expression grim.

"They were already scavenging what was left of the rooftop by time I came out of the tank. Seemed like they came up right after the Enforcers left."

"Opportunistic modder freaks." Vey swore. "Do you think they saw you?"

"One of them was carrying a short-range relay beacon, so I was able to break in, tweak their perception of reality a bit, and slip away." Wisp grinned through her mask of soot and hugged her bear. "They never even knew I was there."

"Do you know if they picked up any of the others?"

The hacker shook her head. "It didn't sound like they found any survivors. Wait, where's Gran?"

"We don't think she made it out," Vey said. "Jack's brother is missing, as are some of the others. We're going to stay here through the morning in case anyone else shows up."

* * *

Morning brought little change to the musty bowels of the building. Scrapes, bruises and burns were tended while the survivors conversed quietly among themselves. Loki and Lyla passed out breakfast rations, and Adrian spent the morning sitting silently against the wall, watching dusty cobwebs sway in the breeze from the vents.

Vey, Libby and Demon moved off to one side, arguing. Occasionally he was able to see their faces well enough to read what they were saying. The disagreement seemed to center around his presence, whether he had deliberately led Enforcement to their location, and whether he posed an ongoing danger.

"How hard could it be?" Libby asked at one point. "He's deaf. Just take him for a walk. Make him go first. It'll take one bullet, maybe two. He'll never even see it coming."

Vey shook her head, and the trio continued arguing. Adrian cautiously stretched his shoulder and considered volunteering to leave on his own.

"I really don't think he should be a part of this," Libby insisted as the three made their way over to him.

"He's proven his loyalty," Demon responded. "Besides, it was his sister that brought them here, not him. And she's dead."

"Mel's dead?" he asked, heart sinking. "You're sure?"

"Not positive. But Wisp saw her go off the edge, and there was no net where she fell. No one survives that far of a drop."

Adrian nodded.

"I'm sorry about your sister," Vey said, sitting down beside him.

"I had no idea she would do something like that for them." Even as he said it, he wondered if Mel had realized just how much death and destruction her actions would cause.

"If you want me to leave, I'll go quietly," he said. "I won't try to follow you."

"No, you've proven yourself," Vey replied. "And where we're going, the information you have is going to be even more useful. I don't suppose you still have your tablet, do you?"

Adrian frowned. He'd put it in an inner pocket of his jacket after the community meeting, and hadn't thought about it since. When he removed the device from his pocket, he was surprised to find it still functional.

"What's going on?" Wisp asked, joining their circle.

"Remember how we've talked about moving the community? Packing up, finding a way to breach the outer wall, and getting out? Well, I think the time has come to give that a shot."

"The old smuggling routes," Wisp guessed. "Snow can't dig that information out of the archives without reconnecting to the network, but he can."

"I'll see what I can do," Adrian promised.

"How's your shoulder?" Demon asked.

"Good, I guess. It doesn't hurt anymore." Images and articles blurred past his view as Snow scanned the archives for a viable means of escape from the city.

"There's a smuggling tunnel behind a hidden door in a control room like this one," Adrian said. "If it hasn't been walled off, we should be able to reach it through the utilidor network."

"Or flooded," Demon added. "Things were getting a bit soggy when I came through last night."

"You're sure this is the way out?" Vey asked.

"Ninety-nine percent sure. It's on the Seventy-Fifth Tier, and it's located right next to the wall. None of the records indicate anything was done about it. From what I can tell, erecting the new wall was of greater importance by that point."

"Let's put it to a vote then."

Vey explained the situation as the tablet went around the room. When it came time to vote, Loki and Lyla's hands were the first to go up.

"Ghost towns! And horses!"

"I want to see a river," Jack said, raising his hand.

"To the great unknown!" Wisp said, grinning.

Gradually, every hand in the room went up.

Vey nodded. "It's decided, then. Let's get packed up."

"What about Gran and the others?" Lyla asked.

"If they were coming, they would have been here by now," Vey said. "I'm sorry."

* * *

The dusty hallway seemed cold compared to the crowded control room, and Adrian was glad for the insulation of his uniform as he stood waiting to lead the way. As the refugees adjusted their packs and spilled out into the hallway, an argument broke out at the back of the line.

"But we can't leave them here!" Lyla said, expression anguished. "The vermin will eat her kittens!"

Vey shook her head and pointed at the control room. When she joined him at the head of the line, her expression was sad.

"I told them they could have a moment to say goodbye."

"Where are the others going?" The refugees were forming into two groups, with himself at the head of one line, and Wisp leading the other.

"We've decided to send a party back to salvage more supplies. Libby and her people volunteered. Demon will guard them, and

Wisp will try to make sure things go smoothly with any scavenging flesh hackers they encounter."

Loki and Lyla reemerged from the control room as Manx passed out portable lights. Soon the groups went their separate ways, Vey and Adrian leading theirs through the utilidors toward the Seventy-Fifth Tier.

***

Demon's comment about flooding had been prophetic. The farther they went, the more often they were forced to detour around submerged sections of passage. Cracks in the ceiling wept, leaving grimy trails down the walls. There was also a peculiar musty smell in the tunnels that made the hair on the back of Adrian's neck stand on end.

Although the utilidor network seemed devoid of life, they often came across strange markings at corridor junctions. Some seemed like hastily scrawled symbols, others little more than dirty smudges.

"What are they?" Adrian asked, as they passed another cluster of indecipherable markings.

"No idea," Vey replied, frowning.

"Modder symbols?" Manx suggested. "They have a strange way of doing things. Wouldn't surprise me if they'd invented their own language."

Vey shook her head. "I doubt any of them write by hand. They're fully digital."

"Well, it's not like any language I've ever seen," Mandi said. "And I studied linguistics as well as programming and engineering."

As they drew closer to their destination, the sogginess of the tunnels increased. Runoff turned the floor slick and treacherous, and murky water pooled in every low spot.

"Must be raining again," Vey noted. "Is there another way around?" Ahead, the tunnel dipped into the water and made a right turn.

Adrian shook his head. "This is it. The control room we're looking for is right around the corner, and it's a dead end."

Manx grimaced. "I'll bet you dinner that tunnel's flooded."

"I'll scout ahead and find out."

Fetid water sloshed around his knees, cold and murky, as he waded around the corner. The tunnel beyond was a jumble of fallen ceiling and broken pipes. One wall had collapsed, spilling crushed rock into the utilidor. Through the tangle, he could make out the twisted shape of a broken door.

Scrambling up the pile, he slithered through the rubble until he could peer into the doorway. The control room seemed to have been the epicenter of the cave-in, and there was little of the original structure left. Rock fill spilled through the broken walls, burying twisted pipes and dusty banks of broken equipment. Part of the ceiling had come down, followed by what he could only guess were the floors above.

A handful of loose pebbles and dust rained down on his back as he lay peering into the ruin. He began to crawl backward, chest tight with panic, as more fine debris rained down around him. His mobility was hampered by having one arm in a sling, and he desperately regretted not unbinding it before he entered.

Strong hands dragged him out of the rubble, and Vey helped him to his feet as something settled deep inside the cave-in. The rubble shifted, setting the water sloshing around their legs as they made their way back to the sea of worried faces that waited for them above the water line.

"Bad news?" Mandi asked.

"Caved in," Vey said grimly. "How far back does the damage go? Could we clear out a path to the tunnel entrance?"

Adrian leaned against the wall, heart pounding as if he had just run for his life, and considered what he had seen.

"I don't think so," he said at last. "It's caved in worse in the control room itself, and it looks like the building above has collapsed. If we start clearing out the rubble, the whole thing could come down on us."

Vey swore. Manx and Mandi exchanged worried frowns.

"Look, this was just the closest and most viable-looking place I found. There are probably others."

"We need to move to higher ground," Mandi said. "I don't like how fast this water is rising."

"There's sewage in it too, judging by the smell," Vey added. "But we can't go far until the others get back."

"We could leave them a message," Manx suggested. "Directions drawn on the wall or something."

"I don't like the idea of marking our location for anyone to find."

As the group moved back up the tunnel, Adrian's sensors picked up a lone figure standing in the middle of the utilidor junction ahead. It was the last intersection they had passed on their way in.

"Vey, there's someone in front of us."

"How many?"

"Just one, at the junction. I can't tell if there are more off to either side."

Vey turned and gave a series of orders to those behind them.

As they drew closer, the group's lights revealed a slight, dark-clad figure unlike anyone they had sent back to salvage from the rooftop community. The figure's face, half hidden beneath a deep hood, was delicate and exceptionally pale. Her hands were joined in front of her body, enfolded in the loose cuffs of the hooded garment. Her eyes seemed to be closed.

A few meters short of the junction, Vey motioned for everyone to stop. Her hand rested on the butt of her weapon.

"What are you doing here, flesh hacker?"

The figure's head lifted slightly, and Adrian noticed a faint, vein-like glimmer of silver. Not flesh, but artificial skin over subdermal nanoprosthetics. The pale lips moved.

"Divert your lights, please. It is too bright to see."

Vey made a lowering motion, and the group's lights aimed at the walls.

"That's better." Wide, dark eyes regarded them, all pupil.

"Where's the rest of your group?" Vey asked.

"I am Emissary Neva. I come alone, bearing an invitation."

"That's very trusting of you."

The Emissary smiled. "We are protected by the threat of mutually assured destruction. I am wired with enough implanted explosives to level a city block. Acts of aggression are not advised."

"If you do us no harm, you have nothing to fear from us," Vey replied. "What's your message?"

"Hero Adrian," the Emissary replied, "our Most Highly Evolved has requested your presence. You may bring your friends."

"We're waiting for the rest of our party," Vey interjected. "We're not going anywhere without them."

The figure smiled again. "Do you mean Emissary Wisp and her companions? They are already enjoying our hospitality."

Vey swore.

"It's a trap," Manx said, stepping to the front of the group. "There's no way to know if she's lying."

"I speak only the truth. Your friends are all alive and safe. I can tell you their names as proof." The Emissary followed the statement with a list of every refugee in the party that had returned to the rooftop.

"But what do you want me for?" Adrian asked, puzzled.

"Or any of us, for that matter?" Vey added.

"We wish to extend an offer of safety, repairs, and upgrades. With the Company reaching this far into the abandoned tiers, there is safety in numbers and a strongly fortified position."

"Give us a moment," Vey said, turning back to the rest of the group.

"If they're lying, they have an awfully good grip on who went back for supplies," Mandi noted.

"We're better equipped to stage a rescue from outside their

community than in," Manx countered.

"It sounds like they're offering help," Adrian said. "We could at least see what they have to say."

"The thing about flesh hackers," Vey said, "is that their idea of help and ours tends to differ. Their guests go to sleep and wake up with upgrades they didn't want or consent to. Then that person can't leave, because the implants require continued maintenance."

Adrian nodded. If these were anything like the flesh hackers he had encountered above the wall, he didn't like the idea of being at their mercy.

"What about Wisp and the others?" Jack asked. "We're not going to leave them, are we?"

Throughout the discussion the Emissary simply stood watching, motionless as a statue.

"What are the terms of this invitation?" Vey asked. "Will we be free to leave if we want, whenever we want?"

The Emissary seemed to consider the question for a moment.

"Yes. According to the direction I have been given, you are invited as guests."

"Do we have your word? Does that courtesy extend to all of us, even Adrian? And Wisp and her group?"

"We wish only to help."

"Let's put it to a vote," Vey said, turning back to the group. "I'm reluctantly in favor of accepting this invitation. At least to make sure the others are safe. Hands up if you're in favor."

Adrian raised his hand, as did most of the others. Manx did not.

"There's nothing to stop them from changing their minds once we're there," he pointed out.

"The longer we wait, the longer they have the rest of our people," Mandi countered. "I'm in favor of the speediest intervention possible."

Manx frowned, and reluctantly raised his hand.

"It's decided," Vey said. "Lead the way, Emissary Neva."

The flesh hacker nodded, smiling faintly, and motioned for them to follow.

# CHAPTER TWENTY

The shadowy figure led them around the curve of the tier, through tunnels knee deep in cloudy water and past tangled cave-ins. Eventually they turned aside and entered the basement utility room of an abandoned building.

"Where are we going?" Vey asked.

"We must go around," the Emissary said, turning to face them.

"Go around what?"

"A fissure in the bedrock of the city. It is very deep, and the edges are not stable."

The smog-choked world above seemed excruciatingly bright after the darkness of the utilidors. They moved through deserted streets washed clean by the recent rainfall, where roofs and awnings still dripped and water puddled in the low spots. They detoured around a sunken intersection, and crossed another of the peculiar bone circles.

"Do your people make these?" Adrian asked, as the Emissary paused to examine the shiny objects arranged on a toppled vending machine as the center of the design.

The only answer he received was a cryptic shake of the head.

"Do you know who does? I've seen several of these now. The first was on the other side of the wall, on the Forty-Eighth Tier."

The Emissary looked up in surprise and removed the full-face gas mask she wore.

"There are circles above the wall?"

"I only saw one. It was in an abandoned district."

"They like their quiet. We surmise that these circles may be displays of prowess, or meeting points, or perhaps they mark a territory. I have always found them fascinating. They are not good places to be at night."

"Why is that?" he asked, but the Emissary had already resecured her mask and moved on.

They descended into the bowels of another building and resumed their journey through the utilidors, eventually coming up beneath the tier's Enforcement precinct. A cadre of hulking guards closed around them as they entered the building's basement. Adrian immediately felt less at ease.

Most of the men were of significantly above-average height, with unnaturally wide shoulders and narrow waists. Their faded gray uniforms fit awkwardly, stretched tight over hard angles that no human body should have, and they moved with a peculiar gliding gait. Several had replaced one or both of their eyes with an array of sensors protected by a synthetic lens.

The refugees were herded up a series of maintenance corridors and utility stairwells to the main floor, emerging just inside the barricaded main entrance of the precinct. A security station lay between them and the rest of the building.

Although bullet holes and fire damage marred the dull gray walls of the lobby, the precinct's power system seemed to be intact and functioning. Air circulated through the vents, doors slid open at their approach, and overhead lights flooded the room with harsh white illumination.

"Security screening." The pale green words popped up in the middle of his field of view, pulsating gently. "Please form a line and proceed through the scanner."

At some point during their ascent from the utilidors, his communication module had made contact with the tower's relay. The exclusion of those without connectivity came as little surprise.

Even above the wall, modders were known for their dislike of those who shunned technology.

Vey nudged his good arm to get his attention. "I don't like this. What's going on?"

"It's a security checkpoint. We just walk through the scanner." Adrian stepped through the white arch and motioned for the others to follow.

More guards stood around the bank of monitoring equipment attached to the scanner, their expressions grim, their prosthetic eyes dead and unreadable. The scanner technician was shirtless, his chest little more than human flesh stretched over a robotic frame. His biological arms ended just below the shoulder, each humerus capped off and attached to the bone-and-tendon framework of an actuator-driven prosthetic limb. His body ended at the waist, attached to a device that resembled a modified a wheelchair.

The technician still had his original eyes, brown, bloodshot orbs that rarely left the scanner screen. Nathan Cerney, formerly of the Forty-Eighth Tier, a factory worker. Missing, presumed dead. He had been diagnosed with late-stage bone cancer a week before his disappearance.

"What happened to you?" Adrian asked.

The guard glanced up at him and smiled, baring a mouthful of dark metal.

"I was sick. These people saved my life. There was a lot that they couldn't save–" he indicated the machine that had replaced his lower body. "But I feel a lot better now."

"How are the hands? Do they work as well as the real thing?"

"Pretty close to it. I'm stronger than I ever could have been with biological parts, and these hands can do anything my old ones could."

"Are you in pain?"

The guard grinned. "They removed my pain receptors. They can do wonderful things here, amazing things. You should let us repair your arm. You could be so much better than you are now."

"I think I'm good. It's not that serious."

Red lights flashed as Vey walked through the scanner. A pair of guards pulled her aside and pointed to her firearm.

"Hell, no. I'm not giving up my weapon. We have your leader's word. We're not prisoners. We're guests."

"It is standard procedure," one of the guards said, the words glowing warning red.

"Why don't you speak?" Vey asked. "Don't just wave at me. Tell me what your problem is."

"I don't think he can," Adrian said, eying the hulking guard. "He's saying it's standard procedure."

"We're not going in if they want to take our weapons," Vey said. "Everybody else hear that? Don't give up your weapons!"

Heads turned toward them all down the line, a mixture of fear, worry, and determination framed in the refugees' faces. Adrian looked around for the Emissary, but she was gone. More heavily modified guards spilled out of the double doors beyond the checkpoint.

"We cannot grant an armed party entry. You must surrender your weapons. They will be returned to you." Adrian repeated the message out loud for those without connectivity.

"If you don't trust us with weapons, we don't trust you to disarm us," Vey retorted. "If your leaders want to meet us, they can meet us here."

Meanwhile, a growing number of the refugees were being pulled aside. Lyla was protesting the confiscation of her bag to the wheeled scanner technician, who was examining the contents. Jack and Loki had joined the protest, blocking Adrian's view of the contraband.

"Please remain calm," the Emissary said, reappearing from deeper in the building. "No one will harm you here. You are perfectly safe without your weapons."

"We've changed our minds," Vey said. "We're leaving now. Give us the rest of our group."

More guards, old-fashioned black Enforcer uniforms stretched over their distorted bodies, had come up behind the line. The refugees were trapped in the lobby, a wall of augmented guards at their back as well as their front. Hands rested on makeshift weapons, and no one looked happy.

Through the crowd, Adrian caught a glimpse of the scanner technician cradling something small, black and furry to his chest, his ruined face split by a wide smile. Adrian suddenly had a feeling he knew what had been in Lyla's bag.

"Where is the rest of our group?" Vey asked, expression darkening. "We're not leaving without them."

"I'm sorry, but that won't be possible," the Emissary replied, expression serene. And then, via message: "Disarm them."

The guards surged forward. Adrian decked the one that moved toward Vey, earning himself knuckles that stung as if he had punched a cement wall. The guard retaliated by seizing the front of Adrian's jacket and tossing him across the hallway.

"Stop!" The pulsating red letters filled his view, an absolute order.

Adrian rolled to his feet and struggled out of the cumbersome sling that had supported his broken shoulder, but the follow-up attack that he was expecting never came. Every flesh hacker in the entrance hall had stopped moving, frozen in place as they grappled with the refugees.

"What's going on here?"

The words were not in the same stark font the rest of the modders seemed to favor. It was a familiar type of lettering, one he remembered from many conversations about weather, news, and the day's patrol.

The Emissary swept an arm toward the crowded the inner hall.

"Behold, the Most Highly Evolved! Look upon her perfection, and aspire to improve!"

The wall of guards parted to allow a figure in gray pants and a blood-stained white undershirt to pass through. Although slighter of stature than most of the flesh hackers, she was just as bald. Her bare skin was a maze of pale scars, the remains of cauterized parasite trails.

"Mel?" Adrian asked, stunned. "Is that you?"

"There will be no disarming of anyone."

"It is procedure," the Emissary protested. "It is for everyone's safety."

"These people are my friends. They're not dangerous. Put that away," she added, glancing at Vey, who looked ready to shoot the guard that had attempted to disarm her.

"You're alive!" Adrian said. "You survived!"

"You seem surprised. I'm indestructible, remember?"

"How did you survive the fall?"

She shrugged. "I came out on top, I remember that much. An Enforcer's armor works against them in a free-fall struggle with someone who knows what they're doing. I don't remember hitting the ground. When I woke up, I was here."

"The Most Highly Evolved is very modest," the Emissary said. "She came to us already remarkably upgraded."

"They were very impressed with my spinal implant," Mel explained. "I have to say, Enforcers get some sweet augmentations."

"Due to the nature of her fall, we had the opportunity to upgrade her arms," the Emissary continued, expression rapturous. "Within hours, her flesh regrew over her new prosthetics! We have never seen a human body so adaptable."

"Are you alright?" Adrian asked.

"Never better!" She held out her right arm and flexed the fingers. "I can hardly tell it from the original. The wider range of movement takes a little getting used to, as does the strength. But I think that if I had drawn before, I would still be able to. Speaking of which, why don't you let us fix you up?"

Vey stepped forward. "What about the other group? Your

Emissary said the rest of our people are here."

"I didn't have anything to do with it, but they're here. Wisp is being repaired. The rest have been placed in quarantine, mostly for their own safety."

"Did Wisp agree to that?"

"She did. Surgical technicians are repairing the tissue damage that occurred during the fire. I can take you to her if you want to see for yourselves."

The inner corridors of the precinct showed fewer signs of battle than the lobby. Stark gray hallways closed around them as they wound their way across the ground floor, reminding him of another tier and another precinct.

Leaving the refugees in the hall outside the infirmary, Mel led Adrian and Vey into a narrow observation room. In the operating bay beyond, the robotic limbs of an automated surgeon cut away the traumatized tissue from the burns on Wisp's forearm. Another device secreted a layer of clear gel over the wound, and a third covered the area with synthetic skin.

"The gel keeps the wound from scarring, while encouraging the subject's body to regrow the missing tissue. The skin-substitute will protect the injury until it's fully healed, and fall off when it's no longer needed."

"And that's all that thing is going to do to her?" Vey asked.

Mel nodded. "She'll be released as soon as her burns are repaired."

"Don't worry, she's going to be fine. I'm going to make sure."

The words appeared in soft purple text at the bottom of his view. Adrian turned around to find a small, bald girl standing just inside the observation room's door with Wisp's red bear tucked under her arm.

The child's face lit up.

"I remember you! You're the Hero that got Annabelle out of the tree!"

Adrian frowned, trying to place where he had seen her before. She wore purple shorts and a black adult hoodie, and her legs ended in stubs just below the knee. The L-shaped composite blades strapped to her stubs seemed to provide her with as much mobility as her original limbs.

Kara Mae Law, resident of the Twenty-Ninth Tier. Parents deceased.

"I'm so glad you're okay!" she yelled, launching herself toward him. Adrian knelt and hugged her.

"You can't hear anymore, can you?" she asked in her pale purple font.

"I can't. It's alright, though."

"They can fix you here," she said, looking up at him earnestly. "They can fix anything!"

"What happened to you?"

"There was a loud noise, and the building caved in. When I woke up at the clinic, my feet were gone."

"How did you wind up here, though?"

The girl looked sad and stroked the bear. "They said mom didn't survive the cave-in. Most of the people on our floor didn't. I don't think Annabelle did either.

"The clinic couldn't afford to keep treating me, but some of the people there were really nice. Mr. Sampson was one of my doctors, and he told me that he knew of a place where he could send me where they might be able to fix me. He told me I was just going to go to sleep for a while, and then things would be better."

She paused and frowned at the bear.

"I thought he was just saying it to be nice. Other kids that were really sick would just disappear overnight. I thought they were going to put me to sleep. But when I woke up, I was here. They gave me new feet, and they're giving me shots that are killing the bad stuff in my bones. The people here seemed scary at first, but they're all really nice. I miss mom and Annabelle, though."

"They have her on some kind of genetic therapy," Mel said. "It seems to be working. They say she's already showing signs of improvement."

"I feel so much better! And I can do back flips!"

Mel chuckled. "Watch out. Those things are like springs. She can just about touch the ceiling."

"I have touched the ceiling," Kara replied. "Want to see?"

They followed the girl out into the hallway.

"You can hold Mr. Red for me," she said, handing the bear to Adrian. "Watch this!"

And she could, indeed, do a perfect back flip.

"Thank you, but we have to go," Mel said after Kara had done three to the applause of the gathered refugees. "We have important business to attend to."

"You'll be back though, right?"

Mel nodded.

"I'll stay with Wisp then. I promised I'd watch Mr. Red for her."

"What was that all about?" Vey asked as they walked away.

"I met her a long time ago." Adrian explained the circumstances as they made their way across the tower. "I'm surprised she still recognized me."

"I think you make an impression on people."

Their group was too large for the lift, so they took the stairs up to the holding and interrogation units. The narrow hallway, lined with closely spaced gray doors, evoked memories he would rather have left buried.

Mel paused at the head of a corridor lined with holding cells. All down the hallway, doors slid open to reveal windowless cells scarcely large enough to hold a narrow cot, a sink and a toilet.

Libby was seated at the back of the first cell, holding her tomato plants. She seemed to have been talking to them.

"She refused to part with those," Mel explained. "In the end, it was easier to just let her keep them. I was never cut out to be an

Enforcer, really. I'm fine with pulling a Hardy on some rapist, but I just don't see the point in hurting people who haven't hurt anyone else. Especially not over a couple of plants."

As the refugees who had returned to the rooftop flooded out into the corridor and were joyfully reunited with their companions, Adrian noticed that one door had not opened. As he watched, the reinforced composite barrier bowed outward and snapped back into place.

"She's still at it," Mel observed.

"If you'd let her out, she'd stop," Vey retorted.

"It might be safer to wait until she runs out of steam."

"If that's who I think it is, your door is likely to break before that happens."

The cell door slid open, revealing a bloody and disheveled figure, leg raised in preparation to deliver another kick to the door. Wide, bloodshot eyes regarded them from a faded mask of blue paint.

"Are you badly hurt?" Vey asked.

Demon shook her head.

"Now that I have all of you assembled," Mel said, "I would like to make you an offer. The modders have invited you to stay. If we pool our resources, we'll all be better off than we were before."

"No, it's already decided. We're getting out. We're leaving the city."

"You've found a way through the outer wall?"

"We did, but it turned out to be caved in."

"Let me ask around," Mel said, expression thoughtful. "Someone here might know of another way."

"There are people here from all over the city," she explained as they descended back toward the main floor. "There are surgeons, biologists, geneticists, neurologists, programmers, hackers, and working class people from more industries than I can count. They all have two things in common: they want to improve lives using technology, and they've become extremely disillusioned with the

Company.

"The residents of this tower have the technical know-how to do almost anything the Company can do, and in the case of prosthetics, sometimes much more. They've created a smuggling and communication network that spans the entire city. And they're building an army."

Her words were underscored by the wall of hulking guards still blocking the building's lobby. Adrian eyed the grim-faced gathering uneasily, wondering why the defenders had not returned to their posts.

"I think I've found something," Mel announced. "Emissary Neva has a hobby of exploring the forgotten corners of the utilidor network, and she says that there is a split in a wall that leads into a network of caves. Water runs through them when it rains, and she thinks that they must lead outside."

"How much water?" Vey asked. "Are we talking a trickle or a flood?"

"It depends on how much it rains," the Emissary said, emerging from behind the scanner. "I've never seen it be more than a little runoff."

"What does everyone think?" Vey asked the gathered refugees. "Do we want to see where these caves go?"

"It's worth a shot," Libby said. "What about our supplies, though? I'm not leaving without our seeds. We were able to salvage additional food, medical supplies, clothing and tent material as well."

"Of course," Mel replied. "It will all be returned."

The Emissary stiffened. "Most Highly Evolved, that is out of the question."

"We can't force them to join us, and it would be wrong to keep their supplies. It would significantly reduce their ability to survive."

Emissary Neva's face twitched into something that resembled a smile.

"Then I propose a trade. They may take their supplies and leave in exchange for Adrian and Wisp remaining here."

"That's absolutely not an option," Vey said. "We're not leaving anyone behind."

"Then you can stay."

Mel folded her arms and scowled at the Emissary. "We're letting them go."

"We are not. You are a newcomer, and you cannot issue orders that run counter to all of our best interests."

The argument was interrupted by the arrival of Wisp, trailed by Kara and a dozen guards carrying bags and bundles. She had traded in her white smock for a gray jumpsuit similar to those worn by the flesh hackers.

"What are you doing?" the Emissary demanded via the local network, her words glowing red with electronic outrage. "Put those back. They are not leaving!"

"Step aside." Wisp's expression seemed strained, her gaze unfocused. "Move to the walls."

There was a general shuffling in the lobby as the guards obeyed, lining up against the walls with stiff, ungraceful movements. Even the Emissary complied, her steps awkward and robotic.

"What have you done?" Neva whispered.

"They wouldn't listen, so Wisp turned them all into puppets," Kara supplied helpfully. "Don't worry, she promised it won't hurt them."

"You can't control us all."

"I have the security system as well," Wisp replied. "Locked doors will hold them."

"We're leaving. Claim your gear and move out," Vey said, motioning toward the pile of supplies.

The group needed no further urging. Packs and weapons were quickly redistributed, and soon refugees were hurrying down the stairs toward the basement and the utilidors beyond.

"Give me five minutes and I'll join you," Mel said.

"You're asking a lot, Enforcer Melbourne," Wisp replied. She seemed to focus on Mel for a moment, as if assessing her intentions, and a restless stirring rippled through the guards. "Go."

Kara insisted on hugging Wisp and the two former Heroes goodbye.

"You don't want to come with us?" Adrian asked, dismayed.

The child shook her head. "They take good care of me here, and Mr. Red is going to stay and keep me safe."

"Snow will look after her," Wisp added. "We need to go now."

They made their exit under the stares of the Emissary and dozens of hulking modified guards. Adrian was not sad to leave the lobby and the army of immobilized flesh hackers behind. Wisp seemed to be having trouble controlling them and focusing on her surroundings at the same time, and he couldn't help but wonder how long it would be before the group broke her control and came after them.

Mel caught up with them at the entrance to the utilidors, two familiar black duffle bags slung over her shoulders.

"The salvage team found this on the rooftop after the attack," she said, handing him one. "I thought you might want it back."

"Thank you. Are you sure you want to come with us?"

She nodded. "I thought they were a little quick to accept me as their leader solely based on my augmentations, and I was right. Their Most Highly Evolved is no more their leader than the Prime Hero was the head of the Safety Division. I doubt I'm going to be welcome here after this."

Wisp became herself again as they caught up with Vey and the rest of the refugees.

"I've locked the doors and disabled access to the building's virtual control panels, but that'll only hold them for so long. We need to hurry."

"I have the tools to set up a couple of electromagnetic pulse devices rigged to motion sensors," Manx suggested. "That'll keep them off our back for a little longer."

"Do it," Vey said.

Mel grinned. "I almost feel sorry for them. What did you do back there, anyway?"

"Virtually everyone who's used the Company's network is infected with a nasty bit of malware known as Marionette," Wisp explained. "I was able to exploit it to hijack every modder on the bottom five floors of the building. While I was at it, I also skimmed directions to Neva's cave system."

"Lead the way," Vey said. "Demon and Jack will guard the rear and make sure no one falls behind."

* * *

They navigated the utilidor system at a brisk jog, Adrian, Mel, Vey and the other stronger individuals of the group carrying the packs of those that were smaller and slower. Soon a dark crevice could be seen at the end of the corridor ahead, splitting the dull gray wall where the utilidor turned a corner.

An ankle-deep stream of dirty water rushed past their feet and through the broken wall, disappearing into the darkness beyond. The jagged gap was scarcely wide enough for a person to turn sideways and slip through. When Adrian peered through the aperture, the beam of his flashlight spilled into a narrow tunnel made of smooth pale brown stone. He took a deep breath and squeezed through the crack.

The water-worn passage was narrow, winding, and knee deep in dirty runoff. After a few dozen meters, the crevice made a sharp right turn and connected with a wider cavern. The runoff spread out across the floor, eventually joining the murky stream that hugged the far wall of the cave.

At some point the cavern had been a conduit for far more water. The forces of nature had carved grooves into the pale walls and a ripple-like pattern onto the floor. Even the arched ceiling bore the marks of erosion.

Adrian walked a little way downstream, noting that the cavern continued on at much the same width. Turning around, he made his way upstream of the crevice. It was there that his light revealed a series of black marks, stark against the pale cavern wall.

Not words, he realized, moving closer. It was more of the strange symbols they had discovered in the utilidors. They seemed to point to a small, semi-concealed recess low in the wall.

The smell of decay struck him before he looked inside. A flesh hacker's body, or at least most of one, had been wedged into the gap. Dull metal and broken electronics protruded through the crushed skull. Whatever had befallen the modder, it seemed to have been a quick death.

Something gripped his shoulder. Adrian surged to his feet as Mel ducked out of range.

"The hell," he exclaimed, clutching his chest. "Warn a guy before sneaking up on him!"

"Sorry," Mel replied, laughing. "Sometimes I forget you can't hear. The look on your face was priceless, though."

"I doubt he thought it was funny." He gestured toward the remains.

Mel's expression turned serious. "Explains where they got the blood to draw their weird symbols. I don't think this a good place to be alone."

Wisp was just emerging from the runoff-carved crevice when they returned.

"The others are right behind me. I didn't want to wait around in the utilidor for the flesh hackers to catch up."

"Well, I don't think we want to wait around in here, either," Mel replied. "I'm beginning to have some idea why Neva suggested this place, and I don't think she had our best interests at heart."

"She didn't. But don't think they'll be in any hurry to follow us here."

More and more refugees spilled out of the tunnel, filling the cavern with light.

"Which way?" Vey asked.

"Downstream, I think." Wisp frowned. "Neva didn't explore the cave system extensively, but that seems most likely to lead outside. The water has to come out somewhere."

"I don't suppose your people would happen to have a portable relay, would they?" Mel asked.

"Mandi and Manx might, but we don't usually use them. We'd be broadcasting our presence to anyone within range."

"I think it would be beneficial to have connectivity here. It's hard to hear over the sound of the water, not to mention the echoes. If we're attacked, I want the people with connectivity to be able to coordinate a defense. Trying to pass directions up and down the line in here is a recipe for disaster."

Wisp nodded. "I'll go ask them if they can set it up."

"What does it sound like?" Adrian asked, curious. To his senses, the cavern was cool, odoriferous from the human waste and industrial pollution in the runoff, and utterly silent.

"Eerie," Vey said. "There are all kinds of rushing, splashing noises, and they echo. So does everyone's voices. And there's a strange sound, kind of a deep roar, underneath it all. I wish I had some of the sensors you do. I keep getting an uncomfortable feeling that we're not alone down here."

"I get the same feeling. I'll be your eyes if you'll be my ears."

Vey nodded and squeezed his shoulders in a brief half-hug.

***

After a brief regrouping, the refugees set off downstream. Adrian and Vey took the lead, with Wisp and the others with connectivity strung out through the line to monitor and interpret for those without. Mel and Demon brought up the rear.

Despite the fact that the twists and turns ahead revealed no signs of life, he was dogged by the feeling that some unseen menace lurked in the shadowy reaches of the cave. Side tunnels and crevices joined the main cavern at intervals, adding their dark discharge to the subterranean river. In places the water had carved the stone into towering columns and fantastical shapes that cast strange shadows across the cavern floor. The tunnel widened out into echoing amphitheaters and split into braided passages carved through multicolored rock, slowly descending toward what Adrian hoped would be an egress from the hollow plateau that held the city.

Up ahead, the floor of the cave ended in an abrupt drop. Darkness lay beyond.

Vey swore, and Adrian peered over the edge. A jumble of rock lay at the bottom, some thirty meters below. The river poured over the precipice, forming a wide pool at the base of the cliff.

"Do we have any rope?" Adrian asked.

"Yes, but not that much."

"I think there's a path over there," Wisp said, flashing her light along the opposite bank.

On the far side of the river, a band of dry ground led to a narrow shelf carved into the cavern wall. A series of large boulders had been maneuvered into the flow to form stepping stones. One stone seemed to be missing, leaving a meter-wide gap in the middle.

Vey frowned at the path and then back the way they'd come.

"Is there another way? Could we go upstream from where we came in instead?"

Wisp shook her head. "The only thing back that way is a place Neva calls the catacombs. It's not a way out."

"I'll scout the other side and see if it goes anywhere," Adrian volunteered, shrugging off his duffle bag.

"Can you swim?" Vey asked.

Adrian shook his head. "Don't worry, I won't fall in."

As he hopped from one spray-darkened stone to the next, it occurred to him that the water posed an unforeseen danger. Neither he, nor Mel, nor anyone else in their group knew how to swim. He was almost certain that no one in the city did. A full bathtub was the largest body of water even the wealthiest citizen could ever expect to see.

His boots left damp tracks on the grainy stone, and a faint breeze brushed his face as he started down the narrow path. The water-worn white and tan stone had been chiseled away to form a trail little wider than a person's shoulders. He followed it far enough to ascertain that it descended all the way to the cavern floor before turning back.

Adrian flashed Vey and the rest of the refugees a thumbs-up before tackling the stepping stones. The boulders seemed more treacherous from this side, their rounded, spray-slicked surfaces resisting the grip of his boot treads.

As he made the leap across the gap in the middle, he realized he had misjudged it. The toe of his boot hit the wet stone and slid, dropping him straight into the flood. Icy water closed around him, dark and polluted, as the current fought to drag him downstream.

Adrian clutched the boulder and felt for the bottom. Surprisingly, the water only came up a little past his waist. A dark shadow landed on the stone in front of him, and he glanced up to find Vey offering her hand.

"It's not as deep as it looks." He cautiously relaxed his grip and tested his ability to stand against the current. "Since I'm already soaked, I might as well stay here to catch anyone else who slips."

"Are you sure?"

"I'm sure. It's cold but tolerable."

She frowned, but continued across.

"Make it quick! And don't fall in," she ordered from the far side. "I want him out of that water as fast as possible."

The others quickly followed, with Adrian passing packs and bundles across the gap. Mel crossed with both their duffel bags, grinning as she hopped from stone to stone and bounded effortlessly over his head.

"Be really careful with that!" Lyla exclaimed as he passed a hefty bundle across to Loki. The contents wiggled under his touch.

One by one, the last of the refugees and their supplies made the crossing. Meanwhile, Adrian had begun to get the feeling that it was more than just the current tugging at his legs. Some of the pressure seemed to come from downstream. When he shifted to pass the last bag across, his left foot bumped into something solid that had not been there before.

Demon crossed last, steel pipe in hand.

"You alright?" she asked as she stepped over him.

"There's something in the water."

It curled around his left leg. He glanced down, wondering if he had caught some piece of large debris, but the murky flow concealed whatever lay beneath.

"Give me your hand."

As he reached for her outstretched fingers, something slammed into his legs and knocked him off his feet. Adrian flailed as the current pulled him under. His last sight was of Demon, face contorted in a snarl, raising her weapon to attack.

Something closed on his forearm with crushing force. Adrian screamed and clawed at his attacker, earning himself a mouthful of water. The thing was slick and muscular, as cold to the touch as the surrounding liquid. Its dead weight gripped him, holding him under despite his struggles, and he fought the need to breathe until his lungs ached.

His feet connected with something that he thought was the bottom. He launched himself toward the surface, gasping for air, only to find nothing but more water. The world was darkness and white sparks. The liquid stung his eyes, nose and throat.

Mel sent him one message after another, ordering him to surface, to put up a hand, to give her something to grab him by. He had no idea in which direction the surface lay.

Vise-like jaws clamped down on his leg. He punched the thing with all his strength, hammering on its slick, boney skull until his knuckles went numb. The current slammed him against something unforgivingly solid, driving the last of the breath from his lungs. Instinct compelled him to breathe, and he inhaled water.

The thing released him just as he went over the edge. He was falling through the darkness, flailing, unable to roll onto his back. The ground waited for him somewhere below, promising an end to the nightmare.

# CHAPTER TWENTY-ONE

No one had needed any urging to gather their packs and run. Mel was already gone, a streak of pale skin and water-stained gray uniform bolting down the stone path at breakneck speed. Vey followed only slightly more slowly. She wouldn't be saving anyone if she slipped off the narrow ledge and broke her legs in a fall.

"You're not saving anyone, anyway," the voice at the back of her mind whispered. She shoved it away.

Glancing over her shoulder, she saw Libby and Demon coordinating the descent from the top of the ledge. Demon was a solid second in command; she could be trusted to make sure no one was left behind.

The pool at the bottom of the roaring fall was dark and devoid of life. There was no gray-clad figure floating among the ripples that lapped the shore. Vey traced the flood of runoff with her light as it rushed across the echoing cavern, noting that the Enforcer's damp footprints followed the river into a dark gap in the far wall.

Behind her, the line of refugees was spilling out into the lower half of the cavern. Vey motioned for them to follow.

The tunnel forked just inside the passage. The runoff filled the narrower left branch, and the Enforcer's tracks disappeared into the water. Vey swore. Both the Hero and his sister were absolutely crazy, possessed by the kind of insanity that led them to put their lives on the line to save another.

Even if that person was most likely already dead.

"Should have gotten him out of the water," the voice said. "You knew it was a bad place to be."

The thing about Adrian was that it was easy to trust that he knew what he was doing. The truth was, as evidenced by his previous adventures, he didn't always know what he was getting himself into.

"Take the dry fork," Wisp said as the group began to catch up. "Melbourne says they come back together further down. If it forks again, follow whichever branch has the strongest breeze."

She took off running through the strange tunnels, hand on the butt of her pistol, light splashing the gritty beige walls. The others were behind her, a roar of ragged breathing, echoing footsteps and shouts of encouragement.

"She says it comes out! She sees light," Wisp shouted, and a cheer went up at their back. Vey ran faster, her sides burning.

Stay out of the tunnels, she remembered her gran saying. Stay out of the dead buildings. Don't go out in the dark without a light.

A friend's older sister told a story about a spindly man who ate anyone he caught out after dark. He liked to collect shiny things. Sometimes, if the spindly man wasn't hungry, his victims could save themselves by throwing something shiny at him and running away.

The things had never been more than an urban legend, a bogeyman to scare unruly children. But sometimes people disappeared. And when the bone circles began to appear, the warring communities below the new wall blamed each other.

Some people accused the predatory groups, traffickers and cannibals with little or no respect for human life. Some blamed the flesh hackers, with their reclusive tendencies and strange customs. Gran thought it might be the Enforcers.

"You wouldn't believe what they'll do to keep us scared," she'd said.

The tunnel turned sharply to the left and reconnected with the river. Wet footprints emerged from the water, already beginning to fade into the beige stone. Vey eyed the dark river with misgiving, noting that there was little more than a meter of dry ground between the wall and the edge of the channel. Was the thing that had attacked Adrian still in the water? Had it stayed above the fall or gone over the edge with him?

"Any word?"

Wisp shook her head.

"Too late," the voice at the back of her head whispered as she pressed on. "Too late."

She remembered bones, bleached white by the smog and rain. She remembered finding her mother's locket, corroded by the weather, amid a tangle of other shiny items on a table at the middle of an intersection.

A dim glow filled the tunnel, and the roar of the water increased. She rounded a bend and emerged into daylight. The black river plunged over a cliff, roaring angrily.

Vey staggered out onto the narrow ledge, blinking and shielding her eyes. Tall, multicolored cliffs in shades of beige, yellow and rusty red rose like the walls of strange buildings on either side of the water-worn channel. To her right, a set of crumbling steps had been chiseled into the cliff wall.

Below, one gray figure was hunched over another. Marks showed where someone had leaped from the ledge, their feet and one hand leaving deep imprints. Tracks led to the edge of the pool, and drag marks showed where the Enforcer had pulled Adrian from the water.

"Too late," her mind whispered as she launched herself down the crumbling stairs. "Too late."

The Enforcer was frantically performing chest compressions. The second figure lay utterly still, boots splayed apart on the soft ground. There were jagged tears in the fabric of his pants and jacket, and his left hand was torn and bloody. How long had he been underwater?

Drowning was something gran had never taught her how to treat. As long as you avoided the utilidors when it rained, drowning was not something anyone needed to worry about. That said, Vey knew it did not take that long for a person to drown. The rule of threes stated that a person could survive three minutes without air. She was certain he had been underwater for much longer.

How long had the gray-clad Enforcer been performing chest compressions? Adrian's face was pale, his lips blue. His eyes were still open, bloodshot and fixed on the sky.

"He's gone," the voice whispered. She shoved it away. She refused to entertain the thought that he was dead.

"Is there anything I can do?" Vey asked.

"Do you know how to perform rescue breathing?" The Enforcer's expression, usually so full of laughter, was grim and focused.

Vey nodded.

"Okay, you breathe for him. Thirty compressions, then two breaths."

His skin was stiff and icy cold. As she tilted his head back, she was vaguely aware of the others spilling out of the tunnel and scrambling down the ruined steps. The community surrounded them, murmuring softly.

They formed a tragic tableau on the damp ground, framed by the blaze of the group's lights. What Vey had taken for bright daylight had actually been the onset of evening. The last glowing rays of sunset were rapidly fading from the sky.

After the third round of compressions and pauses to administer rescue breathing, Adrian convulsed, gasping for air. They rolled him onto his side as he vomited water. Cheers and screams of excitement rose from the bystanders.

"Do we have oxygen?" Melbourne asked.

Vey shook her head, and the Enforcer swore.

Adrian propped himself up on one arm, coughing violently, and retched up more water. A wave of shivering overtook him, and Vey shrugged off her poncho and wrapped it around his shoulders.

"He's hypothermic," Melbourne said. "That water's pretty cold. We need to get a fire going and get him warmed up."

"I would strongly suggest not doing it here," Mandi interjected. "I think this is one of the plateau's main drainages. It looks like this whole canyon floor was under water during the rainstorm."

"So?" The Enforcer looked annoyed. "It isn't now."

"It may not be now, but it will be if it starts raining again. And we may not have any warning."

"There's a path that looks like it leads out of here," Manx said, pointing to a cluster of lights winding their way up the cliff to their right and slightly downstream. "Demon, Wisp, and a couple of the others volunteered to see how far it is to the top."

"He needs medical attention more than we need to go exploring," Melbourne replied, jaw tightening. "If it weren't so far back to civilization, I'd take him back through the caves."

"You and Vey are our medical team," Mandi said. "You're all we've got."

"This is way beyond me. He needs to go to a clinic."

"I'm going to be okay," Adrian rasped. "Did everyone make it out?"

"We're all here," Mandi confirmed.

The Hero smiled weakly and succumbed to another bout of coughing. He was shivering so violently that Vey had to prop him up. Although his skin was icy, the fabric of his uniform was radiating warmth.

"How are you feeling?" Melbourne asked. "You went over two waterfalls, and who knows what else you hit or how hard. That river bed is all stone."

"I can move my hands. I can move my feet. But I'm so cold. I don't think I've ever been this cold." He paused as another coughing fit overtook him. "I think my uniform is broken. I've got the heat on, and nothing's happening."

The Enforcer reached out and felt the collar of Adrian's soggy jacket.

"No, it's working," she said, frowning. "Do we at least have a medical kit for his hand?"

Vey unpacked her kit as the Enforcer used her flask to rinse off the gouges with clean water. She dressed the wounds with antibiotic ointment and gauze bandages, noting that the lacerations had already stopped bleeding. The runoff smelled like diluted sewage, and her biggest concern was the potential for infection.

As darkness began to fall, Vey found herself shivering in the cool, damp air. This strange outside world was shockingly cold compared to the heat of the city. Far above the cliff walls, a web of sparkling stars had spread across the indigo sky.

"Wisp reports that they've found a wide, sheltered space under the overhang of a higher wall," Loki said. "It's only about ten minutes up the path. She says there's clear water running right out of the wall nearby, and it's warmer and drier than down here."

"I think I can walk," Adrian volunteered, struggling to stand. Vey draped his arm over her shoulders and helped him to his feet.

As the Hero paused, wracked by yet another coughing fit, the rest of the group shouldered their packs and began to move up the narrow path. Vey and Adrian took the second-to-last place in line, with Melbourne keeping watch at their backs.

"Sorry to wind up having to lean on you again," Adrian said.

"I'm just glad you're alive."

"Me too. I thought I was dead there for a while." He chuckled softly.

* * *

It was a slow trudge up the narrow, foliage-choked path, much to Adrian's embarrassment. He couldn't seem to catch his breath, and the more he tried, the more he coughed. If he were to count small blessings, however, he was shivering a little less violently. His uniform's climate control feature provided a faint sensation of warmth, and his neural interface had ceased to flood him with oxygen level warnings and crash reports.

Vey nudged him in the ribs as they rounded a corner at the top of the trail, pointing upward. Millions of tiny points of light stretched out above them, a glittering arch that spanned the sky.

"What is it?"

"They're stars. Gran used to tell me about them. The band across the middle of the sky is called the Milky Way."

"I had no idea there were so many," Adrian said, awed. "It's like a river of light."

They rounded another turn in the trail, and the flickering orange glow of firelight could be seen on the cliff above. They climbed higher, finally coming out on a wide ledge sheltered by an escarpment of red sandstone. Makeshift tents had been erected under the overhang, someone had built a fire from scavenged deadwood, and food preparation was underway.

A cheer went up when the group saw him, and someone pressed a cup of hot soup into his hands. He sat by the fire and ate until Mel came by with his bag and Vey offered him a tent. Safe from curious eyes, he stripped off his torn, sodden uniform. Shivering violently, he scrubbed away the grimy remnants of his dip in the river with a soapy cloth and a bowl of cold spring water.

Faded bruises and a few white dimples of scar tissue were all that remained where the thing had savaged his arm and leg. The flexible armor of his uniform had protected him from the worst of the damage. Beneath the bandages, his torn hand was already beginning to heal.

As he put on a clean uniform, a pair of black kittens tumbled under the edge of the tent and attacked his ankles. He knelt and stroked their fur, smiling through chattering teeth as they grappled with his hand in mock battle. He bent to scoop them up, and something shifted inside his right ear. A slurry of liquid and coagulated blood trickled down the side of his face as Adrian tilted his head from side to side.

A series of familiar tones sounded, and a wall of text momentarily obscured his view.

"Auditory systems functional," the automated message concluded.

Suddenly he could hear.

Mittens slipped under the edge of the tent and gathered her wayward offspring. Voices rose and fell outside. Someone uttered an exclamation, and it was followed by muffled laughter. Adrian hastily pulled on the rest of his clothing and bolted from the tent.

"Vey! Mel! I can hear!"

Mel grinned and slapped him on the back. "See? Indestructible! Just don't get any ideas about testing that crowd control weapon again."

Vey hugged him tightly.

"We saved you a spot by the fire," she said.

While he'd been busy, more tents had sprung up along the back of the ledge. A handful of fires burned brightly, ringed by refugees sharing dinner. The tangy smell of smoke filled the air.

Vey sat down beside him and offered him a second bowl of soup. Between questions about what had attacked him and another round of dinner, the shivering gradually subsided. Propped up against Vey's shoulder, warmed by the blazing fire, he began to feel incredibly tired. Across the canyon, the glowing ivory orb of the moon slowly rose above the horizon.

***

He awoke as the first glimmers of approaching dawn began to seep through the tent fabric. Vey was stretched out next to him, braids draped across her pillow, sound asleep. A furry gray lump was nestled between them, purring loudly. When he shifted, Old Tom opened his one yellow eye and yawned.

It appeared that he had slept in his uniform. After carefully scooting out from under Vey's blanket, he stood up and quietly slipped out of the tent.

The eastern sky was turning brilliant shades of tangerine, peach and gold. The cool air held a pleasant, earthy scent that he had never smelled before, an aroma utterly unlike the miasma exuded by the city.

He followed the curve of the cliff until he was out of sight of the encampment before giving in to the wracking cough that had been tickling the back of his throat since he awoke. After coughing up something black, tar-like and utterly disgusting, he felt better.

The first rays of the rising sun peeked over a range of distant mountains, framed by scrubby gray-green brush on the far side of the canyon. To the north, the plateau that held the city towered against the brightening sky. Its rim was wreathed in smog, trailing hazy streamers like the mouth of some restless volcano.

A few cliff swallows, their dark backs and dusty white undersides flashing in the light, took flight from nests high in the escarpment. Their chirps and warbling calls echoed around him as they dove into the canyon below.

Looking out over a landscape that he had never expected to see, Adrian was filled with hope. With Vey, Mel, and the others, he had finally found where he belonged. The wide-open world waited for them, full of possibilities.

## ABOUT THE AUTHOR

Leland Lydecker is a writer, professional driver, and former airline employee. No stranger to the ins and outs of government and corporate corruption, his preferred writing topics are crime, extra-judicial justice, and the future of society. His interests range from the natural world, to space exploration, to technology and medicine with an emphasis on genetic engineering, cybernetics, and artificial intelligence.

For news about upcoming releases, visit LelandLydecker.com.
You can also connect with Leland on social media:
Facebook.com/LelandLydeckerAuthor
Twitter.com/Leland_Lydecker